THE LEMON TREE CAFÉ

Cathy Bramley

CORGI BOOKS

TRANSWORLD PUBLISHERS
61–63 Uxbridge Road, London W5 5SA
www.penguin.co.uk

Transworld is part of the Penguin Random House group of companies
whose addresses can be found at global.penguinrandomhouse.com

First published in Great Britain as four separate ebooks
in 2017 by Transworld Digital
an imprint of Transworld Publishers
First published as one edition in 2017 by Corgi Books
an imprint of Transworld Publishers

A CIP catalogue record for this book
is available from the British Library.

ISBN
9780552172097

Typeset in 11.5/13pt Garamond MT by Jouve (UK), Milton Keynes.
Printed and bound in Great Britain by Clays Ltd, Bungay, Suffolk.

Penguin Random House is committed to a sustainable future for our business, our readers
and our planet. This book is made from Forest Stewardship Council® certified paper.

1 3 5 7 9 10 8 6 4 2

For the Literary Hooters:
Rachael, Miranda and Jo
with love

PART ONE

A Cup of Ambition

Chapter 1

The executive office of Digital Horizons had an amazing view right across Derby city centre, but I wasn't looking out of the window. I was staring at my boss and he was staring right back, waiting for my response. The low March sunshine wasn't helping matters either; lovely as it was, it was shining directly into my eyes and making them water. I hoped he didn't think I was crying because I was a long way from that.

I shifted my chair but there was nowhere to hide in this glass box. Even the internal walls were see-through.

'No means no.' I crossed my legs and eyeballed him defiantly.

My boss, Robert Crisp, the managing director, sighed and loosened the collar of his shirt. As well he might. I wasn't backing down; some things were worth fighting for and this was one of them.

'A few quick strokes, Rosie,' he pleaded. 'Two minutes and it will all be over. No one outside this room need ever know, if it bothers you that much. You're the best at this sort of thing.' He paused for dramatic effect. 'That's why I hired you.'

A thinly veiled threat; I looked away, disappointed in him.

The only other person in the room, sales director Duncan Wiggins, tutted.

'Bloody feminists,' he muttered, so quietly that only I heard.

Duncan was a prematurely balding thirty-something with a penchant for brightly coloured socks. I'd learned early on to rise above his sexist twaddle. If I argued back, it simply fanned the flames. Nowadays I didn't give him oxygen.

And yes, I was a feminist. Funny that, really; in my early twenties I'd probably have said I was your classic fun, flirty female. I'd taken equality as read, assumed that women had the same power as men; I thought feminists were just making a fuss about nothing. I'd also thought I was never wrong; I was wrong about that too.

Ignoring Duncan, I tried to appeal to Robert's better nature. He was, on the whole, a nice man; a father of two teenage girls.

'Sorry, boss,' I said, 'but it's wrong on so many levels. Surely you can see that?'

I pointed at the image on the computer screen, which had been angled so that all three of us could see it. I couldn't believe that they wanted me to manipulate the picture of Lucinda Miller to make her thinner. Lucinda was a pretty young actress and soon to be the face of the online campaign against teenage domestic violence that we were launching at noon today. She had a halo of copper curls, a naturally friendly smile and a feisty sparkle in her eyes. She was also currently in possession of boobs, a tiny rounded tummy and – shock, horror – no thigh gap.

Lucinda had overcome a difficult childhood to become a successful actress and as far as I was concerned, she was the ideal role model to be the face of this campaign. Exactly as she was.

The client, however, had asked for a bit of airbrushing to make her tummy and legs slimmer. Not that she was fat, they'd been quick to add, just that it would give a smoother line to the finished image. The boobs could stay, though. *Surprise, surprise.*

Duncan had already referred to Lucinda as 'the cuddly one from *Raw Recruits*', the gritty police drama she was currently acting in. Which was ridiculous: she was a size twelve, well below average weight and certainly not in need of any digital enhancement by me and my editing software.

'Have a cake.' Robert slid the plate of cinnamon pastries across the meeting table.

I leaned forward to take one and my black bobbed hair swung forward over my eyes. I hooked it behind my ear and gave him a slight smile. 'Buttering me up won't change my mind.'

He massaged his forehead and sighed. 'We don't have a lot of choice, love.'

My expression reverted to glacial. He held his hands up immediately.

'Sorry. *Rosie*. Sorry.'

'Robert,' I held his eye, 'there's always a choice. We can refuse to do it. What sort of a message are we sending out to young women who are looking to this charity for support? It makes us as bad as the media who caused the problem of low self-esteem in girls in the first place. So no, I won't make her thinner. She's lovely as she is and frankly her *not* being perfect makes a much more powerful statement.'

Next to me, Duncan swore under his breath and I tried not to react.

'Of course Rosie'll do it.' He reached for more coffee and raised a sleazy eyebrow at Robert. 'Women always say no. They never mean it. Not in my experience, anyway.'

Especially when the question is: Do you find Duncan Wiggins utterly repulsive? No one could say no to that and mean it, I thought, taking a bite of my pastry.

'Remind me again, Duncan,' I said, dabbing the crumbs from my mouth, 'when was the last time you went out with a woman who wasn't your mother?'

He opened his mouth, evidently couldn't remember and resorted to giving me a withering look instead.

'And for the record, I do mean it,' I continued, addressing Robert, who I noticed was starting to perspire. 'Lucinda likes the picture as it is; I've got an email from her agent to prove it. Perpetuating the myth that women's bodies are open to manipulation is against my principles and I'm not doing it.' I popped the rest of the pastry in and mumbled, 'Sorry.'

'Business is tough at the moment, Rosie,' Robert argued. 'You know how important this client is.'

'Yes. I do,' I said, folding my arms. 'They are important to young girls who are currently being bullied by their abusive boyfriends for allegedly being slags or being stupid or for having NO THIGH GAP.'

'For God's sake, Featherstone, will you clamber down from your moral high ground?' Duncan groaned wearily, with a well-timed look at my fitted skirt and high heels. I resisted the urge to adjust my hemline, which wasn't particularly short; I dressed for me, not for men. So he could go and do one. 'Have you always been such a barrel of laughs?'

No. Not since one night when I realized that the world wasn't full of gentlemen like my dad but, unfortunately, tossers like you.

'Oh, I'm sorry,' I said with eyes wide, 'domestic violence is a joke to you, is it?'

'He's not saying that, Rosie,' said Robert, shooting Duncan a warning look.

'Enhancing Lucinda's assets isn't a crime, and even if it is, it's not *our* crime,' Duncan continued in his slimy voice. 'We obey the client: we airbrush the chubby lass and launch the campaign at noon. End of story. Now let's move on to something more important: the golf day for top clients. I've been looking into venues . . .'

He began droning on about eighteen holes and teams and trophies and corporate backscratching. I glared expectantly at Robert who squirmed in his seat and lowered his eyes.

At midday the social media campaign went live, spear-headed by a doctored picture of Lucinda Miller with a wasp-like waist, flat stomach and pipe-cleaner legs. God knows who did the airbrushing – probably Billy, the junior graphic designer, who, I knew, was desperate for an invite to that golf day. I didn't see because I was too busy typing. Ten minutes later, I handed my resignation letter to my gob-smacked boss and quit my job as creative director for the largest social media agency in the Midlands.

It wasn't just about Lucinda Miller's thighs, I explained patiently, when Robert accused me of being oversensitive. It was the culture of everyday sexism that was so deeply ingrained in the company's ethos that the few women who were employed by Digital Horizons simply seemed to accept it and the men didn't even notice it.

Anyway, I for one wasn't going to accept it any more. I left the keys to my company car with reception, walked out of the revolving glass doors and jumped on a bus feeling immensely proud of myself. I might have lost today's battle, but I wasn't about to lose my principles too.

The bus took me as far as Chesterfield and I jumped in a taxi to take me the rest of the way: I needed privacy to make an important phone call . . .

'So I'm available right away,' I said to Michael, the recruitment consultant who had headhunted me for Digital Horizons. 'The sooner the better, really.'

I didn't do 'unemployed' very well. I rarely even took my holiday entitlement and relaxing was anathema to me.

'Gosh, *darling*! That's very sudden. What went wrong?'

I had every faith in Michael. He knew how ambitious I was, how hard-working; I was sure he'd be on my side.

'A difference of opinion, and theirs was wrong. So . . .' I cleared my throat. No use dwelling on the past. 'On to pastures new. What have you got?'

'Hmm, nothing of your calibre springs to mind. Bear with, I'll do some digging.'

I heard the drumming of his fingers on his keyboard and gripped the door handle as the taxi bounced over the

Derbyshire hills towards Barnaby, hoping he'd strike gold before we came to a halt. I glanced out of the window just as we passed the 'Best Kept Village 2012' plaque on the big oak tree in front of the church.

Barnaby was a pretty village on the edge of the Peak District. Nestled in a valley surrounded by fields of sheep, it oozed *olde worlde* charm. The cottages were built from chunky buff stone with tiny white windows, a quaint row of shops edged the village green and a stream meandered merrily along, parallel to the cobbled main road.

We passed the end of my steep little street. I'd bought a tiny one-up-one-down cottage at the very top of it last summer with the intention of doing it up and selling it on. I'd had to completely gut it: new roof, dinky log-burning stove, hotel-style bathroom, kitchen with all the mod cons . . . In fact, I'd done such a good job that I couldn't bear to part with it. And now it was home.

The children were outside in the playground at the little Victorian school as we passed by, busy with games of hopscotch and football; a few faces were pressed against the railings waving and shouting to attract the attention of passers-by. I smiled to myself as I waved back, remembering how my little sister Lia and I used to do that too.

Michael was still mumbling under his breath as he read through his notes.

'Ooh, I do have a *fab-u-lous* vacancy for a new business director at a full-service comms agency in London. Exciting client list, great benefits package. Interested?'

I was interested. Or rather I would have been had it not been for the location. I'd spent a few months there after graduating from uni and it hadn't ended well. But maybe I'd have to spread my wings a bit if I wanted to get further up the corporate ladder.

'Possibly,' I said vaguely. 'Further north would be preferable.'

Michael sighed apologetically. 'It's fairly quiet at the moment in social media.'

'Keep looking; I'll go mad if I've got nothing to do.'

He rang off after promising to do his best and I dropped the phone in my bag. I slid back the glass screen between me and the taxi driver as we approached the village green.

'Over there, please.' I pointed to the building with the sunny yellow awning over its frontage and a pair of miniature lemon trees in terracotta pots flanking the door. 'The Lemon Tree Café.'

The old-fashioned bell above the door chimed to signal my arrival and I stepped from one world into another. My grandmother's café couldn't have been more of a contrast to Digital Horizons.

Lunch service was over and most of the tables were empty. Doreen, who'd been here as long as I could remember, was rearranging sandwich fillings behind the counter and my seventy-five-year-old Italian *nonna*, Maria Carloni, was sitting in the toy corner, tidying wooden bricks into a crate. She looked up at the sound of the bell, adjusted her black-rimmed spectacles which magnified her eyes to the size of chestnuts and tucked a stray white curl back into her bun before recognizing me.

'*Santo cielo!*' she cried. 'Rosanna!'

'Surprise!' I laughed as she scurried over, arms wide.

She planted loud kisses on my cheeks and I hugged her plump body tight. She smelled as she had done for decades: of lemon soap and almond hand cream.

The café was chock-full of happy memories for me, stretching right back through my childhood to when Nonna used to look after Lia and me after school: sneaking sweets from the jar on the counter, entertaining the customers with songs and made-up dance routines, and food, of course, lots of food. And after the morning I'd had, it was the perfect place to recharge my batteries.

Doreen waved, her pink cheeks dimpling with a smile as she held up a coffee cup. I gave her the thumbs up as Nonna

9

led me to a stool at the counter and I breathed in the café's unique aroma: the coffee, the fresh pots of herbs on each table, the sweetness of freshly baked cookies and, of course, the zingy lemons from the pots in the conservatory at the back. It all added up to a welcoming mix of warmth and love and a sense of community and I felt the tension ease from my shoulders for the first time today.

'Why you not at work?' Nonna's eyes roamed my face, full of concern. 'You working-holic, even weekends. You like your nonna,' she added with a tinge of pride.

'No, I . . .' I paused to smile my thanks as Doreen set a cappuccino and a ham-and-cheese toastie in front of me. 'I quit my job. Walked out.'

They listened, agog, as I filled them in on the morning's events.

'Dicky heads.' Nonna scowled, and Doreen turned away to serve two ramblers who wanted tea and toasted teacakes to help thaw them out after their chilly hike. 'You their top worker. What is wrong with them?'

'They're dicky heads. Obviously,' I said, winking at Doreen.

I loved Nonna's loyalty. She had no idea what social media was, had never even heard of viral marketing and hadn't a clue what I did all day at work, yet despite that, in her eyes, I was the bee's knees.

'Eh.' She flicked her ubiquitous cloth at me, sending a shower of crumbs into the air. 'Language.'

I laughed, dodging the cloth, and she wandered off to clear tables and chat to her customers, leaving me to enjoy my late lunch alone.

'Here.' Doreen tutted, holding out her hand for my cup. 'You can't drink that now.'

'Oh. I see what you mean,' I said, peering into it. The cappuccino had acquired a layer of fluff and crumbs.

Doreen made me another and leaned in towards me conspiratorially.

'Her and that flippin' cloth. I spend half my time clearing up after her. I don't want to speak out of turn,' she whispered, her face flushing, 'but I'm a bit worried about Maria.'

'What do you mean?' I looked across at Nonna who was leaning heavily on one of the tables and wiping an arm across her brow. 'Do you think she's ill?'

Doreen flushed and shook her head.

'Not exactly . . .' She glanced around her nervously. 'I probably shouldn't say anything. It feels wrong. Forget it.'

'You can't just stop there,' I whispered. 'You've got me worried now. Come on, spill the beans.'

'It's just . . . It feels like . . .' She blew out a breath and twisted the corner of her apron round in her hands. 'OK. The truth is I don't think she's up to the job any more.'

'What – running the café?' My eyes widened.

'Hold on a sec—' She broke off to serve some customers who wanted to pay their bill.

I sipped my new cappuccino and frowned.

Doreen was a hard worker and extremely loyal to Nonna. She wouldn't complain without good reason. She shut the old-fashioned till with a clatter and came back over.

'Take this morning, for instance,' she said, checking over her shoulder that Nonna wasn't within earshot. 'She gave out thirteen pounds in change to someone, instead of three.'

'Easy mistake,' I said diplomatically.

'And I caught her filling the salt cellars with sugar last week.'

I glanced over to where Nonna was seemingly wiping a clean table with her dirty cloth and making it ten times worse.

'Perhaps she needs new glasses?' I whispered back.

Doreen shook her head sadly.

'I thought I'd lost her yesterday; I found her half an hour later fast asleep on an upturned bucket in the courtyard. No, it's not new glasses. She's seventy-five. What she needs,' she said, 'is a rest. A permanent one. Called retirement.'

My stomach plummeted. Nonna was as rest averse as me and didn't take kindly to advice, no matter how well intended.

'Have you tried telling her?' I said weakly.

'She doesn't listen to us.' Doreen huffed. 'I can't even make her take a proper lunch break and she won't let Juliet and me take over the evening cleaning, she sends us home at four and does it herself. We do bits when we can without her noticing. But the griddle is in desperate need of a deep clean and the loos . . .' Her bottom lip trembled. 'If the health inspector ever comes in, he'd have a field day. I can't afford to lose this job, neither can Juliet.'

Juliet was the other part-time staff member who worked when Doreen was off. But Nonna had always kept numbers to a minimum, claiming that she did the work of two people. Perhaps those days were gone, but I didn't want to be the one to break that to Nonna.

'I understand and I'm sure it won't come to that.' I gave her a reassuring smile. 'Er . . . shall I, er, mention it to Mum?'

'Not a good idea,' Doreen said hastily. 'Remember the last time your mum tried to help?'

I grimaced. Who could forget? Mum had been made redundant from the council planning department and rather than look for another job had suggested that, seeing as Nonna was at retirement age, she should take over at the café. Nonna compromised and said Mum could work alongside her to learn the ropes. They fell out in the first week and Nonna gave Mum the sack. Things had been decidedly frosty at family get-togethers for the next six months.

'The problem is,' I said, trying to put it tactfully, 'that they both like to be in charge.'

'Don't I know it?' Doreen rolled her eyes. 'Which reminds me: your mum is having her Women's Institute meeting here in half an hour. I'd better go and set up the conservatory.'

I pondered Doreen's problem while I finished my toastie and looked round the Lemon Tree Café with fresh eyes.

None of us had ever visited Nonna's home town of Naples, but she said that the café reminded her of the house she grew up in. She didn't have any living family, and she'd settled here in England with Mum in the 1960s after her husband died young. She came to the café as a waitress initially, then was promoted to manager and eventually took over the lease herself. The café was her little piece of Italy, she was fond of saying, and she never wanted to let it go.

The walls were lined with old Italian posters advertising olive oil, flour and lemons, the tables were heavy and dark, the mismatched chairs were a little worn in places, but comfortable enough. A plain wooden dresser bulged with Italian crockery featuring lemons and an eclectic collection of jugs and vases filled the gaps in between the pots of herbs. The effect was a cross between a Mediterranean garden and an old lady's kitchen: shabby chic with the emphasis on shabby.

I could see what Doreen meant: the café was looking a bit tired and unloved. But it had so much potential. The place was in a perfect spot overlooking the village green; it had room on the pavement for a few tables in summer. It was a shame I was such a useless cook, or I could have offered to help out.

'So what you gonna do now, eh?' Nonna's sharp voice in my ear jolted me out of my reverie.

She propped herself up on the counter to study me and promptly knocked my coffee cup off with her elbow. I caught it in my lap.

Doreen sighed despondently and handed me a napkin.

'Well,' I said brightly, ignoring that last thought about my culinary prowess, 'I was rather hoping you'd let me work for you for a month.'

Nonna's brow furrowed. 'I don't need—'

'Free of charge, of course,' I added. 'You'd be doing me a

favour. You know how I hate not being busy and it'll look better on my CV than doing nothing.'

Doreen put her hands together in a hopeful prayer while Nonna gave my proposal an awfully long consideration.

'Okey cokey,' she finally grumbled and wagged a finger. 'But remember who is boss. No interfering.'

I threw my arms round her neck and kissed her soft cheek.

'Thank you!' I winked at Doreen whose face could scarcely contain her pleasure. 'And don't worry about me interfering, I can't even boil an egg, remember.'

It might have been my imagination but Doreen's smile seemed to slip a bit at that.

Chapter 2

I was quite looking forward to my first proper day in the café the next morning as I pulled up the collar on my coat against the biting wind and headed downhill from my tiny cottage. It would be a change from the deadlines and the demands of unrealistic clients who expected their brand to flourish after just a handful of sponsored tweets. This would be good for me; a bit of manual labour, an opportunity to brush up on my sorry cooking skills and, hopefully, the chance to have a subtle snoop at the running of the café while I was at it.

As I approached the village green, I spotted a woman with a streak of pink hair going into Ken's Mini Mart. That had to be my old school friend Gina. She'd been a colourful character at school too. It would be good to catch up with her now that I would be spending more time in the village. She'd moved back to Barnaby last year, the same as I had, after splitting up with her husband. But what with doing up the cottage and her setting up a new child-minding business, we'd barely had the chance to get together. I waved to Adrian, the landlord of the Cross Keys pub on the opposite side of the green, who was leaning in the pub doorway smoking an early-morning cigarette and chatting away to a couple of people while their dogs chased each other round in circles on the frosty grass.

It was blissfully peaceful compared to my normal

commute into Derby; I could hear nothing but the birds twittering in the hawthorn trees and the gentle trickle of the stream which bordered the green. None of the other shops were open yet. There were four including the café: Biddy's Pets, The Heavenly Gift Shop and Nina's Flowers. I was smiling at a handwritten sign in Biddy's window – *Pregnant rabbit for sale! Eight (approx.) for the price of one!* – when my phone beeped with a text. I grinned when I saw it was from my friend, Verity.

Good luck today! And if all else fails, serve 'em fish finger sandwiches xx

As housemates, we'd hardly spent any time in our kitchen; we'd invariably relied on mountains of toast or, if we were really pushing the boat out, Verity's speciality: fish finger sandwiches. Funny that we'd both ended up in food-related worlds: Verity at the cookery school and living with a chef, and me at the café. Mine, of course, was strictly on a temporary basis but she had always been a foodie at heart. It had only been when her best friend Mimi died suddenly, leaving a husband, Gabe, and little boy, Noah, that Verity had fallen out of love with cooking. Thankfully her passion returned when the opportunity to run the Plumberry School of Comfort Food came along.

The sign on the café door still said 'Closed' but the lights were on. Good old Doreen had come in early to show me the ropes. Which was just as well, I thought, pushing open the glass door and hearing the bell ding, because I was going to need all the help I could get.

While Nonna prepped the jacket potato fillings, Doreen had given me a cursory tour of the kitchen, pointing out all the bits that needed cleaning or in some cases replacing, introduced me to a rather bad-mannered Italian coffee machine and put me in charge of the griddle and making toast. I was surprisingly nervous and very relieved when the first customers through the door were my sister Lia and her six-month-old son Arlo.

'Oh,' said Lia, blinking at me in surprise. She peeled Arlo's coat off him and pulled out various pieces of equipment and toys from a voluminous quilted bag. 'You're working here.'

'I'm volunteering my services for a while,' I said, cursing myself for not texting her last night. I'd been up until midnight working on my CV (and also watching YouTube videos of how to make patterns in the top of cappuccinos). I took Arlo from her and gave him a cuddle while she mixed milk powder with water in a baby bottle. 'Just until I find another job.'

'You won't be on the shelf for long,' said Lia when I'd explained why I'd walked out of Digital Horizons. 'The *job* shelf, I mean,' she added, going pink and then realizing that that made it worse. Her blush spread down her neck to her bosom as she held her arms out to take Arlo back for his feed. 'Or any shelf.'

'Thank you,' I said drily. 'I think.'

My inability to hold on to a boyfriend was a regular topic of conversation in our family. They all thought I was too choosy but the truth was that I preferred short, fun and flirty relationships that ended well before the 'L' word got bandied about. Love did strange things to people, in my experience, and I was better off without it.

'And it'll be lovely to see more of Auntie Rosie, won't it?' she said, smothering Arlo's face with kisses. 'We pop in most days. In fact, I feel a bit bad, Nonna. If I'd known you needed help, I'd have offered.'

'I don't need help,' Nonna muttered darkly, plonking herself at Lia's table.

'Nonna's doing me a favour, to keep me busy,' I said smoothly. 'And you're already busy enough with Arlo.'

Lia looked like she was about to argue, so I swiftly pulled my new order pad out of my apron pocket and grinned.

'So, madam, can I get you some tea and toast?'

'Please. Just one slice, though,' she said settling Arlo on to her lap.

'And espresso for me,' Nonna added. 'Double.'

I hurried off with my first order and crossed my fingers that the coffee machine would be gentle with me.

'I got the toilet rolls you asked for, Maria,' said Doreen, bending to press a kiss to the top of Arlo's head.

'Thank you, thank you,' said Nonna vaguely.

Doreen hovered at the table and cleared her throat.

'They cost four pounds for nine rolls,' she added.

'Good, good.'

Doreen stood there for a few more seconds and then turned away and disappeared into the kitchen, muttering something under her breath.

I took the tray over and set a plate of toast and some curls of butter in front of Lia who held up her hand.

'Don't tempt me with real butter. I'm trying to shift some timber,' she said, sucking in her stomach. 'And I'd better just have half a slice.'

She was still carrying her baby weight, but then Arlo was only little. And she might be a bit rounder in places but I'd never seen her look lovelier.

'Get away!' Nonna flicked her cloth at her. 'You eating for two.'

'I am,' she agreed. '*Still.* That's the problem. He's been eating for himself for some time now.'

My sister was beautiful. She had fine golden curls, soft pink cheeks and a sunny personality which drew people to her like bumblebees to a sunflower. Whereas my black hair was cut into an angular, easy-to-control bob, I was quick-tempered and sharp-tongued. She went with the flow, opting for an easy life, whereas I was more like a spawning salmon: determined to swim upstream even if it killed me. We both had Mum's brown eyes, shared a deep-rooted passion for Tom Hiddleston and ice cream of any flavour and alongside Verity, who I rarely saw these days, she was undoubtedly my best friend.

Arlo made a contented slurping noise and my heart melted at the sight of him. He was chugging away at his bottle without a care in the world, one hand wound in his fluffy curls, the other cradling his bottle protectively. Maybe I was biased, but my nephew was the most adorable bundle of tiny boyhood on the planet.

'I remember your mamma when she was that small.' Nonna's wrinkled face softened at the memory. 'Before she learn to answer back. Happy times.'

'It must have been so hard for you, losing Nonno so young and having to bring up a baby by yourself,' I said, stroking a finger across my nephew's velvety cheek.

Nonna picked up a teaspoon and stirred her coffee so roughly that it slopped into the saucer. 'Long time ago now.'

'I swear I'd have lost my marbles in the first few weeks if I hadn't had Ed there to fetch me a cup of tea during those long night feeds.' Lia bit into her toast and closed her eyes. 'Oh heaven.'

Arlo pushed his bottle away and began to struggle to sit up. Lia crammed the rest of her toast in her mouth to begin the burping routine.

'Don't rush, let me have him.' I put the little boy over my shoulder, snuggling into his neck and inhaling his sweet milky scent.

'Look at you.' Lia brushed the crumbs from her cleavage. 'You're a natural.'

'A natural auntie, maybe,' I said, forcing a smile.

Motherhood had been part of the life I'd imagined for myself once but now I wasn't so sure. For the last ten years I'd thrown myself into my professional life instead and I suppose now I was married to my career. I couldn't see that changing anytime soon either.

A few gentle pats to his back and Arlo produced a couple

of soft burps and we all cheered. At which point he decided to go one step further and vomited down my back.

'Cheers, buddy.' I passed Arlo back to Lia to mop up and Nonna handed me her cloth.

'Welcome to my world, Rosie.' Lia laughed at my wrinkled nose as I peeled off my cardigan and rubbed off the worst of the milky goo. 'That's what I mean, Nonna – how did you cope on your own?'

'I loved your mamma as hard as I could. I kept us both safe and warm and fed. That's all.' She shrugged. 'And as soon as I have money, I come to England and start new life.'

I balled up the cardigan and the dirty cloth, and gave Nonna a hug. 'I'm proud of you. You were so brave.'

There was a ding on the bell and a stockily built young man with a baby-soft face and huge feet entered.

'Morning, Tyson,' cried Nonna. 'One egg or two today?'

'Better make it two, Mrs Carloni.' He rubbed his hands together and chose a table in the corner. 'Busy day ahead at the garden centre, I'm moving all the big terracotta pots to the entrance ready for spring.'

'Coming up. OK, Rosanna, your turn to be brave, eh?' Nonna twinkled her eyes at me as I smoothed down my new black apron. 'Can you do two fried eggs over easy?'

'Me?' I answered with a laugh as I scampered to the griddle for the first time. 'A walk in the park.'

Now they were the ones you had to flip, weren't they, or was that sunny side up . . . ?

'You having fun time?' Nonna asked, refilling the napkin holder on the counter as I took a quick coffee break at an empty table later on. 'Better than that fancy office, eh?'

'It's trickier than I thought,' I admitted, 'keeping up with the orders and trying to have things ready at the same time.'

'When I first take over the café, it is only me here on my own. No other staff.' She shook her head, lost in her memories. 'Now that is tricky.'

The doorbell dinged and Nonna suddenly gasped and turned away from the door.

'Oh no, he's here again,' she hissed, patting her hair.

I glanced at the door to see a rotund elderly gentleman with a white beard and a fringe of hair around a bald patch, holding the door for a departing customer. He was around Nonna's age, carried a newspaper under one arm and had a yellow carnation in the buttonhole of his blazer.

'Who's that?' I asked.

'Stanley Pigeon.' Nonna pinched her cheeks to make them pink and then took an ancient lipstick out of her apron pocket and puckered up to apply it. 'Such a nuisance.'

I blinked at her; I'd never seen her wear make-up. Ever.

The name rang a bell.

'The postman?'

'Retired now,' she said. 'Although he help out sometimes when new boy can't find all the houses.'

I shook my head and tried to suppress a smile. The 'new boy' was Dad's age and he'd already been in this morning for a takeaway cup of tea and a plaster for his finger after an altercation with a particularly fierce letterbox.

'And why is he a nuisance?'

I remembered passing Stanley Pigeon on my way to school every day. He had kept mint toffees in one pocket and dog biscuits in the other. The best way to deal with any difficult situation, he'd told me once with a wink, was to feed your way out of it.

'He always asking me for dates. Silly old fool.' She sighed dramatically and then sneaked a look at him over her shoulder. 'He looking for me?'

None of us knew much about Nonna's husband, my grandfather Lorenzo, other than that he'd been killed in an accident at work in Naples and that he had been her one true love. She had never remarried, nor, as far as I knew, even had a relationship since. And that was over fifty years ago. I'd never even seen her show a passing interest in another man.

'I think so. Shall I go and ask what he wants?' I watched as Stanley settled himself into one of the sagging armchairs near the window. 'To save you having to talk to him?'

'No, no, you too busy.' She peeled her lips back. 'Have I got lipstick on my teeth?'

I shook my head and watched in amazement as she strutted over to him, one hand on her hip, broad bottom swinging from side to side. Stanley got up stiffly, kissed Nonna's hand and presented her with his carnation buttonhole. I couldn't hear what he said to her but she erupted into giggles, tucked the flower behind her ear and sat opposite him, crossing her legs and hitching her skirt up an inch. I was amazed.

Doreen emerged from the kitchen with a fresh batch of scones.

'It's a hotbed of passion in here,' she chuckled, following my gaze. 'Just goes to show, it's never too late to find love.'

'Evidently. Does he normally stay long?' I asked, hatching a plan.

She laughed. 'Stanley's a regular fixture in the mornings, he usually has breakfast and a pot of tea.'

'Right,' I said stealthily, slipping my hands into a pair of rubber gloves and picking up the bleach. 'While Nonna is occupied, I'm going to tackle the toilets.'

I started in the Ladies and gave everywhere a good scrub. The place really needed a makeover: the tiles needed regrouting, one of the taps leaked and the lino on the floor was ripped. Doreen was right; it was far too much for Nonna to manage on her own. If only she'd admit that she needed help, it would make things far easier.

I made my way into the men's loos, trying not to breathe too deeply, and knelt down in front of the toilet brandishing my bleach. I was still pondering my dilemma: how to put it to Nonna that the café was ready for an overhaul without insulting her . . . ?

'Well, you are honoured. Being allowed to work here.'

I retracted my arm from the U-bend and turned to see my mum, leaning on the doorframe with her arms folded, a twinkly smile playing at her lips. The smell of her perfume was a welcome relief after the aroma of my surroundings and I smiled back.

'Hmm. *Honoured*. Yes, that's just the word I was looking for.' I knelt back on my heels and tried to rub an itch from my forehead with a clean bit of arm. 'Scrubbing toilets. For free.'

'It's further than I got,' she laughed, her brown eyes shining at the memory. 'I only suggested adding paninis to the menu and got the sack.'

'Note to self,' I grinned, 'no messing with the menu.'

'Doreen sent me to tell you that Stanley will be off shortly.' She flicked imaginary pieces of fluff from her neat blouse, straightened her skirt and smoothed her hair, which was still thick and dark like mine but threaded with silver. I liked the fact she didn't dye it; she didn't need to, she always looked fabulous. I, on the other hand, probably looked and smelled considerably different.

'Oh heavens.' I climbed to my feet. 'I'd better get back in the kitchen before Nonna wonders what I'm doing.'

'Forgive me for asking silly questions, but what *are* you doing?' Mum wrinkled her nose, either in confusion or at the smell, I couldn't tell.

'Aha. Join me at the counter,' I said, stopping just short of tapping my nose with a bleach-soaked finger, 'and I'll tell all.'

'She's seventy-five,' I whispered, once I'd washed my hands, given Mum a proper hug and fetched us both a glass of water. 'She won't let Juliet or Doreen do anything other than their nine-to-four duties. And it's too much for her. I'm trying to intervene without her noticing but already I can see it's not enough. When is she going to admit it's time to hang up her apron?'

'Darling, I've been asking myself the same question for

23

years,' Mum replied wearily. 'And I still don't have the answer. I love your nonna dearly but she's a closed book to me. She never opens up. Ever. But I do know the café means the world to her. I don't think she can imagine any other sort of life.'

I nodded thoughtfully. 'Perhaps that's the key; helping her to see what else life could hold?'

'It's a nice thought to help out,' Mum said, pulling the it'll-all-end-in-tears face that she used to do when Lia and I bought something between us claiming we'd share it nicely. 'But your grandmother won't thank you for it. I should know,' she added with a sniff.

I gave her a sideways glance. The difference was that I wasn't planning on 'telling' Nonna how to run her own business, I was simply going to help in small subtle ways, without her noticing. I didn't blame Mum for trying, but unfortunately both she and Nonna were strong women, neither liked to back down.

'Anyway, Mum,' I said, sensing that a change of conversation was in order, 'how's your new role on the parish council going?'

'Well, I've only attended one meeting so far,' she said happily. The valuable part she played on her endless committees was her favourite topic. 'Just between you and me, it's a good job I joined. The state of their reports!'

I let Mum talk while I made a cheese-and-tomato toastie, two pots of tea and a latte.

' . . . but I said, we can't have the next meeting then, it clashes with the local history society AGM. Well, you should have heard—'

Just then Nonna and Stanley erupted into laughter and Nonna leaned forward and smacked his arm playfully as she walked him to the door.

Mum's jaw fell open. 'Is she flirting with him?'

'Outrageously,' I said with a giggle. 'Great, isn't it? I think romance is on the cards.'

'Doubt it.' She sipped her water. 'She's been like this before: a man shows a bit of interest and she goes along with it for a while before giving him the brush-off.'

'Shame,' I said, looking at the pair of them waving to each other. 'A boyfriend might be just what she needs to see that there's life outside of work.'

Mum looked at me pointedly and cleared her throat.

'Which reminds me . . .' I said, willing my cheeks not to blush. I reached into my apron pocket for my phone and scrolled through my emails. 'I should really check in with my recruitment consultant and see if he's found me a job yet, or else I'll be stuck here for fifty years too.'

Chapter 3

'We need two more forks and a spoon, Alec,' said Mum, wafting a hand in front of her face.

'Have you got any more forks, Rosie?' Dad asked, his voice muffled.

He had a towel over his face while he rummaged through the cutlery drawer. 'I can only find five.'

'Try the bottom of the washing-up bowl,' I replied, from the doorway of my cottage where I was fanning the room with the door to deactivate the smoke alarm and remove the worst of the smoke.

I'd invited the family to my cottage for Sunday lunch. This was a first for me. Normally at weekends, I'd have some report or other to catch up on or I'd be glued to my iPad answering tweets on behalf of clients, grabbing a quick snack every couple of hours when I felt hungry. But as I no longer had a proper job, I'd decided to make some proper food for once instead.

In all honesty, my invitation to lunch had two ulterior motives: firstly, having spent a few days at the café I was shocked how fumbly and slow I was in the kitchen; and secondly, I was hoping that somehow we'd be able to bring the conversation round to Nonna's future plans for the café.

I was probably being a bit ambitious.

Dad winced as he pushed up his sleeve and plunged a hand into a bowl of grey sludgy water. 'Yuck.'

'Sorry,' I said, unable to stop myself from laughing.

My dad was a lecturer of philosophy at Derby University. Monday to Friday he wore a uniform of tweed jacket, corduroy trousers and check shirt. At weekends he wore exactly the same. Even now he had his jacket on. He had fine blond hair and fair freckled skin, which had always made him stand out on family holidays as the rest of us only had to look at the sun to get a tan.

'Got 'em.' He waved a handful of dripping cutlery triumphantly and squinted at me through the haze as I pointed out the cloth for him to dry them on. 'How is the pork looking?'

I glanced at the black lump, still smoking in the roasting tray. 'Well done.'

I'd thought a couple of minutes under a hot grill would crisp up the skin on my joint of pork nicely. Unfortunately, I'd got sidetracked trying to get my potato purée as smooth as Nonna's and now instead of golden crackling, it resembled a charcoal brick and there was a thick cloud of grey smoke hanging over the dining table.

Lia and my brother-in-law Ed had escaped to the garden with Arlo for some fresh air, Nonna was beating the lumps out of the potato with the back of a wooden spoon and Mum was trying to make room for six adults and a high chair around my tiny table. And Dad . . . well, Dad was just obeying Mum's orders as usual.

The downstairs of my cottage was open plan: kitchen in one half, living room in the other with a dining table in the centre and a small log burner set into the thick stone walls. The stairs ran up the far wall to a single bedroom and bathroom. It was tiny but gorgeous and the views from the window above my bed across the village and way out to the hills beyond made me feel anything but hemmed in when I woke in the mornings.

'Check in the drawers for napkins, will you, Alec?' said Mum, squeezing the gravy boat in between the apple sauce and the buttered carrots.

'Sure.' Dad began rummaging again. He found a handful of battered paper napkins decorated with poinsettias left over from Christmas and began tucking them into the wine glasses.

'I'll carve the meat,' Lia announced, waving her hand in front of her face as she came back inside. 'I've been watching cooking shows. Did you know you can pay over five thousand pounds for a Japanese white steel knife?'

'Dicky heads,' Nonna muttered with a tut. 'More money than brain, some people.'

'See how you get on with this beauty,' I said, tongue in cheek, presenting my carving knife to her as if it was a precious sword.

'Is it Japanese?' Lia said, wrinkling her nose up at my wobbly, plastic-handled supermarket knife, specially purchased for today.

'Close,' I said. 'Made in China.'

'It'll be a squash,' said Mum, standing back to admire the table she'd laid. 'But I've done it.'

'I don't mind squashing up next to you, Luisa,' said Dad, pressing a kiss to his wife's cheek.

'Not now, Alec,' she said, batting him off. 'Can you fetch our two spare chairs from the car?'

He clasped her hands to his chest, filled his lungs and began to belt out, 'Everything I Do,' from the Bryan Adams song from a Robin Hood film years ago.

I dived to the oven to rescue the roast potatoes to hide my giggle. Dad was an enthusiastic singer, but not terribly good. He had a loud, high-pitched voice which Mum normally only allowed him to exercise when he was right at the bottom of the garden.

Mum pressed a finger to his lips. 'You've got many talents, Alec, but singing isn't one of them. Now, those chairs?'

Dad slunk off and my heart leapt for him. He was a man of simple pleasures; his loves were Derby County Football Club, pork pies and Dolly Parton. Not necessarily in that order and none of these passions compared to his unwavering devotion to his wife. But Mum always seemed too busy to give him any of her time. She loved him, but it always seemed to me like he was somewhere halfway down her to-do list.

'Is it safe to come back in?' Ed asked from the doorway.

'Lunch is ready, we can almost see through the smog again and Dad's stopped singing,' I said, 'so yes, it's perfect timing.'

He had Arlo in his hands and was swooping him through the air, much to the little boy's delight. Mum held her arms out to take her grandson from him and Ed rubbed his hands together with glee.

'I'll sort out drinks, then.' He poured out glasses of wine and handed me a generous measure with a wink. 'Here you go, favourite sister-in-law.'

I smiled and took a sip. I liked Ed a lot. He was a gentle soul with big muscles, cropped dark hair and dimples in his round cheeks. He worked hard for his father's haulage company and was a hands-on dad. Lia was lucky, I thought, very lucky.

'Come on, family,' I said, pulling out a chair for Nonna. 'Let's eat.'

I wouldn't go as far as to say that lunch was a triumph, but it was edible and there was plenty of it. My zabaglione had been polished off, although Lia had declined any, and now we were having coffee and dark chocolate truffles to finish.

'How is Rosie getting on at the café, Nonna?' Lia handed Arlo a softly boiled carrot stick, which he mashed instantly into his face. He pointed longingly at the chocolate to no avail. 'Are you pleased with her?'

'She not doing too much yet,' said Nonna, talking about me as if I weren't there. 'I break her gently.'

'I think you mean break her *in* gently, Mamma,' Mum corrected.

'Yeah, yeah.' Nonna huffed. 'She doing okey cokey.'

Lia and I exchanged grins; that was high praise coming from our grandmother.

Actually, Nonna was right first time; the work was breaking me. I was aching all over and my nails were in shreds. Little did she realize that as soon as her back was turned I was hard at work scrubbing everything from the floors to the furniture. On Friday, she'd had a doctor's appointment and had left me to lock up. Between us, Juliet and I had stripped the big oven down and cleaned every part of it inside and out. It had taken two hours to remove goodness knows how many years of grime. I'd never worked so hard in my life.

'I think I've done quite well,' I said, 'considering how different working in the café is to my old job.'

'You always could turn your hand to anything, love,' said Dad kindly, helping himself to sugar. 'Well done, Rosie.'

'Absolutely,' said Mum, picking up her coffee cup. 'Here's to Rosie for sticking to her principles and handing in her notice. I'm proud of you, darling.'

Nonna drained the last of her wine. 'You good girl, Rosie. You do well. As long as you don't start tell me what to do, we stay friends, eh?'

'Oh, Mamma,' said Mum with a frown. 'When are you going to accept that at your age—'

'*Dio mio!*' Nonna thumped the table angrily. 'When you gonna accept that my business is my business, eh? Keepa nose out.'

Mum and Nonna glared at each other. The only sound in the room was Dad crunching on a piece of leftover crackling. Eventually he swallowed it and took a swig of his wine.

'That's one tough pig,' he said, shaking his head.

Ed made a sound halfway between a cough and a laugh; I didn't dare look at him.

'I would love to help at the café,' said Lia wistfully. 'I love cooking.'

Ed wrapped his arm round her waist and pressed a kiss into her hair. 'But you're enjoying your maternity leave, aren't you? Precious time, just you and Arlo. You'll be at the leisure centre again soon enough. There's no need to go back to work earlier than necessary.'

Lia was a swimming instructor at a busy leisure complex just outside Derby. She'd been there for years, going down to three days a week when she found out she was pregnant. I hadn't heard her mention going back to work since Arlo was born. She'd never been particularly ambitious and part of me wondered whether she'd bother going back at all.

She sighed. 'I do love being with him. Obviously. But I'm feeling . . . I dunno. Look, forget it.'

She pushed her chair back and ran upstairs so fast that I almost missed her trembling bottom lip.

For a split second, the rest of the family was silent.

'I'll go after her,' I said, jumping to my feet.

Lia was sitting on the edge of my bed facing the window, fiddling with the corner of one of the magazines on my bedside cabinet. Tears bulged at her eyes.

'What's wrong?'

'Everything. Nothing. This,' she said, grabbing a handful of her tummy and wobbling it.

'Don't be daft.' I nudged her arm. 'You've just had a baby!'

'I mean it,' she said. 'I hate looking like this, I hate turning on the telly or opening a magazine and seeing some size-eight celeb holding a six-week-old baby saying how hard she worked to fight the flab. I hate seeing pretty clothes in the shops that I can't fit into. I have to make do with leggings and baggy jumpers. I'd give anything to be as slim as you.'

'Are you crazy?' I gasped. 'You're beautiful. And you've earned the right to those curves. That body looks like it does because it's amazing. You're very lucky, actually.'

31

Lia's eyes widened. 'That's a lovely way of looking at it, thank you.'

'You're welcome,' I said, meaning it. I might have been the sister with the career, but she had a family, she loved Ed and he loved her back. In my eyes, that was priceless and totally enviable.

'The thing is . . .' she said, not meeting my eye. 'Don't laugh.'

I stroked her arm. 'I won't.'

She lowered her voice. 'Being this shape makes me feel such a failure. A fat failure with a repulsive body.'

'Never say that,' I said fiercely, poking her in the chest. 'Because if you do they've won. Don't be bullied by what the media say you should look like or what you should weigh or how you should behave. That's why I had to leave Digital Horizons; I was in danger of becoming part of the problem. Jesus, it's the twenty-first century and women are still being manipulated and objectified and pressured into doing things they don't want to do with *their own bodies.*'

'OK.' Lia stared at me, straining away from me as if I'd struck her. 'Point taken.'

'Sorry.' I took a calming breath. 'But it makes my blood boil. Anyway, what else?' I prompted. 'You said everything's wrong.'

She stood up, leaned on the window sill and looked out into the distance.

'I'm ready for something new. I'm ready for a challenge. I don't want to go back to being a swimming teacher, but I have no idea what I do want. And as much as I love Arlo, I need some adult time. A chance to be me again. Ed doesn't understand. He goes off to work and as soon as he drives away he's himself again. I've forgotten who I used to be, what I used to do when I wasn't changing nappies or wiping up drool or puréeing minute portions of baby food. My life is ruled by Arlo's sleep and how much I can do during his naps.'

'How about putting him into a nursery or with a child-minder for a few hours a week, to give yourself some head-space?' I suggested.

'I'd love that,' she said with a wan smile, 'but it's the money. I could justify it if I was back at work, but not otherwise.'

'Knock knock.'

Lia and I turned to see Mum's face at the bedroom door. She waggled her fingers in a wave.

'Can I come in?'

We nodded and she crept in to sit beside us.

'Lia, I just caught the tail end of that. And . . . well, I'm saddened that you didn't come to me for help. After all, Arlo is my only grandchild; I'd be only too happy to have him. Any time, just say the word.'

Lia took a deep breath and glanced sideways at me.

'That's lovely to hear, Mum, but if you remember, I have asked you to have Arlo on several occasions. And each time you've been too busy organizing a charity lunch or going to a meeting or collecting raffle prizes or something. So I've just stopped asking.'

Mum's commitment to her committees knew no bounds. I could just imagine how many times Lia had asked for help and been refused. I reached for Lia's hand and squeezed it.

'Well . . . I . . .' Mum's face flushed. 'Gosh. I didn't realize. But now I know I'll make myself available, just give me a bit of notice, darling, because as you know I'm very busy . . .' Her voice trailed off as she caught Lia's resigned expression.

'Exactly. Forget it, Mum.' Lia pushed herself up off the bed and walked out. Mum groaned and I just about managed to hold my tongue, not wanting to take sides.

By the time we'd got back downstairs, the table had been cleared and Ed had given Arlo his afternoon bottle.

'Well done, Superdad,' said Lia, greeting her husband with a kiss.

'You're the super one,' he replied.

He kissed her and my heart squeezed for them both.

See? I mouthed to Lia, catching her eye. Ed obviously didn't think she was a failure and surely that had to mean more to her than some trashy magazine?

'So what have we missed?' Dad asked from the kitchen sink. 'What's the big secret?'

Lia shook her head and looked down at her lap; Mum began a thorough search of her handbag. Ed looked from Lia to me.

'No secrets,' I said lightly, giving Ed a casual smile. 'Just girl stuff.'

Nonna flopped down on the sofa. 'Nothing wrong with keeping secrets anyway. Nobody need to know everything about you.'

'True,' I said, reaching for the last chocolate truffle.

I loved my family dearly, but there were some things about me that would never be aired around the family dinner table. 'As long as we're there when anyone needs us, that's what matters.'

Mum cleared her throat.

'Actually, there is something.' Her voice was more hesitant than usual and we all stared at her.

'I've decided to give up some of my committees, just for a few months, while Lia needs me.'

She walked across and took Lia's hand. 'I'd like to be a more hands-on grandmother, if I may?'

Lia swallowed. 'That would be brilliant, Mum. If you're sure?'

'Absolutely sure. A few hours a day, or a whole day now and then, up to you.' She smiled at Arlo. 'We'll have fun, won't we, darling? Just you and me. Oh, is he all right?'

Arlo's eyes had taken on a determined look of concentration and his little face was scarlet.

'Looks like the fun's begun already, Luisa,' said Ed with a laugh.

He sniffed the baby's bottom and handed him to Mum. 'Yep. Time to be a hands-on grandmother.'

'Of course,' said Mum stoically, holding Arlo rather gingerly. 'Unless, Alec . . . ?'

'Mum!' Lia and I yelled together.

'OK, OK,' she said, slinging the changing bag over her shoulder. 'I'm going.'

A few days later, I was hunched up over a giant block of cheese, grating it for toasties when Dad walked in. I was so startled to see him that I grated my fingertip.

'Hi, Dad. No work today? Ouch!' I said, abandoning the cheese and sucking the end of my finger. 'What can I get you?'

'A date with your mother would be nice,' he said, pulling up a stool at the counter. 'Or failing that a cup of beef tea.'

'Morning, hen,' said Juliet to Dad in her gruff Scottish accent. She handed me a blue plaster from the first-aid box whilst simultaneously checking the cheese bowl for blood. 'Here. The vegetarians will go mental if you drip blood in the cheese.'

Juliet was a wiry Glaswegian in her forties with spiky red hair and a personality to match. She baked the best cakes this side of the Pennines, which went some way to making up for her rather abrasive manner. She gave Dad the once-over as she made him a cup of Bovril, his favourite.

'Good God, man, you're looking like someone's popped your balloon. Cheer up; you'll put the rest of the customers off.'

I grinned at Juliet's way with words.

'You do look a bit down in the dumps,' I said as I scooped the grated cheese into a container and set it down in the salad counter between the sliced cucumber and shredded lettuce.

'I'm fine,' said Dad with a forced laugh. 'It's just that I had a couple of hours spare after a meeting so I thought I'd surprise

Luisa and take her for lunch. But she said she and Arlo have got Baby Percussion at two o'clock and she doesn't have time.'

True to her word, Mum had immediately stepped down from some of her voluntary positions and had made arrangements to have Arlo every day, Monday to Friday, for four hours.

'Honestly, it's feast or famine with her,' Lia had confided last night on the phone. 'I was only looking for a bit of ad hoc babysitting. Mum has organized trips to the river, swimming lessons, play gym . . . The poor little chap has got a schedule more crammed than the Prime Minister.'

'Baby Percussion?' said Juliet, rolling her eyes. 'When I was a wee girl, I had a saucepan and a wooden spoon.'

Nonna appeared from the kitchen with two bowls of baby food she'd heated for a mum of twins, who was sitting in the toy corner trying to keep both of them occupied while they waited for their lunch.

'Luisa like to be busy, busy, busy. Always the same. Just like me.'

'She seems to make time for the things she enjoys doing,' said Dad. 'All I ever seem to do is work and wait for her in an empty house.'

'Then you should do the same, Dad. What do you like doing? Perhaps you need to indulge your secret passion?' I said, turning to serve a new customer. 'Yes please?'

'Hmm,' Dad stroked his chin thoughtfully, 'that's an idea.'

'If you ask me, all babies need is a bit of your time. Just like dogs, really,' said Juliet, who was a big animal lover with no children of her own. 'All these activities . . . waste of money.'

'Here, take these,' said Nonna, passing her the bowls. 'For the twins over there. See if you can help their mum; give them a bit of your time.'

'Twins.' Dad slurped his Bovril and turned to look at them. 'Now that really would be hard work.'

'Twins is double blessing from God,' said Nonna fiercely. 'Two times the joy. Why you think we have two arms, eh?'

'All right, keep your hair on,' Juliet grumbled and stomped off to offer assistance. She came back straight away claiming that no help was required. Although I suspected she'd simply dumped the bowls and run.

'Eh, Rosanna?' Nonna nodded to a recently vacated table. 'Did that man leave without paying his bill?'

'Um.' I exchanged guilty looks with Juliet.

A man had been in earlier for a bacon sandwich wearing a T-shirt advertising him to be 'Peter Pipes the Plumber'. I'd offered him breakfast on the house if he'd mend the leaky tap in the men's loos. 'No, he paid, didn't he, Juliet?'

'Oh aye.' Juliet nodded. 'And left a tap, I mean a tip.'

She high-fived me once Nonna's back was turned. 'This place is already looking so much better, hen. Next job when she isn't looking is to see if we can get rid of the brown goo at the back of the fridge.'

'Remind me not to order the hummus,' said Dad drily.

'So you're going to stay here for lunch?' I said. 'I can recommend the quiche.'

He got to his feet and pecked me on the cheek. 'Actually, I can't stop. I'm going to take your advice.'

'Oh, what was that?' I smiled back, pleased to see him more cheerful.

'I'm off to locate someone who can fan the flames of my smouldering passion.' He tapped his nose. 'But mum's the word, OK?'

A prickle of concern ran down my spine but I nodded. Juliet put my thoughts into words as she folded her arms and watched him leave.

'Oh shite, hen, what have you started there?'

Chapter 4

A week later and crocuses were beginning to pop up through the grass on the village green; their zingy colours of yellow, purple and white made them look like mini Easter eggs peeping through the grass. Spring was on its way along with milder weather and lighter nights. The buds on my flowering cherry tree were almost ready to pop and despite Mum's predictions, here in the café, in amongst the clink of spoons and the hiss and gurgle of the coffee machine, the romance between Nonna and Stanley was blossoming too.

He was here now sitting in his usual spot looking extra smart. He'd had a haircut and a beard trim and if the price tag at the back of his neck was anything to go by he was wearing a new jumper too. He'd ordered a pot of tea for two and had invited Nonna to join him. She'd been snoozing in the conservatory five minutes before he arrived, although she'd denied it, giving Juliet and I the chance to whip every item of crockery off the heavy Italian dresser, scrub down the shelves and replace everything again before she woke up. But now they were sharing a custard tart – one plate and two forks. It was all very sweet.

The breakfast trade fizzled out by half past ten and in the hiatus that followed, Juliet and I had the fairly easy job of serving up teas and coffees. Nonna went into the kitchen to load the dishwasher while Stanley lingered over the crossword, looking hopefully at the kitchen every time he heard her voice.

It was quiet enough that when Verity rang me on my mobile I was only too pleased to pour myself a coffee and curl up in a chair in the conservatory for a chat. She'd got a gap between cookery courses, she said, and wanted to check up on me.

The conservatory was the most private part of the café. There wasn't much in the way of a view; the windows looked out on to the little courtyard at the back, but with the sun warming the terracotta floor tiles and the potted lemon trees softening the hard lines of the walls, it felt like a little Mediterranean paradise.

'Just making sure you haven't burned the place down with your dubious culinary talents,' she said once I'd made myself comfortable.

'You'd be amazed,' I said. 'I've taken to café life like a duck to water.'

'Not amazed,' she said. 'I adore working in the food industry. Everyone arrives expecting to have a nice time; a break from the daily grind. Being at your café could be a treat to themselves after a hard day or perhaps a special celebration. Imagine an old person living alone whose first conversation of the day is with you. Just think of the difference you could make to someone's life. Every day. Which makes it a nice place to spend time in.'

Verity had been a marketing manager in a financial services company before moving to Plumberry in Yorkshire to work at the cookery school and she'd never been happier.

'I never thought of it like that,' I agreed. 'But being in the village has made me realize how much of my family life I used to miss when I worked in an office such long hours.'

'Sounds like someone might stay on more than a month,' she said in a singsong voice.

I looked around me at the faded decor, the tired menus, the sagging cushions, and felt my heart race. There was so much potential here, new houses were springing up all the time on the outskirts of Barnaby, city workers like me were moving further and further out into the countryside, all wanting a cute café for avocado on toast or bircher bowls, or warm salads. If this café were mine, I'd—

I shook myself. It was a ridiculous thought.

'Nooo,' I said, trying to convince myself as much as Verity. 'I'm used to high-pressure pitches and interpreting impossible briefs and coming up with a creative solution so amazing that the client is rendered speechless.'

'You can use all those skills there, can't you?'

I pulled a waxy green leaf off a lemon tree and folded it between my fingers.

'There is the small matter of Nonna and what to do about her,' I conceded. 'Now *that* needs a creative solution. She's kidding herself that she still puts in a full day's work, but she falls asleep as soon as she sits down and half the time when she serves customers she wanders off part way through and forgets what she's doing. She doesn't ever take a day off; she's a workaholic.'

'Sounds like someone else I know.'

I had to smile at that; I was guilty of doing the same. In my last job I'd always been getting email reminders to take my paid leave entitlement.

'She's seventy-five, Verity; even I might have called it a day by then.'

'Or fallen madly in love and had loads of gorgeous dark-haired babies?'

'We both know how unlikely that is.'

'Rubbish, you just need to find the right man. Like me.' There was a pause on the line. 'Sorry, that sounded smug. Carry on. About Nonna.'

I suppressed a sigh. I was delighted that Verity was so happy with Tom, but love wasn't on my agenda, nor did I appreciate being told that all my troubles would be over if only I met 'The One'. And she knew that.

'It's just not fair on Juliet and Doreen,' I began again. 'At the moment we're cramming as many spring-cleaning jobs in as we can without her noticing. But I'm only here for another couple of weeks, and then I'll be off.'

Michael had called me with the details of a job in Manchester last night for a company called HitSquad. It was perfect, a bit further to commute, but I'd get used to it. And this job in the café had only ever been temporary. I was keeping everything crossed that I'd make the shortlist for an interview. It would be weird to wear my smart office clothes again and get on a train or a bus with the other office workers; I'd got quite used to a short hop across a dewy village green.

'Have you got a new job? How exciting.'

'Not yet, but I might have an interview. I need to start earning again. I used most of my savings buying the cottage last year.'

'Hmm.' Verity didn't sound convinced. 'Don't be too quick to dismiss the café, Rosie. Knowing you, you'd have a chain of twenty of them within a year.'

'Maybe,' I said, distracted by a babble of conversation at the door. 'Listen, all the teachers and staff from the local school are arriving for a celebratory lunch. I'll have to go and serve, they've pre-ordered jacket potatoes and Juliet has already got a queue at the till.'

'It's not just a jacket potato, remember,' she laughed, 'it's a *celebratory* jacket potato. Go and make their lunches special.'

'I will,' I promised. 'I'll even chop up some cress for an extra garnish.'

'That's my girl,' she said, tongue firmly in cheek. 'What are they celebrating?'

'Excellence,' I replied. 'Our little village school has just had a visit from the inspector and it has passed with flying colours.'

'Really? A primary school?'

'Yes, the one I used to go to.'

'Your village is lucky; I'm worried to death about the school Noah is supposed to be starting after Easter. Complete disaster, apparently. Gabe says it's had an awful report and has gone into Special Measures.'

I had only met Gabe Green a handful of times but Verity was very close to him in a complicated sort of way. He'd been married to her best friend Mimi who died aged thirty leaving him to bring up their baby son, Noah. It had been desperately sad and Verity had been heartbroken at the time. Gabe had nearly drowned in sorrow too. He chucked in his job with a top law firm, moved on to a houseboat somewhere and now worked as a French polisher. Verity was Noah's godmother and she and Gabe were both directors of the cookery school she ran. She loved that little boy as if he were her own.

'Well, ours is outstanding, tell him,' I said, 'which bodes well for when my nephew enrols.'

'And your own children, of course.'

I said nothing.

'Sorry, sorry,' she cringed. 'I'm going now.'

Juliet and I herded the triumphant school party into the conservatory. There was only one man amongst them: Mr Beecher, who'd been the school caretaker since I'd been there. In my day, all the kids were scared of him. He used to have red hair, a thick monobrow and a permanent scowl. His hair was mostly grey now and his ears were as whiskery as his eyebrows.

'One potato with tuna?' I called above the chattering about displays and assemblies and parent questionnaires.

Mr Beecher raised his hand.

'That's mine,' he said and narrowed his eyes in recognition. 'I remember you.'

'Ditto,' I said, setting the plate in front of him. 'Mayonnaise is on the table. Enjoy.'

It was hardly surprising he remembered me: I don't

suppose there were many seven-year-olds who staged a rooftop protest to allow the ice-cream van into school because it was a hot day. He'd been furious at having to come up to get me. Mum had been furious too – sending me straight to my room after school – but Nonna had sneaked up with a small dish of ice cream, and told me to always stay brave, that if I believed something was right, or wrong, I should always take action and speak my mind. And mostly I'd managed it.

'Thank you.' His hooded eyes roamed the café. 'So you're back. You didn't manage to scale to great heights in the end, then? Ha ha.'

'We make a difference to people's lives every day in this café, in lots of small ways,' I said, paraphrasing Verity. 'Which is quite a tall order, I think.'

'Yes. It is. Sorry.' He nodded meekly. 'It was a joke, you know, because of the roof incident.'

'I know,' I said, allowing my lips to twitch into a smile. 'I was always a bit scared of you after that.'

He chuckled then and his whole face changed and I realized he was just an old man with a lot of hair.

'I was a bit wary of you too, lass. Got any salad cream? I hate this fancy new mayonnaise.'

'Of course.' I smiled.

Mayonnaise was new, was it? Perhaps I was being a bit optimistic with the bircher bowl idea . . .

Half an hour later, the school group was tucking into a cake that the dinner ladies had made as a surprise and Stanley was *still* here. I made two coffees, two pots of tea, a custard tart, soup with soft white bread, a slice of apple pie and ice cream and an Eccles cake.

'Eh, Rosanna?' Nonna yelled from her chair opposite him. 'More milk for Stanley, please.'

'Is Stanley all right?' I asked Juliet as we cleared away the teachers' plates and mugs.

'I was going to ask you the same question, hen,' Juliet said, tugging her bra strap up under her T-shirt. 'He seems a bit on edge.'

She stacked a pile of plates on the arm with the thistle tattoo on it and scooped up five mugs with the hand that had 'Dean' inked across her knuckles. I piled some empties on a tray and followed her.

'And he's been here even longer than usual,' I said, glancing over on my way to the kitchen. Nonna was still talking at him and there was a pile of shredded napkins on the placemat in front of him.

'Where's that milk?' Nonna tutted, trying to catch my eye. 'You milking the cow yourself?'

'Coming,' I yelled back.

The school lot started making noises about getting back before the dinner bell rang. Chairs scraped across the tiled conservatory floor, bags were retrieved from under chairs and people groaned and laughed about eating too much.

I filled a small jug with milk and took it over.

'Everything OK?' I said when Nonna had stopped talking. 'Can I get you anything else?'

'I'll get out of your way in a minute,' said Stanley, adding a drop of milk to the dregs of his tea. 'I'll just, er . . .'

'No rush, no rush.' Nonna flapped a hand. 'You very welcome in the café.'

Stanley turned beetroot red.

'Thank you very much, well, in that case . . .' He paused and reached into the pocket of his jacket.

But before he could find what he was looking for, Tyson barged through the door, pushing all the teachers aside. He ran in, wild-eyed and panting, and lunged at the counter. The teachers tutted and shook their heads until one of them noticed the time and they all galloped off across the green towards school.

'I need brandy. Large. For the shock,' Tyson demanded before bursting into loud rasping sobs.

Nonna and I were at his side in seconds. Tyson was a lovely lad with lovely manners if rather mucky fingernails.

'What's wrong, boy, what is it?' Nonna cried.

Juliet poured him some tea.

'Large, with plenty of sugar,' she said, pushing a mug towards him. 'For the *shock*.'

He eyed the mug with disappointment and sniffed. I handed him a tissue.

'It's Clarence,' he sobbed, a bubble of snot appearing at one nostril. I handed him another tissue. 'He's dead. Lifted a bag of pea gravel into the back of a Land Rover and keeled over.'

'*Signore mio*.' Nonna made the sign of the cross. 'Poor man. Poor Clementine.'

'Oh no,' said Juliet and I together. 'Sounds like a heart attack.'

'Just like that.' He clicked his fingers. 'Fell to the floor with the gravel on top of him.'

Clarence Fearnley was the owner of Fearnley's Garden Centre half a mile away at the edge of the village. Nonna was good friends with his wife, Clementine.

'What's going to happen to the garden centre? What's going to happen to me?' Tyson sobbed into his sleeve. 'Best job I ever had.'

Juliet and I exchanged sympathetic looks; he was only young, it was probably the only job he'd ever had.

'Try not to worry, Tyson,' I said, putting my arm around his broad shoulders.

'He only young. Not even seventy.' Nonna picked up her coat from the coat stand and thrust her arms into it. 'I get down there and stay with her. She has no family. No one.'

The doorbell rang and in stumbled Stella Derry, Mum's deputy at the Women's Institute. She was breathless and perspiring and the button across the front of her blouse had popped open.

'I've got some terrible news,' she gasped, looking round

to check she had our attention. She braced herself on the counter to catch her breath, bent double, as if she'd just completed her first triathlon. 'Clarence F—'

'We know,' said Juliet.

'Already?' Stella pouted, her double chin wobbling with indignation.

'Here,' I said, taking the remains of a cheese-and-broccoli flan from the counter. 'Take this, Nonna. She might not fancy eating but . . .'

Nonna pressed a hand to my cheek and I laid my own over it, thinking as I did so how lucky I was to still have her so very much alive.

'You good girl, Rosanna. You sure you two can manage without me?'

If it hadn't been such a sombre occasion, Juliet and I might have sniggered at that.

'We'll cope,' I said.

She turned to the door and one of our regulars, Barry, jumped to his feet, wiping crumbs from his mouth.

'Wait,' he said, snatching up his keys. 'I'll run you down there.'

'You OK?' I asked Tyson, patting his arm once they'd gone.

He nodded. 'Although I think I need more sugar. Perhaps a chocolate brownie?'

'Make that two,' said Stella. 'On me. Come and tell me all about it, Tyson. It'll do you good to talk.'

I left Juliet serving them a large square of brownie each and went back to collect Stanley's empty plate. He looked distraught.

'I feel awfully sorry for poor Clarence,' he said with a sigh, 'but his timing is dreadful.'

'Oh?'

Stanley laid two cinema tickets down on the table in front of him.

'I've been working up to asking Maria out all morning.' His shoulders sagged. 'And now it's too late.'

46

I could have hugged him; no wonder he'd been here so long.

'Nonna's very fond of you,' I said with an encouraging smile. 'Maybe today just wasn't to be. But I wouldn't give up hope.'

His face brightened. 'Really?'

'Really. It's never too late to start something new. To let someone know that you care.'

I didn't really know if that was right or not, but it was what Stanley needed to hear and it was a nice thought; because it meant that there was hope for me yet . . .

Chapter 5

March was nearly over and spring had definitely given winter the elbow. Trees were cloaked in blossom and men from the council had been out to give the village green its first haircut of the season. It looked very smart out there now except for the few shaggy clumps left long where the wild cowslips were still in bloom.

Juliet had made delicate lemon cupcakes topped with crystallized flowers on pale yellow frosting, and for our younger-at-heart customers, chocolate Easter cakes filled with mini eggs ready for Easter next weekend.

But today was a celebration of a different kind: a celebration of Clarence Fearnley's life and the café was a hive of activity.

'When life hands you lemons, make cake,' said Juliet, whipping the lid off a container with a flourish to reveal a lemon drizzle traybake big enough to feed the five thousand, or fifty mourners at the very least.

'Oh yes,' Doreen straightened up from the counter where she was stacking Eccles cakes, 'we should have that made into a sign for the café.'

Nonna hung her nose over the cake and inhaled. 'My favourite smell in whole world. Remind me of home and the lemon groves near our house and the limoncello we make in big buckets every year. *Delizioso.*'

Limoncello was still Nonna's favourite tipple. She claimed

a glass of it before bed was her secret to long life. There might be something in it too, I thought, watching my grandmother pick up a heavy watering can and carry it into the conservatory. She had the strength of an ox, was rarely ill and was still pretty switched on for her age.

'Tell us about Naples, Nonna,' I said, looking up from slicing cucumbers into translucent slivers, 'and the lemon groves.'

'Long time ago. Can't remember,' she said, clamping her lips shut.

'You had lemon groves at the end of your street?' I prompted.

She glanced sideways to me and then turned to the window.

'*Mamma mia!* Clementine is here and the food not ready,' she said, ignoring the question.

Clementine Fearnley parked her van outside the café, slammed the door and went round to the boot.

'More work, less talk,' barked Nonna. 'You not finish those sandwiches yet.'

'I almost have.' I eyed her beadily and began to slice faster, wondering for the umpteenth time why she changed the subject whenever I asked about Italy. She claimed that the smell of lemons reminded her of home and then in the next breath pretended not to be able to remember it at all. It didn't add up.

Juliet put the lid back on the cake and stacked the box on top of the others.

'The sausage rolls are cooling, Maria,' she said. 'The fruit scones are still baking, but they won't take a minute.'

Clementine had asked the Lemon Tree Café to do the catering for Clarence's wake. Nonna had jumped at the chance to do something useful for her friend. But we'd needed an extra pair of hands so Juliet, who had been baking all weekend for it, had come in on her day off to help me prepare a hundred rounds of sandwiches and two hundred sausage rolls while Doreen served the café's usual customers.

Eighty rounds of egg and cress, cheese and pickle, ham and mustard and coronation chicken were under cling film in the fridge and the tuna-and-cucumber sandwiches were under construction.

Nonna scurried over to open the door for Clementine. She came in with a bag of compost slung over her shoulder as if it weighed nothing. She wore a shabby dark coat that was several sizes too big for her, thick black tights with a small run in the back and a pair of chunky black brogues.

I didn't know her very well and she never normally came into the café because the garden centre took up her every waking hour. It was closed this week, unsurprisingly, and Tyson had come in earlier this morning for a single egg on toast. He was economizing, he'd explained, in case Clementine closed the garden centre for good.

'You think a woman can't run a business, eh?' Nonna had said, flicking him with her tea towel and stomping off to the kitchen mumbling something rude in Italian under her breath. He left soon after that and didn't even eat his crusts.

Nonna tried to give her old friend a hug, but it was a bit awkward with the heavy load on her shoulder so she patted her arm instead.

'Morning, everyone,' said Clementine to the café in general, taking care not to meet anyone's eye.

She was a good ten years younger than Nonna, but she looked old and drawn today. They made an odd pair: Nonna short and plump with long hair wound into a bun, Clementine, tall and spare with short hair which I suspected she might cut herself with secateurs.

'I'm so sorry for your loss,' I said, giving Clementine a sad smile. 'Can I get you a cup of tea?'

'Yes, please,' she said with a sigh. 'Catnip if you've got it.'

I shook my head not entirely sure if that was a joke. 'I don't think . . .'

'Or valerian? Lemon balm? Skullcap?' Her disappointment deepened as I continued to shake my head. 'What *have* you got to soothe and calm nerves?'

'Um.' I looked at Doreen who was chewing her lip in a way that made me think she was stifling a smirk. 'How about camomile?'

'That'll have to do, I suppose,' Clementine replied and turned away to accept condolences from Biddy from the pet shop.

'*Skullcap.*' Juliet tutted, adding with a mutter, 'She's one of those *herbalists.*'

She always had something to say about customers who didn't want a straightforward cup of Twinings. 'Brews her own tonics from plants. Some say she studies witch—'

'But only those who have nothing better to do with their time than gossip.' Doreen glowered at her before sniffing the air. 'And your scones are burning.'

Juliet's face turned as red as her hair and she marched off to the kitchen.

'For your lemon pots, Maria.' Clementine rolled the bag of compost off her shoulder and on to the floor. 'Top them up with a good couple of inches. They'll need a nitrogen feed soon too. Where do you want it?'

Nonna pointed to the conservatory. Clementine dragged it through with Nonna following behind, wiping up flecks of compost from the floor with a cloth.

'Thank you.' Nonna kissed her friend on both cheeks, much to the discomfort of the younger woman, and brushed clumps of soil from her coat. 'Everything okey cokey?'

'I can't take it in.' Clementine looked down at her hands, dirt ingrained in the creases of her fingers and under her nails after years of working outdoors. 'I sprang out of bed this morning and on the way to the bathroom I shouted over my shoulder, "Look lively, Clarrie, no lie-in for you today, it's the funeral." And then I remembered: it's his funeral. He's gone, Maria.'

'I know, *cara*,' Nonna said. 'I remember the pain of it like it yesterday. Like someone tear your heart out with bare hand. Go sit down for minute.'

'Can't. Too much to do.'

Nonna flapped a hand at her friend until Clementine shrugged in defeat and sat at an empty table.

'Clarence was my first boyfriend, you know. Never *known* another man, if you catch my drift. He was a lazy arse, crap with money and had a fondness for a flutter on the horses. But he was my lazy arse. And I loved him.'

Nonna looked over at the counter shiftily and then leaned down to speak in Clementine's ear. I strained to listen as I searched through the boxes of tea for the camomile.

'I also only love one man but I lose him very young.'

A rush of warmth flooded through me for my lovely grandmother; she might be guarded about her life in Italy, but it was good to know that she'd been happy, even if it was only for a short time.

Clementine sighed. 'I don't know how you do it, Maria. Run this business single-handedly. I think you're amazing.'

'It is my life.' Nonna tipped two pieces of hazelnut biscotti on a plate and sat down heavily beside her. 'I don't think of it as work. Even though I always rush, rush, rush on my feet.'

Doreen and I raised eyebrows at each other. Clementine slipped her coat off to reveal bony shoulders and a scrawny neck.

'You're a marvel,' she said. 'And you've always got a steady flow of customers. The garden centre can go for hours without seeing a single soul. I've never understood how we made a profit, but Clarence always took care of that side of things. Oh hell.'

Two large tears dripped on to the table and she covered her face with her hands. Nonna dabbed them up with her cloth, smearing the table with a thin layer of compost as she did so.

'What am I going to do? What if—'

Nonna patted her hand. 'These problems are for another day. And if you need help with business, we all help you, all other shops. Won't we, Nina?'

This last comment was addressed to Nina from the florist's next door, who'd come in carrying a thermos cup and was wrapped from head to toe in layers of wool.

'Course we will, Clem,' she cried, unravelling a long scarf from around her face.

Clementine, who Nonna said hated having her name shortened, scowled and tried to cover up her tears. 'Oh good.'

'I always appreciate that you've never gone into cut flowers like a lot of garden centres; it's hard enough without competition on the doorstep,' Nina went on brightly. She perched her bottom on the empty chair next to Clementine. 'So I'm happy to pass on any tips. Although,' she cupped a hand to her mouth and leaned forward, 'we've never actually made a profit. Anyway. Small businesses unite! Yay!' She punched a hand encased in a fingerless glove into the air militantly.

'Thank you,' said Clementine graciously, leaning away from Nina. 'That is kind.'

'What can I get you?' I called, conscious that Nina was invading Clementine's personal space.

She bounded over and set the cup on the counter.

'Soup, please.' She shivered, peeled off her gloves and pressed her hands round our old-fashioned radiators. 'Working with flowers is a lovely, lovely thing,' she said, examining her red raw fingers, 'but I think it's very inconsiderate of them to wilt if exposed to warmth of over one degree.'

'It is,' said Clementine, with a ghost of a smile now that Nina was further away. 'Which is exactly why I like to work with plants; a lot more resilient to changes in temperature. Disappearing into a polytunnel to hand-pollinate twenty rows of tomatoes on a cold day is such a treat.'

'Blimey. What does that involve?' I said, setting her camomile tea in front of her.

'It's a very delicate operation,' she replied, mashing the tea bag violently against the side of the cup with a spoon to make it stronger. 'One plant at a time.'

Stanley walked in at this point, dressed sombrely in black. He raised a hand and advanced towards his usual chair with a deferential, 'Good morning, ladies.'

'Morning, Stanley,' we chorused.

'Mrs Fearnley,' he said reverently, stopping briefly by her table and removing his hat, 'you have my deepest sympathies. It has been five years since I lost my dear Winnie yet I still feel the pain of her loss as if it was yesterday. Would anyone care for a Werther's?'

His sentiment echoed Nonna's almost word for word and I felt a tug at my heart for them all. He handed round a packet of sweets and both ladies took one.

'Thank you, Mr Pigeon.' Clementine blew her nose and cleared her throat before unwrapping the butterscotch.

'Stanley, please.' He bowed sweetly to Nonna and murmured that she was looking lovely today. She giggled and flapped a hand at him and he left them to it, unwrapping a sweet for himself.

'As I was saying,' Clementine continued, 'it takes a gentle grip, a cotton swab and plenty of stamina. Like this.' She curled her fingers around an imaginary stem and mimed an up and down motion. 'Shaky-shaky. Or if it's too big a job I use an electric vibrator.'

'I like to see that,' said Nonna, who grew tomatoes in her greenhouse. 'I do this sometimes, but mine smaller. I use a feather. A little tickle do the job.'

'Good heavens,' muttered Stanley, choking on his sweet. He sank down in his chair and tugged at his collar. 'Oh my.'

I handed Nina her soup and we stuffed napkins in our mouths to stop ourselves from laughing. Poor Stanley.

'I've just put the greenery into your Clarence's wreath,

Clem,' said Nina, when she'd got her breath back. 'Good choice on the old-fashioned roses, they are to DIE for.'

Clementine gave Nina the biggest stink eye I'd ever seen.

'Oh balls. Sorry.' She pulled a horrified face at me and pretended to put a gun to her head.

'I'd better get back,' she said, handing me some money. 'Still got a couple of the smaller tributes to do. Give me a can of Coke as well. In case I warm up later.'

Clementine pulled her sleeve up and looked at her watch. It was an old-fashioned man's watch with a large face and a stretchy gold strap. 'Ought to be off myself; I've got three thousand courgette seedlings to water before the funeral car arrives.'

'Do you want a hand to the car with these?' said Juliet, who'd boxed up the food for the buffet while I'd been enjoying the tomato pollinating story. She was making an effort to be polite for once, I noticed, probably under instruction from Doreen.

'Two ticks.' Clementine gulped down her tea in one and stood up, slipping her arms into her oversized coat.

There was a revving noise outside and we all looked out to see Lia trying to jam her Mini into a small space behind Clementine's parked van. She waved as she climbed out and held up some carrier bags from a posh supermarket before stowing them in the boot and coming in.

'Been shopping?' I asked.

'Yes. On my own! Now Mum's looking after Arlo I've decided to splash out on something nice for dinner.'

'Lucky Ed.'

We smiled at each other with wonders-will-never-cease looks.

'It'll be our belated Valentine's dinner. I was going to do this fancy lamb thing then, I had all sorts of romantic plans, but Arlo was ill and by the time I got round to reading the recipe I realized it needed four hours in the oven. So that was that. We had beans on toast in the end.'

'I didn't realize you were such a keen cook?' I said, surprised.

I drew her to the counter where I needed to clear up from my mammoth sandwich session.

'I'm more of an armchair enthusiast at the moment, I admit, but,' Lia leaned in towards me, 'since we had that little chat about my body shape, I've realized that starving myself was just making me miserable and actually, when I cook properly, I eat better and feel healthier for it.'

'Good for you, sis.'

'Yeah, well, it's made me think that instead of just watching cooking shows, I should get in the kitchen and go for it.'

I grinned and handed her a damp cloth. 'You can get in this kitchen and go for it right now if you like?'

She pulled a face. 'I was thinking more this side of the counter with a chic little coffee while I research some recipes on my phone. I want to find a couscous dish to go with the lamb.'

'Fair enough,' I said and began to tackle the crumbs myself.

'Before you go, Clementine,' Nonna plucked a ripe lemon from one of her trees and handed it to her friend, 'take this with you to make lemon tea. Do you good, full of vitamins.'

'Ooh, I love lemons,' said Lia. 'In fact, I could eat a slice right now.'

'If you crave lemon, you know what that means,' Clementine said.

Juliet, who'd been valiantly holding a heavy box of food to stash in the van, slumped on the counter over the box of food.

'Here we go, brace yourselves for some hocus-pocus,' she muttered, earning herself a dig in the ribs from Doreen.

'It isn't a pregnancy craving, is it?' said Lia, going pale. 'Because my body hasn't sprung back after the last one yet, another baby would probably just drop straight out.'

'Thanks for that vivid image,' I winced. 'What does it mean, Clementine?'

'The lemon is a powerful symbol in herbalism, mythology and even folklore,' she said, holding up the fruit between her forefinger and thumb. 'One theory is that eating lemons reflects the need to purify yourself.'

'That's me.' Doreen gave a dirty chuckle. 'I had very impure thoughts about Leonardo DiCaprio last night.'

'Don't worry about it,' said Nonna, 'I have those all the time.'

'Nonna!' Lia squealed and jammed her fingers in her ears.

There was a choking sound from behind Stanley's newspaper.

'And another interesting one,' Clementine continued, 'is that they symbolize clearing and cleansing to separate a person from their ties to the past.'

'So you'd surround yourself with lemons, if you wanted to make a fresh start?' I pondered, with a sweeping glance round the café at the lemon trees and the crockery adorned with lemons and the lemon-themed pictures on the wall.

Nonna's eyes narrowed and then she flapped a hand at her friend.

'Juliet is right,' she said with a harsh laugh, 'hocus-pocus. Now come on, everybody; back to work.'

At quarter to two, the church bells began to ring out a solemn toll. It was nearly time for Clarence Fearnley's send-off and both Nonna and Stanley reached for their coats.

'Maria, would you care to come to the funeral with me?' Stanley said, tucking his scarf into the top of his coat.

'Stanley Pigeon!' huffed Nonna as she pinned a black feathered hat over her tidy white bun. 'What you suggesting?'

Stanley looked at the feather in her hat warily.

'Nothing!' he insisted, shaking his head. 'I just thought . . . But nothing.'

To his surprise she tucked her arm through his.

'I go to the funeral. You go to the funeral. We walk to church together if you want. But I not care to come with you, no.'

'Rightio.' Stanley glanced down at Nonna's hand on his arm, looking utterly baffled.

'It is not a date, nothing like that.' She wagged a finger at him.

'Good grief,' spluttered Stanley, 'the very idea.'

They reached the door and he held it open for her.

'Although,' he said in a wavering voice, 'while we're on the subject—'

The door banged shut and the end of his sentence was cut off.

'Oh my God,' Lia giggled, 'he's asking her out!'

We grinned at each other as the pair of them strolled towards the church arm in arm.

'How cute are they?' I said, resting my elbows on the counter.

'Hashtag old-age goals,' said Lia with a sigh. 'Anyway, talking of true love, the way to my man's heart is through his stomach, so forget the coffee, I'd better get home and start marinating that lamb.'

'Good luck with the cooking,' I said, pressing a swift kiss to her cheek. 'I think it's fab that you're trying something new.'

'Oh thanks,' said Lia, going pink. 'That means a lot.'

I walked her to the door and waved her off, then, still smiling, I turned back to the counter to commence cleaning duties. And what I saw sent chills down my spine: Doreen and Juliet were helping themselves to cash from the till and stuffing notes into their own purses.

Chapter 6

My heart raced. How could they steal from Nonna? How long had this been going on? She trusted them, and right up until this second, I'd trusted them too. They hadn't spotted me, too busy counting out notes and coins from the till as soon as Nonna's back was turned.

I looked away quickly and stared out of the window towards the green to collect my thoughts. This would break her heart. Unless, of course, I tackled the problem myself. I could confront them, catch them red-handed and force them to hand back the money and maybe if they promised never to do it again, Nonna need never know.

Mind made up, I whirled round and caught Doreen looking straight at me. She turned puce and nudged Juliet who slammed the till shut. The two of them looked at each other and then back at me. I took a step towards them, my stomach lurching queasily.

Doreen swallowed. 'Rosie, can I just say—'

I held up a hand to silence her.

'I saw what you just did,' I said. 'But I can't believe it.'

'Cooee! Look who I've brought to see you. Look, Arlo, it's Auntie Rosie!'

Mum was holding the door open with one hand and struggling to manoeuvre Arlo's large pushchair over the lip of the step. 'Darling, give me a hand, will you?'

'We'll talk about this later.' I shot the two women a stern

59

look and turned to help Mum. 'In the meantime, can you do a deep clean of the cupboards while Nonna's out, please.'

Juliet frowned menacingly but Doreen pulled her away.

'Oh, what a lovely time we've had.' Mum wheeled the pushchair to an empty table. 'We've just been up to the river to feed the ducks. This little chap loved it. Ducks, Arlo, ducks say quack quack.'

I unclipped Arlo's straps while Mum slipped off her coat. Out of the corner of my eye, I could see Doreen and Juliet conferring animatedly. As well they might. I mean, honestly, what were they thinking? I took a deep breath and smiled at my nephew as he held out a fabric picture book to me chuntering, 'Ba-ba-ba.'

'Do you want me to read this?' I said, picking him up and blowing raspberries into his neck.

His warm body wriggled in my arms and I held him to me, breathing in his baby smell.

'I had to read a great stack of them to him this morning,' Mum said, fetching him a high chair. 'I think he's going to be a bright boy.'

I unzipped his jacket, slipped it off and popped him in the chair. 'You're really enjoying yourself with Arlo, aren't you?'

Her face softened and she blinked in surprise. 'I am. I really am. Shall we have tea? Do you have time?'

'Yes,' I said immediately. Anything to delay my unpleasant chat with Doreen and Juliet. 'But can you go and order it? I've got my hands full here.'

She looked at the small fabric book in my hands. 'OK.'

I flipped over the page and grinned at Arlo. 'What do cows say? Moo, moo.'

Mum came back with two teas and found a rice cracker in her bag for Arlo.

'You know, I only offered to have Arlo to help Lia out, and of course, in my usual manner, threw myself into it wholeheartedly.'

I suppressed a smile; she'd stepped down as president of the Women's Institute, removed herself from the local history society and the parish council and sent her apologies to the school governing body, just so she could clear her diary to help.

'But actually, life without endless committee meetings is very pleasant and I love the look on this little one's face when he sees me every day. It makes me feel needed.'

'You *are* needed,' I confirmed, sipping my tea. 'It's done Lia the world of good having some time to herself and I think Ed is benefiting too, if tonight's menu is anything to go by.'

Mum gazed at Arlo adoringly and sighed.

'Perhaps the time has come to relinquish some of my voluntary roles permanently and spend a bit more time at home, with my grandson – and your father, of course. We could even go away this summer for a few weeks, just the two of us, on an adventure.'

My heart leapt. Dad would love that. He always complained that he had such long holidays from the university but no one to go away with because Mum was always so busy.

'I think that's a brilliant idea. Also, when I've gone back to my proper career, perhaps you'd be able to pop in here now and then and keep an eye on things?'

Like the staff pilfering, for example. I cast an eye over to the counter. Doreen was chatting with a customer, pouring frothy milk into a latte and Juliet was rearranging the cakes under their glass domes. They were both acting like nothing had happened. My heart felt heavy and sad.

'Oh no,' said Mum, recoiling. 'I know she's my mother and I love her dearly, but once bitten and all that. Hats off to you for lasting this long, but Nonna won't thank me for poking my nose in.'

'Hmm,' I said vaguely, worried that I was about to poke my nose in too. 'So are you going to book a holiday, you and Dad?'

She sipped her tea and rolled her eyes. 'We're discussing it. He wants to experience the golden age of British canal transport with a month on a narrowboat.'

'Ah.'

'Quite.' Mum smiled mischievously. 'I said I don't mind canals but only if they're in Venice. And it is high time I explored my Italian heritage. So the debate rolls on, but let's just say I've sent my passport away for renewal.'

We both laughed. Somehow I didn't fancy Dad's chances of getting his way. But he wouldn't mind. He'd be happy anywhere as long as he was with Mum.

Her watch beeped then and she took a baby bottle out of her bag, tipped milk powder into it and went off to the kitchen to warm it through. I took Arlo out of his high chair and cuddled him, thinking how lucky Mum and Dad were to have each other. They might not be the perfect couple, but they truly loved each other and I'd always casually assumed that a relationship like theirs would be easy to replicate.

How wrong could I be? I'd worked my way through various boyfriends at university, some lovely, some less so. I'd learned to love and learned to leave, trying to work out the sort of man who'd make me happy, searching for The One. And then in London I'd met Callum and the search had ended. Not because Callum was The One, but because what I'd found had frightened me. So I'd stopped looking. Too afraid to risk that happening again. Which I guessed meant that I was very unlikely to have an 'Arlo' of my own.

I blinked away the memories and focused back on my mother as she returned shaking the bottle.

I handed Arlo to her and helped her fasten on his bib. 'I ought to get back to work.'

'Before you go, have you noticed anything odd about your father?'

She settled Arlo on to her lap and he pulled the bottle towards his open mouth and was soon chugging away contentedly.

'No. Why?'

'He's behaving oddly. Disappearing without telling me where he's going. It's been going on ever since I've been looking after Arlo. And the other day . . .' She shifted in her seat and went pink. 'I saw him looking at something on the internet.'

I resisted the urge to put my hands over my ears. 'Go on.'

'He was looking at fancy bras. I only wear plain boring ones. When he realized I'd seen him, he closed the lid of the laptop, muttered "It's not what you think", left the room and the next thing I knew his car was pulling off the drive.'

'And what *do* you think?' I asked, laughing. 'Sounds like red-blooded male behaviour to me.'

'I thought nothing at first and then . . . Oh God, this is such a cliché. Red lipstick on his collar. From another woman.'

I raised an eyebrow. 'Couldn't it be yours?'

Although Mum wearing bright colours was as unlikely as Dad having an affair. Mum's lipsticks were all called things like 'mink' and 'cappuccino'.

'Not pillar-box red, no.'

'There could be any number of explanations. A colleague at work, an accident in Boots, or he could be getting you a gift.'

'You don't think he's having an affair?' Mum nibbled her lip. 'That he's found himself another woman who hangs on his every word and doesn't boss him about?'

A tsunami of warmth rushed over me for my mum; she always seemed so confident of her place in his heart and at least she admitted to being bossy.

'Dad would never be unfaithful to you, Mum, it's unthinkable. Far more likely that he's planning to surprise you with some fancy undies. And perhaps while you're having a reshuffle of your committees, you could schedule in a bit more time for him, let him know you appreciate him.'

'Wise words, darling; thank you. I can't think why someone lovely hasn't snapped you up by now.'

I bit my tongue, preferring not to answer that one, and she hugged me tight just as my phone rang. 'Michael' flashed on the screen.

'Ooh, I have to take this. It could be good news about a job.'

Mum blew me a kiss and I slipped outside into the cool grey afternoon to answer my phone.

'How's my favourite creative director?' he gushed. 'Bored with café culture yet?'

'Life here is anything but boring,' I said wearily, thinking of the next conversation I was about to have with my colleagues.

I wandered across the road to the village green, brushed a couple of leaves off a wooden bench and sat down.

'I'd expect nothing less, darling,' he said smoothly. 'I bet you've installed wifi, set up a Facebook page and had the café trending on Twitter.'

'Actually, no, but now you mention it, that's not a bad idea.'

I don't know why I hadn't thought of it before; that was one positive change I could make to the café that Nonna wouldn't see as intruding on her territory.

'You'll be too busy for all that,' he said airily. 'Because guess who's got an interview in Manchester at HitSquad?'

'Me? Yay!'

A job, a proper one where I didn't need to wear rubber gloves or grate cheese, or go in men's toilets . . .

'Now listen to the job spec, Rosie, you're going to WET yourself. The successful candidate will be at the global forefront of . . .'

My pulse quickened as I listened to the job specification. It was perfect. In the month that I'd spent at the café, I think the only time my pulse had raced like this was when Biddy's sister had reversed her new motorized wheelchair into the toy corner and I'd had visions of little Alfie Sargent getting squished under the wheels. Luckily, he hadn't and the incident had soon been resolved with a chocolate-chip cookie for him and a stern word from Biddy to her sister about reading the instruction manual.

'Michael, you're a miracle worker. When's the interview?'

'Next week, I'll email you the details. Ooh, another call's coming through. Laters.'

'Whoop! Thank you!' I said as he hung up.

I'd got an interview, just as I'd hoped. But then I looked back at the Lemon Tree Café across the road. Even on a grey day like today, with its sunny yellow awning, pretty lettering and miniature lemon trees flanking the door, the café looked warm and welcoming. I'd been here nearly a month and despite the ups and downs, I was going to miss it terribly. Which was ridiculous, it couldn't ever replace my career and, besides, Nonna didn't want me to stay. I gave myself a shake and went back inside.

I'd barely shut the door when Doreen and Juliet practically dragged me through the café and outside to the courtyard at the back.

'It's not what you think,' Doreen blurted out.

'So I didn't see you take money out of the till and put it in your own purses?' I folded my arms and stared beadily at them both.

I hoped I looked authoritative because my legs felt as wobbly as one of Stanley's favourite custard tarts.

'Aye, you did, but it was our money.' Juliet jabbed her own chest with her fingertip.

'And if we don't help ourselves we don't get it,' Doreen added.

'True that,' Juliet confirmed with a nod.

'Hold on.' I held my hands up. 'Nonna pays you both in cash, in an envelope. I've seen her.'

She even paid me that way, even though I'd offered to work for free. But she'd insisted, saying fair was fair. I bristled; what these two were doing was anything but fair.

'Aye, that's wages, although goodness knows what she's doing about tax and stuff.'

'But she forgets to pay us for other things,' Doreen explained, lowering herself down on to the chair Nonna kept out here for napping on whenever she got the chance.

'What things?' I retorted.

'Look,' said Juliet, running her hands through her hair until it stood up in clumps rather than its usual spikes, 'I make cakes for the café, right?'

I nodded. She made batches on her days off. She'd made loads for the funeral.

'Well, the money I took covers the ingredients, plus a bit extra to cover fuel for cooking.'

'And I buy supplies when we run out before the whole-saler delivers,' said Doreen. 'Like toilet paper and soap, or eggs. Things like that.'

'We'd never steal off Maria,' Juliet growled.

I nodded again, tears pricking at the back of my eyes as a giant wave of relief and shame came over me.

'I'm so sorry,' I said. 'I should never have doubted you.'

Doreen struggled out of her chair, put her arms round me and squished me to her chest. 'You're just protecting your grandmother's business. Nothing wrong with that. No harm done.'

'Aye, easy mistake,' muttered Juliet.

'But why not just put in a receipt and ask for the money?' I said.

Doreen cringed. 'Maria isn't fond of paperwork.'

'And she forgets,' said Juliet. 'It's easier to sort it out our-selves than wait for her to do it.'

My mind was racing. This was all well and good, but if Nonna wasn't keeping a note of money coming in and out of the business, how was she going to be able to work out the café's finances?

'What about financial records?' I said. 'It's nearly the end of the tax year; won't she have to send the accountant her books soon?'

Doreen and Juliet looked at each other shiftily.

'Come and look at this,' said Doreen with a sigh.

There was a tiny store cupboard near the toilets where we kept the mop and bucket and basically anything that was too big to fit on a shelf in the kitchen.

'Right at the back, behind all this clutter, is a filing cabinet.' Doreen snapped on the light, a single bare bulb hanging from a cable.

I squinted at the harshness of the light. 'I see it. Just about.'

The store room was a hoarder's haven, shelves either side bulged with kitchen paraphernalia and the floor was piled high with stuff.

'That,' said Doreen ominously, 'is where your grandmother keeps all the records for the café. Or rather, doesn't keep them. The accountants got so fed up with her last year that they sent all the paperwork back and told her to find someone else.'

'So who does it now?'

Doreen shrugged. 'I'm guessing it's a time bomb waiting to go off at the end of the tax year. Maria has buried her head in the sand and gets very tetchy when we ask for expense forms to claim our money back. We've given up asking.'

'But . . . but . . .' I stared at Doreen. 'I thought the leaky taps and dusty corners and greasy griddle and unchanged-since-nineteen-eighty-seven menus were the worst problems. This is far worse. There are hefty fines for failing to submit your accounts. The café would never survive.'

She swallowed. 'I'd agree with you there.'

'I'll have to take a look at it.' I sighed. 'Although accounts are not my thing at all.'

'Private,' said Doreen, pointing at the big label stuck on the front of the cabinet drawer. 'She won't like you prying.'

'What she doesn't know won't hurt her,' I muttered, pushing myself into the store room.

Just then a lone church bell began to chime softly in the distance. Doreen and I looked at each other; the funeral was over. Nonna was supposed to be going to the wake, but what if she popped in here for some reason first?

I rubbed my hand over my face feeling very weary and wondering why I'd ever thought working in a café would be so much simpler than my old job.

'I'll have to leave it for now, but I don't think I really have a choice, do you? If anyone finds out about the state of the business's financial affairs, the Lemon Tree Café could be history.'

Chapter 7

The worry over the café's neglected accounts heavily outweighed the relief I felt that Doreen and Juliet weren't thieves after all. And Nonna's lax attitude to doing things properly – in an up-to-date manner – niggled away at the back of my mind for the next few days and all over the Easter weekend.

Things had changed a lot since she'd first taken over in the café. Everything, every tiny thing, had to be accounted for these days and goodness knows what the tax man would have to say about records kept on scraps of paper in a locked cabinet. Or possibly no records at all. It wouldn't have been so bad if she had an accountant on the case, but apparently she hadn't.

I felt anxious for her and toyed with the idea of tackling her on it, but decided in a cowardly way to have a look at the contents of the filing cabinet first. You never know, I told myself, she could have everything completely under control; I could be worrying for no reason. There was nothing else for it, Doreen, Juliet and I all agreed: the very next time Nonna went anywhere during opening hours, I was going in.

In the meantime, several new and exciting things happened. Thanks to a rather jolly telephone engineer who'd put away half his body weight in honey cake yesterday afternoon, we now had internet in the café. We also had a Facebook page, a little devoid of photographs or posts or followers, but I was working on it. And Nonna and Stanley had been out for dinner together!

This morning I'd persuaded everyone to pose for a staff photo and Doreen had come in especially for it. Although given the fact that we were all dying to know about Nonna's date last night, I suspect that she would have called in anyway.

'I can't see that being on Facebook is going to make a blind bit of difference to a village café,' grumbled Doreen, who was redoing her ponytail for her close-up and dabbing concealer on the mole on her nose.

I smiled to myself. I'd handled plenty of clients in the past who'd been suspicious of new media, only to find them days later secretly logging on to see how many 'likes' their picture had got.

'It might not but if we don't try we'll never know, will we? It's free advertising so it can't do any harm. And once it's set up it'll be easy to run even when I'm not here. Which if I get the job in Manchester could be soon.'

'Course you get the job,' Nonna called from the conservatory. 'If not they all dicky heads.'

'I'll tell them that, shall I?' I said. 'At the end when they ask why they should give me the job.'

'Yeah, why not?' She shrugged. 'It's the truth.'

It was only forty-eight hours until my interview with HitSquad. Michael was emailing me every five minutes with articles he'd found online about the company. They seemed like a great bunch to work for. But every time I thought about leaving the café I felt a tremor of an emotion that I couldn't quite place. It also put me under a bit of pressure; I didn't have long to break into that filing cabinet. If only Nonna would disappear for the day and give me a chance to look inside it.

Doreen wandered off muttering something about Facebook being an invasion of her privacy while Juliet rearranged her cleavage ready for her picture.

'This is as good as it gets,' she said, patting her short red hair. It was rigid with hairspray. She shoved the can back in her rucksack and brushed cake crumbs from her chin. 'Where do you want me?'

'Perhaps in front of the cakes?' I suggested, coughing on the fumes. 'Looking natural.'

Juliet positioned herself by the counter and pouted flirtatiously.

I managed to get a nice shot of her with a plate of muffins and then it was Nonna's turn. She posed by one of the lemon trees in the conservatory, sitting in a chair, holding a Lemon Tree Café menu. I don't know whether it was down to the light in there but the pictures of her were very flattering. There was a soft warmth to her smile and a pink girlish glow to her cheeks. Then again, it might have been a certain gentleman who'd put a twinkle in her eye this morning.

'Your turn, Doreen. Pop an apron on,' I said, 'and pick up that tea tray.'

She obliged, checked her reflection in the coffee machine and flicked her ponytail over her shoulder.

'Come on, Maria, spill the beans,' she said, trying not to move her mouth as she spoke. She stared ahead expressionless, while I captured the shot. It wasn't the most welcoming of looks, but I managed to put her in soft focus and train the lens on the pretty china tea pot instead. 'We want a blow-by-blow account of your date.'

Nonna smiled mysteriously and tapped her nose.

'A lady like to have some secrets,' she said.

'*Some*, yes,' I retorted, 'but you've got more secrets than James Bond and the entire Secret Service.'

'Anyway, boss, you shouldn't have gone to the Cross Keys if you wanted to keep a low profile,' Juliet piped up from behind the counter. 'I saw Adrian this morning. He said you and Stanley looked very cosy.'

'Because we sit by the fire that's why,' Nonna said, wiping her cloth over the window sill. 'And no gossip about your boss, thank you very much.'

'I think it's lovely,' I said, lifting my gaze from the camera to smile at her. 'To find love in old age. Or any age, for that matter.'

'Don't worry, love, you'll meet the right man one day, everyone does, even her,' said Doreen, nodding towards Juliet who was giving the milk pipe on the coffee machine a thorough rubbing down and didn't look the least bit offended.

'True that. Did I ever tell you how I met my Dean?' Juliet said. 'One winter, he came round to investigate my neighbour after a report of cruelty to his rabbit, Bobsie. He knocked on my door and when I saw him in his RSPCA uniform and rubber gloves I nearly fainted into his arms.' She fanned her face with a slice of toast. 'What a hero. He whipped Bobsie from her hutch while the owner was out. Unfortunately, her wee had frozen her bum to the bottom of the cage.'

Doreen and I winced.

'Both Dean and the rabbit were traumatized. I took them both in. I remember that bum – as bald as a baboon's. Bobsie's that is, not Dean's. His was peachy.'

Nonna patted my face. 'You will meet one special boy and boom: you in love. It will happen. It will be peachy for you too.'

'Can't wait,' I said, trying to shake off the image of Dean giving Bobsie a Brazilian.

'Like me,' agreed Juliet, retrieving her sturdy bra strap from where it had slipped down her arm. 'What about you?'

This last question was addressed to Tyson, who had called in for lunch. The garden centre had reopened after a week. Nonna had been to see if Clementine needed any help with the paperwork, but she'd said that she was ignoring all the bills for the moment because the bedding plants season had begun and if they didn't sell them before they got too big for their pots, there'd be no money to pay the bills with anyway.

'Me?' Tyson's entire head turned pink. 'I'm not in love.'

'No.' Juliet tutted. 'What do you want to order?'

'Cheese-and-beans toastie, please.'

'And you knew Dean was the one, straight away?' I marvelled.

'Aye, hen, he's a proper gentleman.'

'Like Lorenzo.' Nonna sighed. 'A true gentleman.'

'Stanley's a gentleman too,' I said softly. 'That's two good ones you've managed to meet. That's two more than me. This could be the start of a new love affair, Nonna.'

'Pfft, and piggies might fly.' She began tidying the pots of herbs, snipping off dead leaves and pinching shoots between her fingers. 'Stanley is a good man. But Lorenzo is only man I ever love.'

The faraway look in Nonna's eyes made my heart squeeze; she'd given up on love at an early age, just like me. Mum had been a baby when her father had died, she had no memories of him at all, and now she was fifty-three. And Nonna had been on her own all those years. Thinking that I might spend the rest of my life without falling in love was a sobering thought.

'I don't know whether to be happy or sad,' I said, lowering my camera.

'Be happy. I have my work, my family and my health, at my age I lucky to have all those things.'

'Good,' I said, 'and we're lucky to have you.'

I spent the rest of the morning trying to convince myself that I was absolutely not turning into my grandmother.

By the following morning, we'd got two hundred followers on our Facebook page and I was feeling sufficiently optimistic to have a go at tackling Twitter.

Nonna couldn't fathom why we'd want to bother.

'Why everyone wanna beep-beep-beeping all the time?' she'd scowled, miming pressing the buttons of a phone with her finger.

'Because people keep in touch with each other these days, Nonna,' I'd explained. 'All the time. We're a nation of sharers.'

'I don't wanna keep in touch,' was Nonna's response. 'My

worst nightmare. I want "Private, keep out" written on my Facebook window.'

'Wall,' I corrected.

'My friend Tansy from line dancing is on Facebook. She gets men from Russia saying she looks sexy,' said Doreen, looking over my shoulder as I logged on to the café's page. 'Has anyone commented on my photo?'

'Not so far,' I said, biting back a smile when her face fell. 'Give it time.'

I was convinced that offering free wifi would have its benefits. Teenagers didn't frequent anywhere without it these days. And it would appeal to business customers too: we could let people have the conservatory for meetings and lunches . . . Of course, I wouldn't be here soon, with any luck I'd be at HitSquad by then. I'd have to train Doreen and Juliet up on social media and hopefully steer Doreen away from sex-starved Russians.

But to keep myself occupied until my interview tomorrow, I was focusing my attention on Twitter and had booked a model for a photoshoot . . .

'Can you get him to sit up by the chair, Biddy?' I said, arranging a plate of biscuits tantalizingly close to the edge of the table. 'And sniff the air?'

I'd found out the previous day that it was National Pet Month and in the absence of anything more appropriate like, say, National Cappuccino Day or Eat More Cake Month, I'd decided that we should get on board and be more pet-friendly. I thought a few pictures of a dog enjoying an afternoon at the café would make a nice story for Twitter. Biddy from the pet shop, who was doing her own campaign – a free bag of frozen mice with every snake purchase – had popped in to lend me Churchill, her elderly black Labrador. It wasn't going well. So far he'd trumped so viciously that two people had left and then he'd chewed the edge of my cardigan to bits when I hadn't been looking.

'I'm trying,' said a harassed Biddy, poking Churchill in the tummy. 'Oh, I know! This is his favourite. Come on, boy, frankfurter.'

Biddy was an 'old before her time' sort of woman in her late forties. She had thinning blonde hair and was a whizz with a crochet hook. Mum once said that the decor in her house was wall-to-wall woollen squares. She produced an inch of cooked sausage from her poncho and waved it under Churchill's nose, but he simply yawned and closed his eyes again.

'What *would* tempt him?' I asked, half wishing I'd plumped for National Stress Awareness Month instead; at least I wouldn't have had to look far for models. I fanned my face, still recovering from the aftermath of Churchill's wind.

'Sex mostly,' Biddy replied with a tinkly laugh.

'Ha.' Nonna flicked a cursory cloth over the table, narrowly missing the plate. 'That tempt us all.'

Oh God. I took a picture of a sleeping Churchill and tried not to dwell on my grandmother's innermost thoughts.

The door opened and in came Stanley being dragged by a small white poodle on a pink diamanté lead. Churchill, with a sudden burst of energy, leapt to his feet at the sight of this vision of canine beauty, and wagged his tail so hard that he knocked the plate off the table.

'Sex slave at your service,' muttered Juliet, elbowing me in the ribs.

'Don't,' I murmured, feeling nauseous again. 'Just don't.'

'Hello, everyone. Meet Crystal,' Stanley stuttered, stumbling forward and trying to tip his hat to us without falling over.

'Steady on, Churchill!' Biddy gasped, trying to grab his thumping tail as he darted out of reach.

Juliet snorted. 'Men. All the bloody same.'

The poodle dived through Biddy's legs, causing poor Stanley to end up with his face in her poncho but still determinedly holding on to the diamanté lead.

The two dogs both lunged for the same Bourbon biscuit and managed to get hold of one end each. I took the picture just as their doggy lips met in the middle.

'That was perfect, Biddy!' I said with a grin and great relief. 'If this doesn't get the café's Twitter feed buzzing nothing will.'

Churchill and Crystal began trotting round in circles, nose to tail, sniffing each other's rear ends.

'Ahh,' said Juliet. 'How romantic.'

'So that's where I'm going wrong,' I said.

'Humph,' said Nonna with a gimlet-eyed glance at Biddy.

'Heavens,' said Stanley, looking down at something brown mushed into his hand. He gave it a tentative sniff. 'What on earth . . . ?'

'Frankfurter,' we all supplied.

I handed him a napkin.

'Crystal is my neighbour's new rescue dog,' said Stanley, attempting to detangle himself and the lead from Biddy's legs. 'I'm looking after her while he's away at a conference. I hope she's allowed in?'

'Absolutely,' I said, pointing to a large dog bowl filled with water. 'And very welcome. As are you.'

Nonna flounced away to the store cupboard to fetch a broom, muttering under her breath in Italian. Biddy clipped a lead to Churchill and headed to a quiet table in the conservatory to tackle a raspberry muffin I'd given her as a thank you. Stanley tucked Crystal under his arm and looked nervously in Nonna's direction.

'I'm glad we are a dog-friendly café,' said Juliet. 'Dean says more places should allow animals in.'

'Dicky head. He don't have to clean up,' Nonna grumbled, wielding her broom menacingly at the crumbs.

'Maria,' said Stanley, clearing his throat, 'I've taken the liberty . . . I do hope this wasn't too forward of me . . . and of course if it's not convenient—'

'*Grazie a Dio*,' Nonna muttered. 'Hurry up or I be dead before you spit it out.'

Stanley's Adam's apple bobbed nervously. 'The cinema, this afternoon. There's a special screening of an old Doris Day film. Would you like to come with me?'

'I just check my diary,' said Nonna, charging off to put the broom away with a suspiciously pink face. 'Yes, I'm free.'

'Really?' Stanley's eyes lit up. 'Marvellous. There's a bus from the green in fifteen minutes, I'll just have to pop home to take Crystal back first.'

Nonna patted her hair. 'Wait, I get my coat, I come with you.'

This was it, this was my chance to take a look in that filing cabinet.

'I suppose you'll be gone for hours, won't you, Stanley?' I shot a sideways look at Juliet.

'All afternoon. And afterwards, I'm going to suggest a fish and chip supper on the way home.' He frowned. 'Unless you think that's too much. I'm out of practice; I haven't dated for fifty years.'

Nonna appeared in her coat, handbag and bright coral lipstick. 'Okey cokey, we go. Don't wait up.'

'Have a lovely time,' I said, ushering them out.

Ten minutes later, Juliet and I stood at the window, watching the pair of them reappear without Crystal, cross the village green and sit at the bench at the bus stop.

'Are you thinking what I'm thinking?' I murmured.

'Operation Paperwork?'

'Exactly.'

We looked at each other nervously.

'Maria would kill us,' Juliet breathed, wide-eyed.

'I'll do it,' I said, full of resolve. 'She can't kill me; I'm family.'

A single-decker bus rumbled around the corner. As soon as I saw Stanley and Nonna get to their feet I stealthily made my way to the store room. Juliet followed closely behind, muttering something about the Mafia and concrete overcoats.

I opened the door to the store room and snapped on the light. My route to the filing cabinet was blocked by several bulky objects. With Juliet's help, I shifted the broom, a vacuum cleaner, three buckets, five mops, a set of stepladders and two big food processors with bits missing. Finally, we had a clear path to the old metal cabinet.

'Pull the door to,' I whispered and crept forward.

There were three drawers in the cabinet. Only the top one was labelled 'private', the other two weren't labelled at all. I tried them all. The bottom two were unlocked and didn't contain anything exciting: old food catalogues, some recipe books and manuals for the electrical appliances. The top drawer marked private was locked.

Above the cabinet was a shelf stacked with dusty jars of Nonna's homemade preserves: lemons, jam, chutney and something dark and plum-like. There was a nail protruding from the edge of the shelf and from it hung a key.

Holding my breath, I unhooked the key and slid it into the keyhole. The key turned.

I looked over my shoulder at Juliet who was right behind me, biting her nails.

'I'm in,' I whispered.

'Hardly Fort Knox, is it, hen?'

'Yes, well, that's because she trusts us,' I hissed back.

We looked at each other guiltily.

'You should probably leave me to it,' I said. 'So you're not implicated in my crime.'

Juliet shook her head. 'Maria will be halfway to the cinema by now, don't worry about it. Besides, we're a team, aren't we?'

She patted my shoulder awkwardly, which was the equivalent of a declaration of love coming from her.

'I appreciate that,' I said truthfully.

I tugged open the drawer and stared inside. It was

absolutely stuffed with receipts, invoices, scraps of paper, bank statements . . . It was the end of March now, there must have been at least a year's worth of paperwork in here. And all this was going to have to be sorted out for the tax office.

'Jesus.' I whistled through my teeth. 'I can't believe she's kept all this hidden away.'

'The thing is,' Juliet hissed, 'what are we going to do about it?'

I shook my head, distracted by a thick Manila envelope sitting on top of the other papers. It was marked with a scrawled *privato* in faded blue ink. There was a word below it which started with 'Ben' but I couldn't make out the rest. I turned the envelope over and found that the flap was loose. I peered inside, feeling my stomach tremble as I did so. Nonna was a private person; I knew what I was doing was bad, but I couldn't resist. Just a tiny peep, I told myself. I put my hand in and drew out a few black-and-white photos and some sort of official document.

Suddenly the door flew back on its hinges and crashed against the wall. I dropped the pictures back into the envelope.

'Eh, what you doing?'

Nonna's angry face glowered at us from the doorway. Juliet swore. My mouth went dry. She's your grandmother, I reminded myself reasonably, she loves you.

Nonna spotted the envelope in my hands and seemed to swell in size. 'Put that down,' she bellowed. 'You look at my private things? Get out, get out now!'

OK, maybe I overestimated that.

I quickly shoved the envelope back in the cabinet and slammed it shut.

'We thought you'd gone,' said Juliet, creeping closer to me.

'I see,' Nonna spat. 'You, you snake in the garden, Rosanna.'

Stanley appeared at Nonna's side. 'Hello, ladies. The bus didn't stop,' he explained cheerfully, not picking up on either the terror on our faces or the fury on his date's. 'We're going to phone for a taxi.'

'Let me do that,' said Juliet, stumbling past me, sidling past Nonna. She bore Stanley away, leaving me to face the music.

I held my hands up. 'I didn't see anything. Just a lot of paperwork that needs sorting.'

'You know what private mean, eh?' Nonna narrowed her eyes as I shuffled towards her, past all the clutter still in the cupboard. 'Private things are private for a reason. Now I don't trust you.'

'I'm sorry for prying,' I said meekly. 'But you can't just close your eyes to this. It's got to change. You need help—'

'You just the same as your mamma ten years ago.' Nonna prodded my shoulder with her fingertip. Close up, I could see her hands were trembling. Despite her obvious anger I felt a surge of love for my prickly grandmother and tried to take hold of her hands but she shrugged me off.

'You think you know everything. I don't want your help,' she said stiffly. 'The Lemon Tree Café is mine; I don't want anyone interfering. Not your mamma and not you.'

She stood back to allow me out of the cupboard. I felt totally wretched but frustrated too.

'If caring for you is interfering, then I'm sorry,' I said, swallowing the lump in my throat.

'If you care for me, then you don't go behind my back.'

A look of pain crossed her face then, but she pulled herself together and walked away.

'You finished here,' she muttered over her shoulder.

Everyone in the café was staring at us. Including, I noticed with a sinking heart, Stella Derry, who was already reaching for her mobile phone. The news would be all round the village before I even made it home.

'My month is up anyway,' I said loudly, holding on to my last vestige of pride. 'And I'll probably have a new job this time tomorrow.'

'She'll come round, hen,' Juliet said gruffly as I snatched up my bag and jacket.

I glanced over at Nonna who was snapping at Stanley that their date was off as the café was unexpectedly short-staffed.

'Maybe,' I said, giving her a very quick hug. 'And maybe piggies might fly.'

Chapter 8

The following day, I went to Manchester for my appointment with HitSquad. Compared to my dressing-down from Nonna, the interview itself was a cinch. I'd secretly hoped to be offered the job on the spot so that I could arrive back in Barnaby triumphant but that wasn't to be. However, as I stepped off the Manchester train at Chesterfield and hopped on a bus back to the village, I thought I'd acquitted myself reasonably well considering I'd barely slept a wink all night.

The look on Nonna's face still haunted me; I'd never seen her so angry. She must be aware that the accounts were in a terrible state? Perhaps her behaviour was simply defensive, fuelled by fear? But it was the envelope marked *privato* with the photographs and document in it that had seemed to really fire her up and I couldn't help wondering who was in the pictures. I would love to see pictures of my Italian family and I know Mum would too. But if they were simply family snaps why be so prickly about them? Why the big secret?

Whatever it was, I thought with a sigh, gazing out of the bus window, she'd made it very clear it was none of my business, so the sooner I could move on with my life and get a new job sorted out the better.

My interview at HitSquad had been quite a shock after spending a month in sleepy Barnaby. It was one of the trendiest buildings I'd ever been in: an open-plan glass box with squishy sofas, loud music at one end and a chill-out zone at the other. The whole thing was a world away from the saggy armchairs and tinkle of teaspoons at the Lemon Tree Café.

The weather in Manchester had been relentlessly wet, making the pavements slippery and turning the concrete charcoal grey but as the bus trundled over the hills towards Barnaby, the clouds parted and huge beams of sunlight skimmed the tops of the Peak District, painting them gold.

I'll miss all this, I thought with a pang. I'd miss the bright yellow fields and the acres of green trees, the glint of the river running through the valley, the blossom in the hedgerows and the fat lambs headbutting each other playfully. But there'd be people in Manchester, I consoled myself; lots of people and shops and no grumpy old women.

I stepped off the bus at the village green, steadfastly not looking in the direction of the café. I'd go home and email Michael and tell him how much I wanted the job and then perhaps head off towards the river for a run. I stepped off the pavement and immediately leapt back as Lia's car screeched to a halt in front of me.

I waved to her.

'Fancy coming back to mine for a coffee?' I yelled through the window, before spotting that her face was red and her eyes were like saucers. 'I can tell you all about my interview!'

She wound down the window and shook her head.

'Oh, Rosie, I'm so glad you're here,' she panted. 'I didn't know what to do. Get in!'

She looked so panic-stricken that I didn't argue.

'What is it?' I said, diving in through the passenger door. She bit her lip. 'I'm not entirely sure.'

My heart missed a beat as I glanced at Arlo asleep in his car seat. 'He's not ill, is he?'

'No. It's Dad,' she said grimly. 'I think he's up to something.'

'Such as?' I blinked at her.

'From where I was standing, it looked distinctly like he was meeting another woman.'

'Dad?' I gasped. 'Are you sure?'

'Yeah. Belt up. This could be a bumpy ride.'

Good God, I thought, as Lia crunched through the gears, there was certainly never a dull moment in our family . . .

We sped off out of the village while she filled me in on the details.

'We were having a walk along the tow path just past the little marina and I saw him. He turned into the car park of the Riverside Hotel. I waved but he didn't spot me so I crossed the path towards the hotel thinking we could see if he had time for a drink.

'I got to the entrance of the car park just as another car turned in. And this is where things turn nasty. This second car parked in the space next to Dad's and a woman got out. So I hid myself and the pushchair round the corner of the hotel where I could spy on them. She was much younger than him: very thin and wearing a dress and boots and her hair was tied in a ponytail. Then Dad got out and they laughed and joked and he reached into the car and pulled out a denim jacket. A denim jacket, Rosie!'

The hairs on the back of my neck stood to attention and I shivered.

Last night I'd been round to Mum and Dad's to tell them that I'd been sacked from the café; they'd known already, of course. Ken from the Mini Mart had told Dad when he called in for a Scotch egg on his way home. Ken's wife had told him, who in turn had had a visit from Stella Derry. I shouldn't imagine there was anyone left in Barnaby who didn't know. Anyway, while I was there, Mum asked Dad if he'd like to take her for that lunch he'd been talking about for ages. Dad went bright red and said he couldn't because he had a meeting that he couldn't get out of. The question was: what sort of meeting was it?

'Did you see them – you know – do anything?' I swallowed, not sure I wanted to know the answer.

Lia shook her head. 'They walked into the hotel together and when they reached the door, Dad held it open for her and put his hand on the small of her back.'

'When was this?'

'About half an hour ago. I've had to run back with the pushchair, fetch the car and transfer Arlo to his car seat. I haven't moved so fast in years.'

Dad had a wardrobe full of tweed and wool. He was not a denim man. Or maybe he was. What did I know? Last week Mum had caught him eyeing up frilly underwear and then there was the unexplained red lipstick. I was beginning to think I didn't know my father at all.

'Oh hell,' I muttered. 'Mum said he was behaving oddly.'

I filled her in on the online lingerie ogling and the lipstick mark on his shirt and his claims of being busy today. There was also that other comment he made ages ago about fanning the flames of his smouldering passion. It was all making sense now, but oh, please let it not be true . . .

'Oh God, that's it, then; he's definitely being unfaithful.' Lia blinked away tears and the car tugged to one side as she rubbed her arm over her cheeks. 'And why did Mum confide in you and not me? I'm only two years younger than you, not twenty.'

I gaped at her. 'I was just there; it was circumstance, that's all.'

Lia harrumphed as she turned into the car park of the Riverside Hotel.

There weren't many cars here at this time in the afternoon, half a dozen maybe plus Dad's and the mystery woman's, which was a small blue Nissan. Lia slowed the car right down and we drove past Dad's Volvo and into the far corner between a battered white van advertising French polishing and the hotel's big green recycling bins where we were less conspicuous.

I turned to face her. 'Whatever we find out could change the family for ever . . . Let's face it together, put on a united front?'

Lia let out a long breath and turned off the engine. 'You're right. So. What are we going to do?'

'Let's go into reception, see if we can spot him and take it from there.' I looked at her, trying to smile bravely. 'There's probably some perfectly innocent explanation and we'll all end up laughing about this in years to come.'

Lia slid her eyes to me doubtfully. 'I hope so.'

'Me too.'

I got out of the car and Lia reached into the back to lift out Arlo.

He opened his eyes, blinked at his mum, then rubbed his face on her shoulder and went back to sleep.

My legs were trembling as we marched to the front door. I held the door open for Lia and the handle was sticky to the touch. I hadn't been to the Riverside Hotel for ages. It had been the 'in' place to go when I was a teenager but it was a bit rundown these days. It all felt a bit sleazy and I was seized with sadness that my father, who I'd worshipped since I was small, might be inside with another woman.

'Why come here,' Lia murmured, 'when the chance of discovery is so great?'

'Why would Dad have an affair in the first place?' I replied. 'I thought he was devoted to Mum.'

Lia shrugged.

It all seemed so unlikely, but then in my experience, men were unpredictable, unreliable creatures so perhaps we shouldn't have been surprised at all.

Just then one of the doors further down the corridor opened and Dad appeared from it. Lia and I pressed ourselves up against the wall like the worst private detectives ever. He was tapping an envelope into the palm of his other hand and humming a song that even at this distance I recognized as 'Jolene', one of his favourite Dolly Parton

86

numbers. He crossed the corridor without looking in our direction and went through another door.

'Oh my God,' I spluttered, 'look how pleased with himself he is. I'm going to find out what's going on.'

'Rosie! Wait,' Lia cried, catching hold of my sleeve. 'What are you going to say?'

But I shook her off and ran down the corridor with Lia scurrying behind me.

The sudden movement woke Arlo up and he began to build himself up to cry.

'Oi,' I yelled, barging my way through the door I'd seen Dad go through. 'Alec Featherstone, come out here now and explain yourself.'

'Rosie, that's the Gents,' Lia hissed, yanking me out.

'Oops, sorry, sorry,' I muttered, instantly going into reverse.

We hurriedly backed out of the men's toilets but not before I'd seen two men, one of them Dad, hunched over the urinal, desperately trying to zip up their trousers.

We turned our heads away just as a man scurried out of the toilets hiding a wet patch on his crotch and Arlo let out a full-on wail.

Lia jiggled him up and down to comfort him but he didn't stop.

'Look,' she said, nodding towards the entrance doors as a slim woman with high-heeled boots and a swinging ponytail pushed through them and exited to the car park. 'That's her!'

'Come on. Let's find out who she is.' I lunged in the direction of the doors but Dad appeared from the Gents and I froze, rooted to the spot, my heart thumping against my ribs.

'Hello, girls?' said Dad, with a confused sort of smile.

Lia simply sucked her cheeks in and raised her eyebrows.

I stared at the man I'd loved more than any other all my life. *Please, Dad, please let this be a big misunderstanding . . .*

My throat tightened and I wasn't sure whether I'd be able

to speak. I'd never had grandfathers: even Dad's own father had died before I'd got the chance to know him. Dad had been my only male role model. I'd put him on a pedestal ever since I was a little girl. I could feel a bubble of anger building up; for Mum but also for myself. How could he let us down?

'Good grief, young man,' said Dad, wiggling Arlo's foot. 'That's a racket and a half.'

Arlo stopped crying and launched himself at Dad who took him from Lia.

'What are you doing here?' Lia asked.

'Besides trying to have a private wee, you mean?' he said with a half-laugh.

'Dad.' I pinched the bridge of my nose. 'We've got to know. Are you or are you not having an affair with that woman, owner of a Nissan Note?'

I jabbed a finger in the direction of the doors.

Dad stared down the corridor, his mouth opening and closing twice before he managed to splutter a reply. 'I won't dignify that with an answer.'

'Ha! Bridget Jones,' I said triumphantly. 'Caught red-handed.'

'What?' He frowned from Lia to me.

'It's a line from one of the *Bridget Jones* films,' she explained and then looked at me. 'It looks like we were right to fear the worst.'

Dad ran his spare hand through his fine blond hair, sending it into fluffy peaks. 'You've totally lost me.'

'It's what Mark Darcy says to Bridget Jones when she asks him if he's having an affair with Rebecca. Her friends tell her that if Mark says "I'm not going to dignify that with an answer", then it proves he is.' I folded my arms and looked at Lia. She was trying to look brave but failing, her bottom lip was doing that wobbly thing, which was a dead giveaway.

'So now we know,' I said, tilting my chin up.

Lia leaned to whisper in my ear. 'Only Mark Darcy actually wasn't having an affair with Rebecca, was he? So in theory . . .'

'Shh.' I gave her a sharp look, although she did have a point.

'Does Mum know who you're meeting?' Lia asked, tilting her chin up too.

'No.' He looked shifty and tried to change the subject by murmuring to Arlo.

I wrapped my arm round Lia's shoulder. Like we were comrades in arms. 'You must admit, Dad, it does look a bit weird. You being here. In a hotel. With a woman.'

'In a denim jacket,' Lia added. 'I didn't think you were a denim-jacket man.'

'Well, it might look weird,' Dad went red and then pulled himself up tall, 'but despite everything you know about me, the conclusion my own daughters come to is that I'm having an affair. Well, thanks. Thanks a bunch.'

'So enlighten us!' I said, holding my palms out.

'I will not,' he said, rolling his shoulders back and jutting out his chin.

'I think that tells us everything we need to know. Kindly hand me my nephew,' I fumed.

Dad kissed Arlo tenderly, handed him back to me and took a few paces towards the exit. Then he turned slowly and sighed.

'Girls, have faith in your old dad, OK? Just for a week. One week. I beg you.'

The pained expression on his face broke my heart and I felt my anger beginning to melt.

Lia looked at me, chewing her lip, waiting for me to respond.

'OK.' I took a couple of deep breaths, trying to slow my racing pulse. 'Deal. But this had better be good.'

Dad's mouth lifted into a smile and he planted shy kisses on both our foreheads.

'I can't promise that exactly,' he said wryly. 'But I do think it'll be a surprise.'

He pushed through the doors to the car park and the two of us let out a breath.

'Do you believe him?' asked Lia, leaning her head against mine.

'I want to,' I murmured, watching the doors swing closed. 'Because if our parents can't make marriage work, then I don't know who the hell can.'

Chapter 9

I refreshed the screen on my phone. Again. Still nothing. Oh well. I'd make another coffee and then try again in ninety seconds.

Michael had told me that HitSquad's managing director, Finnegan O'Reilly, was making a decision today, but that I'd made a very good impression. I hoped so; it was only a week since Nonna had fired me from the café, but I was already bouncing off the walls. I didn't even have any DIY to do at home – I'd had everything done that needed doing when I bought it last year. Even the garden was low-maintenance.

Coffee made, I sat on the sofa, switched on daytime TV, turned it straight off again and checked the café's Twitter feed. The National Pet Month tweets I'd continued to do despite being sacked had garnered quite a bit of interest, including a retweet from Dog-Friendly Days Out. I wondered how the café was doing and what the mood was like following CabinetGate. I was tempted to walk down and see for myself, but I wasn't entirely sure I'd be made welcome. I was so cross with Nonna. I thought by now she'd have come to apologize for the way she'd treated me but no . . . That woman certainly knew how to bear a grudge.

My phone beeped with a message and I fell on it hungrily. Please, please say I'd got the job . . .

It was from Dad.

Family night out TONIGHT at the Riverside Hotel
8 p.m. I thought we could all do with a bit of cheering
up. Dress code smart. PS Eat before you come. I'm
not made of money. Love Dad xxx

I couldn't remember the last time we'd all been out together,
I thought, as Mum and I, arm in arm, followed Lia and Ed
along the corridor and into the Riverside Hotel's large func-
tion room later that night.

'This is very unexpected,' Lia said, giving Dad a sly look as
he showed us to our seats. 'To what do we owe the pleasure?'

Dad seemed a bit frazzled: there was a sheen of perspiration on his forehead and he looked pale as he ran a finger
around his collar. 'All in good time, Lia.'

It was a large room with, at a guess, thirty or forty tables.
The chairs had been arranged so that we could all see the
stage and our table was right at the front. Frank Sinatra
songs crooned away in the background and a babble of
chatter and chinking of glasses added a party atmosphere.
As we reached our table and slipped our jackets off the
lights dimmed and a spotlight flicked on to the empty stage.

'I don't mind why we're here; it's just great to be out.' Ed
sighed with pleasure. 'Our first child-free night.'

He and Lia smiled at each other, but they'd both checked
their phones for messages from the babysitter at least half a
dozen times since we'd arrived in the car park.

'Great seats, Alec,' said Ed. 'What did you have to do to
get them?'

Dad turned bright red and laughed so heartily that a
woman at the next table turned and stared at him.

'Ha ha, nothing, nothing at all,' he blustered. 'Luck of the
draw, I guess.'

'*Whose* drawers? That's what I want to know.' Lia sucked
in her cheeks and looked knowingly at me.

My stomach flipped and I ignored her, pulling out a chair for Mum instead. 'Sit here, Mum, it's got the best view.'

'As long as we don't get one of those comedians who likes to pick on people as part of their act,' Mum shuddered, hanging her velvet blazer on the back of the chair. 'I'll be mortified.'

'I'll jump up in your place,' Dad promised. 'Never fear.'

She chuckled and kissed his cheek. 'My hero.'

My heart gave a little bounce as I watched her tuck her dress under her legs and sit down. She looked stunning tonight in a gold shift dress that set off her olive skin perfectly; Dad would have to be insane if he was actually having an affair. Lia and I hadn't said anything to Mum about bumping into Dad here a week ago. I had no idea what he was planning for this evening, but I hoped whatever he had up his sleeve would banish all our concerns once and for all. I averted my eyes as he picked up Mum's hand and kissed it. The room was filling up nicely now and the lights had been dimmed another notch.

'Here are Nonna and Stanley,' said Lia, waving to attract their attention.

I felt my face grow hot and tried to avoid eye contact as Nonna scanned the room looking for us. Tonight would be the first time we'd been in the same room since she sacked me and I'd been really hoping that I could announce my new job in front of her. Unfortunately, HitSquad had got a rush project on and the whole company had been caught up in it all day so Finnegan hadn't been in touch. Michael had passed my mobile number to him on the off chance he'd still get around to calling me, but I didn't hold out much hope for a call tonight.

'At least Stanley has finally got a second date with her after her meltdown and the aborted cinema trip,' I said wryly.

'Been there, got the T-shirt,' said Mum. 'I don't want to say I told you so, but—'

'Yeah, yeah.' I rolled my eyes.

'Talking of which,' Ed teased, 'when did you last go out on a date, Rosie?'

'February,' I replied promptly. 'With a man called Lewis. He took me to play golf at his club. I hated it.'

'Oh, darling, why?' Mum's brow creased with concern.

I shrugged. 'We'd only got to about the fourth hole and he said he knew it was early days but he thought he was in love with me.'

'Ah, that is so sweet,' chorused Mum and Lia together.

'Sweet? It was our first date,' I retorted. 'I called him a weirdo and told him he'd got the wrong end of the stick.'

'What was it – an eight iron?' Ed put in, laughing at his own joke.

Mum and Dad chuckled.

Lia joined in. 'So you could say the date was a little below par?'

'And I bet he didn't get a hole-in-one,' Ed continued, elbowing his father-in-law in the ribs. 'Eh?'

'Too far,' said Lia, giving him a hard stare. She turned to Dad.

'What about you, Dad?' she said slyly. 'When was your last date?'

I sent her a look that I hope conveyed not-in-front-of-Mum vibes. Dad opened his mouth to answer when there was a polite cough from behind.

'Evening, all.' Stanley, with Nonna on his arm, tapped Dad on his shoulder. 'Very good of you to invite me, Alec. Where would you like us?'

Dad jumped up and shook Stanley's hand and settled them both into seats, thankfully not next to me. Nonna blew kisses to Mum and Lia across the table. I gritted my teeth as she pretended not to see me. Fine. Two people could play at being stubborn. It was obvious she needed help in the café; I was motivated by love for her, nothing else; I was hurt that she couldn't see that but getting increasingly cross too.

'Good evening,' said a waiter, depositing a bottle of prosecco and glasses on our table. One bottle didn't go far between seven but he poured a tiny splash into each glass. 'Compliments of the management.'

'Why?' I asked the waiter.

'All the performers get one.' He smiled briefly and swanned off.

'Performers?' I frowned. 'But we're not—'

'Ssshhh! Let's not look a gift horse in the mouth, Rosie,' said Dad, downing his in one.

'Must be some mistake.'

'I'd like to propose a toast,' said Lia, reaching for her prosecco.

Dad pouted. 'I was going to do that. This is my evening.'

'Is it?' Lia opened her eyes wide. 'I thought it was a family night?'

I dug her in the ribs, but she held her glass aloft. 'Mum, I'm so proud of you, you look absolutely gorgeous tonight. Doesn't she, Dad?'

Dad nodded fervently. 'I was going to say—'

'And Ed and I would like to thank you for helping out with Arlo,' she continued. 'So I'd like to toast your health. To Mum!'

We all joined in with the toast and I watched Dad's face for clues, but there was nothing but love reflected in his eyes. *What are you up to, Dad?* I pondered as I drained the last of my bubbles.

'Also I've been thinking,' Lia continued. 'I've decided to change career; I'm going to cook for a living. And Nonna, I wondered if you'd let me come and work at the café?'

'You must think I mad as a kipper,' said Nonna, glaring at her. 'I not having any of you ever again.'

Mum and I exchanged looks.

'Typical,' Lia huffed, flashing her eyes at me. 'That's your fault, that is.'

Ed pulled a face and disappeared off to the bar, leaving

Lia to sulk. Stanley had taken his glasses off to read the small type on the programme and Nonna was staring resolutely ahead. Dad looked anxiously around the room, his leg jiggling under the tablecloth. He waited until Ed was back with two more bottles of prosecco and coughed importantly.

'I'd like to propose a toast to Luisa too.' He reached for Mum's hand. 'Whenever you decide to do something you put your heart and soul into it, whether it be looking after the family or your voluntary work, and you've given me the inspiration to follow suit. I'm proud of you, Luisa, and I hope you can say the same of me.'

'Oh, Alec, of course I'm proud.' Mum looked a bit misty-eyed. 'What a lovely thing to say.'

They kissed, leaning into each other and Lia and I shared a smile. Whatever else was going on with Dad, that wasn't fake. It couldn't be.

And then the evening kicked off. The music changed to some sort of big-band number. Lights flashed and a compère took to the stage and in the next hour we were totally entertained by an acrobatic troupe, singers, a magician and a dancing dog and Mum didn't let go of Dad's hand once.

During an extremely scary martial arts act involving samurai swords and pineapples, Dad pressed a kiss to Mum's cheek and stood up.

I need the loo, he mouthed.

'Get another bottle,' I said, waving an empty one at him. 'And hurry back.'

He nodded, and bending down so as not to obscure anyone's view, he circumnavigated tables and chairs and disappeared from view.

'OK, Mum?' I whispered, patting her hand as the samurai warriors took their final bows and swished their weapons in a figure of eight as they filed off stage.

She nodded, eyes sparkling in the reflected stage lights. 'More than OK. A night out as a family was just what we needed. If only you and Nonna would make up, it would be perfect.'

She raised an eyebrow hopefully and I bit my lip, looking over at Nonna and wondering whether I should make the first move. But the next act to come out on stage was an Abba tribute band. Lia, Mum and I took one look at each other and jumped to our feet, pushing our chairs back to make some room. Nonna and Stanley clapped along more sedately.

'VOULEZ-VOUS, UH-HUH!' We all did a sort of shouty-singing and began to dance.

Ed slunk down in his seat as if he were trying to make himself invisible and drained the dregs of his prosecco.

'Come on, Ed,' I shouted, 'join in.'

He shook his head nervously.

'I'll go and help Alec with the drinks,' he yelled and darted off.

The audience was still wolf-whistling and clapping the retreating Abba lookalikes when Ed returned with another bottle. We all collapsed back into our chairs out of breath.

'Whoohoo,' Lia cried, 'more fizz.' Although she already looked like she'd had enough.

'Where's Alec?' Mum asked, frowning.

Ed shrugged. 'No sign of him at the bar. But I didn't check the Gents.'

Mum sighed. 'He's probably found a newspaper and locked himself in a cubicle.'

The music for the next act started up and we all looked at each other and grinned; nobody who lived with Alec Featherstone could *not* recognize this one. It was the opening bars to Dolly Parton's '9 to 5': his favourite song.

We were all on our feet in seconds, even Nonna, Stanley and Ed. Lia was clapping her hands above her head in time to the music. Out of the corner of my eye I saw a tall stocky blonde dance her way on to the stage.

'Shall I go and check the loo, Luisa?' Ed asked. 'He wouldn't want to miss this.'

But Mum didn't answer; she couldn't drag her eyes off the singer.

'He's right, Mum,' I said, shaking her arm. 'Dad would love to see this.'

Still no response from her; it was as if she'd gone into a trance. I didn't know why; it was Dad who was the big Dolly Parton fan in the family, not her.

'If you wouldn't mind, Ed,' I said, answering for her.

But before Ed could move, the singer launched into the first line of the song and the crowd erupted in applause and whistles, eager to continue their dancing.

'He's brilliant,' Mum breathed, pressing her hands to her cheeks.

'He? Is it a man? Ooh yay!' Lia shielded her eyes, pointing at the stage. 'It's a man in drag.'

'I think the legs were a giveaway.' Ed laughed. 'And the eighties wig.'

'That's not a man,' said Mum in a wavering voice. 'That's—'

'*Mamma mia!*' yelled Nonna. 'It's not Dolly Parton, it's Alec!'

Chapter 10

We danced and clapped as my dad, in a strappy white dress, blonde wig and high heels, strutted his stuff through three Dolly Parton songs. As soon as he left the stage we rushed out and found him in a lively communal dressing room backstage.

Dad was sitting on a stool, wincing as he eased his feet out of a pair of silver stilettos.

I threw my arms around his neck. 'That was amazing! You nailed it. Absolutely nailed it!'

'Did I?' he said, returning my hug. His face was alight with excitement and adrenalin and there were beads of sweat along the edge of his long blonde wig. 'I thought it went a bit wobbly on the second number.'

The rest of the family were right behind me, including Nonna and a bewildered Stanley. Dad found himself being squeezed and hugged and kissed. Mum and Lia cried and even Ed looked emotional. Stanley clapped him on the back and couldn't take his eyes off his hairy cleavage.

The Russian Cossack dancers had discarded their hats and were throwing back vodka shots like they were going out of fashion, and the Abba tribute lot were still doing their dance routines. Others were milling around, mostly half dressed and chatting animatedly about their own performances. Six samurai swords in leather sheaths leaned up against the wall and the dancing dog was spark out in a large basket in the corner.

And there, in the thick of it, was my dad, a university lecturer from Derby, peeling his tights off. I'd never been prouder of him.

'You were ace, Dad,' Lia cried. 'Totally ace.'

'I saw this blonde diva shaking her hips and I had a weird sensation as if she were someone I'd met before.' Mum laughed and threaded her arms round his waist. 'And I was right. I can't believe you kept this a secret. Congratulations, darling, you're a star.'

'Really?' He puffed out his chest. 'I've been taking singing lessons. I'm sorry. I know I've been behaving secretively but I wanted it to be a surprise.'

'My son-in-law, in a dress,' said Nonna, sitting down on the chair Stanley had found her. She shook her head incredulously. 'Whatever float your goat, I suppose.'

'Boat not goat,' said Stanley with a chuckle.

Nonna shrugged.

'It's been my lifelong ambition to sing in front of an audience,' said Dad bashfully. 'But you were right, Luisa, my voice wasn't up to it. So I thought I'd do something about it.'

'You certainly did that, Alec.' Mum giggled, twanging his bra strap. 'And I'm sorry for criticizing your singing. Just goes to show how little I know; you're brilliant.'

Ed stared at him with a mixture of uneasiness and possibly a bit of envy. 'What does it feel like wearing women's clothes?'

Dad tugged at the neckline. 'Tight. Like an oven-ready turkey.'

'Well,' Ed gave a whistle, 'anyone can see you've got balls wearing that get-up.'

Dad grimaced and looked down. 'Can they?'

Lia giggled. 'I think he means you're very brave.'

'You very sexy, I think,' Nonna chuckled. 'You look like a woman from where I was sitting.'

'Yes, you had me fooled too.' Stanley placed a hand propri-etorially on Nonna's shoulder. I half expected her to shrug it off, but she patted it gently. It was such a tender gesture that my heart gave a little squeeze of hope for them both.

'It hasn't been easy. Any of it.' Dad took mine and Lia's hands. 'And I nearly caved in and told you the truth when you spotted me last week with my singing teacher.'

'So that's who she was. Sorry, Dad,' Lia cringed, 'for jumping to conclusions.'

Mum cocked an eyebrow and I explained how we'd con-fronted him at the hotel and immediately thought the worst.

'We'd only come to check out the stage,' said Dad, shak-ing his head at the memory. 'I came out of the loo and walked into the Spanish Inquisition.'

'I'm sorry we doubted you,' I said, kissing my dad's cheek. 'But next time I'll do your make-up.'

Lia creased up with laughter as I wiped the thick orange foundation from my lips.

'And the outfit?' He looked down at his white and silver dress. 'Do you like it? I picked it up from a charity shop, and I managed to get the bra online.'

'We know!' Lia giggled. 'Mum thought you were up to something kinky.'

He clapped a hand to his forehead. 'That was a bit awkward.'

'If anyone had told me a month ago that finding my hus-band in drag singing "9 to 5" by Dolly Parton would be a relief, I wouldn't have believed them.' Mum laughed softly and her eyes shone with pride.

'I chose that song for you,' he said, pulling her close. 'Because it's about letting go of a busy life and doing what makes you happy instead of serving on all these committees.'

'Oh Alec.' She kissed his cheek. 'That's exactly how I feel.'

'But you be bored, Luisa,' said Nonna, shaking her head. 'What you do all day, eh?'

Mum looped her arm through Dad's and met Nonna's gaze.

'That's what I thought ten years ago when I lost my job. The girls had both left home and I felt adrift, no use to anyone, I'd lost my place at home and at work. I thought perhaps I could be useful to you at the café. But of course you didn't want my help. You made that perfectly clear.'

Nonna looked sheepish. 'I like things my way,' she muttered.

'So I filled my days with voluntary work instead,' Mum continued. 'And all of a sudden I was busy again. But now looking after Arlo has helped me to get the balance right. I love my family and that's who I want to spend time with, not to always be rushing from one meeting to another.'

'I'll drink to that,' said Dad, beaming.

'Oh.' Nonna blinked at her daughter. 'I didn't know this is how you feel, Luisa. I didn't know you feel not useful.'

Mum blew out an exasperated breath. 'You wouldn't, would you? Because you were too quick to throw me out of the café, like you've done with Rosie. You spurn help as if it somehow makes you look weak.'

'I just . . . well, I just . . .' Nonna blinked her dark chestnut eyes at Mum and then me and shrugged helplessly. 'I used to doing everything alone. I'm sorry I didn't listen to you. Both of you.'

I gave her a weak smile; this was as much of an apology as I was likely to get.

Mum placed a hand on Nonna's arm. 'Can we try again? To talk to you about the future?'

Nonna swallowed and we all hung on her answer but one of the Cossacks, impervious to the tension, swaggered into our little circle waving a bottle of vodka.

'You lot want to join us for a drink?' he asked in a broad Liverpudlian accent.

'Yes,' Mum replied with some relief. 'Anyone else?'

'Oh rather,' said Stanley, rubbing his hands together.

'Okey cokey,' said Nonna, still looking at Mum.

Glasses were found, shots were poured and the performers took it in turns to toast each other. I downed a vodka in one just as my phone started to vibrate. I looked at the screen to see a message from an unknown number:

This is Finnegan O'Reilly, sorry it's late but we've had a chaotic day. I'd like to offer you the job as New Business Director. Congratulations! Call me back to discuss when you're free.

My heart pounded. I looked at my crazy lovely family swigging vodka shots and felt a rush of warmth for them. Everyone was occupied and it was an opportune moment to slip away.

From the dressing room, I went out into the corridor and pushed through a heavy door marked 'Fire Exit' and followed a path to the garden overlooking the river at the back.

There was a damp coolness to the air but the sky was clear and dark and no moon was to be seen in amongst a million stars. After the bright lights, thumping music and excitement of the cabaret it was the perfect retreat, the ideal place to gather my thoughts.

I wandered across the dewy grass down to the waterfront and the picnic tables. Ahead of me was a row of houseboats, pretty permanent judging by the plant pots on the deck of one and the plume of smoke rising from the chimney of another.

I sat down, watching the lights from the hotel reflected in the ripples in the river and took a deep breath. I took out my phone and read the message again.

The job was mine, so why wasn't I punching the air with joy?

Something in me had changed.

Despite all my bluster about needing a challenge and being wedded to deadlines and thriving on the cut and thrust of commerce, I'd loved being at the Lemon Tree Café more than I could ever have foreseen. If I took the job in Manchester, I'd miss seeing my family every day and watching Arlo grow up. I'd miss the blossoming love between Nonna and Stanley, and the banter between Juliet and our regular customers. I'd miss watching the seasons alter with each different variety of wild flower on the village green and I wouldn't get to hear the news from the other shops.

I hardly recognized myself. I'd always been the workaholic, ambitious member of the family, the one eager to climb the corporate ladder, to do my very best. My family had always cast me as the brave one, the one to take risks and 'go for it'. But what if bravery had got nothing to do with it? What if building my career had simply been a way for me to run away from what had happened in my personal life?

But actually, what choice did I have? I needed a job and Nonna might have apologized, but I couldn't see her having me back. I had no choice at all.

I took a deep breath and began to type.

A cool breeze off the river made me shiver as I sent a text back to Finnegan telling him that I would be delighted to accept the position at HitSquad and would be available to start immediately.

Decision made.

'Here you are!' Lia threw herself on to the bench beside me and handed me a glass of wine. She plonked an almost full bottle on the table. 'I've been looking all over for you.'

'Perfect timing.' I clinked my glass against hers. 'You can celebrate my new job with me.'

'Yay! You got it?'

I took a deep sip. 'Yep. Time to get my career back on track. Retreat into my comfort zone.'

'And she's off again, leaving me behind.' Lia heaved a sigh, staring into her glass.

'What do you mean?'

'I want to work again. And I want to cook.' She blinked her brown eyes at me. 'Don't laugh, but I had this fantasy that you and I would be able to work together at the café. Now you're going and Nonna won't have me anyway. Oh well,' she took a big slug of wine, 'back to the drawing board.'

'I think you should tell Nonna all this,' I suggested. 'Or I will, if you like?'

'There won't be a job for me. Nonna's adamant about that.' She shrugged. 'If she won't have you, I don't stand a chance; you've always been her favourite.'

'I don't think that's true,' I said, uncomfortably, acknow-ledging to myself that it probably was. I nudged Lia with my shoulder. 'And if it's any consolation, I'd have enjoyed work-ing with you too. Although I don't think there'd be enough money to employ both of us.'

'Doesn't matter,' said Lia with a shrug. Her words were beginning to sound a tiny bit slurred; I wondered whether to mention it.

'Perhaps I'm being unrealistic thinking I could do some-thing different anyway,' she said. 'You've always been fearless: leaving home, going to uni. I was too scared to even leave the village. I've settled for the easy life, stayed near my par-ents, married a nice boy, had a baby.'

'You are kidding me!' I cried, leaning away to give her the full force of my amazement. 'When I saw you on Dad's arm entering the church on your wedding day I was in awe. How does she do that, I thought, look so calm and serene on what must be the scariest day of her life?'

Lia looked at me, baffled. 'I wasn't scared; I was in love. I was starting a new life with a man who – cheesy as it sounds – completes me.'

Out on the river the distant *pffut-pffut* of a diesel engine approaching made me glance up. A narrowboat, all lit up, was gliding silkily towards us. The sound of voices echoed across the water. Right now it seemed such a simple existence: just a small boat on a gentle river, none of the twists and turns of normal everyday life.

'But it's for ever,' I said, twisting the stem of my glass in my fingers. 'For ever.'

'I know,' she said simply. 'But you and I are the lucky ones: we've grown up watching the equivalent of a "How to Stay Married" tutorial.'

'Despite the two of us almost throwing a spanner in the works.' I grinned and then my smile slipped again. 'But that just piles on the pressure for me. I see Mum and Dad and I think, I'll never be like that. How do you get the balance right, letting someone in but not too much?'

'What do you mean?' Lia's nose wrinkled. 'There's no such thing as too much. Just let someone into your heart and let love do the rest.'

Let love do the rest . . . She made it sound so easy.

'Who exactly?' I raised an eyebrow. 'All the men round here are either married or widowers.'

'What's wrong with widowers?'

'Nothing if they're under forty. Which in Barnaby, they're not.'

Lia regarded me quizzically over the top of her glass. 'Hmm. I've often wondered about you. Why someone so beautiful is still single.'

'Beautiful? Cheers, I'll drink to that.'

I raised my glass to hide my face; she didn't know the half of it. But maybe it was time she did. I loved Lia, we'd got closer as we'd got older and I'd always been able to tell her things. *Most things.*

My heart ricocheted around in my ribcage. It would be a relief to share what happened with Callum. I didn't at the time, couldn't, I was so ashamed of what had happened, what I *didn't* do and how it ended. And now I saw that sharing it with Lia could be good for both of us. For her to see that I wasn't the perfect sister with the perfect life that she

106

thought I had and for me . . . for me to get some perspective on an event that had shaped my personal life for the last ten years.

'Lia,' I began.

'Oh here you both are!'

We turned to see Mum and Nonna, arm in arm, weaving their way through the tables to reach us.

'Nonna has something to say.' Mum paused and looked at Nonna, both of them looking like they were about to pop with excitement. 'Go on, Mamma.'

'OK, *cara*.' Nonna patted my hand. 'I have been very silly old woman. The café is too much for me, I bury my head in cement for too long, not wanting to let go of my business.'

'No one was trying to take it from you, Nonna,' I said patiently. 'All I was ever trying to do was make your life easier. My mistake was doing that behind your back, but at the time I thought I was doing the right thing.'

'You good girl, Rosanna. I see that now.' She stroked my face with her thumb, her skin rough from a lifetime of scrubbing tables. 'And I see that maybe not working every day is good. If I not working so much I spend time with Stanley instead.'

'I'm pleased,' I said with a smile. 'And I'm sure Stanley will be too.'

Mum nudged her in the ribs. 'Remember what you need to say.'

'And I very sorry for throwing you out of the café. I was angry when I see you . . .' She hesitated.

I willed her to finish her sentence, to mention the envelope marked *privato*, so that I could ask her about it while I had the chance, but she held out her arms.

'You forgive old Nonna?'

I hugged her. 'Of course.'

'So are you selling up, Nonna?' Lia asked.

The thought of the Lemon Tree Café leaving the family

made my stomach churn. Who would buy it? What would they do with it? I shuddered. It didn't bear thinking about.

The pregnant pause made me look up at Nonna again. She was looking at me with a fixed grin on her face.

'Sell? No, no, why I do that?' She flapped a hand at me. 'I just make Rosanna the manager of the café.'

I stared at her, completely speechless, vaguely aware of Lia making little gnashing noises with her teeth.

'Congratulations, darling,' cried Mum. 'You deserve it. You've done such a good job over the last month. The place is unrecognizable.'

'Eh,' muttered Nonna. 'It not that bad.'

'It's fashionable, Mamma,' said Mum with a laugh. 'Lots of people like shabby chic. So everyone is happy. Are you going to come in? There's a snake charmer on next.'

I promised we'd only be a few minutes and off they toddled. Lia refilled her glass and knocked it back in one.

'What was that about you not being the favourite?' she said drily. 'Mind you, I'd be crap at running the café so you're welcome to it. I just want to cook a few pies and stuff.'

'I've just accepted another job, remember?' I dropped my head in my hands and groaned. Now what was I going to do? I'd gone from no jobs to two. 'Do I stay or do I go?'

'Ooh that's a song,' Lia giggled, draining her glass. 'SHOULD I STAY OR SHOULD I GO NOW.'

'You've probably had enough wine,' I said.

'I'll be the judge of that.'

If I took the job with HitSquad, what would happen to the café? Nonna would have to carry on working; she'd probably never sell up. And that would be sad. But if I stayed at the café that would be the end of my career in social media. I already felt out of the loop and I'd only been gone for a month. You snooze you lose in that industry.

'Is that bargey thing coming here?' Lia pressed a hand over one eye. 'I can't tell.'

The narrowboat did seem to be getting closer to the jetty.

There was no point talking to my sister about it. Or anything else. She was probably too squiffy to give me her full attention anyway. I'd been about to tell her about Callum, but after Nonna's announcement, it could wait.

'So clever how they drive boats,' she said, gazing out at the water. 'I struggle with a car and that's got wheels and things.'

'It has got a steering wheel, Lia.' I followed her gaze as the narrowboat aimed for the only free mooring spot at the end of the row.

'There's a little boy on board,' said Lia. 'Shall we shout hello?'

'No,' I laughed. 'I really think you need to slow down with the wine.'

The man jumped down from the boat on to the path.

'Careful, dude,' he called to the child. 'Keep back from the edge.'

'Do you think he's a traveller?' Lia said in a loud whisper. 'Like Johnny Depp in *Chocolat*?'

'All sorts of people live on boats,' I said. 'I know someone who does. Remember Gabe, Verity's friend, the ex-solicitor? Gave it all up for a simpler life as a French polisher. From what I remember he was drop-dead gorgeous in a scruffy-jumper sort of way. What was the name of his boat? It's on the tip of my tongue.'

'*The Neptune*,' said Lia, squinting in the dim light.

My stomach dropped as I followed her gaze. 'That's it. *The Neptune*.'

The man turned at the sound of our voices and a smile spread across his face. He raised a hand.

'Hurry up, Daddy!' The little boy was jumping up and down in excitement.

'Whoa, Noah, wait,' said the man, darting forward to lift him to safety.

Noah? The breath caught in my throat; it had to be. But it couldn't be, could it? I slowly got to my feet and walked towards the man and his son.

'Gabe? Is that you? And Noah?'

He lifted a hand to shield his eyes from the hotel lights. 'Rosie?'

'It is you!' I laughed, waving to Noah. 'Hello.'

'Oh my God,' I heard Lia squeak behind me. 'Gorgeous.'

'This is incredible!' He stepped forward to kiss my cheek and beamed. 'Verity told me where to find you, but I didn't expect to bump into you as soon as we arrived. What are you doing out here?'

'Honestly? My sister is getting rat-arsed and I'm contemplating my future.'

He raised an amused eyebrow. 'Sounds fun.'

Lia nudged me out of the way with her hip.

'Hi, I'm Lia. Her sister. We're here because our dad's inside dressed as Dolly Parton drinking vodka with Russian Cossack dancers and samurai warriors.'

'With real swords?' Noah breathed, eyes as big as saucers.

'Oh yes, and snakes. It's just your average Thursday night in Barnaby,' I said casually. 'What about you two?'

Gabe glanced over his shoulder at his boat and then back to us. 'We've just moved in. This very second. Well, I brought my van down last week,' he nodded towards the car park, 'and took the slow boat to Barnaby after that.'

The white van with French polishing written on the side . . . we parked next to it in the car park when we came spying on Dad.

'And tomorrow we're stargazing, aren't we, Daddy?' Noah piped up.

Gabe was moving to Barnaby? How had Verity forgotten to mention this?

'That's good news, isn't it?' said Lia, pinching my arm.

I shot her a look and bent down to talk to Noah on his level. 'Do you remember me? I'm your Auntie Verity's friend, Rosie.'

Noah nodded.

'Daddy says you look like Katy Perry.' He put a hand to his mouth and whispered loudly, 'He likes Katy Perry.'

Gabe groaned and ran a hand through his wavy sandy hair. 'Cheers, buddy. Sorry about that,' he added softly.

'Do you like stars?' said Noah.

'I do,' I said, melting at the way Noah clutched his daddy's leg for comfort. 'And I especially love the moon.'

'Today is a super new moon,' said Noah, bouncing on the spot. 'Jupiter is bright, bright, bright.'

He made twinkling actions with his hands.

'Yes, I read about that,' I said, smiling. 'This week is a really good time to see Jupiter.'

Lia draped herself over my shoulders and crooned in my ear, 'Somebody is star-struck.'

I could have cheerfully tipped her in the river . . .

'You've made a friend for life now,' Gabe said, a proud smile lighting up his face. 'Right, come on, Noah. It's way past your bedtime and we're going to have to start getting you in a routine ready for school.'

'I'm going to big school,' Noah announced shyly.

'In Barnaby?' I stared at Gabe.

He nodded. 'All a bit last minute, but yes. That's why we've moved here. On your recommendation, according to Verity. Bit of a disaster with the school I'd planned to send him to.'

'We went there,' Lia said with a hiccup and lurched towards him. 'And we turned out all right.'

Gabe grinned at us both. 'I can see that. Well, goodnight. Lovely to see you.'

He took Noah's hand and started towards the boat but then changed his mind and stopped.

'I don't suppose you fancy joining us tomorrow, do you?' He rubbed his face. 'For a bit of stargazing?'

'Yes!' Noah did a bit more on-the-spot bouncing. 'Come, Rosie. Hot dogs will be there and marshmallows on sticks.'

'Ow.' I rubbed my side. Lia was elbowing me so hard that

I'd have a bruise in the morning. 'If you're sure, I'd love to. Thank you both.'

'Some ladies make cakes,' said Noah slyly. 'Are you those ladies?'

'Sorry. Again.' Gabe clapped a hand over his son's mouth and rolled his eyes. 'See you tomorrow then. About seven?'

We grinned at each other; Gabe waved self-consciously and lifted Noah back on board.

Lia looped her arm through mine as we walked across the terrace to find the others.

'I'd forgotten how exciting flirting is,' she giggled.

'That wasn't flirting. That was talking to a friend of a friend and his son.'

'Whatever.' She snorted. 'So tonight you've got two new jobs and a date with a very handsome man. Not bad for a Thursday.'

'*Two* handsome men,' I said, glancing over my shoulder at *The Neptune*. Noah was waving furiously; I waved back. 'And it's not a date. But no, not bad at all.'

Lia looked at me, each of her eyes darting in different directions. 'So what's it to be, Rosie, an exciting new job in Manchester or a life in an apron?'

'You are *so* drunk,' I laughed. 'And I don't know. I guess I'm going to have to sleep on it.'

My career had sustained me for so long, giving it up to manage the café would be a massive change for me. On the other hand, I'd had a feeling of dread at leaving ever since Michael first set me up with an interview at HitSquad.

I took one last look at Gabe before going back inside the hotel. A thrill of an emotion I'd kept long hidden took my breath away for a second and I was smiling as I went through the door. Life in Barnaby had just got a whole lot more interesting . . .

PART TWO

A Storm in a Teacup

Chapter 11

It was the morning after Dad's Dolly Parton debut. The café had opened as if nothing had changed. Except that everything had changed. Despite a hangover, Lia was in the kitchen making soup. I'd suggested to her last night that she came in for some work experience to see if cooking for a living was really for her. I thought she'd forget, but she was here, downing cans of Coke and furiously chopping vegetables as if she was auditioning for *MasterChef.* Dad was in the conservatory giving an interview to a junior reporter from the *Derbyshire Bugle* called Robin Barker. And Mum, with Arlo playing with wooden spoons on her knee, was in deep conversation with Nonna about the university of the third age and all their fabulous outings. Nonna, it seemed, was keen to start her new life of leisure as soon as possible.

And I had taken over as the manager of the Lemon Tree Café.

'One pot of tea and two caramel slices,' I said, sliding a tray across the counter to Mr Beecher, the school caretaker, who'd come to do the crossword with Stanley.

'You still here, then?' he said, eyeing me from under two tremendously hairy eyebrows. 'Thought you'd have been back off to the city by now.'

'And leave all this behind?'

I nodded at the view through the café window. The bank leading down to the stream along the edge of the village green was dotted with pale yellow primroses and children were splashing in the water. The church spire was just visible behind the pub and the striking green and brown slopes of the Peak District in the distance contrasted sharply with the cloudless blue spring sky.

The urban offices of HitSquad could never have come close.

'Good point,' he said gruffly and dropped a pound in our tin marked 'Tips'. 'Have a cup of tea on me.'

'Thank you.' I smiled. 'I shall have an espresso, I think. I didn't get much sleep last night.'

After tossing and turning, drifting in and out of consciousness and mulling over the two job offers I'd received yesterday, I'd finally come to a decision at around five o'clock. With the help of strong coffee, I'd composed a second text to Finnegan at HitSquad, sending my apologies and explaining that, despite accepting his job offer yesterday, I would now have to decline it after all. And I'd typed an email to Michael, thanking him and saying that I regretted letting him down but that I couldn't envisage anywhere I'd rather be right now than at the Lemon Tree Café.

I took a deep breath, enjoying the momentary lull at the counter. Friday was always our busiest weekday and, coupled with the fact that it was the Easter holidays, the little bell above the door had been dinging away non-stop with the arrival of each new customer.

In the conservatory, Dad and the young reporter were getting to their feet and shaking hands.

'Nice chap,' said Dad, when Robin had left. He rubbed his hands together. 'Think I'll have a beef tea to celebrate my five minutes of fame.'

His phone rang as I passed the mug across the counter.

'That'll be Vegas,' Juliet smirked, popping a whole banana into the blender, 'wanting to know if you'll headline at Caesar's Palace this summer.'

Dad's eyes lit up as Juliet turned on the blender and he scuttled off to a quieter spot to take the call.

'Oh that's a shame,' he said, returning two minutes later. He popped his phone in his pocket and produced a pork pie in a paper bag from Ken's Mini Mart.

'No six-figure contract, hen?' Juliet cocked an eyebrow.

'It was Ed. He can't make the football match tomorrow. He's working.' Dad tutted.

Dad and Ed often went to see Derby County together. Dad was a huge fan and had used football as a way of vetting our potential boyfriends. Ed, who in fact was more of a rugby man, had tactfully professed an interest in the game when he first started going out with Lia and Dad had approved of him immediately. My poor brother-in-law still hadn't got round to telling Dad the truth.

The door flew open and Lucas from The Heavenly Gift Shop ran in and headed for the customer toilets.

'Morning, lovelies! A hot chocolate and a sausage roll, warmed until it goes baggy but not soggy,' he called over his shoulder. 'Thank you!'

Juliet and I exchanged surprised glances.

'Where's the fire?' she muttered.

'At least he said thank you,' I said, reaching for a jumbo sausage roll.

'Oh dear.' Juliet jabbed me with her bony elbow. 'That doesn't look good.'

Clementine had pulled up outside. Her assistant Tyson was in the passenger seat. Both of them were holding tissues to their faces. But before I had the chance to comment, Lucas emerged from the men's loos.

'So sorry,' he said, smoothing his hair. 'My own loo is out of action at the moment.'

I liked Lucas. He was possibly the best dressed man in the village and looked like something out of a Burberry catalogue. He also had extremely good taste; since he'd taken over the gift shop last year, it stocked beautiful cards and the sort of items that you bought with the intention of giving to someone else and then found you couldn't bear to part with.

'No problem.' I opened the microwave and removed his steaming sausage roll. 'How's that for bagginess?'

'Perfect,' he said, doing a little shimmy as he handed me some money.

Dad eyed him up doubtfully. 'Don't suppose you fancy coming to the Derby match with me tomorrow? Free ticket?'

'*Football?*' Lucas recoiled as if Dad had invited him to wrestle with starving alligators. 'Gosh, no thank you. It would remind me of my ex-wife too much.'

'Oh was she a Derby fan?' Dad said, discarding the jelly out of his pork pie.

Lucas shook his head.

'She played. "On the wing", whatever that means.' He fanned his face. 'I'm getting palpitations just thinking about Sundays spent on the sidelines, in the freezing cold, watching her and her friends thunder up and down the pitch.'

'I'd have loved that,' sighed Dad.

Clementine opened the door and ushered Tyson in.

'I'll get these,' she said to him, barging ahead to reach the counter. 'A hot chocolate and a cream horn, is it?'

'No,' Tyson said forcefully, chin high. 'Allow me. While I can still afford it. A herbal tea and sticky ginger cake for you?'

Clementine was dressed in a pair of tatty overalls and looked even thinner than usual. Her cheeks were hollow, her eyes were big and red-rimmed and she didn't look like she had the energy to argue.

'All right. That would be lovely.'

Nonna's ears pricked up and she was at Clementine's side within seconds. 'What happen? Dicky-head tax man?'

Clementine and Tyson raised tissues to their eyes again and Nonna waved a hand. 'Never mind. This all on me. Rosie, get them whatever they want.'

Nonna put her arm round Clementine's stiff shoulders and Tyson's head sagged.

'It's not fair,' he mumbled into his tissue. 'She's such a lovely person.'

Juliet and I grimaced at each other; Clementine had hinted that the garden centre had been having money issues. It looked as if things had deteriorated even more since her husband's funeral.

Juliet added the whipped cream and marshmallows to Lucas's hot chocolate while I went digging through the boxes for the herbiest of teas.

'It'll feel better after a cream horn,' Lucas promised, patting Tyson's arm.

Tyson looked him up and down appraisingly and gave him a shy smile. 'Thanks.'

'I know what'll cheer you up, lad,' said Dad. 'Free ticket to Derby County? Pies on me at half-time?'

Tyson shuddered. 'Sorry, not a football fan.'

'Snap,' Lucas said and took a tiny nibble of sausage roll. 'It was one of the many nails in the coffin of our marriage.' He paled. 'Whoops, sorry, Mrs Fearnley. Shouldn't have said coffin.'

Clementine dabbed a tissue to her eyes and waved a hand. 'Forget it. People seem to have some sort of bereavement Tourette's around me these days. The more they try to avoid talking about death, the worse it gets.'

'Come sit down, you look dead on your feet,' Nonna soothed, leading her away to a table.

'*You* were married?' Tyson stared at Lucas, from his diamond earrings to his dainty moccasins.

Lucas pushed the sleeves of his cashmere jumper up to his elbows. 'Yes. To a girl called Tanya until she divorced me for not being butch enough.'

Tyson's jaw fell open. 'How rude!'

'I know!' Lucas pouted.

Both men shook their heads in solidarity.

Lia appeared from the kitchen, two pink spots on her cheeks and a frizz of curls framing her pretty face.

'Minestrone soup, anyone?' She deposited a heavy tureen on the warming plate. 'Genuine Italian recipe.'

I lifted the lid and inhaled. 'Smells amazing.'

Lia took a swig from her Coke can and belched softly into her hand. 'I thought we should make a bit more of our Italian heritage. I might ask Nonna for any old family recipes. On the other hand, a lot of this old furniture should go, Italian or not.'

'Word to the wise, hen.' Juliet banged two lemon-patterned plates on to the counter, plonked a cream horn on one and a slice of ginger cake on the other. 'I tried that before and she bit my head off.'

'True.' I nodded. 'Nonna is touchy about her past. And it's my first day as manager; I don't want to upset her by making too many changes at once.'

'Fine.' Lia sighed, looking down at her hands. 'Just an idea.'

I bit my lip; I'd forgotten how sensitive she was at the moment.

'Ooh, Alec, I've had three customers in the shop today talking about your Dolly Parton act. How did you do it?' Lucas asked, poking his tongue into the cream on his hot chocolate. 'Because, if you don't mind me saying, you're very manly.'

Tyson nodded in agreement and Dad puffed out his chest.

'Ah. You have to locate your inner diva and work it, work it, work it.'

I did a double take as Dad put both hands on the counter. And twerked.

The two younger men stared at him in awe.

'Your inner diva,' Lucas marvelled. 'OMG. I'm not sure I could ever do that.'

I could feel Juliet shaking with silent laughter.

'Anyway, Lucas,' I said, attempting to keep my voice straight, 'when's the plumber coming to mend your loo?'

He took a deep breath and fanned his face.

'There's nothing wrong with my plumbing. There's a giant bumblebee stuck in there. This big.' He pointed at his plate. 'I can't possibly go back in until it's gone.'

'I'm sure,' said Dad, his lips twitching mischievously, 'that with some thought, Lucas, you will indeed find your inner diva. I'll be in the conservatory phoning my agent if anyone needs me.'

He picked up his beef tea and walked off.

'I'm having beef tea next time,' Tyson murmured, watching Dad retreat. 'Lucas, I don't mind bees. I'll come and rescue it.'

Lucas's hand fluttered to his throat. 'Rescue *it*? I'm the one who needs rescuing. But thanks. I accept.'

Tyson asked to borrow a jar of honey in case the bee needed sustenance and the two of them set off back to the gift shop.

'I think that might be the start of a beautiful friendship,' said Juliet, folding her arms. 'Now, Lia, can I finally get in that kitchen? I'm hours behind with the baking and I've got the WI ladies in later; they always want lemon drizzle cake.'

'Ooh!' Lia's eyes widened. 'Rosie, you should take a cake round to Gabe's tonight for Noah.'

I raised an eyebrow. 'You remember that much, then?'

Her cheeks flushed. 'I remember right up until I lost that drinking game with the Cossack dancers. It's a little hazy from then on.'

'Gabe? I don't know a Gabe.' Juliet looked put out; she prided herself on knowing everyone in the village. 'Or a Noah.'

'You mean you haven't heard? Tell her about your hot date!' said Lia.

'You've got a date?' Juliet's jaw dropped.

'It's not a date.' I explained that I'd bumped into a friend of a friend last night and he'd invited me to go round tonight to look at the night sky from the deck of his houseboat.

121

'Well, hen,' she said, patting my arm, 'at least it gets you out of the house. Beggars can't be choosers at your age.'

'Gee, thanks for the pep talk.'

'I'll do you a cake for your date, providing . . .' Juliet assembled a chopping board, sharp knife and basket of lemons and pushed them in my direction, ' . . . you peel all these.'

I opened my mouth to repeat that it wasn't a date, but it would be nice to take a fresh cake with me; I was sure Noah would appreciate it so I thanked her instead. She disappeared into the kitchen to start mixing cake batter and I picked up the knife and began to peel the first lemon.

Clementine stood up and started jingling her car keys, ready to make a move, and Nonna chivvied her to the counter.

'You not eating, I see that,' Nonna was telling her. 'You bag of bones these days. I make up goody bag for you.'

Clementine rested her elbows on the counter and dropped her head in her hands, while Nonna began filling plastic tubs with portions of food.

'Stick a couple of thousand quid in the bag while you're at it,' she said. 'That might bring my appetite back.'

'Oh, *cara*,' Nonna tutted. 'I so sorry you have problems with business.'

'If there's anything I can do to help – some marketing or something,' I said, 'just say.'

'Kind of you, dear.' Clementine gave me a tight smile. 'But I'm going to have to sell up and I think Clarrie knew it. The garden centre has been struggling for a while. Every time we got a letter from the bank about the overdraft, he used to roll up his sleeves and say, "Dig yourself out of this one, Clarence Fearnley."'

She heaved a big sigh. 'I might put that on his headstone.'

'I am very lucky woman,' Nonna said wistfully. 'I never had a man telling me how to run café, and now I have my clever granddaughter to take over.'

'And a second granddaughter who can cook,' said Lia pointedly, pushing a small bowl of her soup towards Nonna.

Nonna patted her hand kindly.

'Don't look now,' Clementine muttered under her breath, 'but there's some serious eye candy at two o'clock.'

Lia and I checked our watches, Nonna looked at the jar of sweets on the counter.

'You lot are useless.' Clementine jerked her head to the other side of the café. 'Over there.'

We all turned at the same time, completely indiscreetly, to see Clementine's eye candy and there was Gabe helping Noah out of his jacket. How they had managed to get in without us hearing the bell or noticing them was a mystery. Noah pointed to the toy corner and jumped up and down. Gabe caught us all staring at him and raised a hand.

'Gabe! Welcome to the Lemon Tree Café,' I said. 'Hi, Noah.'

Noah smiled shyly before running to play with the toys and Gabe approached the counter. I made the introductions to Nonna and Clementine who both flirted shamelessly and he ordered some drinks and a cookie for Noah from Lia to take away.

'Excuse me for eavesdropping, but I couldn't help over-hearing about your troubles. I'm so sorry for your loss,' said Gabe to Clementine. 'I'm an ex-solicitor, if I can help at all, reading over paperwork for you, looking at your lease . . . I'd be only too happy to help. Also, I know what it's like to lose a partner. Things can get a little overwhelming.'

It was the perfect thing to say and not a hint of bereavement Tourette's. Clementine swallowed hard and managed to nod. I handed her a tissue. At that moment Juliet popped her head out from the kitchen.

'Solicitor?' She stared at me. Clearly Gabe wasn't the only one who'd been eavesdropping. 'I expected one of those new-age scruffs with grass seeds in their hair, living on lentils.'

Ground, swallow me up . . .

'I don't know why!' I said, hoping no one noticed my pink cheeks.

Gabe's eyes sparkled. 'I suppose this jumper has seen better days.'

'No, you look great!' I protested, glancing too late at his attire, which looked like it had been attacked by a plague of giant moths.

'Ahem.'

We all turned as Dad, who'd presumably finished talking to his agent, tapped Gabe on the shoulder.

'I'm Alec Featherstone, lecturer in philosophy at Derby University. And you must be Gabe, the fellow my daughter was talking about last night,' he said with a sniff.

'That would be his other daughter, Gabe. Not me. I haven't mentioned you at all,' I said, wishing my entire family would disappear.

'May I ask why a solicitor chooses to live on a narrowboat?' Dad raised both of his eyebrows.

Gabe's grey eyes twinkled and he looked down at the floor briefly before answering. 'The same reason that a lecturer chooses to dress up as Dolly Parton on his nights off, I guess.' He shrugged. 'Because I can.'

Dad went red, opened his mouth and then shut it again. I hadn't seen him so flustered since the time he bumped into Hugh Bonneville near the London Eye and mistook him for Colin Firth. He hadn't missed an episode of *Downton Abbey* since.

'And as I was saying to Mrs Fearnley,' Gabe paused to smile at Clementine who smiled coyly back, 'I'm an *ex*-solicitor; I renovate furniture these days.'

'I see,' said Dad stiffly. 'A joiner.'

'French polisher, actually,' Gabe said amiably. He scanned the café. 'You have some lovely pieces here, Signora Carloni.'

'Thank you. Lot of people like shaggy sheep.' Nonna patted her hair and batted her eyelashes.

Gabe's eyes widened.

'My grandmother means shabby chic,' I said, smiling at him.

'That what I say.' Nonna flicked her cloth at me.

'Local lad, are you?' Dad asked.

'When you live on a boat, home can be anywhere,' said Gabe. 'It's the thing I love most about it, the freedom. But I'm Nottingham born and bred.'

'Which team do you support, Nottingham Forest or Notts County?' Dad asked, narrowing his eyes.

Lia and I exchanged looks. Nottingham Forest and Derby County fans were sworn enemies.

'Neither.' Gabe ruffled a hand through his sandy wavy hair. 'But I enjoy watching a live game now and again. And my son Noah loves football.'

'Really?' Dad clapped a hand on his shoulder. 'As luck would have it I have a spare ticket for the Derby match tomorrow. Come with me, I insist, it will give us a chance to get to know each other. I can sort one out for the boy too.'

'Thanks, Mr Featherstone.' Gabe looked genuinely touched. 'We'd love to. Noah has never been to a proper match.'

Dad beamed at him. 'Call me Alec.'

The two men made some rough arrangements to meet tomorrow. Dad bid us all farewell and this time shook Gabe's hand heartily. Lia slid Gabe's drinks and a cookie in a bag across the counter and Gabe paid her and called Noah to let him know they were going.

'You're well in there.' I smiled. 'You've made my dad's day.'

'Despite being a lowly boat-dwelling joiner,' he said.

'Ignore him,' I said, 'he's like that with all my boyfriends.'

Gabe raised an eyebrow.

'Not that you're a boyfriend,' I stammered. Was it getting warm in here or was it just me? 'And when I say *all* I don't mean—'

Gabe grinned at me, waiting for me to wedge the rest of my foot in my mouth.

'Rosanna, what you think about getting your friend to do work on our tables?' said Nonna. 'You always say they too scruffy.' She held the sweetie jar out for Noah who took one politely.

Gabe's eyes lit up. He looked at me and I nodded, relieved to change the subject.

'And the dresser,' I said.

'That would be great,' he said. 'I've got workshop space sorted at the Riverside Hotel, I can start straight away.'

'And I might take you up on that offer of help with the paperwork too,' said Clementine, not to be outdone.

'Looks like you're going to be busy,' I said, pleased we could all help him get settled in so quickly.

'Talking of busy,' said Gabe, reaching a hand out to Noah, 'I've got some packing cases to collect from the courier's depot. But are you still on for tonight?'

I nodded, conscious of everyone looking at us. Noah scooted over and tapped my leg. 'Dad says Katy Perry is foxy. Are you foxy?'

Gabe's eyes met mine and my heart jolted. Lia sniggered, Gabe groaned and Nonna whispered, 'Who is Katy Perry?' to Clementine.

'Well, I er . . .' I laughed awkwardly.

'Annnd we're out of here,' Gabe said, opening the door. *Sorry*, he mouthed over his shoulder.

'See you later, I'm looking forward to it,' I said, waving them off.

I really was, I thought, as I watched man and boy cross the village green and climb into a tatty white van.

Lia pressed a hand to her heart. 'How cute are they?'

'Nice lad,' Juliet agreed. She tapped the chopping board. 'Now hurry up with those lemons.'

I picked up the knife and began to peel.

'It reminds me of the folklore about peeling lemons,' said Clementine.

'Here we go again,' Juliet muttered.

126

Nonna elbowed her sharply and she retreated to the kitchen.

'Folklore says,' said Clementine in a low mysterious voice that made us all lean in, 'that if you can cut the peel from a lemon in one strip, you'll meet a new love within the period of the moon.'

'Oh my GOD!' Lia clapped a hand over her mouth. 'Gabe could be it: your new love. It's obvious. Today's a new moon, Noah told us that, remember?' She looked at me, wide-eyed. 'Gabe walked in while we were discussing it *and* you're going stargazing with him tonight.'

'You don't believe in all that, do you?' I said, feeling myself go hot.

Lia just opened her eyes even wider. 'Got to be worth a shot.'

I had one more lemon left. Everyone stared at my hands. How utterly ridiculous.

'Oh all right,' I tutted.

I picked up the lemon, my knife poised.

'Everyone quiet,' Clementine ordered.

I held my breath as I peeled the lemon, carefully sliding the blade under the yellow skin without cutting off the white pith. Round and round the knife went, the yellow spiral growing longer and longer and heavier and heavier. Lia squeaked and I could feel tension radiating off all of them.

'She nearly there,' Nonna hissed. 'Come on, Rosanna!'

The lemon was almost entirely white now but as the knife reached the sticky-out bit at the bottom it slipped and cut through the peel. The strip collapsed to the chopping board in a heap. For a moment nobody spoke.

'As Juliet says, it's just a load of hocus-pocus,' said Clementine, patting my arm awkwardly.

'Aye, never mind,' said Juliet, scooping the pile of lemon peel into a pan. 'When life hands you lemons—'

'Yeah, yeah,' I sighed, feeling unaccountably disappointed, 'make cake.'

127

Chapter 12

The sun had already set when I headed out of the village on foot to Gabe's boat, but the clear sky still held an orangey glow and the air was fresh and cold. A few tables were occupied outside the Riverside Hotel, and lights and music spilled from the bar out on to the terrace. I carried on along the tow path to the jetty where the narrowboats were moored.

'Hello,' I called, spotting Gabe on deck.

He was unpacking the contents of a cardboard box, one of several heaped up and taking up most of the space.

'Welcome aboard *The Neptune*,' he said, holding out a hand to help me climb across. 'Our first visitor in Barnaby.'

'Thank you. I've heard all about it from Verity. But it's my first time on a narrowboat.'

I wobbled a bit as I stepped on to the deck and I gripped his hand for balance. There wasn't much space and my nose was almost touching his jumper. He bent to kiss my cheek and I caught the scent of his aftershave: ruggedly masculine with a hint of leather and wood. I had the urge to bury my nose in his neck and sniff to my heart's content. I'd been single for too long, clearly.

'Sorry. *Narrow* being the operative word on here at the moment.' He nodded towards the boxes. 'A delivery courtesy of my mother.'

I glanced at the boxes labelled with words like: 'Gabe work suits', 'Mimi books', 'G&M wedding' . . .

'She's been storing stuff since Mimi died and now she's decided she hasn't got room for it any more.'

I looked at the tower of boxes and then through the cabin doors into a tiny galley kitchen. 'What are you going to do with it all?'

'No idea.' He scratched his head. 'There's more inside, Noah is sifting through it like a prospector panning for gold. Come on in, I'll give you the tour.'

'Cake as requested,' I said, holding out a bag, 'and wine.'

'You can come again.' He grinned and gestured towards the cabin door. 'After you.'

We walked into the kitchen and through the living area. Gabe pointed out all the mod cons, albeit in miniature, the curtains he'd sewed himself, Noah's artwork Blu-Tacked on to the door of the larder and a photo of him and Noah at Verity's cookery school.

'Which reminds me,' I frowned, 'it's odd that Verity didn't mention you were coming to Barnaby.'

'Ah.' Gabe looked sheepish. 'I haven't told her yet. I love Verity to bits, but she and my mum won't be happy until they've organized my life and married me off. Mum is currently sulking because I didn't move back home with her; hence returning my stuff. I haven't plucked up the courage to break the news to Verity yet. She wanted me to move to Plumberry.'

'I'll have to tell her I've seen you,' I said, 'or she'll never speak to me again.'

He pulled a resigned face. 'I'll ring her tonight. Promise. OK, onwards with the tour. The smallest master suite ever,' he said with a grin, opening a narrow door.

A double bed filled most of the space, a shelf above the bed held a single picture frame containing a wedding photograph, and a box, marked 'Gabe's books', sat in the corner.

'But big enough,' I said earnestly.

'Oh yes,' he said. 'Big enough.'

We both blushed. Gabe looked at his feet.

'So. You're a big reader?' I said, changing the subject swiftly.

'Yes, I am,' he said with a gush of relief. 'Once Noah's asleep I tend to go to bed early and read. The walls are so thin that the TV would wake him. Although, on nice nights I sometimes go mad and sit on deck with a beer. Rock 'n' roll, hey?'

My heart squeezed for him; it sounded quite a lonely life.

'It sounds good to me,' I said, smiling up at him as he closed the door and opened the next one, which led to a shower room.

'What does, an early night?'

I punched him playfully and decided not to answer that one. Although an early night with Gabe . . . I could see definite benefits to that. I'd been too busy over the last month to think about men, but now, in close proximity to one, my hormones were waking up very quickly. I gave myself a shake; this was Gabe, a friend, not someone whose heart I could play fast and loose with. Besides, Verity would kill me. Gabe was not 'fun fling' material. Not at all.

The shower room was immaculate and my heart did another flip when I saw a big and little toothbrush nestled together in a mug above the sink.

'And last but by no means tidy,' Gabe knocked on the last door before opening it, 'my son and heir's room.'

'Dad!' Noah yelled excitedly from beneath a heap of baby clothes. 'Look. From when I was little. I remember this.'

He still looked little to me. He held up a tiny yellow and grey cot blanket in his chubby fingers. He had dimples along his knuckles, his hair was as unruly as his dad's and his smile just as infectious.

'Oh dude.' Gabe groaned and rubbed a hand over his face. 'What a mess. I remember it too. Say hello to Rosie.'

'Hello,' Noah said dutifully without looking up. 'Why did I have a dress?'

He pointed to an ivory lace gown on the floor.

Gabe swallowed. He picked it up and stroked it tenderly.

'This was Mummy's when she was a baby,' he murmured. 'And you wore it for your christening too.'

'I don't want the dress,' said Noah, looking horrified. 'But I'm keeping the rest.'

Gabe shook his head. 'There's no room, mate. You can keep a few things, but not all of it.'

Noah's face crumpled. 'Oh but—'

'Hey, I've brought cake,' I said, holding my hand out to him. 'Do you want some?'

'Thanks for the distraction,' Gabe murmured a few minutes later after I'd pacified Noah with a slice of Juliet's cake. 'I want him to be able to hold on to some of the things, especially the ones that belonged to his mum. But it's just the space issue.'

We were standing in the galley kitchen watching Noah finishing his cake whilst also digging into the box marked 'G&M wedding'. Gabe handed me a glass of wine and pointed to the box Noah was rifling through.

'I'm pretty sure Mimi's wedding dress is in there. I got rid of most of her clothes, but I didn't . . . I couldn't . . .'

'What about a memory quilt?' I said, suddenly remembering something I'd seen on Pinterest. 'A patchwork quilt made from squares of the fabrics you want to keep.'

Gabe raised his eyebrows thoughtfully. 'That could work. And as you've already seen, I'm quite handy with a sewing machine.'

Noah jumped to his feet, snapped off the TV and stacked his plate in the sink.

'Thank you,' he yelled over his shoulder as he ran back to his room.

'Do you want to help cook the hot dogs?' Gabe called after him.

'You can do it,' said Noah, as if he was doing his dad a favour. 'But I'll do the marshmallows.'

131

Noah's bedroom door shut firmly. Gabe and I looked at each other, amused.

'He's four,' said Gabe. 'Imagine how much control I'll have over him when he's fourteen.'

I chopped and fried onions while Gabe grilled the sausages and set the table. Within twenty minutes our supper was ready. We chatted while we ate, or rather listened as Noah told me all about his dinosaur collection and what colour his new school uniform was and that he'd really, really like a bed with a slide but the ceiling in his bedroom was too low.

'Perhaps you could have a slide out of the window straight into the river,' I suggested with a wink.

Noah's eyes grew wide. 'Yeah!'

Gabe gave me a horrified look. 'You're supposed to be on my side.'

At which point I went pink and couldn't help wondering what side of the bed he slept on, or had he simply got used to sleeping in the middle on his own?

'Do you want more cake, dude?' Gabe asked. 'Or are you saving yourself for marshmallows?'

'Marshmallows. Please may I get down from the table?' he asked, already scrambling down and heading back to his room.

'Yes,' Gabe called. 'What are you doing in there? You'd better not be making more mess.'

'It's a surprise. Don't come in.'

Gabe clapped a hand over his face and groaned. 'The words no parent wants to hear. Ever.'

'Perhaps he's trying to squeeze himself into that christening dress,' I laughed.

'Or maybe he's making a slide to fit through his window,' he said, raising an eyebrow.

'I meant well,' I said.

'Yeah. Everyone always does.' He stared at me for a moment. 'Fancy getting some fresh air?'

The night air was cool and I shivered as we climbed back out on deck. Gabe handed me a blanket and I took it gratefully, wrapping it round my shoulders. I sipped my wine while he slid two of the boxes as far inside as he could to make more room. Then he jumped on to the jetty and untied the ropes.

'Ooh,' I said, snuggling under my blanket. 'I wasn't expecting a trip.'

Gabe gave *The Neptune* a push and jumped back on board before starting the engine.

'I promised you a dark sky for stargazing, we need to move away from the lights of the hotel for that.'

The gentle chug of the engine was mildly hypnotic as we glided slowly through the water and towards the blackness of the countryside. I felt myself start to relax, cosy under the blanket, while a gentle breeze lifted my hair from my face. After only a few minutes we had completely left civilization behind and the only lights were the ones inside *The Neptune*. Gabe steered us towards the bank and cut the engine. There was a velvety silence; all I could hear was the faint slapping of the water against the hull of the boat and the distant hoot of an owl.

Gabe climbed on to the bank and I threw him the rope, which he secured around the trunk of a slim tree. He jumped back and ushered me through the boat and out on to the bow where he lit the log burner. Once the fire was blazing, he topped up my glass and we sat side by side watching the flames.

'Poke me if I go to sleep,' I said, stifling a yawn. 'I'm so chilled out.'

'Whoops. Is that my cue to liven up?'

I choked on my wine, worried I'd offended him, but when I looked at him his eyes were sparkling with humour.

'Not at all,' I said, relieved. 'I'm enjoying myself. The last few weeks have been hectic; an evening like this is just what I needed.'

The moon was the merest sliver in the sky, barely visible over the treetops against a backdrop of midnight blue. At first I only saw a handful of stars but as my eyes became accustomed to the dark, more and more of them popped into view.

'I love the night sky,' he murmured after a few moments. 'Especially when it's a new moon like this.'

'Me too,' I agreed. 'It puts you in your place, doesn't it, the sheer majesty of it. We're just a tiny speck in the universe, so therefore our problems must be microscopic too.'

'Quite a philosopher under that pretty dress, aren't you?' Gabe grinned.

'Never you mind what I've got under my dress.'

I caught his eye and we both laughed and I reminded myself that flirting with Gabe was probably not a good idea.

'What do you love about the night sky, then?' I asked, breaking eye contact.

'Oh, I dunno.' He shrugged. 'I guess the sun shows up every bit of a blue sky – it's just there for you. But at night-time you have to be patient to see it properly, and if you do, you're rewarded with thousands upon thousands of stars revealing themselves like hidden treasure. I think it's magic.'

I tilted my head back and stared upwards, letting my eyes adjust to the blackness after the bright orange glow from the log burner.

'Thanks for inviting me,' I said softly. 'And you're right, it is magical.'

Our eyes met and we smiled at each other, his handsome profile lit by the reflection of the flames and a deep feeling of peace washed over me.

'It's a metaphor for life really,' he continued. 'The darker the sky, the brighter the stars. Sometimes when Noah asks me about his mum I tell him that she is up there sparkling away, shining a light for us, and she will always be there keeping an eye on us. I say it for his benefit but that thought has pulled me through many a dark night.'

I truly felt for him. To lose the love of your life at such a young age must have been awful. There was that old saying, about it being better to have loved and lost than never to have loved at all. Was falling in love really worth the heart-ache? My experience so far had told me that it wasn't but, despite that, deep down I hoped I hadn't completely given up on love, that maybe one day I'd find the courage to try again.

I nudged his shoulder with mine. 'Don't take this the wrong way, but can I suggest if you ever get to share a romantic moment with a woman under a starry sky, that you don't mention that your wife is keeping an eye on you from above or you'll never get your leg over again.'

His eyes crinkled with humour. 'Thanks for the advice; I'll bear it in mind. What about you?'

I spluttered on my wine. 'Me?'

'Yes, have you got anyone to share romantic moments with?'

'Oh no,' I said airily. 'I don't really do romantic. I got my fingers burned once. Didn't like it and have no desire to repeat the experience.'

Gabe topped up my wine and, after a moment, cleared his throat.

'I'd love to repeat the experience,' he said. 'I want to be half of a couple again, to be part of something special, but I don't know where to start.'

My heart literally ached for him. That had to be one of the sweetest things I'd ever heard a man say.

'I think you've done pretty well. You've only been in the village twenty-four hours and you've already lured a woman to a dark riverbank and persuaded her to sit next to you under the stars. Not bad for starters.'

'You're right,' he said, perking up. 'I'm better than I thought.'

'There you go.' I clinked my glass against his. 'You've impressed yourself.'

'I don't feel impressive.' He frowned. 'Sometimes I think I jacked my old life in too easily. I gave up my job – the career that used to make my heart race – the house . . . everything. I just walked away. I feel like I should have moved on by now.'

I set my glass down and turned to face him, taking his hand in mine.

'Sometimes *moving on* has to wait its turn until you're ready,' I said firmly. 'Adjusting to being a single parent and grieving for the person you lost, for the *life* you lost . . . that was enough to be dealing with. You did the right thing for you.'

Gabe nodded. 'That is the best description of my situation that I've ever heard.'

My insides pinged with pride and I looked back into his soft grey eyes and smiled. 'And one day you'll be ready for your heart to race again. And when that day comes, you'll know.'

'Actually,' he said in a low husky voice, 'it's racing now.'

Ditto. His face was so close to mine that I could hear his breathing and his mouth looked so kissable . . .

Oh God. This was not meant to happen. Gabe was a friend, someone very special to Verity, and not someone who I could afford to have a meaningless fling with. A gentle breeze brushed against my skin making me shiver, and I broke his gaze.

Gabe reached for my hand. 'Rosie—'

A clatter of footsteps from behind us startled me.

'Dad? Is the fire hot now? Is it time to do the marshmallows?'

Gabe and I sprang apart as Noah forced himself into the gap between our chairs and I took a deep breath, not sure whether I was happy or sad that Noah had broken the moment.

'I think so, dude,' Gabe said with a grin. 'It certainly feels hot from where I'm sitting.'

You and me both, I thought, pressing a cool hand to my face. *You and me both.*

Chapter 13

I spent the whole of the weekend with my head in the café's accounts. Nonna hadn't recorded so much as a single payment since parting company with her accountant a year ago and I needed to put everything in order to avoid getting into trouble before the tax office began asking awkward questions.

She had called in to my cottage with two shopping bags full of pieces of paper on Saturday and I'd given myself a headache trying to sort them into date order and input everything into a spreadsheet. But by Monday I was more or less straight and had even contacted an accountant friend of Dad's to take a look at it. All this extra work meant that it was the following Tuesday before I had the chance to call Verity and tell her about hanging out with Gabe and Noah.

'I know all about it and I am so proud of myself,' said Verity smugly. 'Gabe was moaning about their local school being rubbish and yet refusing to entertain any sensible suggestion I came up with. And then you mentioned your village school inspection. I dropped a few meteor-sized hints about Barnaby's primary school being successful *et voilà*! Plus, he's always had a soft spot for you. That helped.'

'Has he?' I asked casually.

'Yeah. Since that time in the hospital last year. You were brilliant with Noah when Gabe and I were so upset.'

I cast my mind back to that awful night in Plumberry.

Verity and I had been having cocktails in a restaurant when the call came through that Gloria, who was Gabe's mother-in-law and Verity's good friend, had been rushed to hospital. Gabe and Noah were already there when we arrived and I'd played with Noah while Gabe and Verity spoke to the doctors.

'I was glad I could be of use. That was such a tough night.'

'It was,' Verity sighed. 'But back to you and Gabe; tell me everything.'

I craned my neck to look into the conservatory, checking up on our business customers. Three men and one woman had been here for at least an hour having a meeting and I was chuffed to bits. I'd created a LinkedIn profile for the café last week in a bid to attract more business lunches and it seemed to be working. We never normally had customers who spent so much and stayed so long.

I laughed. 'I've been round to the boat for hot dogs, Verity. That's all. As friends.'

'Oh I know, I know,' she said blithely, 'but even so. He invited a woman to *The Neptune* and he cooked for you.'

She said 'cooked' as if that was just the sweetest thing.

'Verity Bloom,' I said calmly, 'he was glad to see a friendly face in a new place. That's all. Nothing happened. Honestly.'

I was glad she couldn't see my face right now; I was grinning from ear to ear remembering the fun the three of us had had toasting marshmallows under blankets and gazing up at Jupiter, pointed out ably by Noah.

There was something so intrinsically good about Gabe: his manner with Noah, the way he'd offered to help Clementine, even though he wasn't a solicitor any more, and the way he'd accepted Dad's invitation to the football, even though he must have had a million and one more pressing things to do. (Dad had had a great time with Gabe and Noah on Saturday, and he was already talking about the next home game.)

A man like that . . . well, even I'd be safe, wouldn't I?

'Of course nothing happened,' she laughed. 'He's not your type. But do me a favour, will you?'

'What?' I said, feeling miffed that she'd dismissed the idea of Gabe and me so easily. Was I really that bad a prospect?

'Introduce him to some single girls. Try to fix him up. It's time he got back out there.'

I opened my mouth to argue that perhaps Gabe would prefer it if people stopped interfering in his life, but thought better of it; she just cared, that was all.

'Sure, sure,' I said, my eyes flicking to the door as Stella Derry helped her elderly mother inside and made the international sign for tea. I gave her the thumbs up. 'Although I can't think of anyone offhand.'

Anyway, the thought of another woman taking my place on his boat under the stars made my toes curl.

'Well, keep your eyes peeled. And isn't Noah just the best boy in the world?'

'He's a star,' I agreed, remembering how he'd entertained me on Friday with his theory of why dinosaurs were 'stinked'.

Noah had been in charge of the marshmallow toasting, getting far too close to the flames for my liking, and I had said as much to Gabe. He had been totally cool and said sometimes you have to learn the hard way. And then he'd said, "God you're right, Mimi would have killed me . . ." Then he'd grinned and apologized for talking about Mimi again and I'd reassured him that I was glad she still managed to talk sense into him. And he'd kissed my cheek secretly when Noah wasn't looking and said that he was pleased to have a friend in Barnaby.

'Rosie?' Verity said sharply. 'Are you there?'

'Hmm? Yes. I'm here. And Noah looked so cute in his school uniform yesterday.'

It had been the first day of the summer term and Noah had been the only new starter at the village school. He'd looked so little but, at the same time, grown up in his shirt and tie. They hadn't come into the café, but Gabe had tapped on the window so that Noah could give us a twirl.

Verity fell quiet.

'I'd have loved to have been there on his first day of school,' she said after a pause. 'As Mimi couldn't be. Children need a mother figure in their lives, so badly. Oh well, you're there now to help him. I'm sure you'll do a great job.'

I laughed nervously and brought the call to an end. In the space of two minutes, Verity had successfully recruited me to be a matchmaker for Gabe and a mother figure for Noah. That woman should be running the country . . .

An hour later the party of business people were still there. Which was fine; they'd ordered plenty of drinks and now food, but they weren't very friendly and covered up their documents when we went near them. I'd looked for company logos on their paperwork for a clue as to what they were up to but had spotted none. I was intrigued.

'I've been thinking,' said Lia, emerging from the kitchen with a tray of crispy jacket potatoes. Her cheeks were pink and tendrils of golden hair had slipped from her bun.

'Have you?' I raised an eyebrow. 'Do you need a lie-down?'

She giggled. 'I know! I think my baby brain doesn't know what's hit it. Talking of my baby. Look.'

She took her phone out of her pocket and showed Doreen and me a picture of Arlo wearing a big inflatable jacket and a striped swim nappy. 'His first lesson. I don't know who enjoyed it more, him or Mum.'

'Ah,' Doreen and I chorused dutifully.

'Anyway.' She stuffed her phone back in her pocket. 'I was thinking that we could perhaps be a bit more adventurous with the menu.'

Doreen paused from cleaning the coffee machine.

'We are adventurous,' she said, looking put out. 'Half the people round here had never had sourdough bread until we started doing it as an alternative toast option.'

'Toast is not adventurous,' Lia scoffed. 'That's what I'm talking about. We've got a proper kitchen through there but most of what we do is simply an assembly job: quiche with a salad garnish, jacket potatoes with bog-standard fillings, rolls filled with the usual suspects. Everything is fresh and delicious, but we don't stand out from the crowd as much as we could.'

Doreen flicked her plait over her shoulder and stared at Lia. 'Why would we want to stand out?'

'We're an Italian café in a Derbyshire village,' I said. 'I think that makes us already stand out.'

'Italian decor, maybe. But if we're going to attract more of those sorts of people,' she nodded towards the conservatory, 'we should jazz things up a bit.'

She had a point; the table of business people had scanned the menu rather despondently when ordering lunch. I'd steered them towards the pasta salad in the end, suggesting that it was easy to eat with one hand, seeing as none of them seemed able to put their phones down for more than two seconds.

'Refreshing the menu is a good idea,' I said diplomatically, 'as long as we don't upset our regulars with too much change.'

'Fine.' Lia sighed and trotted back to the kitchen.

'She's right.' Doreen picked up her cloth and started attacking the dried-on milk splashes on the coffee machine with gusto. 'The whole café is ready for an overhaul. I s'pose you'll be wanting to get rid of an old-timer like me soon too.'

'No way!' I cried. 'The café wouldn't be the same without you. Remember when Lia and I used to come in after school to see you?'

She chuckled and nodded. 'You both always wanted a

fresh crust thick with butter and I used to have to cut both ends off a new loaf.'

I smiled at the memory. 'Best part of my day that was.'

'That's nice to hear.' She heaved a deep sigh. 'And I'm glad; I'd hate to leave. This café has been the hub of the community for donkey's years. Whenever there've been problems, the whole village has always congregated here to get things sorted. Like when the sewers got blocked with disposable nappies years ago and the village green flooded.'

'What did you do?'

'Clarence Fearnley drove down from the garden centre on his little digger. He scooped out the blockage into a big mound.' She winced at the memory. 'Not a pretty sight. Or smell.'

I shuddered. I'd had the pleasure of changing Arlo's nappy once or twice and that had been bad enough.

'And then everyone helped with spades and big black bin bags,' she went on, misty-eyed. 'Anyway, the point is that your nonna made this place the centre of it and, despite the stench and the state of the floorboards, it was great fun. Really brought the village together.'

I liked the idea of the Lemon Tree Café being the hub of the community. It was what I wanted social media to achieve, but it looked as though we'd been doing it for years anyway.

'And,' she tapped her nose, 'the till didn't stop ringing all day. We sold out of everything.'

'Excuse me,' said one of our business customers, waving her hand in the air to attract our attention. 'Could you clear? We're ready for coffee now. Four Americanos with milk. Oh sorry!' she said with an apologetic laugh. 'That's just four normal coffees.'

'Thanks for explaining that,' Doreen muttered under her breath.

'And can we have another couple of chairs? We'll be joined by two others shortly.'

'Of course,' I said, wiping my hands on my apron.

'I'll clear and bring chairs from the table right next to them,' said Doreen, picking up an empty tray. 'You get the *normal* coffees on.'

I set four cups into saucers and felt a presence at my side. Lia whistled under her breath and pointed out of the window. 'Isn't that Gabe?'

A tall man was striding purposefully to the door. It was Gabe, but dressed so differently to the last time I'd seen him in his jeans and T-shirt that I had to look twice. He pushed the door open, checked his watch and scanned the café.

In a navy linen suit and soft pink shirt, he exuded style and assertiveness, helped in bucketloads by those intelligent grey eyes and confident smile. I couldn't take my eyes off him.

'Check you out,' I said.

'Scrub up all right, don't I?' Gabe held his arms out to the side. 'Good old Mum; those boxes of stuff turned up just at the right time. I haven't dressed like this since I was an office boy. Although the least said about the patchwork quilt Noah decided to make while you and I were out on deck, the better. Fabric scraps everywhere.'

'Sorry,' I cringed, imagining Mimi's wedding dress in tatters. 'My fault for suggesting it.'

'Don't apologize,' he said, giving me a look that made my insides melt. 'It kept him occupied all weekend. And making a memory quilt is a lovely idea. Thank you.'

'So you had a good weekend?'

'Yes. Busy. Football on Saturday with your dad, then Clementine came round on Sunday, asking for help. Before I knew it, it was Monday, Noah started school and I took Clementine to see her bank manager.'

So she had taken him up on his offer of help; I was so pleased.

'How did we all manage before you arrived?' I said playfully.

'It's a nice feeling to be useful,' he said shyly.

A man like Gabe could be very useful in all sorts of

imaginative ways, I reflected, noticing a pinging in the pit of my stomach.

'Why are you grinning like that?' he asked.

'Nothing.' I shook myself. 'Are you going to order something?'

'Actually, I'm here for an appointment.' He inclined his head discreetly to the business meeting in the conservatory. 'With Clementine's bank and an . . . other person.' He cleared his throat, as if realizing he'd given too much away. 'And Clementine will be here any moment too. I suggested holding it here rather than at the bank or the garden centre. I thought it would make a traumatic meeting less emotional for her if it was on neutral territory.'

'Oh right.' I blinked. So much for thinking it had been my amazing marketing skills that had brought them in. 'A lovely thought, thanks.'

'You're welcome. Here she is now.'

Sure enough, the door opened slowly and Clementine, looking pale and gaunt in a black dress and pearls, glided towards us, her head high.

Gabe held out his arm and she clung on to it. 'Are you ready?' he asked.

'Not really.' She exhaled a shaky breath. 'But let's get it over with.'

Chapter 14

'*One pound?*' Nonna and Mum exclaimed together.

Their indignation was so fierce that the two cyclists who'd pinched Stanley's usual spot in the window paused from chewing their flapjacks.

Mum handed Arlo to Lia, who covered his face in kisses after their time apart. Mum's hair had gone frizzy round her hairline and smelled of swimming pools; she looked tired but happy. Much like Arlo.

'Is that all?' Doreen scowled, her eyes taking in Clementine's dishevelled appearance. Her short wiry hair was sticking up in all directions; I could see Doreen itching to smooth it down.

Clementine nodded wearily. 'The bank has sold the garden centre, or rather passed its debts on to an investor of some sort. And all that changed hands was one pound.'

I felt sick; they'd just spent upwards of eighty pounds on refreshments.

'Dicky heads,' spluttered Nonna, passing Stanley a cup of tea. 'That a good business.'

Clementine raised an eyebrow. 'Hardly. As has now been proven.'

The business meeting had finished at three o'clock. The four suited strangers had swept out with curt nods of thanks after settling their substantial bill just as Mum had returned with Arlo from their swim. Gabe had dashed off to collect Noah from school, leaving Clementine alone at the table amongst the debris of abandoned crockery and a plate of lemon shortbread. Nonna sat down next to her with an espresso.

'Daylight robbery,' said Doreen, stacking the bankers' plates together angrily and piling them on a tray. 'And those are the sorts of people you want in here, Rosie?'

'No, of course not.' I picked up the copy of the receipt they'd left on the table; it was the largest bill we'd had since I'd been here. 'But I'd rather they spent money with us instead of some city café.'

Nonna and Stanley had not long arrived after a day out together at the market in Chesterfield and Nonna had been carrying a bunch of tulips from Nina's flower shop.

Stanley hovered near the cyclists for a few minutes, willing them to leave his table, but eventually he gave up and brought his tea over to the little circle of commiserators gathered at Clementine's table.

'I know it's very traumatic,' I said. 'But at least you know where you stand now. You can stop worrying about what's going to happen.'

'True,' Clementine acknowledged. 'It can't get any worse.'

'If they've got money, why haven't they paid a fair price for Fearnley's?' said Doreen over her shoulder as she stomped to the kitchen with the tray. 'And so much for Gabe's expert help. I'm sure I'd have done better than that myself. A *pound*.'

'Gabe Green was brilliant,' said Clementine, rallying slightly. 'Such a lovely boy.'

'Oh I'm so pleased.' I breathed a sigh of relief. Even though I trusted Gabe to do his best, I'd been thinking along similar lines to Doreen. I looked up to find Mum watching me, a smile playing on her lips, and I felt my face heat up.

'If it hadn't been for Gabe, I'd have lost the house too,' Clementine continued. 'It was mortgaged up to the hilt. Gabe was adamant that I be allowed to stay in my home. At least I've still got a roof over my head and I own it outright. I bet he was a great solicitor. Firm but fair.'

'But only a pound. For all that land. It does seem a little parsimonious of them,' said Stanley, eyeing up the leftover shortbread. 'Anyone mind if I . . . ?'

Clementine nudged the plate towards him with a shaky hand. 'Take it. I couldn't swallow a thing.'

'I made those,' whispered Lia to Stanley. 'What's parsimonious?'

'Miserly.' He bit into a piece of shortbread. 'Whereas these are utterly butterly.'

Lia smiled proudly and helped herself to half of one. 'Quality control.'

Nonna tutted at the pair of them. 'Stuffing faces is not helping Clementine.'

'It's too late for help.' Clementine's teeth began to chatter. 'It's over.'

'Shock,' Mum whispered in my ear.

'I'll make her some sweet tea,' I said, glad of something to do. I darted behind the counter and rummaged around for something reviving amongst the boxes of herbal tea.

'Not tea,' said Nonna gravely, following me. She reached into the back of a cupboard and brought out a small bottle of limoncello. 'Something stronger.'

'But we're not licensed—'

I shut up, recognizing the look on my grandmother's face. It was the one she reserved for traffic wardens and people who leave dogs in cars without air and water.

'This is emergency.'

She poured a generous measure into a glass and put it into her friend's hand. 'Sip slowly.'

'Life's a bugger and then you die. Cheers,' said Clementine.

She knocked it back in one, gasping as the alcohol hit the back of her throat. She brought the glass down on the table with a thump and eyed the bottle. Nonna sighed and gave her a top-up.

'Last one. You in shock.'

'Course I'm in bloody shock. When Clarrie died I thought

I'd sell up and retire to the coast. Now I'm going to have to get a job. Me! Even I wouldn't employ me. And I'll have to . . . Oh, too many things to contemplate. It's the end, the end.'

She slumped forward and rested her head on the table.

Stanley pulled up the chair recently vacated by the woman who thought that us country bumpkins wouldn't know what an Americano was – not that I was still annoyed about that – and took Clementine's hand.

'I know you're grieving for Clarence,' he said, 'but it's not the end, believe me.'

'Mine and Clarrie's entire life's work is gone,' Clementine said, tears welling up in her eyes. 'All gone. Lock, stock and barrel. Well, I say stock, that chappie never even bothered to walk round everywhere. That's what makes me so sad. He's probably from a firm of property investors. The place will be bulldozed. All our nursery beds, our polytunnels, gone.'

Nonna's dark eyes blinked rapidly behind her glasses. 'So they not know what they buying?'

Clementine shrugged. 'I dare say they're more interested in the land than in all my lovely plants and shrubs. There are trays and trays of unsold seedlings and more covering every surface at home. I suppose technically I should take them back to the garden centre. They're not mine any more.'

The doorbell dinged and a couple of mums came in with their children; school had finished and the café would be busy for the next hour.

'I'll go and serve,' said Doreen.

'Thanks.' I took the chair next to Lia at Clementine's table and made faces at Arlo. 'When does the garden centre change hands?' I asked.

'Midnight officially. The investors will be there tomorrow doing some sort of stock inventory. But I suppose once we finish trading today . . . Oh God.' Clementine covered her face with her hands. 'I need to tell Tyson he's redundant. I ought to get back.'

'Wait a minute. I have idea.' Nonna frowned. I could almost see the cogs whirring in her brain. 'If they don't know what stock is there, they not know if anything is missing, do they?'

Clementine smiled, although it didn't reach her eyes.

'I don't have any lemon trees, Maria, if that's what you're thinking. In the forty years we've been in business the only ones we've ever sold have been to you.'

Nonna waved a hand. 'I not think of that. I think of you. How many seedlings you have?'

'Hard to say. Five thousand? More?' Clementine shrugged. 'There are some in the big polytunnels, the new greenhouse, the old greenhouse, the ones outside hardening off . . .'

'Take them,' Nonna hissed, hunching over the table. 'They never know. And they better with you than left to die at garden centre. What if they not come quickly enough to water, what then? They all die and worth nothing. So. You take them.'

'But then I'd have tomatoes, courgettes and green beans coming out of my ears. What am I going to do with them?' Clementine grumbled.

'Oh!' Lia's eyes lit up. 'Ratatouille?'

Clementine gave her a withering look.

'I'll get my coat,' Lia murmured and kissed me goodbye. 'Home time.'

I sucked my cheeks in to hide my smile. Stanley chuckled too until Nonna flicked him with her cloth. 'Eh. This not funny.'

'Sorry,' he said contritely. 'But listen, when I was a postman . . .'

Nonna rolled her eyes. 'Not the story about when big spider run up your trousers and you have to strip off in graveyard?'

'Maria, that was private,' he said, flushing. 'No. I was going to say that I noticed that most houses in the village have greenhouses. Perhaps we could get the seedlings fostered, ask people to look after them until . . . ?'

'Exactly.' Clementine shrugged. 'Until what?'

'Until we organize a village event,' I said suddenly, trying to shake off the image of an elderly trouserless postman. 'So that you can sell them and at least get something for your efforts. Not enough to retire to the coast, but at least maybe a holiday at the seaside.'

'A holiday,' Clementine said wearily. 'What's one of those?'

'A village event,' said Mum with a twinkle in her eye. 'Barnaby's good at those. Remember the Queen's Jubilee, the Millennium New Year's Eve party? And I'll help.'

Nonna slapped the table. 'It settled then. We go tonight. In the dark.'

Stanley's eyes gleamed. 'An undercover mission.'

The pair of them were relishing the drama. I, on the other hand, was desperately trying to think up what sort of event I could run from the café involving five thousand delicate seedlings . . .

Just then Noah ran in, closely followed by Gabe who placed an order at the counter with Doreen. Noah waved a book in the air and made a beeline for me.

'Rosie, I can read!' he said, forcing his way on to my lap and making himself comfortable.

'You're a genius,' I said calmly, even though my heart was looping the loop at his gesture.

He held up his book and flicked through the pages, which had one word on each. I kissed his cheek; his jumper smelled of school but as I leaned closer I caught the smell of shampoo and grass and biscuits.

'Hello again.' Gabe grinned at Noah sitting on my knee. 'Sorry for the intrusion. Looks like you're all up to something.'

'We are,' said Nonna, grabbing an unsuspecting Gabe by the shoulders and kissing his cheeks. 'We planning a burglary. Are you in?'

'Bloody hell!'

Noah regarded his father severely. 'Daddy! That's fifty pence in the swear box.'

'That's steep,' said Clementine with a whistle. 'You can buy half a garden centre with that.'

At seven thirty a crack team of seedling thieves in a convoy of vehicles crept up the long lane leading to Fearnley's Garden Centre, next door to Clementine's house. I was with Dad in his Volvo with the back seats folded down. Lia had reluctantly stayed at home to put Arlo to bed but Ed had brought a van home from work and had given Nonna and Stanley a lift. Doreen and Juliet had roped their husbands, Alan and Dean, in to the mission and the other businesses around the village green had turned up to help too: Adrian from the pub was there in his posh Range Rover, and Ken from the Mini Mart, Biddy and Nina all had vans. Lucas only had a tiny Smart car so he'd stayed at the café with Mum. She was phoning round the village to find foster parents for the seedlings and Lucas was going to keep in touch with Clementine to direct vans to the right houses.

Only Gabe hadn't made it.

'I'd love to lend a hand, but Noah fell asleep at the dinner table,' he'd explained on the phone, sounding disappointed. 'School is tiring him out and I don't know the people in the boats next door well enough to ask them to babysit him yet. I'm missing out on all the fun.'

I pictured him alone having an early night, with a book, in that bed . . .

'I could come round later, if you like?' I found myself saying. 'Tell you all about it.'

'Really?' I could hear the smile in his voice. 'Great. Oh and be careful. If anyone asks, you're collecting pre-ordered stock. OK?'

We drove in, past the public car park and along the driveway marked 'Deliveries' and parked in front of the longest polytunnel. There was a bit of a breeze and the sky was dark and cloudy but spirits were high.

Nonna had borrowed a black hoody from Ed and Stanley had put the hood up on his cagoule and pulled the drawstrings in tight. The pair of them looked like jolly Grim Reapers.

'I so excited, I already need to pee,' Nonna said in a low voice, scuttling off to the customer toilets.

Clementine and Tyson were waiting for us, side by side in front of the garden centre entrance in matching padded gilets, jeans and work boots. They made quite a pair: Clementine so tall, thin and pale, Tyson, chubby and pink.

'I doubt that the buyers would send anyone round tonight,' said Clementine, making us all squint as she shone a torch in our faces. 'But I've turned the outside lights off just in case. Have you all got your torches?'

We all flashed our lights on and off.

'We can take a few trays off you to sell in our shops,' Ken offered. Biddy and Nina nodded their agreement.

'I've been thinking about that,' I said swiftly. 'We could make a big day of it. Like a village fête but led by us, the businesses.'

Everyone murmured their interest and Clementine cleared her throat.

'It's cold and dark and quite possibly muddy,' she said in a wavering voice. 'And yet you've all turned out to help a silly old woman who has made a total mess of things. I can't thank you enough.'

We all began to dispute her claims and Tyson threw his arms round his boss and pressed his face into her bosom. 'I'll miss you,' he said in a squeaky voice. 'You did your best.'

She patted his head awkwardly. 'I did. I just wish my best was better.'

'Well, I can't think of a more fruitful way to spend an evening,' said Stanley, taking Nonna's arm and looping it through his.

'Talking of fruit,' Clementine wiped her eyes on her

sleeve, 'if you and Maria would like to start on the strawberries, while I head for the sweet peas . . .'

She divvied up the jobs and we all set off. Tyson showed Dad and me to a row of handcarts and we took one each.

'Follow me to the marigolds,' he said, steely-eyed. 'Let's do this.'

Chapter 15

Two hours later, it was mission accomplished and we called it a night. We left a few packs of bedding plants to avoid raising suspicion as Gabe had advised and around five thousand tender seedlings had been secreted in numerous cold frames and greenhouses around Barnaby. Clementine had written watering instructions down for people and made promises to give advice if anything looked like it was getting too 'leggy'. Everyone was so fired up with the drama of it all that no one had wanted to go home, so Adrian invited everyone back to the pub for a drink 'on the house'.

I made my excuses and walked along the dark lanes through the village to the river. The lights on the other narrowboats were off, but there was a welcoming glow from inside the cabin of *The Neptune*.

'There's a real sense of community in this village,' said Gabe, after I'd filled him in on the capers amongst the courgettes. 'Barnaby is a lovely place to live.'

It was too breezy to sit comfortably on the little deck tonight so we were in his cosy living area instead. He handed me a mug of tea and slid a stool under my feet. It wasn't particularly comfortable – a built-in bench-style arrangement – but I was so tired that with gentle music playing in the background, soft light from one solitary lamp and the lulling motion of the boat on the water, plus the warmth of the small space, I soon began to relax.

Noah was fast asleep and the two of us kept our voices low.

'Everyone is talking about you, singing your praises.' I slipped my shoes off and made myself more comfortable. 'Clementine, Nonna, even my dad.'

'Really?' He sat down next to me on the sofa. 'It's mutual. I've been made to feel really welcome in a short space of time. And I want us to fit in, it's important to me.'

'You'll no doubt have made quite an impact at the school gates too. A new face and a single man with a cute . . .' I sipped my tea and looked at him over my mug. 'Boy.'

'I did feel the weight of a few stares.' He rubbed the back of his neck awkwardly. 'I hate that, to be honest, although I'm getting used to it now. It happened at Noah's nursery too. All the curious looks and the wondering what happened to Noah's mum.'

'Sorry.' I bit my lip, touching his arm lightly. He was wearing a denim shirt with the sleeves rolled up and his skin was warm. 'I didn't mean to make light of it. I should have thought of that and come with you. At least on Noah's first day.'

'That would have given them even more to speculate about.' He grinned. 'Anyway, it's fine. Moving somewhere different is always going to be difficult at first. We'll soon be old news.'

I peered at him surreptitiously as he gazed into his mug; somehow I doubted Gabe Green could ever be old news. Unless he left, which, I realized with a jolt, I didn't want him to do.

'You mentioned liking the freedom of boat life to Dad. Does that mean you're not planning on staying in Barnaby for long?'

He puffed out his cheeks and didn't answer straight away.

'Million-dollar question. The whole narrowboat life . . . it has served me well for three years, but at some point I've got to put down roots, build us a better life on solid ground. A family life.'

His eyes held mine for a second and my heart thumped.

'Being here has given me a taste of what I could be part of again. I want to get back on track. Rejoin the real world.'

'Verity would applaud that.' I grinned. 'I should warn you that she has asked me to introduce you to all the eligible women in the village.'

He groaned. 'All of them?'

'Don't worry, there aren't many.'

'I'm only interested in one.'

'So you've been looking already?' I raised my eyebrows, wondering who the lucky girl was.

'It's not just about having a girlfriend.' He laughed softly. 'It's a whole lifestyle change and I need to be part of a community again. Until I moved here I thought that working as a French polisher would see me through life and I'd stay living on the boat with Noah but now . . .'

'I know what you're thinking,' I said, sitting up straighter.

My heart leapt with pride for him; Gabe was ready to kickstart his career and it was being in Barnaby that had done it.

'Do you?' His grey eyes searched mine and he twisted his body towards me.

I nodded. 'And I think you're absolutely right.'

It must have been helping Clementine out that had reawakened his interest in law. And, of course, working as a solicitor would be demanding; he'd need a support network around him for that to work. And I didn't mind helping out.

'Thank you for making it easy for me.' He exhaled. 'Because this is a big thing.'

'Of course it is!' I said encouragingly. 'I have a theory that we should be the very best version of ourselves and I think for you that means getting a proper job again.'

'A *proper* job?' He stared at me, his expression telling me that I'd got the wrong end of the stick.

'That wasn't what you meant?' I stammered.

'No, I . . .' He raked a hand through his hair. 'Actually, I was working up to asking you out on a date.'

He looked so deflated that it was all I could do not to hug him.

'Me?'

'But I can see now that that wouldn't work,' he said flatly. 'Especially as I haven't got a *proper* job.'

I was mortified to have insulted him and my stomach lurched.

'Forget I said that. Of course you've got a proper job,' I said hurriedly. 'I thought I was doing the right thing, trying to encourage you and I misunderstood you, that's all.'

He sprang to his feet. 'No, *I* did. Put it down to lack of practice. I'm really sorry. And you're right. It is time I got my act together. Why would a girl like you . . . ? Look, forget it.'

I stood up too, feeling awful. 'Gabe, let me explain.'

'No need.' He plastered on a smile. 'Honestly. Message received and understood.'

He pressed a kiss hastily to my cheek and ushered me to the door. 'You must be tired. Long day. I know I am.'

He faked a yawn and stretched his arms above his head.

I stood my ground and stared at him, forcing him to make eye contact.

'Gabe, listen.' I tucked my hair behind my ears. 'I'm really flattered and I do really like you but—'

I could see Gabe's chest rising and falling with every breath, waiting for the end of my sentence and my heart went out to him. It wasn't his fault, it was mine. He'd done nothing wrong. I was preparing to flee as usual. It was a shame because Verity loved him, all my family seemed to like him and he'd done nothing but help everyone around him since he'd been here. And on top of that, there was no denying it, Gabe Green was totally gorgeous.

He wasn't the problem, I was.

'It's OK,' he said stoically. 'A widower plus a four-year-old boy isn't much of a catch.'

'No. It's me who isn't a catch. I know enough about you and Mimi to know how happy you were and that you've had your heart broken,' I said softly. 'But what you don't know is I have a past too.'

An image of Callum's stricken face flashed through my brain, his pleading with me to give him another chance, that this couldn't be the end. I shuddered at the memory.

'We're in our thirties,' Gabe shrugged. 'Who doesn't have a past?'

'Not like mine.' I shook my head sadly. 'Verity will confirm it: as soon as someone starts to get close, I run a mile. I can't help it. It's the way I am. I can't . . .' I swallowed. 'I can't take the risk. Not again. And you deserve better, Gabe, believe me, you and Noah.'

'What happened to you?' he said, reaching out gently to take my hands.

His eyes bore into me as if he was searching my soul for answers and my heart thudded in case he found them.

I looked at the floor between us. 'Don't. Please don't ask.'

'OK.' He nodded and stepped closer until I could smell his lovely smell and feel the warmth radiating from his body. I squeezed my eyes shut. *God, I was so fickle and idiotic.* I wanted to meet someone but it was almost as if I activated a self-destruct button as soon as a glimmer of romance came my way.

Gabe pulled me into a quick friendly hug instead.

'Friends?' I said, relishing the feel of his arms round me.

'Yeah,' he murmured, pressing the swiftest kiss into my hair. 'Friends with benefits.'

'Gabe!' I gasped, pulling back to gawp at him.

'What?' He shrugged innocently. 'I'm a French polisher who's collecting a load of your furniture tomorrow. What did you think I meant?'

I was still smiling when I climbed into my bed an hour later.

Chapter 16

The next morning, I was frying eggs at the griddle with one hand and jotting down ideas for a village event with the other when Lia approached me, holding out a spoon.

'Taste this,' she said.

I blew on the food and opened my mouth for her to pop the spoonful in. It was packed with flavour: aubergines, tomatoes, garlic and herbs with a cheesy breadcrumbed crust.

'Seriously good,' I confirmed. 'What is it?'

'Aubergine Parmigiana. I thought I'd try something different, even though you're resisting all my attempts to revamp the menu.'

I looked at my sister, her face animated and her smile wide, and felt a wave of pride for her.

'I think you've found your talent, you know,' I said, putting down my pencil and giving her a one-armed hug. 'Cooking makes your eyes sparkle. Oh BOGOF!'

I released her and scribbled the word down.

'I was going to say thank you,' said Lia wryly, 'but on that note . . .'

'Not you. Buy one get one free,' I said, turning my attention back to the griddle. 'Juliet?'

I peered over my shoulder and waited for her to catch my eye. 'Two eggs sunny side up for Barry, to go with the beans on toast.'

Juliet swooped into the kitchen with a warmed plate and some new orders and bore Barry's breakfast away.

'I'll take over,' said Lia, wrestling the spatula from my hand. 'You go and scribble insults on your pad.'

I breathed a sigh of gratitude. 'Thanks. I can't relax until I know how we're going to help Clementine make money from those seedlings with an event like I promised.'

'Shouldn't the café be your priority, now that you're the manager?'

'The café still is my priority; we're having all the furniture renovated this week,' I said, picking up my notebook and pencil. 'Gabe should be here any minute.'

My heart gave a little leap. I'd made such a mess of last night. I'd made him think his job wasn't good enough when really I admired all he'd achieved. I'd have to make it up to him today somehow.

'Funny,' she said slyly, cracking two more eggs into the pan. 'I've never heard you say that the furniture needed work. Then Gabe turns up and hey presto.'

'It was Nonna's idea, not mine,' I said, concentrating on keeping my features neutral. I checked through the café to see if he'd arrived. Not yet. *Friends with benefits.* I stared at the words I'd written and tried to ignore the fizzing in my stomach: 'free plant with every purchase' and 'BOGOF'. Hardly thrilling.

'Plus,' I said, 'he needs the work; we're doing him a favour.'

'With absolutely no ulterior motive,' sniggered Lia.

'Absolutely none. Anyway,' I continued, blithely, 'back to this event. If I'm smart about it, I can put the café on the map *and* help Clementine. I just need to come up with a plan.'

'You'll think of something,' Lia said airily. 'You're brilliant like that. That is *your* talent. Besides, you'll have to; the whole village is counting on you.'

'No pressure then,' I said with a groan and headed out of the kitchen.

The café was busy this morning and a huddle of customers queued at the counter; the weather was damp and drizzly and the people of Barnaby had obviously decided that a warm café was infinitely preferable to the chilly outdoors.

Juliet looked up from sprinkling chocolate powder on two cappuccinos and jerked her head towards a man behind the counter.

'Just sign for that parcel,' she said. 'He's been waiting ages.'

The courier held a large plastic bag out to me. 'Name?'

'Rosie Featherstone.'

'Signature here, please.'

I signed for the parcel, which was addressed to Dad from a posh lingerie company, and dialled his number.

'A parcel of ladies' undergarments has just arrived, Dad. Is Dolly Parton making a comeback?'

'Dolly? No! That was a one-night-only performance. This is a surprise for your mum. I couldn't have them arriving in my office. People jump to all sorts of conclusions.'

They certainly do, I thought, remembering how Lia and I had done just that where Dad was concerned.

After a rather tongue-in-cheek write-up in the paper on Sunday about how midlife crisis affected professional men, featuring Dad in his sparkly dress, he had consigned his drag act to history. His agent, who it turned out was just a chap from a working men's club in Sheffield, had been gutted; he'd already lined Dad up to sing at a stag party. Dad had appeased him by passing on the number of the Russian Cossack dancers from Liverpool. Now Gabe had got him interested in narrowboats and he'd bought himself a book on the history of English waterways. Mum wasn't sure whether to be pleased or not.

'How lovely,' I said. 'What's this in aid of?'

He lowered his voice. 'Remember when she caught me looking at bras online and she said to you she only wore plain boring ones?'

'Yes?'

'Well, not any more. I thought she deserved something beautiful, just like her.'

I felt a lump in my throat suddenly. How lovely to have someone to dream up little ways to brighten your life. I thought back to how I'd woken up with stomach cramps this morning; I'd have loved to have been able to nudge someone and ask if they wouldn't mind fetching me some tablets or simply have given me a cuddle to make me feel better.

I shook myself; that wasn't going to happen, was it? Not while I dispatched every suitor who came my way with a curt 'thanks but no thanks'.

'She'll love it, Dad, and she'll love you for thinking of her.'

I was still smiling about it when Stanley came in for his breakfast.

'Awful out there,' he said. 'But I step in here and it's like being on holiday.'

'Glad to hear it.' I helped him out of his wet anorak and he looked round automatically for Nonna.

'And when Maria smiles at me, it's like the sun comes out. Where is she this morning?'

My heart lunged again: someone else whose day was brightened by the existence of another.

'Gone to see Clementine,' I told him, as he settled himself into his armchair with the crossword. 'For moral support when the new people turn up at the garden centre next door.'

'Maria is a dear soul,' said Stanley. 'Such a good loyal friend.'

'And always at the centre of any trouble,' I added with a grin.

I could just imagine the pair of them at Clementine's front window waving their fists in defiance as the buyers arrived to claim their investment.

'In that case, I'll have a bacon sandwich with both slices of bread buttered please,' he said with a wink and spread his paper out on the table. 'But don't tell your grandmother.'

Nonna had been keeping an eye on his cholesterol since Clarence's heart attack. Stanley pretended not to like it, but it was obvious he loved being cared for.

'Sneaky,' I replied. 'Your secret's safe with me, but in return, if you have any bright ideas to help Clementine sell those seedlings, do share them. I'm really struggling. All I've got so far is a buy-one-get-one-free promotion and I can't see that attracting much interest.'

Stanley withdrew a pen from the breast pocket of his blazer and pulled the cap off.

'Sometimes the harder you try to solve a puzzle, the more elusive the answer becomes.' He took his glasses off and swapped them for another pair. 'And when that happens I stop thinking about it and the answer always comes in the end.'

'So I should try to forget about it?'

'Exactly.' He smiled and his blue eyes, magnified in his reading glasses, crinkled at the corners. He ran his fingers down the clues and began to read. 'Fourteen down: just an obstruction of the heart; ten letters. Hmm. Aneurysm? No, too short . . .'

Out of the corner of my eye, I saw Gabe's van drive slowly past looking for a parking spot. I had an obstruction of the heart too, I thought with a sigh, rendering me completely incapable of letting anyone in, and I had no idea how to get rid of it.

Gabe had picked Nonna up on his way to the café and she was full of news from Fearnley's when the two of them came in.

'All the plants being packed up and taken away on big lorry!' she said, pausing to pinch a fresh basil leaf from a pot on a table and lift it to her nose. 'We should have taken more; they not even checking what was there, just doing job as quick as possible. Dicky heads.'

Gabe nodded to the conservatory where every spare inch of space was covered in seed trays. People who couldn't help us last night had promised to come in and collect them later on and we were storing them in the meantime. 'You did pretty well, Maria. Besides, where would you have kept them without raising suspicion?'

'True, you smart boy,' Nonna admitted and went to say hello to Stanley, leaving me face to face with Gabe.

'Hello again,' I said.

My stomach gave a little flip. We'd parted as friends last night, but if I hadn't been so quick to fob him off, perhaps things would have ended differently. And looking at him now, with a gentle smile lighting up his handsome face, his eyes studying me with such intensity that it felt as if he could read my mind, I felt a pang of regret.

'Hello,' he said, pulling the end of his tape measure out and then letting it zip back in. 'Where shall I start?'

'I have no idea,' I admitted with a grin. 'We've got customers at almost every table and tomato plants at the rest. How about I make you a coffee first?'

'You see what I mean?' said Gabe, nudging me softly with his shoulder. 'Friends with benefits are the very best sort.'

'Give me a flapjack with that,' said Nina a bit later on when she came in for a toastie. 'I need a sugar hit.'

I popped the largest square into a paper bag and pushed it across the counter. 'Stressful morning?'

'With knobs on,' she confirmed. 'The shop's as dead as a dodo in this rain. Luckily we've had three Fone-A-Flower orders for big bouquets to do. But it's not that. Fone-A-Flower have also sent me a weird email, wanting to renegotiate my terms. From next month, my territory will be reduced, so we'll get far fewer orders.'

Juliet screwed the lid on to the smoothie maker, folded her arms and scowled. 'Haven't used Fone-A-Flower since I ordered some flowers for my mum. They arrived late, half dead and looking nothing like the website.'

Nina's frown deepened. 'My bouquets are always bursting with life and we're never late.'

'Just saying.' Juliet turned the smoothie maker on and Nina poked her tongue out at her back.

'I hate to break it to you,' I said as I walked Nina to the door, 'but it sounds to me like you might be getting a new competitor.'

'My worst nightmare.' Nina heaved a sigh. 'There's little enough business to go round as it is. And Juliet's right, unfortunately: some florists do give Fone-A-Flower a bad name. They don't seem to do proper checks on shops, you only have to fill in a few forms and send some pictures of your work and they add you to their stockist list. I don't like them, but I couldn't survive without them. Then again, I probably can't survive with a new competitor either. Let me know if you hear anything on the grapevine, won't you?'

'Of course,' I said, giving her arm a comforting squeeze as she opened the door.

As Nina left, a man came in I hadn't seen before. He flicked his wet hood down to reveal a handsome face, bright eyes and a neatly trimmed beard.

'Welcome to the Lemon Tree Café,' I said, smoothing my hair down and hoping I didn't smell of fried eggs.

'Thanks.' He looked round, nodding appreciatively, and gave me a warm smile. 'Nice to be out of the rain.'

He shrugged his arms out of his raincoat and looked around for somewhere to hang it.

'I'll take that,' I offered, admiring his outfit of tailored polo shirt, jeans and jacket.

'Thanks.'

He handed me his coat and I found space for it on one of the coat pegs.

'Mmm, what a lovely aroma! What coffee is this?'

My spirits lifted; we'd had a flurry of new likes on our Facebook page over the weekend and I'd even had some interest from food bloggers who reviewed cafés on their blogs. I had an inkling he could be one of those. He certainly seemed very interested.

'We have it roasted exclusively,' I said, tapping my nose. 'It's a secret but I can tell you it's an Italian roast.'

He raised his eyebrows. 'Impressive.'

We approached the counter together and he took a small notebook out of his pocket. I slipped behind the counter, leaving him to study the menu and the cakes under the glass domes.

'So,' I smiled at him, 'anything tempt you?'

He raised an eyebrow playfully.

'The *exclusive* coffee, obviously, black please,' he said. 'And what else do you recommend?'

Juliet looked up from slicing rolls.

'I recommend that,' she said, pointing to the blueberry crumble cake. 'Our bestseller this week.'

'Is that so,' he said, writing a note in his book and slipping it back in his pocket. 'I'll have a slice of that, then, please.'

I chatted about what else sold well and he asked me where most of our customers came from while I made the coffee.

'And how did you come across us?' I placed his Americano on to the tray.

'Word of mouth,' he said, folding his arms and leaning on the counter with a smile.

'The best form of marketing,' I said happily.

'You said virus marketing was the best sort?' Juliet argued, cutting him a far slimmer slice of cake than I'd have done.

'Viral,' I corrected. 'And it's sort of the same thing; viral marketing is simply spreading the word digital-style, through blogs. Wouldn't you say?'

I smiled at our charming customer.

'I guess so.' He held up a menu. 'Mind if I take a copy?'

'Be my guest,' I said, pleased we seemed to be getting his approval. 'Our Instagram and Twitter details are at the bottom, as is the wifi code. Anything else you need, let me know.'

'Sure.'

I'd had the menus reprinted to give them a fresher look and I was really pleased with them.

'You probably aren't interested in lunch,' I said, pointing to the blackboard, 'but we do have an aubergine Parmigiana special on today. And feel free to take any photos.'

He looked amused. 'Right,' he said, picking up his tray. 'The proof of the pudding, as they say . . .'

'He's as slippery as an eel, that one,' Juliet hissed darkly as soon as he was out of earshot.

'He's a blogger; he's just remaining aloof, that's all,' I whispered.

'Aloof, my arse,' I heard Juliet mutter under her breath. 'If anyone wants me, I'll be in the kitchen washing up.'

I rolled my eyes at my colleague; sometimes I despaired, I really did.

I had agreed with Gabe that he would take eight tables at a time to strip back and revarnish. He had driven four tables away in his van. I was expecting him back any minute for the others.

'I've got it: impediment,' I said, looking over Stanley's shoulder at the crossword.

'What's that, dear?' He lowered his reading glasses to peer at me.

'Fourteen down. Just an obstruction to the heart. As in, if you know of any cause or just impediment why these two . . . blah, blah, blah, speak now or for ever hold your peace.'

'Yes!' He gave a bark of laughter. 'It fits, thank you. I was thinking medical like angina or something.'

Stanley looked over at Nonna as she bustled to the door

to let Gabe in and gave a little sigh. 'Most of the time we are our own impediments, holding ourselves back from the things we most want.'

'I agree,' I murmured, unable to drag my eyes off Gabe as he tried to fend off Nonna's attempts to feed him. 'Daft, aren't we?'

'Absolutely.'

We both sighed.

'Rightio, that's it,' Stanley said abruptly. He levered himself out of his chair and folded his paper. 'I'm off.'

'Where to?' I asked, startled by his sudden movement. I held his coat out for him and he slipped his arms in before replying.

'Bristol.'

It seemed a bit sudden but I kissed his cheek and waved him off.

'Where he going in a hurry?' Nonna demanded, watching her beau stride across the village green.

'Bristol, apparently,' I said, throwing Gabe a smile before going to help Juliet with the washing-up.

'*Mamma mia*,' said Nonna with a groan. 'What he have to do that for?'

I blinked at her; perhaps 'Bristol' was some sort of old person's code.

'He didn't say,' I said with a shrug. 'But he seemed very definite about it.'

Nonna tutted and shook her head and Gabe and I exchanged confused looks.

Whatever it meant, it seemed to be important to both of them. I would have stopped to find out, but the lunch rush was about to commence and I wanted to get the kitchen sorted.

'Right, troops,' I said, reaching for a tea towel, 'help is at hand.'

Juliet had the radio on in the kitchen, much to Lia's disgust.

'I wouldn't mind if it was something I could sing along to,' she moaned.

'Shush,' said Juliet harshly. 'It's *Gardeners' Questions*. The expert is just helping a listener choose plants for clay soil. That's what we've got: a wet bog in winter and hard as brick in summer. I could do with some advice.'

'That's it!' I started with a gasp. 'That's our event: Barnaby does *Gardeners' Questions*. Stanley was right, I stopped thinking about my problem and now I've got a solution. We can build a massive publicity campaign and bring loads of people to the village with their questions.'

Juliet looked sceptical. 'Only one problem, hen. How is that going to make money?'

'Details, Juliet, mere details,' I said confidently. 'Barnaby might have lost its garden centre, but we've still got our resident expert who was the heart and soul of the garden centre anyway.'

'Yay! Well done, sis!' Lia hugged me. 'I knew you'd do it.'

Just then Gabe and Lucas poked their heads into the kitchen, both looking very grave.

'Sorry to barge in,' said Gabe.

'But we think we know who the new owner of the garden centre is,' said Lucas, pressing his fingertips to his lips.

'Who?' we demanded.

'I had a call from a greetings card supplier today, saying I'd no longer have exclusivity in this area for their range because a *big player*,' Lucas added sarcastic air apostrophes, 'is moving in.'

'Nina had something similar happen to her with Fone-A-Flower,' I added.

'I hope it's Waitrose,' said Lia dreamily. 'It's a nightmare getting preserved lemons round here.'

I shot her a look.

'It's not Waitrose,' said Gabe. 'I asked my old boss from the law firm to look into that investor we met yesterday.

Turns out he's a scout for Garden Warehouse, he sources new sites for a fee.'

'Oh no,' I said, my heart sinking.

Garden Warehouse was a big retailer originally based up in the north, buying up cheap locations and erecting huge shed-like buildings. They sold everything under the sun, with the emphasis on the outdoors.

'They have a huge gift section,' said Lucas. 'Cards, wrapping paper, the lot. I'll fold, I just know it.'

Tears pricked his eyes and he turned into Gabe's chest. Gabe patted his back stiffly.

'There, there,' he murmured.

Juliet's eyes narrowed. 'Don't they do pet stuff as well, and fresh flowers?'

'And don't forget the café,' I said, feeling sick with dread. 'They always have a café.'

'What are we going to do?' Lia said in a shaky voice. 'This could spell the end for our little business community.'

I blinked at her, trying to absorb the news: Garden Warehouse, the biggest chain of garden centres in the country, was coming to Barnaby.

'I don't know exactly,' I said firmly, 'but we will be putting up a damn good fight, that's for sure.'

Chapter 17

Everyone had an opinion on the imminent arrival of Garden Warehouse. Unsurprisingly, most of the business owners were worried, but some could see a plus side to having a big store so close to home.

'It will be nice to have somewhere nearby to go for a mooch on a rainy day,' said Dad, cheerily, rubbing his hands together, until I glared at him.

'I've been to the one in Derby,' Doreen admitted. 'Alan bought me a lovely solar-powered light-up gnome for my birthday.'

'Which is reason enough for me never to set foot in the place,' Juliet muttered.

'What always worries me about these chains,' Biddy fretted, brushing dog hair off her crocheted tunic, 'is who looks after the pets when the shops are closed? All my animals come home with me.'

Except the rats and chicks in the freezer, presumably, I thought.

'Fearnley's was a bit pricey,' whispered the vicar when he came in for a toasted teacake and then blushed for being disloyal.

'Expertise comes at a price,' said Nonna, glaring at him. 'Like Jesus.'

'Right,' said the vicar, looking baffled.

'I'm with you, Vic,' said Barry. 'I want something cheap

and cheerful along my back wall. Does anyone know when they're opening?'

We didn't have long to wait to find out; the following Monday, every person in the village woke to find that a leaflet had been pushed through their door (including all the shops, which we agreed was a bit below the belt) advertising the reopening of the garden centre in a week's time, and job vacancies for part-time staff.

I invited every one of the businesses, plus Stella Derry representing the Women's Institute, to a meeting to discuss tactics at eight o'clock that night in the café.

Mum was the first to arrive at half past seven. She tapped on the door and let herself in.

'Only me!'

I looked up from setting up the conservatory for our meeting and felt quite underdressed in my jeans and hoodie. She was wearing a soft jersey dress and boots and her wavy hair framed her face, which was free of make-up except for a slash of nudey-colour lipstick.

'You look fantastic,' I said, lifting my cheek up for a kiss.

'Ditto,' she said, taking my chin in her hand and scrutinizing my face. 'I think this new job suits you. And Nonna seems to be taking to retirement very easily. You were right about her and Stanley; they do seem to really care for each other. It's so nice to see her with a male companion. It's a first for me.'

She shook her head incredulously as she helped me push two tables together to make one long one.

'Gosh, yes, of course,' I said with a pang of guilt for not thinking of it sooner. 'And you're all right about it?'

'Absolutely,' said Mum fervently. 'It's not as though I knew my father. And you know how frugal Nonna has always been with details. Lorenzo worked in the lemon groves in Naples, both young when they fell in love, killed in an accident when I was only a baby. And that's it. All I know.'

I nodded. 'Poor Nonna. And poor you.'

'I'd love to have met him, even talking about him with her would be something, but she claims it upsets her too much to rake up the memories,' said Mum with a sad smile. 'I've never even seen a photograph of him; Nonna said she was only able to bring the essentials from Italy, which mostly meant my baby stuff. There's nothing to remember him by.'

'Oh Mum, I can't imagine that.' I abandoned the cups and saucers I'd been laying out on the table and gave her a hug. 'I'm so lucky to have you and Dad.'

A thought struck me with such force that I felt my lungs contract. What if there *was* something to remember him by? What about those black-and-white photographs in the envelope marked *privato* in the filing cabinet? Although I hadn't had a chance to study them before Nonna had burst in on me and thrown me out of the café, I felt sure that there must be one of my grandfather in amongst them. And if that was the case, why had Nonna kept them from Mum?

My eyes flickered to the cupboard where the filing cabinet was; it wouldn't hurt to sneak a quick look at that envelope while no one else was here, surely Mum deserved to see them?

I glanced out of the café windows; there was no one to be seen.

'I can't be sure,' I said nervously, 'but I think Nonna might be hiding some pictures in there.'

I nodded towards the cupboard. Mum followed my gaze and gasped.

'Really? Why would she do that?'

'No idea. Shall we take a look?'

Mum swallowed and nodded. The two of us crept over to the cupboard and I switched on the light. I'd had a clear-out of this cupboard, under Nonna's watchful eye, and most of the clutter had gone. This time the path to the filing cabinet was clear. I stepped forward, feeling my stomach flutter with nerves.

'You keep watch,' I whispered.

She nodded. She looked even more anxious than me.

I took the key from the top shelf, unlocked the drawer and slowly opened it.

'Can you see it?' Mum hissed, looking over her shoulder.

It was empty. I shook my head, frowning. 'It's gone, perhaps—'

'Rosie,' she stammered, 'quick, someone's coming!'

Oh hell! The last thing I wanted was for Nonna to catch me prying again. My fingers fumbled as I shut the drawer and replaced the key just as I heard the ding of the bell and voices enter the café.

I grabbed the nearest thing to hand – a large glass jug – and darted out of the cupboard.

'This will do,' I said brightly, not catching Mum's eye. 'It will be perfect for water.'

'I'll give it a wash,' said Mum, grabbing it from me.

It was Ken and Nonna who had arrived. Nonna's eyes narrowed at seeing me appear from the cupboard, but luckily Stella Derry came in bursting with news of a snake escaping from the pet shop. Everyone was hanging on Stella's every word wondering where the snake had gone. Everyone except me; I was more concerned with what had happened to that envelope.

By eight o'clock everyone had arrived and was tucking into the plates of sandwiches and cakes that Doreen had prepared.

'We can't compete with Garden Warehouse on price, so let's focus on quality, quirkiness and our quaint village appeal,' I said, aiming for a positive start to the meeting.

'Well said,' Ken agreed in his unhurried thick Derbyshire accent.

Ken had kindly offered to chair the meeting on the grounds that, as Garden Warehouse posed the least threat to his business, he was less likely to get overemotional. Although looking at him, slumped in his chair, with his striped

174

hand-knitted tank top, flared jeans and open-toed sandals, it was hard to imagine him getting worked up about anything.

'Before we begin,' said Clementine, eyes blinking rapidly, 'this is all my fault so may I apologize for this whole debacle?'

'No you may not,' said Nonna fiercely. 'You victim of this same as anyone.'

Clementine's chin wobbled. 'But if we hadn't made such mistakes—'

Lucas reached forward and took her hands in his. 'Don't dwell. The hardest times in life are the ones that make you stronger. My divorce lawyer told me that when he handed me his bill.'

'Thank you,' said Clementine uncertainly, sliding her hands out from his.

'And I haven't forgotten about my promise to help you sell your seedlings,' I added. 'Hopefully tonight's meeting will kill two birds with one stone.'

'Whatever we do, we need to do it soon,' she said with a worried frown. 'They'll be getting ready to pot on. Leave them too long and they'll outgrow their trays. Mr Beecher has already had a few problems with the mangetout.'

Adrian, the pub landlord, poured himself a glass of water from the jug on the table.

'Listen, folks, I feel like the cuckoo in the nest here; I might actually benefit from having a Garden Warehouse down the road.' He winced and ducked as if expecting us to all throw sausage rolls at him. 'People will be stopping in for a quick drink or a pub lunch on a Sunday. So I'm sorry too. But I'm on the village's side; anything you do, count me in.'

The pub and café had a symbiotic relationship: they only offered lunch on Sundays when we were closed and, of course, we didn't open in the evenings. They did do coffee and tea all day long, but quite frankly, you couldn't tell which was which, so we didn't worry about it.

'Thanks, Adrian, but nobody need apologize,' I reiterated. 'We are all on the same side. We can't stop Garden

Warehouse, but what we can do is put up a united front and make sure we preserve our villageyness. Garden Warehouse is going to put us on the map whether we like it or not. It's up to us to make sure that people don't overlook our businesses for their cut-price offerings.'

'Found it!' Biddy bounded in, red-faced, and chose an empty chair next to Stella, resting her handbag under the table. 'Little blighter had snuck into my bag.'

Stella clutched at her throat. 'I presume it's not in there any more?'

'Oh Stella,' Biddy laughed, helping herself to a sandwich. 'You are funny.'

Mum and I exchanged looks; Stella didn't look like she was finding it very funny at all.

Ken coughed to call the meeting to order.

'I'll probably get more customers too,' he admitted. 'Not that I want 'em. I like my Mini Mart as it is: steady trade and no surprises. I don't want to be running out of stuff all of a sudden and have to start restocking shelves every five minutes.'

I wasn't sure Ken's wife would necessarily agree with that sentiment; she was in here yesterday looking at holiday brochures with her sister and I overheard her say that if only Ken would pull his socks up they could afford Benidorm instead of Blackpool again for the fifth year on the trot.

Everyone started talking at once then about how Garden Warehouse was going to ruin everything: Lucas mithering that he'd lost his best card supplier, Nina complaining about the inferior quality of their cut flowers, Stella declaring that none of their cakes would be freshly baked and Biddy saying that she couldn't move for extra-large rabbit hutches and Garden Warehouse only sold hutches that were too small to swing a cat in.

Ken banged a spoon against his mug.

'The thing is,' he began, 'we all have to move with the times. It happened to me years ago. Once upon a time people came to Ken's Mini Mart for a week's worth of shopping. Now I see home-delivery vans driving into the village on a daily basis and people getting off the bus staggering under the weight of supermarket carrier bags.'

Adrian, Mum and Stella shifted in their chairs awkwardly.

'So they pop in for the one thing they've forgotten. And that's just the way it is. So look for your niche.' He sat back and folded his arms. 'That's what works for me. In my case, I carry the everyday essentials. For all of you, it will be different.'

I smiled to myself. Ken's definition of essentials must be huge; his catchphrase was 'I've got one of those somewhere', and he'd start burrowing into the back of shelves and invariably find what you were looking for. He stocked everything from, well, just everything . . .

'Good long-term advice,' I said. 'We specialize. Focus on making our businesses stand out. Food for thought, everyone. In the short term, we need action now. This week. They'll be planning a big PR campaign to reopen the garden centre with a bang. I suggest that we get in there first and hold a Barnaby Spring Fair this weekend.'

'A Spring Fair!' Biddy clapped her hands and there were interested murmurs that I took to be a positive response.

'My granddaughter,' Nonna beamed round the room. 'Such a clever girl. Went to university.'

'They know, Mamma,' whispered Mum, patting Nonna's hand.

Mum and I smiled at each other, both pleased to see Nonna in a better mood. Stanley had gone away to visit his daughter and she'd been fractious and grumpy ever since. His daughter lived, unsurprisingly, in Bristol . . .

'If we all join together,' I continued, 'the Spring Fair will be able to offer a lot of what Garden Warehouse can but with the added bonus of being set around our lovely village green. It won't stop them running their own opening event but if we go first, people will have already spent their money with us.'

'But we don't have any plants,' said Nina.

'We have five thousand bedding plants, including flowers, fruit and vegetables, and that's what most people will be buying at the moment, isn't that right, Clementine?'

She nodded. 'I could set up a little stall.'

'Stalls. Plural,' I said. 'And perhaps not run by you. I thought the Women's Institute might be able to help there?'

'Oh yes!' said Mum and Stella together.

There was a moment of awkward silence; on the whole Mum was coping well with not running every committee in the village, but sometimes she forgot she'd abdicated her roles to focus on her home life.

'Sorry,' said Mum, going pink. 'Go ahead, Stella.'

'We'd love to be involved,' said Stella. 'I mean, usually we'd run a cake stall but—'

'Cakes are rather our domain,' I pointed out.

'Jam and chutney?' she asked hopefully. 'A sort of fruit and vegetables "before and after"?'

We all agreed that would work well. Mum suggested setting up some games for the children on the green too and Lucas came up with the idea of a teddy bears' picnic. I found myself wondering whether Noah had got any teddy bears or would he bring one of his dinosaurs instead . . .

'And what about me?' Clementine frowned, looking put out.

'I've got other plans for you.'

I outlined my idea to make Clementine's plant sale the central focus of the Spring Fair, covering the village green with marquees, and to make Clementine our resident gardening expert both on the day and in the local press. I thought she might be resistant to that, but on the contrary, she loved the idea.

We chatted then about spring-themed promotions, giveaways, little competitions and Adrian suggested that, weather permitting, he could set up a mini-beer festival on the village green too.

Biddy raised her hand. 'And how will we attract visitors?'

'Leave that to me,' I said, tapping my nose. 'But in the meantime, I want you all to set up a Twitter account and get as many people to follow you as you can in the next forty-eight hours.'

'Are we nearly done?' asked Adrian, checking his watch. 'Only we've got the meat raffle in the pub in ten minutes.'

I nodded at Ken and he brought the meeting to a close. Nonna, Mum and I cleared up between us and a few minutes later, the café was neat and tidy and ready for tomorrow.

'Who wants a lift home?' said Mum, rummaging through her bag for her car keys.

'Actually, Nonna,' I said, slipping my hand through her arm, 'I thought you and I might walk back to your cottage. If that's all right with you?'

Nonna narrowed her eyes. 'Why, what you want?'

'Information,' I said, leading her to the door, 'about Bristol.'

Nonna tutted. 'Nothing interesting about Bristol.'

'I'll be the judge of that,' I said, jerking my head out into the blustery night. 'Let's go.'

It was too blustery to chat much on the short walk through the village to Nonna's cottage, so we kept our heads down and concentrated on getting there as quickly as her seventy-five-year-old legs could manage.

I breathed in the familiar smell of Nonna's home as she unlocked the old oak door and ushered me in. The aroma reminded me of the almond biscuits she'd baked for us when we were little and took me straight back to my childhood.

'Coffee?' she asked, taking off her headscarf and shoving it in her coat pocket. Apart from a few strands at the front, her hair was still in its neat bun.

'And biscuits please,' I said, grimacing as I ran my fingers through my own knotty bob.

Nonna led the way through to the kitchen. I'd always

loved this cottage. It had been the village bakery a hundred or so years ago. There was a room at the back which used to house the old ovens, a tiny door in the side through which flour deliveries would have been made, and – my favourite feature – a trapdoor under Nonna's bed, for lowering supplies to the ground floor.

I sat at the table, covered as ever with a plastic cloth, and watched as Nonna spooned coffee into an ancient coffee pot and sat it to boil on the hob. There was a pile of post in one corner and it reminded me of the missing envelope from the café. It must be here in the cottage somewhere. I reached a finger out to the pile and surreptitiously lifted up the edge of one or two, trying to find that thick Manila one.

'It's lovely to have company, especially as Stanley is not here,' said Nonna.

She gave me such a big smile that I felt instantly guilty about snooping. Right, no more. I reached for the biscuit tin instead.

'So Stanley's gone to visit his daughter?' I said, shaking some biscuits on to a plate. She'd got some almond ones. Hurray. 'That was a bit sudden, wasn't it?'

One minute he was contentedly doing his crossword, the next he was off to book a train to the south-west.

'He suddenly decide he should let his family know.' She took her glasses off and polished them on a tea towel and sighed. 'About me.'

Not much bothered Maria Carloni, but tonight she looked fearful and worried.

'That's good, isn't it?' I said encouragingly. 'I think he's being gentlemanly and respectful.'

'His Winnie only died five years ago. What if they think I some floozy after his money, eh?'

She sat down heavily at the table, knees wide as usual, her thick tan tights wrinkled at the ankle, and folded her arms over her bosom. Floozy was not the word I'd use. Feisty maybe or full of life . . .

'Then they'd be wrong because you've got your own money.' I picked the almond out of a biscuit and crunched on it. 'And what if they're glad he's got some company again? Which is far more likely.'

The coffee pot started to boil. Nonna began to get up but I beat her to it and placed the pot on the table.

'And what he going to tell them, eh? I been to dinner with old lady, I hold her hand, I buy her flowers? There is nothing to tell. I think he make big thing out of nothing.'

'Maybe he's *planning* a big thing,' I suggested.

'Yeah, well.' She banged cups on to the table and gestured for me to get some milk from the fridge. 'That's another problem.'

'Oh?' I poured the coffee and passed her the sugar and waited for her to elaborate.

She dumped two large spoonfuls into hers, stirred it roughly and slurped.

'He wants to . . .' Nonna paused and then mumbled into her cup, ' . . . sleep over.'

I choked on my coffee. Nothing in my previous thirty-two years on the planet had prepared me for a conversation like this.

'It is a long time since I been with a man. I have admirers in my day, but I always stop before it gets, you know . . .'

'Yes I know,' I said hurriedly, not wanting too much information. 'But why? Why stop?'

She cast her eyes down to the table and to my horror I saw a tear drip on to the plastic cloth.

'Oh Nonna, I didn't mean to upset you.'

She shook her head and wiped her eyes with a handkerchief. 'Don't be sorry. I need you to hear this. I stop because last time it end badly. Since then I scared to try again.'

I frowned. Was she talking about Lorenzo? She couldn't blame herself for his accident, surely?

'But Stanley is adorable,' I pointed out. 'What can go wrong?'

'I know that. I silly old woman. Don't make my mistakes, *cara*. Always afraid to share your heart and show other people how much you care.'

'I'm not afraid,' I said defensively.

Nonna raised an eyebrow.

I felt my cheeks colour, wondering how much she noticed about the lack of men in my life.

'So what are you going to do?' I asked. 'About Stanley?'

'Do you think I should let him stay over?' She blinked at me.

'Um.' I swallowed, feeling unqualified for the job of relationship advisor. 'Yes.'

She mulled that over for a moment.

'OK, but if he snores,' she jerked her thumb, 'I open that trapdoor under my bed and get rid of him.'

'I like your style,' I said with a grin.

'And you?' She peered at me over the top of her glasses. 'What you going to do about Gabe? He is adorable too.'

I blinked at her and felt my face heat up. 'Pardon?'

'Come on, Rosanna, I might be old, but I not blind.'

'He's just arrived in the village,' I said, flustered, 'and I'm so busy with the café and then there's Noah to consider . . .'

'Doesn't matter.' Nonna reached for the limoncello bottle and poured us both a shot. 'If I can take risk at my age, so can you. Be brave, *cara*.'

Was she right? I wondered, as I walked home minutes later, hunched up against the cold wind. Should I take the risk? Maybe if Nonna could take a chance with Stanley at her age, so could I.

Back home, I made a mug of tea, created the best social media plan of my career and then fell into bed and had the loveliest dream about a man with soft grey eyes and a smile that warmed my heart like summer sun . . .

Chapter 18

Gabe manoeuvred the newly renovated table back into position next to the toy corner and straightened up. He had worked so speedily on the café's tables this week, sanding, stripping, revarnishing, and they looked really good. The place still had its lived-in Italian-family-home look, but none of the sixth-form-common-room scruffiness that had begun to creep in. I still wanted the large dresser sprucing up, but it was too big to go in Gabe's van so he was going to have to do that in our little courtyard. He'd be here for a whole day as soon as he could manage it. I'd be lying if I said I wasn't pleased about that; I'd enjoyed his company over the past few days and had begun to look forward to his visits.

'There. Good as new.' He wiped an arm across his forehead.

'I wouldn't go that far,' I quipped. 'I actually quite miss the drawing that Alfie Sargent did of Nonna on this one with a Sharpie.'

Gabe scratched his chin to hide a smile; the little boy's drawing had been less than flattering but completely unmistakable, right down to the ample bosom, apron and thick glasses.

'What does it take to impress you?' he said with mock sadness.

'I'm teasing; I am impressed really.' I ran a finger around the edge of a table. 'I was worried they'd look too perfect. Actually they look just as welcoming, but the rough bits at the edges have gone.'

I glanced up at him. Perhaps he could do the same for me?

'The rough bits are my favourite, more of a challenge.' Gabe traced the grain of the wood with his fingertip and met my gaze. 'No matter how badly wood has been treated, the grain will always be there under the surface, every pattern as unique as a person's soul. I love making it shine again, revealing its natural beauty.'

My heart thumped; were we still talking about wood? The moment was broken as Lia joined us.

'Look at you two gawping at each other,' she snorted, bringing us each a cappuccino. 'Get a room.'

We leapt apart guiltily.

'Lia!' I hissed, utterly mortified.

'If not a room, then a smooth table?' she continued, seemingly amused at my discomfort. 'Is Noah looking forward to tomorrow, Gabe?'

It was now Friday afternoon, the day before the Barnaby Spring Fair.

'He's very excited. It's looking great out there,' said Gabe, nodding towards the activity on the village green.

Under a wide blue sky, members of the school PTA were setting up marquees, the Women's Institute were allocating tables to each one and Mr Beecher was unloading stacks of chairs from the school minivan. Luckily, the buffeting winds from earlier in the week had dropped and the air held the promise of summer warmth.

The last few days had been completely manic: I'd managed to get Clementine a radio slot just before the news later this afternoon. She'd be taking readers' calls about gardening problems and I'd coached her to mention the seedling sale on the village green at every opportunity.

I'd corralled every single village social group I could find into organizing a part of the Spring Fair, from the Mums and Toddlers group to the Allotment Society, and I'd even persuaded the local cancer charity, The Chestnuts Cancer Hospice, to get involved; I'd bought goodness knows how many miles of bunting to string around the village; and I'd set up a Thunderclap social media promotion to coincide with Clementine's radio appearance.

'All Rosie's idea,' said Lia proudly and then waltzed off to the kitchen with a wink.

'You've worked very hard,' said Gabe, taking a seat in the window. 'More impressive than sanding down a few old tables.'

'Nah.' I wrinkled my nose and sat opposite him. 'It isn't far removed from what I used to do in my previous job.'

'Do you miss that life?' said Gabe. 'I sometimes miss mine.'

He scooped some froth off the top of his cappuccino with a teaspoon and put it in his mouth. He had a nice mouth. Kissable lips. I could kiss him now, just lean forward and press my mouth to his and lick that tiny smear of chocolate powder off—

'Rosie?' He looked at me, amused.

'Yes!' I said with a jump. 'I mean no. What was the question?'

'Never mind.' He shook his head and laughed. 'Are you free for the next hour?'

I looked round the café. We weren't too busy; everyone would manage perfectly well without me.

'Possibly, why?'

He leaned forward and smiled cheekily. 'Fancy an adventure?'

I quirked an eyebrow. 'Always.'

Gabe stowed Noah's booster seat in the back of his van, brushed crumbs from the passenger side and ushered me in.

'Are we going where I think we're going?' I asked as we drove past the village green, along the Chesterfield Road and stopped at the grass verge opposite the entrance to what had been Fearnley's Garden Centre only a few short days ago.

'Know your opposition,' said Gabe with a wink. 'I learned that on day one in law school. Let's sneak in and see what they're up to.'

The grass was dotted with tiny purple and yellow flowers. Beyond the verge was a long, neatly trimmed hedge and over it I could see sheep munching on sweet spring grass and small wobbly legged lambs chasing each other in gangs.

This rural idyll was in stark contrast to the other side of the road.

Lorries and vans littered the driveway leading to the tiny car park and there were people everywhere: forklift trucks shifting crates, men erecting signage, a woman on her knees filling up two huge wooden planters with primulas and conifers, people pushing tall trolleys with plants bulging out of the edge of their shelves and the sound of hammering coming from inside the main building. And overhead, casting a shadow over all of the activity, was a ginormous black and yellow sign that read 'Garden Warehouse: everything you need for the outdoors and more!'

I couldn't get over how much the place had changed in such a short time.

'Is this wise?' I said doubtfully.

'I promised you an adventure,' he grinned, yanking on the handbrake and twisting the keys from the ignition, 'not a walk in the park.'

'But what about that?' I pointed to the metal security fence straddling the entrance. Just beyond it, unless I was very much mistaken, was a man with a clipboard who looked terribly official.

'What about it?'

Gabe got out of the van, took a bag of tools from the back and pulled a baseball cap down low over his eyes.

'Act confident. Don't make eye contact and stride as if you're late for a meeting,' he murmured as we approached the fence.

And so I did, and miraculously, when Gabe nodded to Clipboard Man, he nodded back and let us pass without a word, although he did give my Lemon Tree Café apron a quizzical look.

'So what are we actually doing here?' I murmured as we

hurried along the path, past a long polytunnel and towards the main building.

'Intelligence gathering.' Gabe tapped his nose. 'Thought you might be curious to know what they've done so far.'

I was.

The two of us marched round the entire site at a brisk pace: through the front doors, underneath yet more black and yellow Garden Warehouse signage, past the shelves being stocked with packets of seeds and plant pots and big displays of cheap and cheerful plastic gardening sets, along the rather smelly aisle selling every type of pet food for every type of pet and out of the back plastic flappy doors and into the courtyard. Two men were hoisting up a plastic sign above a long plastic table next to a fixture of empty metal buckets: 'Fresh Flowers'. My heart sank. Poor Nina. This one area was bigger than her entire florist's shop.

Out in the open air were aisles of low wooden tables, empty now but with signs boasting multibuy deals of 'five for a ten-ner' on bedding plants and 'buy one get TWO free' on terra-cotta plant pots. There were neon signs advertising opening offers everywhere. We didn't go into any of the greenhouses, but we did slow down when we reached the big wooden cabin that had used to house Clementine's bonsai collection. Work was already underway to convert it into a café. The sight of it made the hairs on the back of my neck prickle.

'Very professional,' I said as we made our way back to the original car park. 'But soulless.'

Gabe nodded. 'And that's where the Barnaby shops score highly. I can't see that wooden cabin being able to compete on any level with the Lemon Tree Café. Certainly not the beauty of its staff.'

That did cheer me up. I nudged him with my shoulder and grinned. 'I'll pass that on to Nonna.'

It was almost time to collect Noah from school and Gabe asked me if I'd mind tagging along with him. We approached

187

the van to find cars parked either side of it and the lane seemed to be even busier than before.

'I wonder what poor Clementine thinks of it all.' I glanced up at her house; there was no sign of life at the windows, which was just as well because she should be on her way to Derby to the radio studio now for her very own *Gardeners' Questions*.

'I know exactly what she thinks of it, the vicar told me,' he said with a wry smile. 'And it's too rude to repeat.'

He stowed his tools in the back while I leaned on the side of the van and stared up at the garden centre. 'It already looks tons bigger than Fearnley's ever was somehow.'

'They do seem to be utilizing every square centimetre,' he agreed. 'But then, they're famous for piling high, selling cheap, so they would.'

'By why us?' I frowned. 'Why here?'

Gabe opened the passenger door for me.

'Imagine if Garden Warehouse was one of your clients. You'd probably be able to come up with a dozen reasons why it could be good for the village. Jobs, customer choice, more visitors to the area . . . ?'

I shook my head firmly and climbed in.

'I can't allow myself to go down that road. I stand for Barnaby and our little community, and whatever measly benefits we might get – like more trade at the pub, for instance – will be greatly outweighed by the disadvantages. And our event tomorrow will hopefully show Garden Warehouse that we won't be bullied and we're not going to make it easy for them to take our customers.'

Gabe closed his door, plugged his phone into the charger and stuck the keys in the ignition.

'But after the Spring Fair? What then? Garden Warehouse will still be there. Don't you think you should try to find ways to work together? Turn their arrival into an advantage? In my experience, most big companies are all too keen to get into bed with the locals.'

'Really?' I raised an eyebrow at that and we shared a smile.

'All I'm saying,' he added softly, 'is that if I were to be offered a job when I needed one, it would be difficult to turn it down.'

I looked at him swiftly. I thought about Noah and him on *The Neptune* and the uncomplicated life they'd made for themselves and remembered how I'd put my foot in it the other night talking about a proper job.

'Do you need a job?' I asked softly.

He opened his mouth, seemed to change his mind and exhaled sharply instead.

'I was talking about Tyson,' he said.

Lucas had offered him a couple of shifts a week at the gift shop, but he needed more than that and had tied himself in knots with guilt before applying for a part-time job at Garden Warehouse. He started on Monday, working in the timber department, and was dreading it.

'You're probably right,' I conceded reluctantly, 'but let me be outraged for a little while longer. I can only listen to what my heart tells me to do on this one, not my head.'

Gabe looked at me, his gaze intense, and the corners of his mouth turned up in a gentle smile. 'Is your heart telling you anything else?'

The low afternoon sun filtered in through the van window, lighting up Gabe's smile and giving his hair a golden glow, and my heart did a double beat as he reached across and stroked my cheek with his thumb, my skin tingling deliciously at his touch.

I nodded and took a deep breath. 'Although mostly I ignore it.'

'You're vibrating,' Gabe said, looking at my lap.

'Sorry.' I shook my shoulders to release the tension. 'Talking about personal stuff always—'

'No, your pocket. Something's vibrating.'

'Oh.'

It was my phone, doing its best to alert me to an incoming call even though I'd put it on silent. I pulled it out of my apron pocket and jumped when I saw the name Robert Crisp from Digital Horizons flash up on the screen. There also seemed to be a flurry of other alerts: voicemails, texts and Facebook notifications. What had I missed?

'It's my old boss,' I said, frowning at Gabe. I swallowed. 'I'd better . . .'

'Sure, sure.'

He offered to get out of the van to give me some privacy but I shook my head.

'Hello, Robert, this is a surprise,' I said.

'Rosie! How nice to hear from you!' He cleared his throat. 'Except I called you. How nice to hear your voice, is what I meant.'

I stole a glance at Gabe who was pretending to scroll through his own messages. I pressed a hand to where his thumb had been and wondered what might have happened if we hadn't been interrupted.

'What can I do for you?' I asked.

'Well.' There was an uncomfortable silence. 'Yes. Nobody has been in touch asking for a reference for you and part of me was glad and the other part a bit suspicious. A woman—' He coughed. 'A *person* like you should be snapped up like a hot cake and now . . . I'm waffling, but I regret having lost you.'

'That's encouraging to hear,' I said diplomatically.

'It was a shame you chose to leave.'

Gabe started the engine, nodding towards the clock.

'Time to pick up Noah,' he whispered.

I fastened my seat belt while Gabe turned the van round and headed back to the village.

'Robert,' I said sternly, 'you asked me to touch up Lucinda Miller.'

I caught a glimpse of Gabe just as his jaw dropped. I turned to the window to stop myself from laughing.

'Hmm,' Robert said glumly. 'Bad decision, as it turned out. Lucinda wasn't happy about it and has refused to do anything else with the charity. The charity retaliated by sacking us.'

I bit my lip and just about resisted saying I told you so.

'Anyway,' he cleared his throat, 'then when your name came up today, I thought: Ah, so that's what she's doing. Setting up her own business.'

We passed Gina Evans, my old friend from school, pushing a twin buggy with a small child on each side holding on to the handles. I gave her a wave. She flicked her pink hair out of her eyes and waved back. She never made it into the café; too stressful, she told me on Facebook, with all those inquisitive fingers . . .

I tuned back in to Robert, who seemed to think I'd set up my own social media agency.

'I am?' I said, staring at the phone.

'Supporting local businesses. Looking after the squirrels.'

I frowned some more. 'Robert, what are you talking about?'

'Sorry.' He gave a bark of laughter. 'I always think of clients like animals. You get your big clients: the elephants, we all need an elephant or two on the books. And antelope – fast, medium-sized and keep us on our toes – and then squirrels. Digital Horizons is too big to deal with squirrels. Not enough meat on them for us. But I've often thought that get enough squirrels and you could, you know, have a feast.'

'Ri-ght.'

Gabe drew the van up outside Barnaby Primary School and I crinkled my nose and circled a finger round my temple miming to Gabe that I thought Robert had gone completely mad. The playground was empty and we still had a couple of minutes before the bell went. Gabe turned the engine off and undid his seat belt.

'Hold on,' I said, sitting up straight. 'You said my name came up. When and who with?'

'On the BBC news, of course,' Robert replied. 'I must say I was quite—'

'What?' I demanded, grabbing Gabe's arm and squeezing it. 'What did they say?'

My jaw dropped as Robert explained that he'd heard on the three o'clock news that I was using the power of social media to pull in an audience for the Barnaby Spring Fair.

'So well done,' Robert finished. 'And good luck. Today squirrels, tomorrow, um . . . elephants!'

'Thanks, Robert, I'd better go,' I said and ended the call.

'Well?' Gabe's eyes were wide with intrigue. 'I'm on the edge of my seat here.'

'My Thunderclap has just been on the national news,' I said, my voice breathy with excitement.

'Thunderclap? Jesus.' He looked appalled as if it was some sort of contagious disease.

'It's a social media campaign,' I laughed, pulling him in for a squeeze. 'A type of online rent-a-crowd to spread the word about tomorrow's Spring Fair.'

'So . . .' He looked doubtful, although he seemed not to mind the hug. 'It's good news?'

'The best,' I said, struggling to keep my grin under control. 'We're going to have so many visitors that the Women's Institute may well run out of jam. Listen,' I said, releasing him and slipping my phone back into my pocket, 'I'm going to have to dash back to the café. I've got some serious tweeting to do. Give Noah a big kiss from me, won't you?'

I reached for the door handle, brimming with purpose and eager to press on with the next stage of the campaign, but Gabe caught hold of my hand.

'So Noah gets a kiss,' he said softly, his eyes crinkling with humour. 'What about me?'

I let my heart answer that one.

We only came up for air when the giggles from some of the mums arriving to pick up their precious little ones became too loud to ignore.

Chapter 19

It was the day of the Barnaby Spring Fair. I was up at seven and practically ran out of the house at eight, smiling whenever I thought about that kiss in Gabe's car yesterday. I hadn't felt like this about a man for years. In fact, I don't think I'd ever felt this way about anyone, certainly not after only one kiss.

But what a kiss.

The connection between us had been . . . well, I wasn't usually the romantic type, but it had had enough electricity in it to power the whole village. For a week. At Christmas.

My eyes searched the village green for him now amongst the helpers and spotted him in the middle with Noah, doing something with a pile of old pallets and a hammer.

As I raised my hand to wave at him, my phone rang. The sight of Verity's name flashing on the screen made my stomach flip.

Did I tell her about the kiss or not?

'How's it going?' she squealed. 'I heard you on the radio yesterday.'

'Really well!' I said, smiling at Mr Beecher as he struggled past dragging a huge bag of cones for the children's obstacle race. 'The sun is shining and we're expecting the whole village to turn out.'

'And have you fixed Gabe up yet? He hasn't mentioned anyone – well, no one except you.'

I bit my lip to stop myself asking what he'd said about me.

'Well, no, busy week, hardly seen him.' I squeezed my eyes shut and tried not to picture the moment when our lips met yesterday and golden sparks of happiness had danced around our heads. 'But don't worry, leave it with me.'

'Now, I want you to promise me something,' Verity said, her voice turning serious.

'Anything.' I crossed my fingers.

'I love Gabe and Noah. They mean the world to me. I love you too, of course,' she added.

'Ditto,' I said softly.

'It's none of my business really, but please take care of my darling friend. For him to get close to someone again after Mimi will take a huge leap of faith. Think carefully before you let him take that jump. Make sure whoever you fix him up with is someone who won't break his heart. Promise me that.'

Her words hit me like a hailstorm and I sat down heavily on a bench on the village green, gripping the phone to my ear.

This was why I'd pulled back from Gabe the other night on his boat. Everything Verity said pointed to me being absolutely wrong for him. I had form for pulling back, with-drawing from relationships as soon as things got serious. And this time it wouldn't just be Gabe who got hurt; I could possibly let Noah down too. A wave of sadness washed away the mood of the day and for a moment I couldn't speak.

'Oh I think I've lost her,' Verity muttered to herself.

'I'm here,' I said hoarsely. 'And yes, I promise.'

Just then Doreen ran out of the café in a flap looking for me. There was a BBC van parked right outside.

'Rosie?' she yelled. 'Help!'

'Crikey,' I said with a gulp. 'I'll have to dash. Looks like the BBC might have arrived for breakfast!'

The response to our social media campaign, coupled with Clementine's stellar performance on the radio, had been incredible. Last night we'd been almost overwhelmed with enquiries via our Facebook page and Twitter feeds and had had to have an emergency convening of the Spring Fair committee to deal with everything. Our anticipated numbers were so high that Barnaby's two community police officers had got the wobbles and had requested back-up from the local force, and a makeshift car park had been set up in a spare field at Jericho Farm. The Riverside Hotel had asked to be in on the action as well and had offered Clementine an evening edition of her *Gardeners' Questions* along with an opportunity to sell any remaining seedlings. Clementine was on cloud nine and not a little bit tearful at all the lovely messages of support she'd received after the radio presenter had probed into her background yesterday. I had a feeling an unexpected star of the village had been born.

Also unexpected, my friend Gina had called into the café after all her little charges had gone home last night. She and another childminder friend of hers had offered to run a cress heads egg decorating stall with eggs from Jericho Farm and packets of snaffled seeds from Fearnley's old stock. And as we wanted to appeal to families, we'd readily agreed.

The morning flew by getting the café ready for its busiest day in history and dealing with last-minute queries and I managed to push my conversation with Verity to the back of my mind.

Were only teddy bears eligible to come to the teddy bears' picnic? (No, Lia replied, all cuddly friends were welcome.) Did anyone mind if Ken's son Martin sold bags of his home-made rhubarb fudge from a stall on the village green? (Nobody minded, although most people thought there might not be many takers particularly when they saw the colour of it.) And would it be all right if the local TV station did a spot of filming for their *Derbyshire People* programme? (A wholehearted YES! was the jubilant response to that one.)

There were a host of other late additions to the programme too, like Biddy's idea of a dog show, with prizes for the prettiest eyes, waggiest tail and best rescue dog, and the day promised to be an unforgettable one for the folks of Barnaby.

And then suddenly it was midday and the narrow roads through Barnaby began to hum with the arrival of dozens upon dozens of cars. One minute, Dad and Ed were securing the last string of bunting around the pub's outdoor beer tent and the next, the village green seemed to fill up with eager bodies waving their money, queuing for artisan beer, choosing between a fairy, a superhero and a tiger at the face-painting stall, pointing at the peculiar pink fudge (which those brave enough to try declared delicious) and pottering around the many plant stalls which formed a circle around the edge of the green. Someone handed Clementine a megaphone and she pronounced the first Barnaby Spring Fair to be open and everyone clapped furiously, except Nonna and Stanley, freshly returned from Bristol, who were secretly sharing their first kiss behind the lemon trees in the café's conservatory.

I welled up with tears when I spotted them; it looked as if they were over the moon to be back together and I couldn't help thinking of the other night and Nonna's dilemma about letting a man back into her life. From where I was standing, it looked like her concerns were well and truly relegated to the past . . .

Everyone was being their best and brightest self today, due in no small part, I reckoned, to such a heavy press presence. The BBC TV crew had been joined by Dales FM and the local TV news station. Robin Barker, the junior reporter who'd interviewed Dad about his short-lived Dolly Parton tribute act, was back too. As I hadn't had the chance to organize our own photographer, I bunged him fifty quid and a bacon sandwich and asked him to snap away to his heart's content. He was as happy as a pig in clover, especially when I gave him, and all the other members of the media, special press passes hastily laminated by Mrs Murray, the school secretary.

I paused from clearing the pavement tables and smiled to myself as Gabe and Noah lined up with a crowd of other adult-and-child pairs for the piggy-back race.

Mum caught my eye from inside the café and waved the teapot at me. I stuck my thumbs up and moments later she came out with a tray. She was helping out today, thank goodness, it had been 'all hands on deck'.

'Perfect timing,' I said, taking it from her and putting it down on a table in a sunny spot.

'What a success!' She plonked a smacking kiss on my cheek.

'Isn't it?' I agreed. 'And yet if you'd have asked me at the beginning of the year what success meant to me, I'd have probably said a promotion, a ten-thousand-pound pay rise and adding a million followers to a client's Twitter account. Not a village plant sale. I've quite surprised myself at how delighted I am.'

Mum laughed. 'I'm not surprised; you've always fought on the side of fairness.'

'Have I?' I gave her a quizzical look as she poured us both a mug of tea and passed me one.

'Remember the rooftop ice cream protest?' She looked at me over the rim of her mug. 'When you said it wasn't fair not to let the ice-cream van into school on that hot day?'

'Everyone remembers that. Mr Beecher still has nightmares.'

'And the xylophone mallets in the Nativity?'

'No?' I sipped my tea, grinning. 'Remind me.'

'Gina was picked to play "Silent Night" on the xylophone and Jimmy Dillon was jealous so he stole the mallets just as the parents filed into the hall and Gina got blamed for losing them.'

I laughed at the memory. 'It's all coming back to me now.'

I'd marched to the front of the hall, crashed my cymbals together and made everyone look for the missing 'bongers', as I'd called them. They'd been found in the boys' toilets, in the hands of Jimmy Dillon who was doing his own rendition of 'Silent Night' on the radiator.

'You must have been mortified when I did that.'

She pulled a shocked face. 'No! I was proud; you were standing up for what was right. And the Barnaby Spring Fair is no different. It's about being fair. And judging by how few seedlings are left and the depleted cake selection inside, I think you've done pretty well.'

'Thanks, Mum.' I leaned my head on her shoulder.

I'd set out simply to help raise some money for Clementine, to help her through the next few months, but we'd done much more than that for her. Clementine was in her element, talking to fellow gardeners, poring over various plants. The school had asked her to run a gardening club for a small fee. Dales FM had been quick to snap her up for a regular weekly slot on Friday lunchtimes, too. She had been about to shake hands on the deal when Gabe had stepped in and pointed out that there was indeed no such thing as a free lunch and that expertise like hers came at a price. Clementine and Tyson between them had had so many enquiries that they'd decided on the spur of the moment to set up their own gardening business. 'And I'll tell Garden Warehouse where to stick their timber department,' Tyson had said, chin tilted defiantly to the sun.

I did like things to be fair. And it *was* unfair that Clementine had suffered so much loss in such a short time and it did seem unfair (regardless of how sensibly Gabe put it) that Garden Warehouse could stomp all over Nina's flowers and take her Fone-A-Flower territory and nab Lucas's best greetings cards range and undercut Biddy on her pet supplies. And in time, when the café in the cabin was ready, they'd do the same to us too.

'It has gone well,' I agreed. 'But there is one thing that we can't get away from and that is that the new café is almost certainly going to affect our business when it opens.'

Mum shrugged casually. 'It is what it is. But focus on the

positives: we've all had the most profitable day any of us can remember and more than that, the entire village has done something together. I can't remember the last time that happened.'

'The nappy blockage, according to Doreen.'

Mum winced. 'Thank you for that reminder.'

One of her friends called her name and after pressing another kiss to my cheek, she waved back and went to join her.

Mum might have a point about fairness, I thought, stacking our mugs and the teapot back on the tray. It had always been something that I'd striven for. I'd even walked out of my job at Digital Horizons because I didn't think it was fair to alter Lucinda's photo.

So why when I broke up with Callum hadn't I fought for fairness then? I'd acted like a coward, too scared to do the right thing, too desperate to sweep the whole mess under the carpet and move on. But I hadn't moved on, had I? I'd remained just as scared: scared of making mistakes and of history repeating itself.

And now, today . . . ?

I caught a glimpse of Gabe with Noah hanging on tight, galloping across the village green towards the finish line. Even from this distance I could hear shouts and cheers and Noah's excited squeals as they finished first.

The promise I made to Verity echoed through my brain; I had to be fair to them too.

I raised a hand as Gabe pointed me out to Noah and I crossed over to the green to meet them.

'We came first!' Noah danced on the spot showing me his winner's medal.

'You're the dream team,' I said, ruffling his hair. 'Well done.'

I stooped to give him a hug just as Lia's voice came over the megaphone. 'Teddy bears' picnic is about to start in two minutes. All hungry bears this way!'

'Dad,' Noah tugged Gabe's sleeve, 'where's Jorvik?'

Gabe pulled a tatty green toy dinosaur from inside his jacket and handed it to his son. Noah tucked it under his arm and kissed its head.

'Tell me about school,' I said, rubbing a chocolate smear from his chin with my thumb.

'S'OK.' He looked down and scuffed his shoe on the grass. 'But I've got to go back again next week.'

'The concept of "for the rest of his formative years" hasn't sunk in yet,' said Gabe, placing a hand on his son's shoulder.

'What's the best bit about it?' I asked.

Noah thought for a moment.

'PE. And sandwiches.'

Across the green, the teddy bears' picnic music started up and a crowd of children surged towards Lia and Mum, anxious to secure their places at the long trestle table laden with snacks. Noah flung an arm round his dad's leg and gave it a hug.

'Bye, Daddy,' he called over his shoulder.

'Don't you want me to come with you, dude?' Gabe shouted after him.

Noah threw his dad a look of disgust. 'I'm not a baby.'

'He's not even five,' Gabe muttered under his breath with a sigh. 'Which means he *is* a baby.'

'Your sandwiches must be good,' I nudged him with my shoulder, 'if they're the best bit of school.'

'Tuna and sweetcorn. No mayo. He has the same everyday. He doesn't really embrace change, my boy.'

We held our breath as Noah struggled to find a place at the picnic table and then sighed with relief when he sat down and made Jorvik shake hands with the teddy bears around him.

'He looks like he's doing all right to me,' I said, feeling as proud of the little boy as if he were my own.

'Rosie,' Gabe ran a hand through his hair nervously,

'Noah might not like it but, I'm ready to embrace change. I've been doing a lot of mulling since I've been in Barnaby and after yesterday in the van with you, I think . . . no, I *know* that mine and Noah's lives are ready for something seismic to happen.'

My pulse quickened; I had to stop this.

Whatever seismic thing Gabe had in mind, somehow I thought it probably involved more kissing. And while I did really like the kissing, could quite happily agree to more than that, I couldn't. It wasn't fair.

'Are you OK?' He peered closer. 'You've gone pale, but at the same time, you look hot.'

'Hot in a Katy Perry way?' I teased, pressing a hand to my chest as if that was somehow going to calm things down.

'Hotter,' he murmured, touching the back of his hand to my face.

'I've got something to say,' I said, taking a deep breath. 'About my breakfast.'

His lips lifted in an amused smile. 'Go on.'

'This morning I ran out of bread to make toast. And butter. So I toasted a bagel and spread it with peanut butter instead. A toasted bagel with melting peanut butter. It was amazing. Delicious.'

Gabe was trying really hard not to laugh. 'Sounds great.'

'It was.' I exhaled again. 'Most people would think, Ooh that was nice, forget boring old toast, from now on I'll have bagels. But not me. I thought: I'd better not have that too often or I'll get addicted and it will lose its deliciousness.'

'So much angst. At breakfast,' he marvelled.

'I know,' I said, as if I couldn't believe it myself. 'It's almost as if I can't let myself get too attached to something in case it goes wrong. And then you came along.'

'I like this story,' he said, his lips twitching. 'Not what I expected, but I like it.'

'Well, you're my toasted bagel with peanut butter; very special.'

I looked at Gabe and my mouth went dry. His face was lit up; eyes dancing, a smile as wide as an ocean.

I exhaled, a feeling of dread making its way from my toes right up through my body. I was about to wipe that smile from his face.

'But here's the thing,' I said, bracing my hands against his firm broad chest, 'I'm scared that if I let you get too close to me and something goes wrong, you'll stop being special. Like the bagel.'

Gabe scratched his head. 'This conversation has gone off at a tangent that, never in a million years, could I have predicted.'

'I'm sorry,' I said, feeling awful. 'But I needed to get it off my chest before you made your seismic change.'

'Um.' Gabe scratched his head again and seemed to be sifting back through the conversation to where he'd left off before my bizarre bagel analogy.

'OK,' he said as if he'd come to a decision. 'Consider this: what if it's OK to have something special every day? In fact, I'd go as far as to say that we owe it to ourselves to make sure we do.'

I slid a sideways glance at him. He made it sound so simple. Perhaps it was? Perhaps I could have someone special in my life, every day.

I shook my head slowly. 'But that's not real life, is it? And I can't, I won't take that risk.'

'So you don't even want to try?' he said sadly. 'Because, you and me, I think, we could—'

I never got to hear the end of the sentence because there was an almighty crash, accompanied by squeals and screams from the teddy bears' picnic table and we looked across to see Noah on the grass. It looked like he'd fallen backwards off his stool taking the tablecloth, a pile of sandwiches, a bowl of Wotsits and an entire jug of orange squash with him. The children's shouts rapidly turned to laughter as Noah began to kick his legs in the air, shouting for help whilst simultaneously stuffing handfuls of food into his mouth.

Gina ran to pick him up and Mum looked round frantically for Gabe.

'And for his next trick . . .' said Gabe with a groan and ran off to rescue him.

I watched as Gina and Gabe dusted Noah down and led him away to dry off.

Gina and Gabe. As much as it pained me to consider it, there was an idea . . .

Chapter 20

After the chaos and mayhem of Saturday, Monday proved to be our quietest day ever. Not even Stanley had been in, although, oddly, he had reserved a table for this afternoon – something he'd never done before. By lunchtime, the café was so deserted that we agreed that Doreen might as well go home. Lia left to go shopping with Mum and Arlo, and for the next two hours, I coped perfectly well alone. It wasn't difficult. I had a student who'd managed to make one hot chocolate last for three hours, the mum and her twins who'd all had a snooze in the toy corner, and two women from a cosmetics company discussing winter highlighters over green tea until the water in their mugs had gone stagnant.

Mum, Lia and Arlo came back at half past two and we stood in the café windows looking out at the carless road around the green.

'They all must be at Garden Warehouse,' I said with a shrug.

Mum and Lia looked at each other. Mum laughed awkwardly.

'What?' I said, looking from one to the other. 'Am I right?'

Mum nodded. 'The car park was so packed that everyone was parking on the lane.'

'Really?' I had to admit, I was curious. And a bit bored.

'I think I'd better see for myself,' I said. 'Lia, please can I borrow your car?'

'What are you going to do?' She hid her car keys behind her back. 'Because I don't think you should get into any arguments.'

'As Gabe would say, I'm going to get to know my opposition. Would you mind hanging on here until I get back?'

She handed the keys over, extracted a promise from me to be careful and made me untie my apron before I set off. No sooner had I left the village than I hit the traffic. There were cars attempting to mount every available surface and one lone man in a fluorescent yellow jacket fruitlessly trying to prevent cars parking illegally.

I crawled through the traffic jam and pulled the car on to Clementine's drive. The front door of her house flew open and she charged towards me waving her fist, her face puce with fury.

'Oh it's you,' she said with a scowl as she came to a halt by the car door.

'Do you mind?' I said as I climbed out of Lia's car. 'It's just that there is literally nowhere else to park.'

'You don't say,' she grumbled, folding her arms across a pair of worn dungarees, adding more kindly, 'and of course I don't mind *you* being here.'

'Oh God, how awful for you.' I looked at the sea of cars surrounding her house.

'I've been round and complained,' she said. 'The car park extension will be ready in about a week to coincide with the, er,' she coughed, 'café opening. They're calling it the Cabin Café, by the way.'

One week. I felt a prickle of nerves down my spine.

'Well,' I took a deep breath, 'at least this gridlock situation is only temporary.'

'They were rather decent about it,' Clementine conceded. 'They've given me an inconvenience payment of five hundred pounds – which will help pay some bills – and another hundred pounds in vouchers to spend in store.'

'It's the least they can do after everything you've been through,' I said huffily.

'To be honest,' she tugged her sleeves down over her bony wrists, 'I feel a bit disloyal.'

'Why?'

'I went in to have a nosy and spend some of my vouchers and came away with some wild bird food and a gift for one of Clarrie's nephews. I had quite a nice time. Haven't had money to spend like that in years.'

I felt a wave of sympathy for her, imagining the life of debt that she and Clarence must have been wading through without any of us knowing.

'Don't feel guilty. And it isn't as if it's money you could spend in the village.'

'Hmm.' She chewed her thumbnail. 'I know how important it is to support the village shops, especially after all you've done for me. I should have bought things from Biddy and Lucas.'

I pushed down a stab of dismay. What if the rest of the village, and the neighbouring villages, started doing their shopping here? It wouldn't take long for us all to start feeling the pinch.

'Business has been a bit flat for all of us today,' I admitted, 'but it gives us a chance to catch our breath after Saturday's triumph.'

'What are you doing here anyway?' She frowned. 'Come to collect your free cappuccino like everyone else?'

I froze.

'What?'

Clementine pointed across the dividing fence to a small sign a few metres up the drive at the entrance to the car park.

'Free cappuccinos to our first FIVE HUNDRED customers!' I read out loud. *'Five hundred*! That's more than we serve in a week. Two weeks, probably!'

'The coffee wasn't very nice either,' added Clementine indignantly. 'Tasted like burned soil.'

I narrowed my eyes. 'You drank one?'

'I *took* one,' she corrected, her eyes darting left and right. 'Look at it this way: one less for someone else to have. Don't worry, they'll run out eventually.'

I pulled a face, too furious to speak.

She eyed me critically and plucked a huge sprig of mint from a bush at the edge of the drive.

'Calms inner fire,' she said, pressing it firmly into my hand with a knowing look.

'Five hundred free cappuccinos,' I fumed. 'The café isn't even open. How are they doing it?'

'Serving it from a mobile catering truck. Bacon sandwiches this morning too, and biscuits. Free biscuits, actually.'

I glared at her.

She swallowed. 'I didn't have one of those, I promise.'

'This I have got to see.'

I stomped off to investigate.

It didn't take me long to locate the free coffees; the queue was easy to spot. I marched through the black and yellow store and out into the courtyard where a gleaming stainless-steel catering van was dispensing refreshments. A line of customers snaked back to the fresh flowers counter and my heart sank when I spotted one or two familiar faces in it, including the postman, some of the mums who'd caught Gabe and me kissing on Friday afternoon and Martin, Ken's son, who was probably spending his fudge money from Saturday.

Traitors. I graced them with a tight smile and walked straight up to the counter, skirting the queue.

'Just looking at the menu,' I said loudly as a chorus of tuts flared up behind me.

The van had a long serving hatch down one side and there were two women and one man in uniform inside it pouring drinks, shouting orders, taking money and pointing out the sugar and stirrers at the end of the fold-down counter and generally getting in each other's way.

'NEXT PLEASE!' yelled the man. His face was flushed and there was a big frowny crease between his brows.

'What cake is that?' asked a plump lady at the front of the queue, pointing to something I couldn't see.

She had a small beige dog under her arm whose tongue was doing its best to lick the frosting off the nearest cupcake.

'Blueberry crumble cake,' said the man, scratching his beard. 'Our bestseller.'

What a coincidence, blueberry crumble cake was our bestseller . . . At which point, I realized where I'd seen the man before.

'Hey!' I gasped, squeezing in next to the lady with the dog. 'I recognize you.'

It was the stylish man who'd been into the café the previous week asking about our menu, the one I'd stupidly assumed was a blogger.

'Hello?' He looked startled and then raised his eyebrows. 'Oh hello.'

As slippery as an eel, Juliet had said. I should have listened. If I'd thought for one moment he was an industrial spy . . . I groaned . . . and I'd even given him a copy of the menu.

'Oi!' A man with greased-back hair and an e-cigarette dangling from his lips tapped me on the shoulder. 'There's a queue, love.'

I smiled sweetly at him. 'I'm not a customer.'

The server had a badge pinned to his black and yellow uniform. *Jamie Dawson, Catering Manager.* Great.

'And *you* are not a blogger.' I narrowed my eyes at him.

He blinked innocently. 'I never said I was.'

He was right, I thought irritably; I'd just assumed. And then proceeded to give him as much information about the café as he could scribble into his notebook.

'How much is the blueberry crumble cake?' asked the lady with the dog.

'A pound,' said Jamie. 'But you'll have to take that cup-cake as well, I'm afraid; your dog has just licked it.'

Crumbs, we charged double that . . .

'Princess!' The lady frowned at the little dog. 'I'll just take the free cappuccino, thank you.'

'That same cake at the Lemon Tree Café is twice the size and home-made,' I whispered, omitting to mention the price. 'And we have a dog bowl for Princess.'

The lady made an ooh shape with her mouth, took her coffee and moved off.

'For God's sake,' Jamie muttered under his breath, dumping the licked cake in the bin.

'You said you'd heard about us through word of mouth,' I said crossly, folding my arms.

'I did. Now please move along, you're holding up the queue. NEXT.'

I stood my ground. 'Oh yeah? Who?'

Jamie rolled his eyes and looked over my shoulder. 'Him.'

I whirled round to see who he was looking at. The air squeezed from my lungs as if someone had punched me. Gabe and Gina were here. Gabe was pushing a trolley and Gina was holding up a tray of plants for inspection.

They haven't wasted any time, I thought bitterly. I'd only passed Gina's number on to Gabe on Saturday afternoon at the Spring Fair and now here they were. Together. Looking all . . . coupley.

A sob formed in my throat. I felt betrayed in every way.

'Gabe?' I said with a croak, pointing at him. 'Him?'

'Yep, that's the one,' said Jamie.

Suddenly I found myself jostled out of the way by the man with the slicked-back hair and I marched off to Gabe and Gina.

'Thank you very much!' I said angrily, willing back the tears as I tapped him on his shoulder. 'You Judas.'

'Rosie?' He blinked nervously and looked at Gina. 'What's wrong?'

'Oh hi, Rosie!' Gina smiled, leaning in for a hug.

Gina had always been a larger-than-life character at school, loud and dramatic. Today's outfit consisted of orange dungarees, a striped ethnic jacket and an orange bandana tied round her pink hair.

'Hi,' I managed to say.

'What's up, mate?' asked Gina, putting her arm round my shoulders.

All day I'd been blaming the lack of custom on the fact that everyone was having a rest after such a busy Saturday, spending their money at the Spring Fair. Now I could see that that had nothing to do with it; Garden Warehouse had taken our business. On their first day. Everyone was here. Everyone was drinking free cappuccinos while we, *we* who did our best to make every customer feel valued and welcome, stood around wiping non-existent crumbs from our tables . . .

And Gabe, who had given me the kiss of my absolute life on Friday – three tiny days ago – was shopping with Gina like they were auditioning for *Mr & Mrs* or something after having sent the enemy right into our camp.

I looked from Gabe to Gina and then to Jamie Dawson doling out free stuff from his shiny stainless-steel wagon and felt my throat throb with unshed tears.

'What is it?' said Gabe tenderly, placing a hand on my lower back. 'Tell me?'

I jumped away as if he'd burned me.

'Get off. I've got to go,' I muttered. 'I need to get Lia's car back to her.'

'Rosie?' Gabe's shoulders sagged. 'Can we talk about this?'

'Not now.' I began to walk away.

I heard him swear and Gina call my name, but I kept on going towards the exit. My head was swimming and I felt sick. This could possibly be the worst day of my life. Except for . . . I pushed thoughts of Callum away. I wasn't going to let him intrude. Not today.

I ran through the car park, down the path and back to the car. But before I'd even unlocked it a text came through from Lia.

Get back to the cafe asap. It's all kicking off!!!

I walked into the café a few minutes later to find quite a crowd gathered round Stanley's usual spot. Doreen was back, Juliet was here too, Lia was feeding Arlo in his high chair and Mum and Dad were assembling a tray with champagne flutes and an ice bucket. Stanley was in his armchair and Nonna was fidgeting opposite him.

'Ah!' Stanley beamed when he spotted me. 'Good. We're all here.'

Juliet narrowed her eyes when I squeezed in between her and Doreen. 'You look shite.'

'Thanks,' I muttered. 'What's going on? Because the last thing I feel like doing is celebrating.'

'What all this about, Stanley, eh?' Nonna cried. 'You won the lottery or what?'

'Patience, my dear lady, patience,' he chuckled.

Nonna took Stanley's glasses off his face and polished them on a napkin. 'What you clean these with?' she tutted, looking through the lenses. 'Olive oil?'

Stanley put his glasses back on and took a deep breath. 'You look even more beautiful now.'

She pretended to tut again and batted her eyelashes.

'Now then. Alec,' said Stanley, 'would you mind? My grip isn't as firm as it was.'

He nodded towards the champagne bottle and Dad dutifully tore the foil off and began untwisting the wire.

'What's going on?' I murmured to Mum, but she shrugged.

'Stanley came to see me this morning and asked me to arrange all this,' she whispered. 'That's all I know.'

Stanley cleared his throat and took Nonna's hand.

'Over the past few weeks, Maria, you and I have become much closer and I've come to realize that the best moments of my day are the ones I spend with you. And I'd like more of those moments.'

'I'd like that too. But,' she lowered her voice to a stage whisper, 'do we have to do it in front of all my family?'

'I am honoured to call you my special lady,' Stanley continued.

'Okey cokey.' She smiled self-consciously. 'And I call you my special man.'

'Cork primed and ready to pop,' said Dad, setting the bottle back on the table.

'Rightio,' said Stanley in a wobbly voice.

He released his hand from Nonna's and, grasping the edge of the table for support, he slid forward on his chair until his knees were touching hers. And then in a move remarkably agile for a man of his age, he whipped a small velvet box from his blazer pocket and dropped down on to one knee.

'Maria Carloni . . .' Slowly and carefully he lifted the lid of the little box to reveal a diamond ring. Nonna's eyes widened to the size of tennis balls. 'Will you marry me?'

Mum and Lia gasped. We all looked at Nonna and I clapped a hand over my mouth as my eyes filled with tears. What a perfect end to a terrible day.

Dad picked up the champagne bottle, waiting for the word to pop the cork. Mum was clutching her chest, tears of happiness bulging in her eyes. Lia's hand froze in mid-air on its way to Arlo's mouth and Juliet and Doreen, in a rare moment of solidarity, reached for each other's hands.

The colour drained from Nonna's face.

'Maria?' Stanley prompted.

'What you do that for?' she said hoarsely. 'I already say you can sleep over.'

I heard Juliet stifle a snort.

Stanley blinked at her, glanced over his shoulder at us and

then said quietly, 'I have too much respect for you, my dear. I'd rather wait until after we are married.'

'*Santo cielo*,' she muttered. 'No, no, no.'

'Oh dear.' Stanley's chin dropped to his chest. He levered himself up and Dad offered him a steadying arm to help him back into his chair.

Nonna wiped her eyes and sat up straight.

'Stanley,' she said, looking down at her hands, 'I am very sorry but I cannot marry you.'

Dad crept away from the table with the champagne and put it out of sight. Doreen and Juliet clung to each other, shocked into silence.

Poor Stanley. His face was beetroot red and he looked dangerously close to tears.

'I've rushed you,' he blustered, slipping the ring box back into his pocket. 'My own silly fault. Getting carried away at my age.'

'Wait.' Nonna held up a hand. 'I cannot marry you because . . .' She turned to Mum and a single tear ran down her wrinkled face. 'Because I think I still married.'

'Good grief.' Stanley pressed himself flat against the back of his chair.

'What?' Mum gasped. 'My father is still alive?'

'Nonna,' I said, trying to stay calm, 'Lorenzo is alive?'

'No. Lorenzo is dead.' She covered her face with her hands. 'He not my husband.'

'Bloody hell,' muttered Mum, who'd gone completely pale. Dad shoved his way round the table and took her in his arms.

Nonna took a deep breath. 'And I not Maria Carloni. Also I not from Naples. My name is Signora Maria Benedetto from Sorrento. I married to Marco.'

'Will somebody please tell me what the hell is going on?' said Lia, scooping Arlo from his high chair.

'The party is over,' Stanley said solemnly, blinking back tears from his pale blue eyes. 'Goodbye.'

'We'll be off too,' Doreen said, dragging Juliet with her towards the door. 'Come on, Stanley, we'll walk you home.'

The two women linked arms with Stanley and led the subdued old man from the café and across the village green. That left just us, the family, unsure quite who was who any more.

'I do love Stanley,' Nonna whispered hoarsely. 'Now is too late. I always leave it too late.'

My phone beeped with a text. It was a message from Gabe.

Rosie, are you OK? I'm worried about you. Are we still friends? Gabe xx

I closed my eyes for a second trying to conjure up his presence, his soft smile and lovely manly smell. What I'd give right now to feel his strong arms around me, pulling me into his chest, pressing kisses into my hair and telling me that whatever happened, he'd be right there at my side, every step of the way. I could have had that; like Nonna, I'd left it too late.

But did it have to be like this? Wasn't there something I could do?

'Nonna, we can sort this out,' I said urgently. 'We can find out if Marco is still alive. This doesn't have to be the end of you and Stanley.'

'Really?' Nonna's dark eyes searched mine. 'You help me?'

I nodded, looked down at the message on my phone and felt a flicker of hope. And perhaps it didn't have to be the end of Gabe and me either . . .

PART THREE

Tea and Sympathy

Chapter 21

I opened the front door of my cottage and drew in a sharp breath as a gust of wind tossed a confetti of shell-pink blossom from my cherry tree over my head and into the house. Poor tree; it was little more than a bare twig after the gales that had blown through the village last night. I crossed the threshold and peered down to the village and beyond. On a clear day, at the top of my steep hill above Barnaby, I could see right across the Derbyshire Dales. The sheer beauty of their rugged peaks, sweeping green valleys and tumbling navy streams could take my breath away. But today the view was hazy, and the weather, just like today's agenda, carried an unpredictability that made me shiver.

The morning air was cold, I noticed, as I picked up my pace downhill, colder than yesterday when Garden Warehouse had opened its door for the first time and pinched all our customers, tempting them with free drinks and copycat blueberry crumble cake. It was colder than Saturday too, the date of our Spring Fair, a day filled with sunshine and flowers, cakes and kisses (well, no kiss for me, but Nonna and Stanley had definitely kissed). When the people of Barnaby had come together as one happy community to celebrate all that was good about our village. That jollity was so far from the here and now, amongst my family at least, that it almost felt like a cruel joke.

Today the sun was missing in action. Instead, gloomy

clouds lumbered across the sky, tipping a month's worth of rain down on the hills approximately every hour, and Dales FM, the local radio station, was full of flood warnings and news about the latest road closures. The weather, however, was the least of my problems.

Funny how life can seem full of trials and tribulations one minute and then – whoosh – along comes something new to worry about and all those other niggles fade into the background.

Well, Nonna's revelation last night was that 'something new'.

And everything else had to wait. Because until our family got to the bottom of Nonna's secret life, none of us had the headspace to cope with anything else.

After Doreen and Juliet had escorted a rather bewildered Stanley back home yesterday, Mum, Dad, Lia and I had closed the café and listened as Nonna confirmed what she'd blurted out to Stanley. In 1964 in Sorrento, on the picturesque Italian Amalfi coast, she'd run off from her husband, Marco Benedetto, taking her baby and nothing more than a small case of belongings and had managed to deceive everyone, including her own family, that she was the widow of Lorenzo Carloni from Naples. And after she'd confessed a few scratchy details, she dissolved into such heart-rending sobs, joined to a lesser degree by the rest of us, that Mum, ashen-faced, had insisted on leaving it there for the day, driving her home and sitting with her until she fell asleep.

Dad had phoned me last night, worried about the effect this was going to have on Mum.

'She's grown up thinking she's Lorenzo's daughter, she's never even heard of this Marco chap. And running off from your husband like that and fleeing the country . . . Mum doesn't know what to think any more.'

Lia was the least fazed by the whole affair.

'Ancient history,' she'd said philosophically, as I'd bundled Arlo's pushchair into the back of her car, while she strapped him into his car seat. 'Mum is still Mum, finding out that a different man is your father after all doesn't alter who she is. At the end of the day, what does it really change? Does it actually matter?'

I'd pointed out that if Marco was still alive, Arlo was now in possession of a great-grandfather and Mum, quite understandably, might like to meet him. At which point it occurred to us both that tracking down Signore Benedetto should be priority *numero uno*.

I also privately thought that the real changes would come when we, as a family, got to the bottom of the reason for all this subterfuge. And that was the plan for this morning. Ed couldn't make it as he was in the middle of moving his dad's company to new premises, but Dad was bringing Mum and Nonna to the café and we'd asked both Doreen and Juliet to work the morning shift between them, while Nonna picked up her tale from where she'd left it last night.

I slowed as I rounded the corner past the churchyard and raised a hand to Clementine and Tyson, who were already hard at work chopping back the climbing roses.

'Might pop into the café later,' Clementine called, waving her secateurs at me. She was wearing mud-caked old boots, a pair of scruffy dungarees and a waxed wide-brimmed hat. But beneath the brim, her smile was unmistakable, and lovely to see.

I dithered at the iron railings which circled the church grounds, not really in the mood for small talk.

'For our first board meeting.' Tyson's proud face appeared between the thorny branches.

Clementine rolled her eyes good-naturedly. 'For cappuccinos, I was going to say. You know,' she looked around amongst the gravestones furtively, 'to make up for yesterday.'

'No need,' I said flatly.

She raised an eyebrow questioningly.

I lowered my eyes and attacked a patch of moss with the toe of my shoe. Almost impossible to believe that less than twenty-four hours had passed since I'd parked on her drive and ranted about Garden Warehouse's invasion of her personal space and the underhand tactics of their catering team.

'There's every need,' Clementine insisted, rubbing her pointy nose with a gloved hand. 'I haven't even thanked everyone for their help on Saturday yet. Do you know the plant sale raised over two thousand pounds? Stella Derry appeared at the crack of dawn this morning with a big tin of cash.'

'Oh.' I shuffled my feet, anxious to get on before she asked me any questions that I wasn't ready to answer like: *How's your nonna?* Or should that be: *Who's your nonna?* 'Good.'

'Good?' Tyson and Clementine retorted in unison.

'It's fan-bloody-tastic,' Tyson corrected. 'We're going to buy one of those whopping great petrol hedge trimmers, aren't we, partner?' His eyes glinted.

'*Clementine.* And yes.'

'Great,' I said weakly, forcing a smile, wondering why on earth we'd thought that airing our dirty linen at the café was a good idea when customers were likely to be in and out. 'See you later.'

I continued on briskly, over the village green, along the main street, past the school until the houses began to thin out, making sure to avoid further conversation with my purposeful stride.

Five minutes later I was stamping my feet to keep my circulation flowing outside a bungalow, tucked away at the very edge of the village.

I glanced down at the scrap of paper which Nonna had given me to check I'd got the right place. I had. Not that there was any doubt that this was Stanley's bungalow in amongst a cul-de-sac of similar properties. The neat little front garden with a freshly mown square of lawn edged with a narrow border of perfectly symmetrical tulips couldn't belong to anyone but him. There was even a genuine red Royal Mail postbox on display in the garden.

I blew on my frozen fingers and gave the door one last hammering. I'd already knocked and rung the doorbell several times but Stanley hadn't answered and I was at the point of walking away and abandoning my quest when I heard a faint scraping sound coming from the hallway.

I bent down to the letterbox, forced it open and caught a glimpse of a rough brown doormat.

'Stanley? Please open up. It's Rosie.'

Quick as a flash, a small face with two bright black eyes leapt up at the door from the inside and I fell backwards with a yelp.

'Crystal! Bad girl!' Stanley opened the door instantly and scooped the poodle under his arm. 'I do apologize; my neighbour hasn't taught his dog any manners at all. Are you all right?'

He helped me to my feet, which wasn't easy given that Crystal was trying to corkscrew her way free from his grasp.

'I'm fine,' I said, giving Crystal a rub behind her ears. I eyed Stanley closely. 'Are you?'

He wasn't his usual dapper self – that was immediately evident. His skin had a yellowy pallor as if he hadn't had much sleep last night. His fringe of white hair was standing to attention at the back of his head, there were crumbs in his beard and his cardigan buttons were all askew. He had a napkin tucked into his shirt collar.

Stanley took a deep breath. 'I will be. And how . . . how's Maria?'

'Worried, exhausted and totally mortified to have caused anybody any pain.'

A blotchy blush crept from the collar of his checked shirt to the crown of his head, his Adam's apple bobbed up and down a couple of times, but he didn't speak.

I gave him a sad smile. 'Part of her is relieved to be getting things out in the open and the other is terrified that she's alienated everyone she loves. I've told her not to worry about that.' I met his gaze. 'We'll love her whatever she has to say. Won't we?'

The question hovered in the air between us like a rain-cloud. I covered his hand with mine and I was pleased when he didn't pull away. He tightened his grip on the dog and she panted in my face, resting her front paws on my arm so that we were all connected in an odd trinity.

'I've only asked one woman to marry me before yesterday,' said Stanley in a considered voice. 'So I wouldn't claim to be the most experienced in these matters, but finding out that the lady you've been courting was already married must go down as one of the more unsuccessful proposals of all time. And because of my desire to make a public declaration of my intentions towards her, I've caused untold damage to your family.'

He hadn't said that he loved her; I thought my heart would break. Once again it struck me how fickle love is; our emotions can waver even within a day.

'None of that is your doing,' I said sadly. 'None at all.'

Stanley shot me a look that implied that he begged to differ. A sudden icy blast of wind whipped round us, making my eyes water and Crystal's ears flap.

'Come on in,' he mumbled and turned back to the house. I followed and closed the door behind us.

The hallway was small and square with a worn wooden floor and cream painted walls. A neat collection of jackets hung from pegs on the wall, below which was a shoe rack filled with a row of perfectly buffed brogues and a slightly muddier pair of walking boots. A side table held an avocado-green telephone with a tangled cable, a photograph of an unsmiling couple in their early forties with two dark-haired, freckly children and a brass vase filled with silk flowers that had seen better days. The air in the bungalow smelled musty and stale and Stanley's loneliness touched me like a physical presence.

Crystal trotted over and sat on my feet and Stanley clasped

his hands in front of him and waited. This new stilted Stanley was so unlike the man I was so fond of that my heart ached for him.

'Nonna is still the same woman,' I said gently. 'And she cares about you very much.'

He tilted his chin and aimed his gaze at a point somewhere above my head.

'One of the answers in my crossword this morning was "hoodwinked".'

'Oh Stanley,' I murmured.

He blinked rapidly and smoothed a hand down the front of his cardigan. 'And that's just how I feel. Hoodwinked. She led me to believe that she was a free agent.'

'And she is,' I said. 'She is. Almost certainly.'

While Ed had taken Arlo up for his bath and bedtime story last night, Lia and I had sat on their sofa with her laptop and spent a couple of hours doing a bit of digging on the internet and although we couldn't be absolutely one hundred per cent certain, we had found details of a man called Marco Benedetto born in 1939, who died in 1997 and was buried in a Sorrento cemetery.

Stanley's eyebrows twitched. 'Maria seemed very unsure about that last night.'

'I know, I know,' I soothed, 'and we are going to get to the bottom of everything today. Right now, in fact. And she'd very much like you to be there. You're part of this family now. Whether you like it or not.'

I smiled, hoping he'd smile back, but he simply dropped his gaze to his slippers.

Actually, Nonna hadn't said she'd like Stanley there – she'd just asked me to check on him – but I felt sure she would. Besides, I wanted to include him. Nonna had her family supporting her (although it had to be said Mum was being a bit restrained with her affection) and we all had each other. But Stanley had no one to turn to and he deserved to hear the truth as much as we did.

Crystal yawned and swapped allegiance to Stanley's feet, leaning up against his shins.

'You can bring her too?' I said.

'I don't think so,' Stanley said gruffly, bending down to scoop the dog up into his arms. 'I'd rather steer clear of the café today. I'd thought that this was a new start for me. It took me a long time to pluck up the courage to ask Maria to become more than just friends. It's no fun getting old, you know, half your friends are dead, and the other half are mostly doolally. But not Maria, she has a spark in her that has made me feel young again. Now I realize I didn't really know her at all. Has anything she's ever said to me been the truth, I wonder?'

'I don't have all the details yet myself. But I know my grandmother and she doesn't have a bad bone in her body. I think that if she felt the need to hide the truth from her family, she did so for a good reason.'

'But if you let secrets fester,' he said, shaking his head, 'it can only bring you unhappiness.'

I felt a pang of sorrow at his words.

'Believe me, I know. I know that more than anyone.' I shrugged helplessly and hoped he didn't notice the tear that had sprung to my own eye. 'So what shall I tell her?'

I held my breath while he scratched his beard.

'Tell her . . .' His eyes softened. 'Tell her that there are no hard feelings. Life is too short to harbour those. Anyway,' he laughed softly, 'these past few weeks have been the happiest time I've had for years and I will always be grateful for that. When the air has cleared, if she still wants someone to keep her company, then I'll be waiting. And I promise never to propose to her again.'

It was the best I could hope for under the circumstances. I darted towards him for a quick hug, half expecting him to leap back and shut the door in my face. But instead he leaned against me, patted me on the back and gave a shuddering sigh before releasing me and smiling bravely as I waved and told him I'd be back to visit him soon.

Nonna had been super-cautious about letting a man into her life and now it was obvious why. But after more than fifty years of being alone, she had chosen Stanley to open her heart to. That had to mean something; it had to mean their gentle love was worth saving.

And that was exactly what I intended to do.

Chapter 22

By the time I reached the door to the café it had started to rain heavily but before I had the chance to escape the downpour, I heard a voice call my name. It was Gina. The sight of her made my heart pound as I recalled the shock of seeing her with Gabe yesterday at Garden Warehouse.

She was coming out of Ken's Mini Mart in full-on child-minding mode, pushing a double buggy containing a snoozing baby and a little girl under a plastic rain cover. Two sturdy boys clung on to the sides. All of them were wearing wellies and enormous raincoats, including Gina. She steered her little party towards me as the two bigger boys did their utmost to stamp in every drop of water and I stepped back to escape their splashes, plastering on a smile.

'Disaster!' she said cheerily, from underneath a bright yellow hood. 'Ken says he's fresh out of stale bread.'

'Quack, quack,' cried the little girl from the pushchair. 'Quack, quack, quack.'

The boys joined in with her, getting louder and louder and more and more splashy with their feet.

Gina gave me a helpless look and we both laughed.

'Let me guess, you're going to feed the ducks.'

'Correct.' She took off her glasses and tried to dry the lenses on a damp tissue.

'And paddle in puddles!' added one of the boys gleefully.

'Still bonkers, then,' I said with a pointed look at the charcoal sky.

Gina rolled her eyes heavenwards. 'I'd be even more bonkers after a day shut inside with this lot. Believe it or not they find the water calming.'

I had a sudden flashback to mine and Gabe's night stargazing, the only sounds coming from the gentle lapping of the river against the hull of the boat and the distant cooing of a wood pigeon. That had been calming. Until Noah had thrust his cheeky face between us. I felt a rush of affection towards the pair of them and grinned at Gina's two charges.

'I can believe that. Actually,' I said, remembering all the bread we hadn't sold yesterday, 'we can probably help you out. Come in.'

'With this?' She waggled the double buggy to demonstrate its girth. 'Easier not to.'

I left them outside singing a lively version of 'Five Little Ducks Went Swimming One Day', which didn't sound in the least calm to me, while I fetched them some bread.

'This is tough stuff,' I said, handing over a bag of rolls to each of the boys. 'Hit a duck on the head with one of these bad boys and you'll knock it out.'

Gina groaned. 'Don't give them any ideas. Thank you for that, though, you're a lifesaver.'

'Good luck with the calming.' I smiled and turned to go but hesitated. I had to mention it . . . 'You and Gabe looked like you were having fun yesterday?'

She smiled. 'He came over to talk about some childminding, but I'm swamped at the moment, felt really bad about it. Nice guy.' She cocked an eyebrow under her soggy hood. 'Even offered to come and buy plants with me. It's a nightmare trying to get big stuff home without a car.'

My heart zipped about joyously. 'There was me thinking that you and him . . . ?'

She smoothed a strand of pink hair out of her eye and

tucked it into her hood. 'Chance'd be a fine thing. Anyway, you looked upset, you OK?'

'Not really.' I pulled a face. Understatement of the century.

'Come on, Gina,' said one of the boys, tapping at her sleeve.

'I'd better go.' Gina smiled. 'Oh good news, I nearly forgot. Tell Gabe I can do Friday now; I've had a cancellation. I missed him at the school gates this morning. Don't eat it all.'

This last comment was aimed at the boys, whose small jaws were valiantly trying to make a dent in yesterday's bread. I reached into one of the bags and tore a roll in three, passing the smallest piece inside the rain cover to the little girl.

'Friday?' I frowned.

'Babysitting,' she said. 'He's taking someone important for dinner, apparently.'

My heart double-dinged like a target in a pinball machine; it was the first I'd heard of it. Perhaps he'd met someone he liked at the school gates after all.

'Sure,' I said, intrigued. 'If I see him, I'll be sure to pass the message on.'

Inside, I breathed in the warmth and welcome of our little café and cast a proud eye over our newly polished tables, the pots of fragrant herbs, the vibrant Italian crockery gleaming on Nonna's old dresser and the framed posters adorning what little wall space we had either side of the counter. The old chalk blackboard declared our soup of the day to be a warming tomato and basil and the smell of freshly baked banana muffins wafted through the air enticingly as Juliet transferred them from the cooling rack to the cake stand.

I was glad we were meeting here after all. The comforting surroundings of the café gave a semblance of normality to what could possibly be the most abnormal day our family had ever encountered.

Someone had made a sort of barrier with the lemon trees across the entrance to the conservatory to offer us some privacy and I pushed my way through.

I was the last to arrive, although I'd already shouted my hellos when I collected the bread. Dad had his arm around the back of Mum's chair. She was shredding a napkin into a million pieces, Lia was uploading a picture of Juliet's fresh muffins to the café's Instagram page and Nonna was fussing with a watering can round the lemon trees.

'Sorry, everyone,' I said, hanging my coat over the back of a chair. I kissed everyone before sitting down next to Lia. 'No Arlo?'

Lia pointed to the toy corner where my nephew was holding court on a play mat with two other little ones. 'Over there with Naomi, the twins' mother. Socializing.'

The café didn't have quite the same *Marie Celeste* air to it today, although it was still quieter than usual. Doreen was in the kitchen cooking breakfasts and Juliet was serving the vicar with his usual Tuesday order. But Stanley's chair looked very empty without him.

Nonna let out a sigh before sitting down between Mum and Lia. 'How's poor Stanley? What he say?'

She looked every day of her seventy-five years today: her white hair wasn't as neatly coiled into its bun as normal and her eyes were dull and tired.

'He said you make him feel young and he looks forward to keeping you company again soon.'

'That so sweet.' She sighed, pressing a hand to her chest. 'After everything I done to him.'

'But first things first,' said Mum, taking Nonna's hand. 'We need to know if Marco is still alive.'

Nonna looked down at her lap. 'I know, I know. I should never have led Stanley on like that without knowing.'

Mum took a deep breath and I could see she was fighting to keep her temper under control.

'Not just because of that, Mamma,' she said, withdrawing

her hand. 'If my father is alive, I'd quite like to meet him, if that's all right with you?'

I looked at Lia and pulled a face. I didn't think there was much chance of that.

Nonna's chin wobbled. 'Oh Luisa, *cara*, what a mess.'

Dad's arm slid to Mum's shoulders and she leaned against him heavily.

Lia looked at me as if to say 'you're the eldest' and began to examine her fingernails.

'We think we may have the answer to that,' I said and outlined what Lia and I had discovered on the internet last night.

'It could be him,' said Nonna, her hand fluttering up to her neck. She twisted a gold crucifix round in her shaking fingers. 'He was two years older than me.'

'So I'll never know him now,' said Mum flatly. She pulled a tissue from her sleeve and dabbed at her eyes.

Nonna drew herself up tall and met her daughter's eye. 'Then you are lucky, lucky girl. That man was dicky head. Worse. He was *evil*. I know you angry now, but he was. And if he is dead, I not sad. Not at all.'

The feisty old lady I knew and loved was back.

'Tell us why, Nonna,' I urged. 'Tell us what happened.'

Nonna looked at me gratefully. 'I lie awake last night, thinking, thinking, thinking. How to make you understand what it is like for me, why I do what I do, where to start my story. It not easy.'

'How about starting with breakfast,' said Doreen from behind the waxy leaves of the potted lemon trees. She pushed her plump bottom through and set a tray of bacon sandwiches on the table. 'I bet none of you has eaten.'

She was right, I hadn't been hungry earlier. My mouth watered.

'Doreen, you're a marvel,' said Dad, picking one up and chomping straight into it.

She went pink and her cheeks dimpled.

'And as you know this is proper Derbyshire bacon.' She flicked her plait over her shoulders. 'Not like the stuff they serve up at Garden Warehouse, all fat and gristle.'

'Tea up!' Juliet called, her wiry frame also backing through the greenery.

Mum made room for a second tray and both Doreen and Juliet hovered while we helped ourselves to mugs of tea and bacon sandwiches and showered them with gratitude.

Nonna took a couple of mouthfuls and pushed her plate aside.

'Why don't you start at the beginning, Nonna?' I suggested. 'We know so little about your life back in Italy.'

Because whenever we asked you about it, you always changed the subject . . .

'And what we thought we knew, we actually don't,' Mum added, nostrils flaring.

Lia widened her eyes. 'What about . . . ?' She jerked her head towards Doreen and Juliet who seemed to be stacking the empty plates in slow motion.

Nonna lifted a shoulder. 'I have no secrets from my staff.'

Dad cleared his throat.

'Well, no more than from anyone else,' Nonna muttered, folding her arms.

'Hello? Anyone serving?' called a familiar voice from the counter. 'Ooh, hello? Am I missing something?'

The makeshift barrier of potted lemon trees was no match for Stella Derry's nosiness and her beady eyes darted round us all.

'Yeah, your invite.' Juliet scowled at her and marched her back through to the café. 'Tea?'

'Well!' said Stella, adding resignedly, 'Earl Grey, please.'

Doreen glanced at her colleague's retreating back and nibbled her lip.

'We, Juliet and me, well, we wanted to say that we understand that things are a bit tricky, so don't worry about the café. We'll manage it between us.'

'True that,' Juliet agreed gruffly, rejoining us after dispensing the fastest pot of tea in history. 'This is a proper family business in every sense of the word. The way you rally round to support each other—'

'Yes, like when Rosie stepped in to help here even though she thought the job was beneath her,' said Doreen with a ghost of a smile.

I opened my mouth to argue but Juliet ploughed on.

'Aye, and when you all went to watch Alec sing Dolly Parton songs.'

'In a dress and heels.' Doreen's eyebrow lifted a fraction.

'When he had his midlife crisis.'

Dad ran a finger round his collar. 'I wouldn't go that far.'

'And you all let Lia take over the kitchen for hours using every utensil we own just to make one pot of soup,' Juliet added innocently.

Lia frowned. 'Not *hours*.'

I didn't look at her. Three to be exact.

'And that's what makes this family special. We feel privileged to be part of it, don't we, Juliet?' said Doreen, looping her arm through her colleague's.

'Aye. Now, every family has a story to tell, I reckon,' she said, checking we all still had tea in our mugs. 'And we're going to leave you to tell yours.'

The two of them disappeared back through the branches to the counter without another word and for a moment we were all silent. It was the longest speech they'd ever made without bickering and certainly the most heartfelt.

I looked at the faces I loved most in the world and felt my throat tighten; this family *was* special and whatever it was that Nonna had to tell us, that would never change.

'Mamma?' Mum said calmly. 'Rosie's right, I think you should start at the very beginning.'

'OK.' Nonna took a sip of her tea and set the mug carefully on a coaster while she gathered her thoughts. 'I was born in Sorrento in nineteen forty-one. My mother was

Isabella and my father was Salvatore De Rosa, Sav for short. My brother was older than me, he is Sav too. We live in apartment over the family business.'

'A café?' Lia asked.

Nonna shook her head. 'A bar called Bar Salvatore.'

Dad chuckled.

She caught his eye and her lips twitched. 'My family like that name. Papà worked hard – too hard – and died suddenly when I was only young. Mamma took over until Sav left school. Then, of course, he run it because he is *man* of the family.'

Nonna told us about growing up in the pretty town of Sorrento: diving off the rocks and swimming in an emerald Mediterranean Sea, watching the fishermen bring in their fresh catch at the Marina Grande, playing in the narrow streets around the Piazza Tasso when the square filled up with people dancing and drinking during festivals throughout the year. And, of course, the lemon groves which she had always hinted at but had never wanted to discuss until now.

'When I sixteen,' Nonna began, 'I leave school and start to work in the bar. I cook and clean and waitress. Sav was in charge. He did as little as possible.'

'If I ever have another baby and it's a girl,' said Lia, folding her arms, 'they'll be treated exactly the same.'

'Hear, hear,' I murmured.

'Every day, I meet my girlfriends in the lemon grove in the middle of Sorrento. We sit in shade, talk about boys and escape our mothers and our jobs for an hour. Our little bit of freedom.'

I gazed at Nonna, transfixed. The sounds and smells of the café behind me disappeared and I found myself transported to 1950s Italy and inside the head of a sixteen-year-old girl, on the cusp of falling in love . . .

One baking hot day when the air was thick and still, Maria was sitting with her friends, talking and drinking lemonade as usual in the lemon grove, when suddenly there was a cry as a ladder, which had been leaning against a nearby tree slipped, a pair of legs appeared amongst the branches and a wooden crate of lemons came crashing to the ground. The legs belonged to a boy who landed with a thud at the girls' feet. Her friends laughed as the lemons rolled everywhere and the boy darted left and right to collect them but Maria didn't laugh. She stared. She had never seen such a beautiful face in her life. His eyes were so dark, they were nearly black, he had wild curly hair and a strong proud nose and when he smiled at her, her heart . . . well, it was like having a choir of angels singing inside her head. She jumped to her feet and helped him pick up the rest of the lemons.

The boy introduced himself as Lorenzo Carloni and asked if he could walk her home when he finished work. Maria, scarcely able to string a sentence together with nerves, said yes.

After that they barely spent a day apart. Maria was in love. And for a reason she never understood, Lorenzo loved Maria fiercely too. He was only two years older than her but he had seen so much more life. He was loud and boisterous and made friends everywhere he went. He had nothing: no family, no home, no one. His mother and father were already dead and his grandmother had brought him up in a poor part of Naples. When she died, he travelled to Sorrento to earn a living and got work picking lemons. It didn't pay much but it was a job and Lorenzo was grateful for what he had.

Maria was besotted. It was as if she had been living in a world of black and white before and now it was in colour, like the movies. The sun always shone when Lorenzo was around. Her mother liked him too. He lived in a shared room in a boarding house, but he began to spend all his time with Maria's family. Lorenzo's dream was to escape the poverty of post-war southern Italy. He told Maria stories of

234

men he knew who had got work and a free passage to England. Lorenzo and Maria made plans to go as soon as they were married, but Maria's mother said she wasn't allowed to marry until she was eighteen. So until then, both of them saved up what little money they had ready to build their new life together. The weeks before her eighteenth birthday, they talked of little else. When the day finally came, she waited for Lorenzo. He'd promised to come after work and said he'd have a special birthday present for her. She was sure it would be a ring.

She giggled with her friends all afternoon, doing her hair and dressing in her best clothes; she was so excited to see him. By nightfall, he hadn't come. Nor had he sent a message. At midnight still nothing. Maria went to bed worried and uneasy; it wasn't like him to let her down.

In the morning, the police arrived. Lorenzo was dead. He had been robbed and stabbed, dying instantly in an alley behind the cathedral. Maria was beyond devastated. The light in her heart went out and with it all her hopes and dreams of marrying the love of her life. She barely left her bed for a month. Sav went back many times for her to ask the police if they had discovered who had killed him. But they never found out. The police told Sav that the last person to see him was the owner of a jewellery shop and that the thief must have been watching him. Maria dragged herself from her bed to talk to him, desperate to find out about Lorenzo's last movements. The jeweller confirmed that Lorenzo had been planning to propose to Maria that night. The jeweller showed her an identical ring to the one Lorenzo had chosen. It was gold and set with two tiny diamonds — one for each year he had loved her. Maria broke down in tears and the jeweller was so affected by her grief that he gave it to her to keep.

'But I could not bring myself to wear it.' Nonna sighed. 'Lorenzo bought me a ring and it cost him his life. I never really get over that.'

'Nonna,' Lia wiped her eyes, 'that story breaks my heart. Why aren't you more upset?'

The old lady patted her hand. 'This happen nearly sixty years ago, *cara*. And in my head, I already tell it a thousand times.'

'Then why not tell it to me, Mamma?' Mum demanded, raking both hands through her hair.

'And why keep it a secret?' I asked, sipping the last of my cold tea. 'It doesn't make sense. You didn't do anything wrong.'

'I must say, Maria,' said Dad, his brow creasing in confusion, 'it's a terribly sad tale, but he was just your first love, what has all this got to do with Marco Benedetto?'

'Because Lorenzo taught me how to love.' Nonna's features turned to stone. 'And then Marco taught me never to let a man into my heart again.'

Beads of perspiration formed along my forehead and my heart began to pound. I'd learned that lesson too. I prayed to God that she hadn't learned it the same way as I had.

'Coffee this time?' Doreen smiled sweetly, plonking a tray of coffee and almond biscuits on the table.

I let out the breath I didn't realize I'd been holding.

'Thank you,' I said shakily. 'And Doreen? You'd better find the limoncello.'

She pursed her lips. 'That bad?'

'Worse,' said Nonna blackly.

Chapter 23

Over coffee, and limoncello for Nonna, she told us that as far as she was concerned, from the age of eighteen, she *was* Maria Carloni – Lorenzo's widow. She had his ring, or at least one like it, she knew he had loved her and in her heart she was as good as married. And although her future plans were shattered, she was thankful for all the happy times they had had. So for the next few years, she simply carried on with her life; she watched her friends marry and have babies. But for her there was no one else, she wasn't interested in sharing her life with a man who wasn't Lorenzo. She lived with her mother, she worked in the bar and tried to bring in new customers, to make people feel welcome in Bar Salvatore, just like when her father had been alive.

Throughout Nonna's story, she kept her chin up, showing me every inch of the proud young woman she would have been all those years ago.

'I can't imagine anything keeping you down for too long,' I said, pouring us all a top-up.

'That's true, Mamma,' said Mum. 'You have always been a very determined woman.'

'Lia?' Juliet appeared holding Arlo at arm's length in front of her. He was kicking his legs and looking very pleased with himself. 'Naomi and the twins are ready to go and I think Arlo might need a change.'

Lia stood up, waved to the twins' mum and shouted her

thanks. Taking Arlo from Juliet, she caught a whiff of her offspring.

'Oh poo.' She pouted. 'Now I'm going to miss the story.'

I handed her Arlo's changing bag and winced at the smell. 'I'd offer to do it, but . . . No, actually, that's a lie.'

Nonna's face had gone a peculiar colour. 'We come to part of the story which isn't for the children's ears. Or yours, Alec.'

Lia tutted. 'Arlo isn't going to understand.'

'I meant you and Rosanna. I'm gonna talk about sex.'

Mum swallowed hard.

Dad sprang to his feet and slipped his arms into his anorak. 'I might stroll over to Ken's for a pork pie.'

Part of me wanted to laugh at being referred to as a child. I was thirty-two. The other part couldn't leave the table quick enough.

'Wait for me, Dad.'

After Dad and I had dodged the puddles fetching him two mini pork pies, I spent the next fifteen minutes making myself useful, collecting empty mugs, loading the dishwasher and making toasties. Lia and Dad took Arlo out in his pushchair to get him to sleep and I kept sneaking looks at Mum and Nonna, trying to guess what was going on.

They were sitting together, hands joined on the table, heads almost touching and at one point I spotted Nonna dabbing Mum's tears away with a tissue. My heart went out to the pair of them.

I made up my mind: I was going back in, sex or no sex. I had to know what Marco had done to Nonna. But before I had the chance to act on my decision, Verity phoned me.

'Just taking a break from watching Tom teach the Sushi for Beginners course,' she giggled. 'I shouldn't laugh but a man who's been a right know-it-all the whole morning has just eaten a teaspoon of wasabi paste and now he's making a noise like an elephant in labour.'

'Sounds painful.'

'There's always one,' she said pragmatically. 'He'll survive. Anyway, has that attractive blogger been back in, has he posted his article yet?'

'No he hasn't,' I said. 'Because he's not a blogger and he's barred. Permanently.'

I filled her in on the latest goings-on with Garden Warehouse, bogus blogger boy's blatant sabotage of the café's business, copying our menu and our current downturn in customer numbers.

'Keep the faith,' she said. 'That place has novelty value at the moment, that's all. Whereas the Lemon Tree Café has the Carloni family. And you don't get more authentic than that.'

Except that we were, in fact, *Benedettos* . . . But I couldn't tell Verity that. Nonna had asked us to keep it in the family for the moment.

I glanced at the mostly empty tables. 'I hope you're right. They're cheap and cheerful whereas we're just—'

I was about to say cheerful but at that moment Mum gasped and shouted 'Bloody HELL' as presumably Nonna filled her in on more details of her sex life than Mum had ever wanted to know and I couldn't imagine that she was feeling too cheerful at all.

I nearly leapt out of my seat when Doreen tapped my shoulder.

'Your mum's calling for you, love.'

'Hang on, Verity, I'll just see what Mum wants.'

I walked through to the conservatory to find Nonna's head buried in Mum's neck. Mum rocked her back and forth making shushing noises against Nonna's white hair as she wept.

I lifted the phone to my ear to tell Verity I'd call her back later but the look on Mum's face stopped me in my tracks.

'Mum? What is it?'

Her eyes burned with fury. 'That monster, Marco. He

killed my twin brother and could have killed your nonna and me too.'

My jaw dropped. 'Your *twin*?'

She nodded tersely. 'I had a brother, Gennaro. But my father, Marco,' she spat his name out through gritted teeth, 'made sure he never even got to take his first breath.'

'Oh my God.'

- My skin prickled with goosebumps. I wrapped my arms round her and Nonna. Mum looked up to the ceiling and I could see she was trying to be strong.

'It gets worse. He forced himself on her.'

Blood rushed to my head. No. Not Nonna.

'I'm sorry, Luisa,' Nonna wept.

My stomach twisted; she had nothing to apologize for.

Mum lowered her voice. 'Mamma was attacked by Marco Benedetto. He got her pregnant and her family made her marry him. And she has been keeping this secret all my life.'

I was barely aware of my movements as I jumped up, stumbled backwards into the branches of a lemon tree and ran out of the café. I stood on the pavement letting the rain wash over me, my heart pounding fiercely in my chest.

'Hello? Rosie? Are you there?'

I looked down to see my phone in my hands. Verity was still on the line.

'What's going on?'

'Nonna was raped too,' I blurted out, wiping the rain from my face.

'OH MY GOD. Who would do that to an old lady?'

'No. Not recently. When she was . . . I don't know, early twenties, I guess,' I corrected her.

My entire body was trembling: legs on the verge of collapse; hands shaking so much I could barely hold the phone to my ear.

'Jesus. Even so. Poor thing. I can't imagine – wait, you said "too"?'

240

For a moment I didn't understand what she meant. 'What?'

'You said Nonna was raped *too*? Who else, Rosie?'

My lungs felt as if they'd been jammed in a vice; I couldn't breathe. I gulped at the air, desperate for oxygen. Across the street on the village green was a bench. I'd go over and sit, regardless of the rain. I stepped off the pavement blindly between two parked cars.

'Forget it,' I said. 'Forget I said anything.'

I didn't see the van approach. It drove straight through a big puddle and a huge plume of water from the cobbled street hit my lower half.

'Oh my God, it's you. It happened to you too, didn't it?' Verity said with a gasp.

'I have to go.' I glanced down at my wet jeans.

'Is this something to do with Callum? Is that why—'

But it was too late; I'd hung up.

Chapter 24

The rain was hammering down, lashing against the café's windows and bouncing off the pavement, and the drains at the edge of the road were gurgling as they struggled to cope with the volume of water. My clothes were plastered to my skin but I was rooted to the spot. Besides, I didn't care about the rain; it disguised my tears. Out of the corner of my eye I saw Dad and Lia huddling in the doorway of the pet shop. Dad was waving to me and Lia was laughing and shouting something about a drowned rat.

The van skidded to a halt and the driver jumped out and slammed the door. Someone shouted my name.

Memories that had been packed tightly away where they couldn't hurt me were thrashing around in my brain, making a bid for freedom, and I pressed my hands to my head, trying to keep them in.

I'd never named it. I'd been shocked and then angry, incredibly angry. But I'd never named it. Until now.

Nonna was raped too.

Gabe was at my side, holding something over our heads to shield us from the rain. It smelled of wood shavings and oil and showered me with sawdust. I stared blindly up at him. My mouth was dry and my tongue felt numb.

'Rosie.' Gabe ran a hand through his hair. 'I'm so sorry, I couldn't stop.'

'That's what he said,' I said with a harsh laugh. I sniffed back my tears.

His brow furrowed. 'Are you all right? You don't look well.'

'Shock.'

'Right. You're soaked. My fault. Oh God,' he stared at my hair, 'now I've covered you with sawdust too. Come on, let's get you inside before your hair turns to papier mâché.'

He nudged me towards the door of the café, but I wouldn't budge.

'Not in there,' I said, shaking my head.

I didn't want anyone to see me like this. Couldn't face the questions. I swallowed hard to force down the lump in my throat.

'I'm not leaving you out here.' Gabe looked round, sizing up the options. 'My van?'

I shrugged, which he took as a 'yes', and he pulled me towards it, our feet splashing through the puddles. We got in and condensation began to gather on the windscreen.

Normally this would be my cue to make some sort of joke about us being so hot we steamed up the windows but not today.

'Your place or mine?' said Gabe, starting the engine.

I shot him a look and he flushed.

'I've never said that to a girl, I mean, woman before.' He gulped. 'And I didn't mean it like that now either.'

I thought about his big bed in his little cabin and felt my own face blushing. I stared out of the window.

'Mine,' I murmured.

The van started to move. We passed Dad and Lia with the pushchair. She was straining her neck to see through the misted windscreen, no doubt wondering what was going on.

'I don't know about you,' said Gabe in an attempt at jollity, 'I'm cold and wet and could do with a cuppa.'

No, I thought, turning away from him, *you don't know about me. Not at all.*

The drive to my cottage was so quick that the windscreen hadn't even cleared by the time we arrived. I kept a spare key in a bird feeder hanging off the cherry tree and I shook it to get it out.

'Aha, now I can break in,' Gabe grinned.

'I'll change my hiding spot,' I replied without thinking.

'I'd never actually break in,' he said, hurt.

I opened the door and let us in. 'I know. Sorry.'

'Nice place,' he said, looking round my little home. 'I love *The Neptune*, but there are times when it would be nice not to have to walk in single file or bang my knees on the bedroom wall when I get out of bed in the morning.'

'Thanks.' I stood in the centre of the living room and shivered.

'Better get you out of those wet things,' he said, taking a step towards me.

I jumped back. 'No way.'

Gabe looked mortified. He held his hands up. 'Of course not. Sorry. I'm out of practice. Only used to dealing with small boys. If Noah was here I'd peel his clothes off, wrap him up in a blanket in front of the fire and make him hot chocolate.'

I nearly sobbed; that sounded heavenly.

'I'd better . . . um.' I pointed upstairs.

'Right.' He rubbed a hand over his face and seemed surprised to find it wet. 'So what can I do to help?'

The way he was looking at me, so eager to please, so desperate to do and say the right thing, made my eyes feel hot. I turned and ran up the stairs before he could see me cry.

'Hot chocolate and a fire please,' I said in a wobbly voice.

When I came back down, Gabe had lit the fire and was stirring a pan like mad with one hand and rubbing his hair dry with my kitchen towel with the other. It was so lovely to have another person here looking after me that my breath caught in my throat.

Not that I wasn't perfectly capable of looking after myself. I sneaked another glance at him. But once in a while didn't hurt . . .

I knelt as close to the fire as I could get, added some more kindling and let the flames warm my bones.

'One hot chocolate.' He handed me a dripping mug covered in a mountain of cream. 'Noah once asked for the best hot chocolate in the world, I googled exactly that and now I've made him this recipe so many times I'm an expert.'

'And so modest with it,' I said, smiling.

He looked relieved to see my improved mood and sat down with his own mug perched on the edge of the armchair.

I sipped at it. It was thick and sweet like pure melted chocolate and completely delicious.

'Oh my.' I licked my lips. 'Thank you. *That* is better than s—'

The word 'sex' died on my lips and my stomach flipped. Why did I always go for those sorts of comments?

I smiled brightly and scrabbled round for something nicer to say.

'It's like a hug in a mug.'

'Um.' He scratched his chin. 'Are you OK? Because yesterday at Garden Warehouse . . . and now . . . well, obviously you're not OK, but—'

'Gabe, can we just . . . can you give me a minute?'

'Sure.'

We drifted into silence. Me lost in my thoughts, letting the hot chocolate work its magic, Gabe alternating between jiggling his leg and prodding the fire with a stick.

For ten years I'd worn my sexuality like a suit of armour. A hard impervious shell. I'd never shied away from talking about my body or about sex (unless it involved older members of my family) and I wasn't afraid to show men that I

245

found them attractive. Why should I? What's sauce for the goose is sauce for the gander, I reckoned. I'd always enjoyed men's company, often more straightforward, less angsty than women's. I'd had boyfriends too. I wasn't going to live like a nun just because of him.

Because of Callum.

But if anyone got too close, demanded more commitment than I was prepared to give, down came the protective visor. I'd had *lovers*, but I'd taken care not to fall in *love*. I, like Nonna, had been too hurt to allow that to happen.

My thoughts shifted to Nonna; poor thing, raped and then forced to marry her attacker. She'd kept that trauma to herself for five decades. Now that I'd admitted it out loud to myself, I was determined not to do the same.

I looked at Gabe, his damp hair sticking up in peaks where he'd rubbed it, his eyes watchful, patient, full of concern.

'You're shivering,' he said.

He took a blanket from the arm of the sofa, the one I wrapped myself in when I couldn't be bothered to light the fire, and tucked it round my shoulders.

'I've never seen your bossy side,' I said, smiling with my eyes over the top of my mug.

'There are lots of sides to me you haven't seen,' he said.

I wondered if he was flirting with me. I looked at him for clues but his grey eyes were as deep as pools and I couldn't read them. There was a warm sensation in the pit of my stomach that I hadn't felt for such a long time that I didn't recognize it at first. I let my eyes roam over his handsome face, his soft friendly smile and jaw studded with sandy-coloured stubble.

He was a lovely man.

But we were friends, that was all. And I treasured his friendship, I didn't want to risk losing it.

'Look.' He caught me staring and my insides fluttered with the same feeling again. This time I was pretty sure it was attraction. 'I don't mean to pry, but whatever it is, you can trust me with it.'

I blinked at him. 'Really?'

He moved from the armchair to the far end of the sofa, still keeping a respectful distance.

'Really.'

'It's a secret,' I said. 'Not even Verity knows. Not properly.'

'It will be safe with me. Promise.' He made a cross on his chest. 'I'm actually brilliant at keeping secrets.'

'Well . . .' I let out a long breath and thought about it.

I'd come so close over the years to telling someone: Mum, Lia, Verity . . . It had never dawned on me to tell a man. But now, cocooned in my cottage, with the fire flickering, the rain tapping softly at the window, a mug of hot chocolate and Gabe's kind eyes cheering me on . . . maybe I could.

'OK. But you might not think so highly of me afterwards.'

'Who says I think highly of you now?'

'Oh,' I said, embarrassed. 'Good point.'

'Rosie, I'm sorry, that was mean of me. For the record, I think very highly of you and I doubt very much you'll change that.' He reached for my hand and squeezed gently before releasing it. 'I'm sorry. Again.'

'OK. I had a boyfriend called Callum,' I began. 'Nothing serious, we were only together a short time . . .'

Gabe sat mostly in silence, occasionally shaking his head, sometimes frowning while I told him how I'd met Callum. We were both interns at a media buying agency in London's Canary Wharf. The company didn't pay much but they did cover our accommodation; six of us, all new graduates, shared a flat in Putney. We were a happy gang and Callum and I somehow became an item. He wasn't my normal type, he was quiet and shy, too quiet at times, but that drew me to him even more. We were young, completely penniless, but we were living in London and life was brilliant. After three months, our internship came to an end, Callum was offered another one somewhere else and wanted me to join him.

But I'd decided to go home back to Barnaby. Dad's aunt had died and left me some money and I thought I'd give property developing a go while I looked for a proper job. Before we went out to celebrate my last night in London, I packed my things and had 'the talk' with Callum which I thought he'd be expecting: I said I didn't think we could make it work long distance, it had been fun while it lasted and I hoped we could stay friends.

He was devastated, declared his desperate love for me, begging me to give it a chance, to try to make it work. I couldn't believe it; it was obvious to me that we'd split up when I left London. We were both only twenty-two, just starting out, and we weren't in love, or at least I wasn't and I'd thought he felt the same. Callum got hideously drunk that night, telling everyone how I'd broken his heart, how he couldn't live without me, that I'd been his soulmate.

Callum's drunken behaviour aside, it had been a good night involving dancing, cocktails and a bag of chips on the night bus home. We didn't get back to the flat until the early hours and my train was leaving at noon the next day. We all went to bed but Callum pleaded with me to let him into my room, 'just to cuddle', but I refused. We were over and I didn't see the point of dragging it out and giving him false hope. Besides, he was so out of it I thought he might throw up. An hour later I must have fallen into a really heavy sleep, because I didn't even hear him come into my room. I only woke up when I felt his weight on me, his hot breath on my face and his hands tearing at my T-shirt, pushing it up.

I struggled. I tried kicking out, grabbing his face, pushing at his shoulders. But he was too strong for me and I was trapped. I started to cry, Callum was crying too, saying that he loved me, over and over. I shouted but everyone in the house had had too much to drink, and no one came to my rescue.

When he rolled off me I thumped him so hard I heard his jaw crack and nearly broke my own wrist. I was so shocked I didn't move; I just lay there gasping for breath.

When I woke up the next morning, I stormed into his room but his bed was empty, he wasn't anywhere in the flat, he'd simply vanished.

'I left that day, caught the train as planned and never saw him again.'

I looked up at Gabe and there was such anger in his eyes that for a moment I was quite taken aback.

'Nice bloke,' he muttered, his face stormy with anger. He leaned forward, resting his elbows on his thighs and rubbed his face. 'There's no excuse. There's never an excuse. If a girl says no, no matter what the circumstances – even if she'd said yes the day before, or even five minutes before, that's all a man needs to know. I hope you haven't in some way laid the blame at your own feet?'

I stretched my legs out towards the fire to feel the warmth and glanced sideways at him.

'I did at first. For ages I blamed myself for getting it so wrong with him, for not realizing how strong his feelings for me were. Then I blamed myself for not fighting him off hard enough, but above all I felt sick that he'd used his physical power to force me to do something I didn't want to do. It was an unfair fight. For the first time in my life I felt like the weaker sex and I hated him for that.'

'You're anything but weak.' His gaze met mine so fiercely it brought heat to my cheeks. 'In fact, you're one of the strongest women I've ever met. I . . . I think a lot of you; Noah does too.'

My heart melted at that.

'I made myself strong. From then on I decided not to let any man have power over me again.'

'Love is a powerful force,' said Gabe softly.

He moved to the log basket, feeding more wood into the flames.

I shrugged one shoulder. 'Exactly. That's why I don't let relationships get that far.'

'That's a shame because you're missing out. That power is

249

a force for good far more often than for bad. Being loved by someone is one of the greatest privileges of life.'

His voice was low and thick with emotion and I wondered whether he was thinking of Mimi.

'It is also one of the biggest risks,' I said softly.

He knelt back on his heels and looked me squarely in the eye. 'There are good men out there, Rosie. I'm sorry this happened to you. But give us poor men another chance. If you never take the risk, you'll never find out.'

I wondered if he'd ever take the risk again.

'Oh I know; my dad, for instance. You know where you stand with Alec Featherstone.'

Gabe cocked an eyebrow.

'Yes, OK,' I admitted, 'perhaps not when he's dressed as Dolly Parton.'

We both laughed at that and suddenly I realized that I'd done the thing that I should have done years ago. I felt like a rain cloud had lifted from above my head.

'Ooh,' I said, remembering suddenly. 'Gina says she can babysit on Friday.'

'Oh? Right, good.' He nodded and rubbed his neck and started jiggling his leg again. 'I'll, er . . . yes, thanks for passing that on.'

Poor man; he looked so awkward. All he did was offer to get me out of the rain and he'd ended up giving me a counselling session. I bet he hadn't expected his morning to turn out like this.

'You'll probably want to get off now,' I said, making it easy for him.

He made a whistling sound through his teeth.

'Actually, I wanted to, I wondered if you . . .' He blinked his grey eyes at me and let out a long breath. 'I wanted to give you a hug. But after what you've just told me I understand if you'd rather not.'

'Please do.' I swallowed. 'Do hug me.'

He didn't need asking twice; the next second I was

wrapped in his arms, my face buried into the soft place between his chest and his cheek, his damp hair tickling my face. He smelled of woodsmoke and a faint hint of spicy aftershave and it was so intensively masculine that it made me realize how long it had been since I'd been so close to a member of the opposite sex.

'Thank you for telling me, Rosie; I'm honoured.'

'Thanks for listening. You're a good friend, Gabe,' I murmured into his neck, dabbing at a stray tear.

He said something so quietly that I couldn't quite catch it, but I think it was something about a good start.

I closed my eyes and allowed myself to relax against him. The sounds of the fire crackling, the rain dripping from the trees and the birds singing drifted away until all I could hear was the gentle beat of Gabe's heart through his shirt. My eyes brimmed with tears.

Peace. Total peace.

I'd done it. After ten years, I'd faced up to the fact that what had happened to me was rape. That *no* means *no* whether you know your attacker or not. That just because we'd done it before didn't mean it was OK for Callum to do it against my will. And not only had I admitted it to myself, I'd shared it with someone who cared about me.

I felt better for it. I'd let someone in on my deepest secrets and instead of feeling exposed as I'd feared, I felt brave and hopeful. Maybe this was a new start for me and my fragile heart.

Chapter 25

The next couple of days were completely bonkers. Derbyshire had snow. Only a sprinkling but even so, it was almost
May! The peaks looked postcard-perfect and when the sun
came out, everywhere looked so beautiful that we forgot to
moan about the cold and the damage it was doing to everyone's gardens and just enjoyed the scenery instead. I even
spotted Noah playing with his new friends on the village
green after school one day, trying to make snowballs and
miniature snowmen while Gabe stood in the middle of a
crowd of mums. I was pleased to see him making friends,
but nevertheless spent a long time wiping down tables so I
could keep an eye on him from a distance. I wondered
which one, if any, he'd be taking out on Friday night.

I was massively grateful to him for being the one to help
me unlock the memories of what happened with Callum,
but before he'd left to pick up Noah from school, I'd made
him promise – again – never to breathe a word of it to anyone, even Verity. I decided that no one in my family would
ever find out that my relationship with Callum had ended so
badly. Nonna's story was enough for everyone to cope with
and now that I'd confided in Gabe, I felt as if I had everything I needed inside me to cope with it myself. Just having
one person validate my feelings about that night was all it
took and the fact that Gabe had been so lovely and support-
ive about it made me like him even more.

I did tell a small white lie to Verity.

I sent her a text saying that Nonna had not only lost a baby, but had been raped *too* and that I'd been so shocked at hearing the news that I'd got a bit flustered and that I'd fill her in properly soon. Maybe one day I would tell her, but for the moment my story could wait; right now, Nonna needed me.

Because suddenly, after more than fifty years, Maria *Benedetto* couldn't wait to go back to Italy and none of us had the heart to argue. What mattered more than anything, to all of us, was to readjust to our new family tree and what better way to help Nonna lay her ghosts to rest than by going back to where it had all begun. To visit her family's graves, to be certain that the Signore Benedetto we'd found on the internet really was her husband and for Nonna to reconnect with the country that ran as strongly through her veins now as it had always done.

Nonna had asked me to go with her. I was honoured, but at the same time worried that the rest of the family would feel left out. But it was fine. Mum might have wanted to go with her but she still didn't have a valid passport. Dad didn't want to leave Mum, Lia couldn't leave Arlo and as Nonna was too impatient to wait any longer than she had to, it made sense for me to accompany her. I booked us flights and a hotel and three days later, on Friday evening, we were making a flying visit to Sorrento.

'Please ensure your tray tables are in the upright position, window blinds are fully raised and stow all loose items under the seat in front of you.'

I glanced at Nonna. After discovering that the cabin crew on the flight from Luton to Naples couldn't supply her with a glass of limoncello to calm her nerves, she had opted for a double brandy instead. She had knocked it back in one and had been snoring softly for the last hour. Her chin was tucked into her chest and her hands clasped tightly across the front of her new lilac dress and matching jacket.

'I wanna look my best when I go back to Italy,' she had said firmly, ignoring Mum's suggestion that the most important thing when travelling was comfort.

She was a remarkable woman, I thought, watching her soft puffs of breath and the rise and fall of her chest. She was taking her first flight at seventy-five years of age to return to a period of her life she had been trying to forget for more than fifty years and even though I knew she was nervous at what, or who, she might find in Italy, she was determined to face the consequences.

The brandy had really knocked her out; despite the various bongs telling us to fasten our seat belts in readiness for our descent, and the pilot's announcement that the weather in southern Italy this evening was a balmy sixteen degrees, she still didn't move a muscle. I did up her seat belt and then my own before pulling the bus timetable from my bag to check it for the umpteenth time. Nonna had assured me that the best way to get to Sorrento from Naples was by bus. Privately I'd thought that her travel tips were possibly out of date so I'd looked it up on TripAdvisor only to find that she was right. I'd bought tickets online for the last bus of the day and we'd be arriving in Sorrento at just before eleven tonight.

Looking at her faded features, slack now in sleep, it was almost impossible to reconcile this dear time-worn face with the feisty young woman who I'd learned about ever since Stanley's proposal.

My eyes pricked with tears and I blinked them away as the plane dipped its nose and began its descent. Nonna stirred and I took her hand in mine.

Hers was a story that, even now, I was still coming to terms with. And I wasn't the only one. The entire family had been shell-shocked by Nonna's revelations.

I looked at Nonna's hand and twirled the worn gold band around her finger. Her wedding ring. *Signora Maria Benedetto.* Married to Marco and not to her first love, Lorenzo Carloni, as she'd led us to believe all these years. Although if I'd been married to a man like Marco, I'd have been tempted to erase it from my memory banks too.

I looked out of the window as the aeroplane swooped low across the water. The sinking sun had set the sky alight with pink and orange stripes and the sea below shone like liquid gold. Now and then a light winked from a tiny boat and then suddenly the plane banked, we turned and the coastline appeared, its jagged edges of burnt-orange rocks glittering with lights.

My stomach flipped; in a matter of minutes Nonna would be back in Italy and together we'd be heading to Sorrento to face her past and say her final goodbyes.

For the first hour of the flight, Nonna had been as excitable as a child. She'd read every word on the safety card tucked in the seat pocket in front of us, she'd checked that both she and I really did have a lifejacket under our seats, she'd visited the loo twice and had even knocked on the door of the cockpit and asked to see the pilot. She had been escorted back to her seat after that.

'I like aeroplanes. Last time I make this long journey, with your mamma,' she chuckled, choosing an espresso and chocolate muffin from the menu when the trolley passed by for the first time, 'I was on train with hundreds of others. Nothing like this.'

'Tell me,' I urged, handing her an extra sugar packet, which she tore open and tipped into her cup. 'Mum told me the bones of the story, but tell me how you ended up with Marco. And how you managed to escape.'

Nonna frowned, stirring her coffee for ages before meeting my gaze.

'I'm ashamed.'

'Don't be.' I swallowed and covered her hand with mine. Understanding completely how she felt, but knowing now, thanks to Gabe, that shame had no place in what had happened. 'I have always loved you. Always. And now I know what you've been through, I'm even more proud.'

'Okey cokey.' She glanced across at the passengers on the other side of the aisle. Nobody was paying us any attention and the seat next to me was empty. It was just her and me, thirty thousand feet up in the air somewhere above Europe . . .

'If my days with Lorenzo are like being in heaven,' she began, 'then life with Marco is the worst kind of hell . . .'

For a couple of years after Lorenzo died, it was obvious that she was simply not interested in men and Maria's mother was worried about her. Her brother Sav and his wife Sofia had moved their two children into the apartment above the bar and now Maria and her mother were sharing a room. It was cramped and Sofia was making it very clear that Maria was not welcome.

One day Marco Benedetto came into the bar and asked Maria to go to a dance with him. She didn't want to go, but Sav and her mother told Marco that she would. Everyone knew Marco. He ran his family's ice-cream business and made lots of money selling gelato to the tourists in the Marina Piccola at the water's edge.

He came to collect her on his motorbike and they rode to Piano, a town just along the coast road. The dance was full of young girls trying to attract men and men showing off to the girls. Maria hated every minute of it and detested Marco. Where Lorenzo had been full of life, he was just full of himself. His breath smelled of Turkish cigarettes and garlic and his skin smelled so strongly of aftershave that it made her choke. He had hooded eyes and a square jaw. She knew others found him handsome, but his looks left her cold; she could see only steel in his heart and couldn't wait for the night to be over. He threw her round the dance floor, laughing when he spun her so fast that she stumbled.

She told him that he had bad manners, which made him laugh more.

'Foreign girls find me irresistible,' he'd said with a grin. 'I have to fight them off down at the beach.'

'And yet you are still single?' she'd replied feistily.

Maria asked to go home, but he made her wait until the end of the night. Outside he walked her back to where they had left the motorbike and under the streetlight, he had grabbed her around the waist.

'Just a little kiss. I deserve that?' His eyes had glinted menacingly under the sodium light.

She should have just kissed him, but Maria had never despised someone so much in her life and couldn't bring herself to do it.

'You have the manners of a filthy street dog and you deserve nothing from me,' she'd said proudly and turned her head so that his harsh lips had only found her jaw.

'A dog?' he'd snarled.

Enraged, he dragged her into a stone passageway hidden from view. He tore away every bit of her dignity along with the hem of her dress and she was powerless to stop him. Afterwards he pressed his hard mouth against hers, every touch of his skin on hers a torture after the tender, innocent caresses of Lorenzo. He took her home and as he left her at the door, he gripped her face in his hand until her eyes watered in pain.

'You see,' he'd laughed, 'you're just like the other girls. You want Marco too.'

She bit his finger and ran inside, his laughter ringing in her ears, mocking her for her tears. After that he kept coming round and Maria kept trying to avoid him until three months later when her mother spotted her swollen stomach.

The priest and Maria's mum scared her into marriage, telling her that her baby would be taken from her if she didn't comply. Marco's family were keen to see him marry, thinking that becoming a father would be the change he needed to make him settle down and Marco, deciding at his age that he should have a wife, flippantly agreed to make an honest woman of her.

Maria's wedding day dragged by like a bad dream. If only Lorenzo had not been killed, none of this would have happened, she told herself. She thought her life couldn't get worse. Her family were relieved to see her get married and her mother told her she was only emotional because of being pregnant. No one was listening to her.

When the midwife heard two heartbeats Maria suddenly found her strength. This wasn't just about her any more; she had two extra lives to take care of. Marco was more full of himself than ever, insistent that fathering twins proved what a man he was. He wouldn't leave her alone, wanted to go everywhere with her, convinced that she was cheating on him. But who would want her now? Her legs were swollen, her body was bloated, she was always tired and sick. Some women bloom like a flower when they are with child. Not Maria; she faded and faded until all the colour was bleached from her skin. Her stomach grew and the day the babies were due to be born got closer. As time went on, the air between Marco and her got more and more heated, like the approach of a thunderstorm. Then one day he came home to take her to the hospital for an appointment.

Before they left, Marco lost his wallet and blamed her for moving it. By the time he found it in his jacket pocket, they were running late. As he locked the door to their apartment Maria told him to hurry. His fury burst to the surface and he hit her jaw so hard she thought it had cracked. She stumbled sideways and slipped down the stairs, screaming with fear that she was going to hurt the babies. Marco tried to grab her back but it was too late. She broke her wrist trying to save herself and the unborn twins, but she landed heavily on her stomach. Marco pulled her to her feet and shoved her in the car. She was speechless with pain as he drove to the hospital. Gennaro and Luisa were born eight hours later. Luisa screeched the place down, but Gennaro was still and blue.

A doctor was called but nothing could be done. A piece of Maria died with her son.

She could never prove that Marco caused the death of their baby boy, but until that moment there had been nothing wrong with the babies. After the funeral she was silent, she looked after Luisa and she kept them both away from the monster as much as she could. He said that if she told anyone what had happened he would call her a liar and say that she was mentally ill. When Luisa was only two weeks old, Marco forced himself on Maria again in the night while the baby cried in the crib at the end of the bed.

And that was the moment Maria knew she would rather die than carry on living like this.

It took her a month to plan their escape. A friend from her school days, Edoardo, knew someone who could help her disappear. He arranged everything for her: a fake passport, transport to Milan and from there a passage on a train full of brick workers on their way to a new life in England.

This was what she and Lorenzo had dreamed of all those years ago. Edoardo asked her to give him a name for the false documents.

Suddenly she could see a way to be the person she'd hoped to be. Being Lorenzo's widow was a million times better than being Marco's wife. So she decided: from now on she would live life the way she wanted. She couldn't have Lorenzo, but she could take his name.

Leaving her mother was the hardest thing she had ever done and travelling across Europe by train with one tiny baby, still grieving for the other, wasn't easy either. But as the distance between her and Marco widened, she gradually began to breathe and knew in her heart she had done the right thing.

As soon as she arrived in England she went to a women's charity for help. Scared that Marco would come after her, she had changed her surname officially and the charity helped to ensure that he would never discover her whereabouts. She and Luisa moved around for a while before finally settling in Derbyshire. Even though she had never left England, she had always kept her passport up to date, just in case she ever needed to get away again.

'The first year was hardest,' she said, shaking her head now at the memory. 'I miss the sunshine and the sea, the smell of lemon blossom in the air and my mamma, most of all I miss Mamma. For one year, I don't dare write to her. Then a member of Italian community is travelling back home to Salerno. I give him a letter for Mamma. After that we keep in touch secretly and she send me money to help me buy our first home. But I never see her again, she die in nineteen seventy-five. Now, I not know what family I have any more.'

My heart ached for her. She must have felt so alone in a strange country with no one to turn to for support. And yet she had survived.

'You are the bravest woman I have ever met,' I said softly, squeezing her hand.

The cabin crew came past at that moment with the trolley for a second time and Nonna winked at me.

'Brave or not I think I have a limoncello to calm the nerves, eh?'

I shook my head as she accepted the brandy instead of limoncello and I held her hand, stroking my thumb against the wrinkled skin on the back of her hand until she slipped into sleep.

The plane touched down at Naples International Airport and passengers clapped as the engines roared and the force of the brakes thrust us back in our seats.

I turned to Nonna to wake her up, but her dark anxious eyes were already trained on me. She blinked blearily from behind her thick glasses.

'*O mio Dio.*' She stared out at the dusky evening as the aeroplane taxied along the runway and came to a jerky stop. 'We here. No turning back.'

'Welcome to Naples International Airport, ladies and gentleman, where the local time is eight thirty and I'm pleased to inform you that you may now disembark from the front and rear doors.'

Around us our fellow passengers began scrabbling for their belongings, unsnapping seat belts and reaching into the overhead lockers. Nonna and I stayed seated, and I leaned across and pressed a kiss to her soft cheek.

'Once you face your past,' I reassured her, 'you'll be free to move forward. It's the right thing to do.'

She nodded. 'I have Stanley Pigeon to thank for this. If he not propose, I not be here now.'

'Stanley is the bomb,' I said with a grin.

She chuckled and then looked at her hands.

'I never thought I love again. I think I am too old. But I love Stanley, and I wish I'd told him. Being with him, these last few weeks, make me realize how much I miss out on. Someone to kiss goodnight, someone there when I open my eyes in the morning. Someone to share little things with.'

My stomach fizzed.

'I know what you mean,' I said truthfully; I often woke up and felt the same.

Her eyes searched mine. 'But I break his heart. Do you think he ever talk to me again?'

Stanley had been incommunicado all week; Nonna had been round to see him, but either he had not been there or he had not wanted to speak to her. In the end she had popped a note through his door to let him know she was going to Italy to sort out her affairs. His lack of contact bothered her, but my theory was that his ego was still a bit bruised; I was sure that by the time we got home, he'd be ready to see her again.

'Stanley Pigeon adores you,' I said confidently. 'And after you find out once and for all what happened to Marco you can go tell him exactly how you feel about him.'

'It's time to go, ladies!' A tall blonde member of the cabin crew beamed at us.

'It is time,' I agreed, realizing that we were the last ones on board. I stood up and helped Nonna up from her seat. 'Italy awaits.'

Chapter 26

'Dicky head.' Nonna took her seat next to me on the bus after showing the hotel address to the driver and asking him to drop us off outside. 'That boy laugh at my Italian. Say I have English accent.'

The driver winked at me in his rear-view mirror and in deference to Nonna I managed to smother a smile. With his black curly hair, mischievous eyes and cheeky smile, he looked like fun. He winked again and flashed his white teeth at me.

I dipped my head quickly, not wanting to encourage him. From what I'd heard about this part of the coast, with its winding narrow roads perilously close to the edge of cliffs, the last thing we needed was a bus driver who paid more attention to his female passengers than the road.

I focused on my phone instead and sent Lia some pictures of the amazing food I'd seen in the airport café: paninis lavishly filled with salami, slices of ripe tomato, air-dried ham, pungent cheeses and bright green basil, huge folded pizzas loaded with black olives, artichokes and roasted red peppers and pastries sprinkled with almonds and stuffed with fruit.

Menu ideas? I typed and pressed send.

Nonna glanced over my shoulder at the pictures.

'Best bread in whole world. When I start the café, you can't buy Italian bread and I no have time to make it.

Anyway, English people only eat soft white bread back then. Now it different story. English eat anything and panini as common as rolls.'

Paninis should definitely go on the Lemon Tree Café menu, and we could make them as generous and abundant as these, much more tempting than the standard cheese-and-ham ones back home . . .

'We could go more Italian, don't you think? Make us stand out? Do less of the soup and jacket potato style lunches?'

'Mmm.' But she wasn't concentrating; she had reached into a plastic wallet containing all her official documents and was anxiously fingering her wedding certificate. I gave her arm a squeeze.

I knew she was worried. I was a bit nervous too. What if we'd got it wrong and Marco was still living and, worse, *livid*? Or what if he was a changed man and was desperate to see his daughter? The list of 'what ifs' was endless . . .

'Tomorrow we visit cemetery,' said Nonna, reading my mind. She slipped the certificate back into its wallet and smiled bravely at me. 'Then we know for sure.'

The driver started the engine and closed the doors and the bus headed towards the barrier at the exit of the airport.

'How long will it take to get to Sorrento?' I asked, doing up my seat belt and unscrewing the cap off a bottle of water before taking a sip.

She shrugged. 'One hour.'

As the barrier lifted, the driver accelerated out into the traffic, Nonna and I were thrown back in our seats and I spilt water over the pair of us.

She wiped a hand across her wet face and gripped the seat in front. 'Maybe less.'

The journey took us on a motorway, and then through several small steep towns, across a bumpy bridge over a river and around a series of hairpin bends, all at startling speed.

And an hour later we pulled in at the roadside on the edge of Sorrento.

'Hotel Roseto,' shouted the driver.

Nonna and I unloaded our cases from the boot and the bus trundled on.

'Wow.' I stared up at our home for the next two days.

Hotel Roseto was a pretty building painted a soft pale yellow. It was three storeys high with a small wrought-iron balcony at each of the upstairs windows. The façade was smothered with bougainvillea in full fragrant bloom and the large front garden was a riot of pink and purple geraniums, spilling from pots and hanging baskets. Orange and lemon trees woven with lights formed a canopy over tables and chairs, and candles glowed in tall glass jars.

We stood for a moment, stunned by its beauty, and inhaled the sweet night air.

Nonna twinkled her eyes at me. 'Maybe Stanley and me come here for honeymoon.'

I grinned back at her; she had to be the most irrepressible old lady in the world.

'Let's just deal with one husband at a time, shall we?' I said, leading her indoors.

Next morning the sky was the sort of perfect cloudless blue that made you feel that anything was possible. Which was handy given that we had quite a big day ahead of us. Nonna and I, fortified by a good night's sleep in sturdy twin beds with crisp cotton sheets and a breakfast of boiled eggs, crusty rolls and strong coffee, left the hotel just after nine.

We walked along the main road heading towards the centre of Sorrento and stopped at a little flower stall where Nonna bought roses for her parents and a bunch of lily of the valley for her son, Gennaro.

The cemetery sat high up a steep road overlooking the town and we were both out of breath by the time we reached the entrance. Despite the sunshine and the warm morning air, Nonna shivered as we passed through a tall pair of handsome gates.

'*O signore mio*,' she muttered.

I felt her anxiety vibrating through the fabric of her dress like a force field. Visiting her mother's grave for the first time was going to be tough for her, seeing where her little boy was buried again would probably break her heart and on top of that she was hoping to discover that her husband was dead. Not your average mini break, was it?

'Would you like me to go and ask about Marco?' I offered. 'You could wait here.'

She shook her head. 'I want to see with my own eyes.'

The cemetery was nothing like any I'd seen at home. For a start there wasn't a blade of grass anywhere, nor were there any wonky headstones of varying sizes and materials, no gargoyles or angels or garishly showy sculptures. Instead, rows and rows of evenly spaced identical graves were marked with pale grey marble crosses, each one engraved with the person's name and date of birth and death. It could have looked stark and forbidding, but it was as far from that as it could possibly be. Each and every grave appeared to be beautifully cared for and decorated. Pot plants, candles, flowers, framed photographs . . . there were personal items on every one. This was a place people came to celebrate the lives of the departed, to relive happy memories and keep their love alive. The dead in Italy, it seemed, were gone but not forgotten.

'The Benedetto family is buried up there,' Nonna said, pointing to a raised area up to our left. 'I came with Marco to visit his grandfather's grave one time. If Marco is dead, he will be with them. But first we see my boy. This way.'

'So Gennaro is not with the Benedettos?'

She gave a harsh laugh.

'Marco had nothing to do with the funeral. Afterwards he said he was too upset. But that had nothing to do with it.' She blinked at me and two angry pink spots appeared on her cheeks. 'It was guilt. Gennaro die because of him and he know it. Anyway I am glad because now he buried with my family. All these years I been thankful that he was near people who loved me and loved him too.'

Nonna knew exactly where to find Gennaro's grave. She marched ahead and I followed, nibbling my lip. If her family was dead, who would be left to look after Gennaro's grave? It would break Nonna's heart if his was the only untended plot in the cemetery.

An elderly lady in a headscarf carrying a wicker basket passed by as we reached the end of the row.

'*Buongiorno*,' she murmured, inclining her head.

'*Buongiorno*,' Nonna replied, too busy scanning the names on the graves to pay her any attention.

'*Buongiorno*,' I said, peering into her basket.

It contained a pair of secateurs, a cloth, a soft brush and a packet of LED candles. There were also some loose green cuttings as if she'd been pruning foliage.

She caught me staring, frowned and then dipped her head before hurrying away. She emptied the greenery into the rubbish bin and then took the steps up to the upper level.

Ahead of me, Nonna gasped. 'Gennaro!'

She dropped to her knees, talking softly in Italian, whispering words of love to her only son.

I stood behind her and read the engraving on the marble cross. Gennaro Benedetto, Mum's twin brother, had been born and died on the same day in 1963.

'I blame myself when he didn't survive,' said Nonna. 'A mother's job is to protect her babies. I no protect Gennaro. When I find I was pregnant I was so *angry*. My head full of terrible thoughts. I didn't want to marry Marco, I blamed my family, my babies, everyone. I want it to all just go away. Later when I start to feel them kick, I knew I love them even though Marco was their father. It not their fault. I would give my life for either of them.'

There was nothing I could say. Tears pricked at my eyes as

I stroked Nonna's back. Poor little thing. He didn't even live long enough to feel his mother's arms around him.

But someone had been caring for him recently; the grave was as immaculate as its neighbours. There was a silver hurricane lantern which someone had obviously been polishing, inside of which a battery-operated candle flickered. Two matching white pots held neatly trimmed evergreen shrubs and the marble itself was spotless. My heart squeezed with relief.

Nonna found an empty metal vase to the side of the gravestone and took it to the tap. She filled it with water and began arranging the lily of the valley.

'I wonder who has been looking after his grave,' I said idly, picking up a stray leaf which looked like it had been newly snipped.

Nonna didn't answer, there were tears on her cheeks and she seemed to be lost in prayer.

I turned back to look at the old lady we'd passed. She was at the top of the steps staring at us.

'Nonna,' I said gently, 'where did you say Marco's family was buried?'

'Up,' said Nonna, jabbing a finger. 'Where that woman stands.'

'Thought so. See you in a minute.'

I left Nonna whispering to the baby boy she never got the chance to know and headed for the steps.

It probably wasn't the done thing to run in a cemetery, I thought, so I simply lengthened my stride to cover the distance between here and the upper level as quickly as I could. But even before I made it to the bottom of the steps, I lost sight of the woman in the headscarf. There were more levels above and paths heading off in every direction; this place was like a marble maze.

I frowned and shielded my eyes, looking left and right for any sign of movement but the lady must have been niftier than she looked. And she had obviously left in a hurry; her basket lay abandoned on top of a gravestone. I was almost sure she had been tending Gennaro's grave before we arrived and now she was amongst the Benedetto plots, which meant she must be one of them. Perhaps she had recognized Nonna, and for some reason that had prompted her to disappear.

I approached the grave where the basket had been set down and held my breath, hardly daring to look . . .

The basket sat in between two white pots containing the same green shrubs as the ones on Gennaro's grave. There was an identical silver hurricane lamp too, but the door of this one was open and the candle had been taken out. A pair of secateurs had been left sticking out of one of the pots, a few dead leaves snipped into a neat pile.

I lifted my eyes to the cross and translated the Italian inscription: *Marco Benedetto born in 1939, died in 1997.*

So our internet research had been right. A wave of relief washed through me. At least there was no chance of us bumping into him. I hadn't admitted it to Nonna, but I'd been quite nervous of that. And now Nonna was free, free to move on with her life – in fact, she'd been free for nearly twenty years. I waited for sorrow to kick in; I was standing in front of the grave of my grandfather, after all. But nothing, not even a twinge.

There was a small framed photograph of Marco just under his name. His eyes were as dark and hooded as Nonna had described, but his hair was sparse and white, his face jowly and rumpled. Nonna had said he was a handsome man, but he hadn't aged well.

I clenched my fists.

You forced yourself on her. You used your strength to take what you wanted. But you didn't break her spirit. You lose, Marco.

'Granddad Benedetto,' I said out loud, 'or *Nonno*, I suppose you would have been to me. I hope you're sorry now for what you did. But I'm not sure any of our family will ever forgive you.'

'Rosanna?' Nonna was huffing her way up the steps towards me. 'What you find?'

'Peace.' I smiled as I wrapped my arm around her shoulders. 'For you, I hope.'

'I never thought I be so happy to find out my husband is dead,' said Nonna as we made our way back down the hill twenty minutes later. 'I terrible person.'

'Rubbish. He was a baddie,' I said, pulling a face. 'I could tell just by looking at him. I'm glad you escaped from him, I'm glad you came to England with Mum.'

'Me too,' she said, stopping to pinch my cheek. 'And he had uses. I have all of you to love.'

'I wonder if anyone loved Marco after you left?' I peered up a side street as we walked by.

While she had spent a few private minutes sitting quietly at Marco's graveside, I had walked around the whole cemetery fruitlessly looking for the old lady, wondering where she fitted in to my family, if at all.

'I hope so, *cara*,' Nonna sniffed. 'But somehow I doubt it. Zebras never change their spots.'

'No,' I said, hiding my smile. 'They don't. Can you hear that?'

An awful wheezing sound from behind us, along with rapid footsteps made us both stop and turn round. It was the old lady with the headscarf running to catch us up.

'Maria?' she gasped, pressing a hand to her hip as she caught her breath. '*Sei tu?*'

I moved instinctively closer as Nonna stiffened. '*Sì?*'

'Alba.' The woman tapped her chest. '*Sono* Alba Benedetto.'

Nonna began to nod slowly, her eyes raking the woman's face, taking in the lined cheeks, the hooded eyes and pointed chin.

'*Santo cielo!*' she murmured.

Alba tentatively reached out to grip Nonna's hands. Nonna looked at me amazed.

'Rosanna, this is Marco's sister. Alba, *mia nipote*, Rosanna.'

Both women began to speak as quickly as gunfire. I didn't

have a clue what they were saying, but it seemed friendly enough so I stepped away and sent Mum and Dad a text message while I waited. By the time I'd finished my update, Nonna was kissing Alba's cheeks and exchanging numbers. Both women had tears running down their cheeks.

Nonna sighed as we watched Alba make her way back to the cemetery.

'OK?' I said, scrutinizing my grandmother's face for clues.

'They guessed,' she said, shaking her head softly. 'Marco's family guessed that I run away to safety. He had always been violent. You see. Zebras.'

'He'd never have changed,' I agreed.

'And they feel guilty. Alba said they wish they help me after the babies are born but she and her mother were scared of Marco too. Alba's mother was very sad not to be a *nonna*, but she understand. But the best bit,' Nonna gulped back a sob, 'is that nobody blame me for leaving. Alba say they glad I escape.'

There was something heartbreaking about watching an old lady cry. I hugged her close while she worked her way through her sorrow and we stood like that with seagulls circling overhead for several minutes before she dabbed her face with a tissue and gave me a watery smile.

'Let's go,' she said, looping her arm through mine. 'I feel like a door has closed finally. Like now I have the opportunities to do what I want, to love who I want.'

'You mean a door has opened,' I said with a grin. 'When one door closes another one *opens.*'

'No. I mean closed. Because when I run away from Marco, I leave a door open. I should have been brave and faced up to him, tell him I want to end our marriage, to close the door on it. Instead, the door has been open all this time. And now it is closed. See?'

I thought about that for a moment.

'So you're saying that you can't go through the new door until the old one is closed.'

'Exactly. You gotta go back and shut the door.'

I stared at her as a light bulb pinged on in my brain. A big neon light bulb, pouring light on to the thoughts that had been skulking around in there for a decade.

'YOU are a genius,' I spluttered with laughter. 'When you put it like that it's obvious.'

'*Grazie*,' she said, sucking her cheeks in and patting her hair. 'Come, we deserve espresso after all this excitement. And maybe cake. I take you somewhere special. I not sure it is still there, of course, after all these years but . . .'

She described a bar she had always gone to to drink coffee with friends, away from her family's prying eyes. She told me she had always associated that coffee with Sorrento and home and how difficult it had been to find rich smoky coffee in England. I tuned out for a moment and I drifted off inside my head.

What Callum had done to me had made me feel so violated, so powerless, that I'd refused to let myself love or be loved ever since. I'd put my heart on ice. But hearing Nonna's story had given me the key to unlock mine.

And I had closed a door, just like her.

Gabe's words came back to me: *being loved by someone is one of the greatest privileges of life*.

I deserved that privilege and next time love came knocking, I would do my best not to close the door in its face.

We turned into a narrow street and Nonna pushed open a shabby door. The aroma of freshly roasted coffee sent my senses heavenwards.

'Wakey wakey,' Nonna tutted, waving a hand in front of my face from the doorstep. 'I seen more life in that cemetery. Choose a cake and then we off to library to look at old newspaper.'

'How exciting.' I laughed, closing the door behind me. 'First the cemetery, next the library. Some tour guide you are.'

Chapter 27

Later that evening, Nonna and I shared our hotel bedroom's little dressing table while we got ready to go out. I was trying to disguise my sunburned face with make-up and she was redoing her bun. Fifteen minutes ago she had been fast asleep after our busy day. But then the little gold alarm clock she'd brought with her from home had rung out and she'd woken up immediately and changed into a smart yellow dress.

'My hair as black as coal when I was a girl, and even longer than this,' said Nonna, setting her grips aside and brushing out her hair. 'Always I left it down until I married Marco. He liked to pull it hard, so after that I keep it in a bun.'

I paused from patting concealer on to my nose and looked at the thick white hair tumbling over her shoulders. Her face was pink from the sunshine too and there was a sparkle in her eyes that had been missing for the last week. She might be an old lady now, but that girl was still there.

'You should leave it down; it suits you, you look very youthful.'

She tilted her face from side to side and studied her reflection in the mirror. 'Why not? Come on, let's go.'

We stepped out of the hotel into the dusk. The evening air was warm and fragrant and the snowstorms of Derbyshire felt like a million miles away. We'd only been here twenty-four hours and already Sorrento felt like home.

We'd had a packed day. Our trip to the library revealed that Bar Salvatore had never been sold, and therefore had either gone out of business or was still in the family so we decided to try to go there for dinner tonight. Then at lunchtime, while we'd munched our way through slices of the most delicious pizza I'd ever tasted, Alba had called and invited Nonna for coffee before our flight home tomorrow. After that we spent the afternoon exploring. Nonna showed me around Piazza Tasso, Sorrento's main square, and we'd done some shopping in the narrow cobbled streets which led from the magnificent cathedral. Nonna picked out a mug for Stanley with lemons on it and I bought some lemon-scented candles for Mum and a cookery book of traditional Sorrentine recipes for Lia. From there we'd peered into the lovely church of San Francesco with its tranquil Moorish-style cloisters and emerged into some pretty sculptured gardens edged with ornate railings.

'The sea!' I'd cried excitedly, pointing beyond the railings to the wide expanse of blue.

I'd taken my phone out and snapped away with the camera while Nonna pointed out the landmarks. To our far left was the little island of Capri, and to the right, around the bay, Vesuvius smouldered away in the distance, rising green and blue above the horizon with the sprawling city of Naples around its base. Directly below us was a bustling harbour teeming with life: bars, hotels and tavernas hugged the water's edge, all with tables lined up facing the water. Passengers queued for a ferry which every so often tooted its horn and sent up a plume of smoke, and a collection of smaller boats bobbed up and down in the sea. There were people splashing about in the waves on the edge of a small strip of beach. It was like looking down on a movie set.

I'd filled my lungs with salty air as my eyes took in the long sweep of coastline with its pink and orange houses perched on the cliff tops. This was a truly magical place and it hit me exactly how much Nonna had had to sacrifice to escape her unhappy marriage.

She was gazing far out to sea, her eyes cloudy and seeing things and people I couldn't even begin to imagine.

'Take me somewhere else,' I said gently, to bring her out of her reverie. 'Show me somewhere happy.'

She'd thought for a moment and her face dissolved into a smile. 'The lemon groves, where I meet Lorenzo.'

I'd held my arm out and the two of us had meandered contentedly back through the streets until we'd found the Giardini di Cataldo, and beneath the dappled shade of the ancient lemon trees, Nonna had sat and reminisced about the man she had loved and lost.

Bar Salvatore was at the opposite end of Sorrento to our hotel and after a long day on her feet, Nonna was soon tiring. As soon as we reached the main road, I flagged down a taxi and Nonna gave the driver directions to Via Vittorio.

Less than five minutes later we were standing on a narrow cobbled street outside the De Rosa family home.

I read the sign above the doorway set into a high wall. 'Bar Bufalo. Are we definitely in the right place?'

'Of course. This is Bar Salvatore,' Nonna frowned. 'Or was.'

Lush greenery cascaded over the top of the wall, and I could hear the gentle strains of harp music. The aroma of garlic and something deliciously meaty filled the air and my stomach rumbled with appreciation.

I opened the door and gestured for Nonna to go in front of me, but she shook her head.

'After you.'

'No one will recognize you,' I said, sensing her nerves as I went ahead. 'Just let me do the talking and if you want to turn around and leave, that's what we'll do.'

'Okey cokey.'

A flight of stone steps led to a large terrace set out with

simple wooden tables, mostly occupied with diners. Trees formed a natural canopy over the dining area and small glass jars lit with candles hung from their branches. Modern square terracotta pots of varying sizes were arranged in clusters and brimmed with myriad different plants, from herbs to cacti, and in a clearing in the centre, a young woman with pale blonde hair and a long floaty dress was playing a harp. Huge patio heaters, one at each corner, threw out enough heat to keep the evening chill at bay and the atmosphere was incredible.

'*Mamma mia.*' Nonna turned on the spot to take it all in. 'It is so different.'

'It's gorgeous,' I said, putting an arm around her shoulders and pointing her towards the door to the bar. 'I can't believe this is where you grew up. How does it feel to be home?'

'I can't believe it.' She gave a small hiccup. 'I need a drink.'

Inside, a long bar lined with bottles took up most of the space. Two men were drinking beer at the bar and several couples sat at small wooden tables, sipping wine and perusing menus. Waiting staff dashed backwards and forwards to an open hatch in the back wall, ferrying plates of food at head height out to waiting diners. Close up the smell was even more tantalizing.

Behind the bar, a slim man in a black shirt open almost to his navel dropped his cloth to the countertop and flung his arms out wide.

'Hey, beautiful ladies, I am Paolo, welcome to Bar Bufalo!' He grinned, showing a set of very white teeth. His face was tanned and he had a pattern shaved into the side of his light brown hair. He winked a brown eye at me. 'English, yes?'

I heard Nonna harrumph at my side, but she said nothing as we approached the bar; she was too busy taking everything in.

'I am half Italian,' I said proudly.

'Ah,' he dipped his head and pointed, '*parla italiano?*'

'Er, just the odd word,' I said, making a mental note to sign up for Italian conversation classes as soon as I got back to England. 'And they're mostly rude ones, learned from my grandmother.'

I nudged Nonna but she appeared to be transfixed by some old black-and-white photographs on the wall at the end of the bar.

'You come for dinner, yes?' He handed us menus, not pausing for a reply. 'You have a drink first. Don't tell me, don't tell me, let me guess.'

He stroked his chin and looked at us in turn.

'White wine for the *signorina*,' he winked at me, 'and red for your sister.'

'Dicky head,' Nonna muttered, trying to flutter her eyelashes and look cross at the same time.

'Good guess!' I pulled a bar stool out for Nonna but she ignored it, she was still squinting at the photographs, trying to see the details.

'What can I say?' He grinned again, raising both hands up. 'I am an expert.'

'This was Bar Salvatore once, wasn't it?'

Paolo, who I thought was about my age, paused from pulling a cork out of a wine bottle and cocked an eyebrow. 'You been here before?'

'*Santo cielo!*' Nonna muttered with a sharp intake of breath. She pushed the stool out of her path and made a beeline for the photographs.

'Not me.' I looked at my grandmother and then back to him. 'But my grandmother, Maria De Rosa, grew up here.'

'*De Rosa?*' Paolo's jaw dropped. '*Maria* De Rosa?'

Nonna nodded and smiled sheepishly.

He whooped with delight and everyone looked at us.

'I am Paolo De Rosa!' he cried, tapping his chest. 'You are my family?'

Nonna was trembling.

'*Tua famiglia, sì.*' She pointed to one of the photographs. 'Rosanna, come and see your great-grandfather.'

And then Paolo was round the bar in a flash, kissing Nonna's cheeks, holding her hands and crying, actually crying. Nonna and I shed a tear too as she pointed out members of her family in the pictures taken in Bar Salvatore as it was then, even including one of herself as a little girl. Paolo announced to the room that his *zia* Maria had returned and everyone whistled and clapped and raised their glasses.

'Rosie, like the rose, full of perfume and promise,' said Paolo, holding me at arm's length and kissing my fingertips.

'Are you always this flowery?' I asked with a grin.

He laughed. 'The tourists love it. I can't help myself.'

'Well, I'm not a tourist,' I said, feeling all tingly and proud. 'I am family.'

Nonna and Paolo chatted away in Italian far too quickly for me to follow and I was happy to sit and sip my wine while they sorted out how they were related (Nonna was Paolo's great-aunt, Paolo was her brother Salvatore's youngest grandson).

In no time we had established that Paolo had taken over two years ago from his mother. He had changed the name and changed the menu and given the bar a new lease of life and now it was winning awards and busy every night. His mother had retired with her new toy-boy husband and was now spending her days sailing around Sardinia in their yacht. Paolo was astounded when Nonna filled him in on her whereabouts for the last fifty years and whistled in disbelief as I flicked through photos on my phone to show him the rest of the family.

As soon as the harpist stopped for a break, Paolo dragged her over to meet us. Her name was Alice, and she was Paolo's American girlfriend. She looked tiny without her harp and was painfully shy and such a stark contrast to her exuberant and boisterous boyfriend that I wondered what drew them together. Alice blushed when Nonna complimented her on her playing and she escaped back to her harp as soon as she could.

Next Paolo took us on a tour of the apartment upstairs where Nonna used to live with her family, including a peek into Nonna's old bedroom where Paolo's eight-year-old daughter Adriana was fast asleep in bed.

'Here is the real boss,' Paolo whispered, the pride on his face shining through the darkness. 'That one wraps me round her finger.'

Nonna patted his back. 'And that is how it should be, she a very lucky girl to have you.'

'So,' Paolo clapped his hands when we arrived back at the bar, 'ready to find out what makes Bar Bufalo so special?'

It had been hours since lunch so we followed him eagerly out into the garden where he found us a table near a heater and kept fussing round Nonna to check she was warm enough.

'What's good to eat, then?' I asked as we finally got a chance to peruse the menu after all the excitement. 'Let me guess, pizza?'

Paolo wagged a finger.

'No pizza at Bar Bufalo. To stay in business in Sorrento, you must do something different. That is why we change the name. Everyone boast that they serve the best pizza in town. So we don't serve it at all. It is not called Bar Bufalo for nothing. Our house specialities are buffalo mozzarella salad to start followed by our award-winning buffalo steaks. No one can do it like us; we are unique in Sorrento.'

He puffed out his chest and looked at us, waiting for our order.

'Then I guess I'll have that.' I grinned.

'Me too,' said Nonna.

'*Fantastico*,' he beamed, taking the menus from us.

'Eh, Paolo?' Nonna shook her empty glass at him.

He collected it from her and laughed. 'Just like your brother.'

We watched him walk away, stopping at nearly every table to talk to his customers, and Nonna's eyes shone with pleasure.

'I have my family back again, *cara*,' she said, lifting up her glasses to dab at her eyes. 'I feel like luckiest woman alive.'

'Me too,' I said, smiling broadly.

Dinner, as promised, was incredible: the setting, the food, Alice's harp music and Nonna talking non-stop about her childhood and growing up in such a beautiful place combined to make it one of my most memorable meals ever. After sharing a melt-in-the-mouth rum baba, the chef, a tall man with a streak of silver in his black hair, came to offer Nonna a tour of the kitchen and while she quizzed him on the rum baba recipe, I caught up with Paolo at the bar.

'Hey, cousin!' He grinned, wiping the bar top and flipping the cloth over his shoulder. 'You like your buffalo?'

'Best steak I've ever had,' I confirmed. 'You've got me wondering what we can do differently for the Lemon Tree Café.'

Paolo nodded proudly and poured me a tiny glass of dessert wine. 'I will have to come and visit and see this place.'

'Definitely!' I took a sip; it was sweet and very cold and made my mouth tingle. 'I just need to work out what people will eat every day that will set us apart.'

'I spent a summer working in a pizza restaurant when I was a student. I make the lightest dough in Sorrento and I know the best meats, the best sauces and herbs and which combination of cheeses to use. But when I took over here, I knew that I'd never beat the competition by doing exactly the same as them, even if mine was the best. I stopped doing the food that the De Rosa family had been serving for years. Mamma thought I was mad. And for the first month I thought she might be right; customers took their time deciding they like the new menu. Very risky.'

He whistled through his teeth at the memory.

'I have the same problem,' I said and explained about

Garden Warehouse opening up a café half a mile from ours.

'You have to do what inspires you, fills you with passion. If you love what you do, the customers will know and they will keep coming back. For me it is the buffalo, for you,' he shrugged, 'maybe, I don't know . . . what do the English eat, fish and chips?'

I laughed. 'Totally. Morning, noon and night. I'll ask my sister Lia what she thinks – she's the cook in the family.'

He grinned. 'And then tell me what you decide and don't be afraid to take risks. I want to know all about your English café from now on.'

'I'll drink to that,' I said, raising my glass.

Alice appeared at Paolo's side then and kissed his cheek. '*Ciao*, darling. I have to go home to Bella.' She smiled apologetically at me and held her hand out for me to shake. 'It was nice to meet you. I'd love to stay and chat but my babysitter can only stay until ten o'clock.'

'I thought her name is Adriana?' I said, confused. I looked into my glass; perhaps I'd had more to drink than I realized.

'Paolo's daughter is Adriana, mine is Bella,' Alice said with a shy laugh.

She blushed and shook my hand firmly. For a small girl she had very strong fingers. It must be all that harp-plucking.

'I must go. *Ciao*.' She waggled her fingers, kissed Paolo again and hurried off.

Paolo and I waved as she disappeared down the steps that lead from the restaurant back down to street level.

'Sorry.' I cringed. 'I just assumed; I didn't mean to embarrass her, or you.'

Paolo waved a hand dismissively. 'Don't worry. Alice is still getting used to telling people she has a boyfriend. My wife – Adriana's mother – left us three years ago. I woke one morning and she had vanished.'

'No!' I said, shocked. That poor little girl waking to find

her mother had gone. 'What an awful thing to have to deal with.'

'Terrible,' he admitted. 'But part of me wasn't surprised. When I met her she was the most beautiful creature I had ever seen. My mother warned me that she wasn't the kind to hang around, that she wouldn't be content as a wife. She was a free . . . what do you say?'

'Free spirit.'

'Exactly. A free spirit. But I didn't care at the time. I decided that I would be content to love her for as long as she stayed. I couldn't believe my luck when she agreed to marry me. And when Adriana came along I had everything I could wish for. Oh excuse me.'

A glamorous woman wafted up to the bar in a cloud of heady perfume and Paolo went to serve her, making a show of pouring glasses of prosecco from a great height, kissing her hand and laughing with her.

I adored my cousin already. It would be so easy to dismiss him as a cheeky barman who loved to chat up his female customers, but there was so much more to him than that. He had been burned in love but he had bounced back. He had a business he was passionate about, a lovely new girlfriend and I bet he was a great dad too. The lady sashayed back to her friends with the glasses on a tray and Paolo rejoined me.

'So,' he said with a sad smile, 'we were very happy for six years – well, I was *still* happy. Obviously she wasn't. So she packed her things and disappeared without a word and I was left wondering what had gone wrong, whether it was something about me, or us, that had caused her to go.'

'You mustn't blame yourself,' I said fiercely, fighting the urge to crush him to me in a big hug and then run upstairs and do the same to Adriana.

'Human nature,' he said simply, lifting one shoulder. 'I dragged myself through the days. My work suffered. I was an engineer at the Sorrento council back then. It was almost impossible to look after Adriana and do my job. My little girl was the only light in my life. It became her and me against the world.'

'I've got a friend like you at home,' I said, thinking of Gabe. 'Although his wife died suddenly. Their baby boy was only one at the time and I know he struggled to cope at first. I think he's a brilliant dad.'

'A boyfriend?' Paolo arched an eyebrow.

'Just a friend, a special friend,' I said, shaking my head.

'You sure?' he said playfully, poking my shoulder, 'because my cousin is going pink.'

'He's a lovely man, but we're friends, that's all,' I said, feeling embarrassed suddenly. 'His son is called Noah. He's just started at the village school. He's only four but such a cutie and he knows loads about the planets. And dinosaurs.' I laughed fondly, remembering Jorvik the dinosaur that Noah had taken to the teddy bears' picnic last Saturday. Goodness – only a week ago!

Paolo was smiling knowingly at me, arms folded. 'Go on. I want to know more about your *friend*.'

'Well, he listened to me when I needed someone to talk to. He's *very* easy to talk to. And I trust him and I think because he understands what it is to be hurt, he is a good listener. And he's a very kind person, he only moved into the village a few weeks ago, but already everyone loves him.'

I was talking too much. I sipped at my wine but the glass was empty and I just ended up making a slurping noise. Paolo poured me another and grinned.

'Everyone?'

'Mostly.' I swallowed, feeling my face get redder and redder. I pressed the back of my hand to my cheek. 'Sunburn.'

'And he's just a friend.' Paolo grinned slyly, picking up a beermat and fanning my face with it. 'Right. It sounds to me like maybe you want more from him.'

'No,' I protested, cursing my squeaky voice and wondering

why I was blathering on about Gabe and wondering even more why it was making me so twitchy. 'It's never even crossed my mind.'

He nodded decisively. 'You should go for it. If a man can make you go so hot just by listening to you, imagine what you'd do if he—'

'Anyway,' I said loudly, 'back to you. How did you cope?'

'A year after she left I had a letter from my wife.' His gaze met mine. 'One letter. Saying that Adriana and I are better off without her and that she met someone new in France. That letter changed everything. I stopped feeling sorry for myself and felt sorry for her instead. She would never get to know her daughter, never feel her little arms round her neck and see her smile first thing in the mornings to light up the day. So I decided to move on. I said to myself that I'm not going to be the man who gives up on life because of this. I quit my job as an engineer and took up my mother's offer to buy the bar from her. I threw myself into renovating this place and although it was tough, living and working here made it easier to look after my little girl and then one year ago I met Alice.'

'You make it sound easy.'

He gave a harsh laugh. 'Not at all. It took me a long time to trust. I thought I'd never be able to let someone get close to me again and I was worried what Adriana would make of a new woman in our lives.'

His story touched my heart. More than that, it resonated so closely with mine – and Gabe's, come to that. I wondered whether Gabe thought about women in terms of how it would affect Noah. I tutted at myself; of course he did. He'd have to be cautious. Just like Paolo.

'How did you meet?'

'Alice was heartbroken too. Her husband died in a boat accident three years ago. Bella was only a baby. She came into the restaurant looking for work last year and when she played her harp, it was so beautiful and haunting that I fell in love with her straight away.' He grinned sheepishly. 'My heart was broken, but I met someone who understood sorrow and knew how to fix it. A bit like your friend.'

'Paolo,' I murmured, unable to resist giving him a hug this time, 'I'm proud of you and happy that you have met someone.'

Shortly after that, the chef brought Nonna back into the bar, both of them chattering away in Italian, Nonna rubbing her eyes and doing her best to stifle a yawn. It was time for us to leave.

'Why don't you cancel your flight tomorrow?' Paolo suggested as he escorted us down the steps and on to the cobbled street. 'The restaurant is closed until night-time on Sundays and we have promised the girls a trip to the beach. I would love you to meet Adriana.'

'Tempting, very tempting,' I said, giving my new cousin a hug. 'But we need to go home. I have a family café to revolutionize. You have completely inspired me to achieve greatness.'

Paolo puffed out his chest. 'Then I am honoured.'

I had had a long chat with Lia while Nonna was sleeping this afternoon. Garden Warehouse had erected a huge billboard at their entrance advertising the opening of the Cabin Café 'very soon' and I had no time to lose if I planned to do something to combat the effect they were bound to have on sales.

'I am so happy,' said Nonna tearfully, grabbing Paolo by his cheeks after he had found us a taxi. 'I never think I see my home again. Or my family.'

'You must come back,' he said, looking from me to Nonna. 'I mean it, bring all the family. It is not too late for us all to be a proper family.'

'We will,' I promised, sneaking a look at Nonna. 'In fact, one of us has already suggested coming back for her honeymoon.'

She sighed. 'If it's not too late. I not sure if he ever speak to me again.'

I frowned. Mum had been to Stanley's bungalow on Nonna's insistence to check he was all right and had found the curtains closed but no one at home. His neighbours hadn't seen him either. I hoped he was OK and that he'd simply gone to visit his daughter again, but I'd feel happier when I knew for certain.

Paolo was hugging his great-aunt so tightly she was gasping for air.

'Then you must go to this man, *zia* Maria; tell him how you feel, what is in your heart.'

Paolo looked at me and winked. 'You too, Rosie.'

I was glad it was too dark to see my blushing face.

The taxi bore us away and we both waved to Paolo out of the back window.

'I will have sweet dreams tonight,' said Nonna, smiling to herself as she closed her eyes and the taxi hurtled across the Piazza Tasso. 'What a lovely, lovely young man.'

'Absolutely lovely,' I agreed distractedly and then wondered whether I was thinking about Paolo. Or Gabe . . .

Chapter 28

I spooned fresh coffee into the Lemon Tree Café's old Italian coffee machine and smiled fondly at it. It might be grumpy and fractious and completely unpredictable, but just seeing the little Italian flag on its shiny chrome front made me glow inside. I'd always been proud of my heritage, but now having spent some time there, I felt a deep connection to my Italian roots. I fetched two mugs and glanced outside while I waited for the machine to come up to pressure.

Outside the café windows, the sky was heavy and grey and couldn't have been more of a contrast to the glorious weather I'd woken up to this morning.

We had packed our cases, deposited them with the concierge and had left the hotel straight after breakfast, determined to make the most of our last couple of hours in Sorrento. I'd accompanied Nonna as far as the Piazza Sant'Antonino where she'd arranged to meet her sister-in-law Alba. The two old ladies soon made themselves comfortable under the shade of a parasol for coffee and a catch-up. I'd left them to it and had spent a lovely hour exploring the marina, soaking up the sun reflected off the water and gazing out at the magical sight of Mount Vesuvius across the bay. I'd been tempted to hop on a ferry to Capri, but I'd have to save that for another time. Because there would be another time; Sorrento had got under my skin and I felt refreshed and energized.

It had been an amazing two days, I mused; emotional, but amazing. But now my short sojourn in Italy was over and I was back to earth with a bump. I mentally ran through what I had to do in the next two days and the sheer enormity of it made my stomach loop the loop.

Dad had collected Nonna and me from the airport, and I'd asked him to make a detour past Garden Warehouse on our way home. It was open, of course, as it was every day of the year except Christmas Day, and there were plenty of cars parked either side of the road. Clementine had placed a row of orange traffic cones at the end of her drive, I noticed, and customers were trundling back to their vehicles with big black and yellow carrier bags and trays and trays of plants.

But what had completely floored me was an enormous billboard advertising the opening of the Cabin Café with 'special celebrity appearance' on Tuesday. As in the day after tomorrow.

I'd felt sick when I saw it.

Less than forty-eight hours from now the Lemon Tree Café would cease to be Barnaby's only café. And with a celebrity on the premises, to boot, there'd be no surprises as to who would have the most customers on Tuesday.

Unless, that was, I came up with something even better very quickly.

Which meant there was no time to waste, so after I'd unpacked, I'd gone straight to the café and asked Lia to meet me there. I was so fired up after my trip that I couldn't wait to start planning. I didn't have time on my side but I did have determination, a head full of ideas and my talented sister.

I took our coffees to the conservatory and sat down opposite her. I'd left her scrolling through the pictures of Sorrento on my phone. She handed it back to me and picked up a teaspoon to scoop up the froth from her latte.

'Buffalo,' I said, noticing which picture she'd been looking at. My mouth watered as I conjured up the memory of last night's dinner, which Paolo had insisted was on the house. 'That's Paolo's secret. The most amazing steak I've ever had. You should try it.'

'Yeah, I'll remember to look for it in Asda next time I go,' she muttered.

'Good point,' I said, choosing to ignore her tone. 'It might be more of a specialist butcher thing, I'll google it.'

'I wouldn't bother; I can't see buffalo catching on in Barnaby somehow,' she said, raising a sceptical eyebrow.

She was in a bad mood, which was unlike her; she was normally such a sunny person.

'Look at this one.' I showed her a picture of Nonna trying to fit a huge slice of pizza into her mouth. The corners of Lia's mouth twitched. 'The pizza is fantastic. Light crispy base, loaded with flavour. Even the simple tomato, mozzarella and basil was amazing.'

'Stop,' she groaned, rubbing her stomach. A stomach which, I noticed with a jolt, was an awful lot smaller than it had been a month ago. 'I'd kill for a slice of pizza right now. I can't remember the last decent one I had.'

'Sorry,' I said with a grin, 'I'll stop talking about food now.'

'So you had a good time by the look of it?'

I pulled a face and rocked my hand from side to side.

'There were some tough moments. Visiting the cemetery was hard for Nonna and I thought she was going to have a heart attack when Marco's sister Alba chased us down the road. But she enjoyed being back in the lemon groves and, of course, going back to the family home on Via Vittorio has made her so happy.' I smiled at Lia. 'The main thing is that she has finally closed the door on a very unhappy time in her life. I was glad I was there for her.'

'Rosie Featherstone to the rescue,' she said, blowing on her latte.

'Hardly!' I said, hurt.

I hadn't meant it like that. Having only just confronted

my own unhappy time, I knew how it felt to draw a line under something, to feel like a weight had been lifted from your shoulders. But of course I couldn't say any of that, so I bit my tongue and steered the conversation back to something lighter instead.

'You'd love Sorrento.' I sighed, reaching for the milk and adding a splash to my coffee. 'You'll have to go – you, Ed and Arlo – this summer, before it gets too hot. Honestly, the sea, the mountains, the lovely square and the shops! Talking of which . . .' I pulled the present I'd bought her from out of my handbag. 'For inspiration.'

She smiled her thanks and took the recipe book out of its paper bag and began flicking through it.

I sipped my hot coffee. It was nice but not as nice as the one I'd had this morning at the harbour.

'And the coffee in Italy,' I said, eager to tell her all the details, even if she didn't seem too impressed. 'Seriously. It is an art form over there. I had this one called *caffè alla nocciola*: espresso with hazelnut cream. It was so delicious I almost wept.'

Lia let out an exaggerated sigh as if she had heard enough about Sorrento to last a lifetime.

'Sounds great,' she said flatly, closing the book and sliding it away from her. 'But I hope you didn't drag me into work on a Sunday evening to brag about your trip? And I say *work*, but of course, only one of us gets paid for being here, so, technically—' She broke off and smiled sweetly. 'Anyway, thanks for the book.'

I stared at her, confused. I'd suggested that she do some work at the café as experience to help her decide if a career in food was something that she'd really like. And I certainly didn't think I was bragging. I didn't like the way this conversation was going at all.

'You're welcome,' I said stiffly. 'And no I didn't *drag* you in for that. Paolo says that we need to revamp our menu to see off the competition and I'd really value your input.'

Lia gave me a hostile look. 'I said we should do that ages ago. I suggested being more adventurous. You ignored me.'

A niggle of guilt crept over me.

'I'm sorry, I didn't ignore you; I was just, well, being cautious. But that was before we had competition. Now we need to stand out. You were right.'

There was a moment's silence while Lia eyed me warily, chewing the inside of her cheek.

Finally, she shrugged a shoulder dismissively. 'So what are you thinking?'

'Well,' I cleared my throat, 'Paolo's success comes from doing something unexpected, offering what nobody else does. So while everyone in Sorrento claims to serve the best pizza in town, he lets them fight it out amongst themselves and serves buffalo steak. We already know that the Cabin Café menu is almost identical to ours—'

'Except not such good quality,' Lia put in.

'Exactly.' I nodded, grateful that she hadn't bitten my head off again. 'So I thought you could help me think of something that tastes fabulous but is cheap, quick and easy to cook which people can't get elsewhere.'

'I don't know,' said Lia, sounding bored, 'chips?'

Ed had dropped her off outside the café earlier and driven straight off without returning my wave. I'd thought at the time he simply hadn't seen me, but now I was beginning to wonder.

'Perhaps we could do some research.' I took a deep breath. 'Let's have a look.'

I reached for my iPad, but Lia finished her coffee and set the mug down heavily.

'It's Sunday, Rosie.'

'I know. Thank goodness.' I flashed her a grin. 'It means we can spend some time on this without the café being open.'

'Bank holiday weekend?' she reminded me.

I blinked. 'Gosh, I'd forgotten about that. Oh well, even

more time to get our heads round trying out a new menu tomorrow. Brilliant! My thoughts are these. The Cabin Café opens on Tuesday serving the bog-standard menu: soup, sandwiches, cakes, etc. Our customers have been eating that kind of stuff for donkey's years. So we launch a brand-new super-duper-never-been-seen-in-Barnaby-before menu, which will put theirs totally in the shade. What do you think?'

'Go for it,' she said, inspecting her nails.

'Lia, is everything OK?'

She shrugged and refused to meet my eye.

'Ed says I should stop working at the café; he says you're taking advantage of me. I argued with him, but he's right, isn't he?' She sank lower in her chair and pushed her hair roughly out of her eyes. 'I'm always going to be the little sister, hovering in your shadow, while you stand in the spotlight, the star of the family. I thought it might change once I started at the café. But it hasn't; now that you're the boss and I'm just the skivvy, it's even worse.'

I felt like I'd been slapped. Tears pricked at the back of my eyes. Not for myself, but for her. I couldn't believe that was how she felt, how *I'd* made her feel.

She scraped at a mark on the table with her thumbnail.

'Lia, you're right. It's not fair that you're working for free when everyone else is getting paid. And it's not fair that I've asked for your help on a Sunday. I'm so sorry. I didn't think it through.'

I reached across the table and took her hands and she gave me a wan smile.

I was truly sorry. The problem was that I didn't know what I could do about it. I'd seen the takings for yesterday while I'd been waiting for Lia to arrive. We had broken even. Just. In theory, now that Nonna wasn't taking a wage, there should be enough to pay Lia, but Nonna had never taken much as a salary. I was only paying myself a fraction of what I'd earned in my last job, but I needed something to live off.

And we'd had to get Juliet and Doreen in for extra shifts over the last week when I'd been so preoccupied with Nonna's saga. There simply wasn't enough in the pot to pay for an extra pair of hands. And when the Cabin Café opened on Tuesday, there could be even less.

'It's not all your fault.' She sighed. 'I was chuffed when you suggested I come and work in the kitchen. I know you were doing me a favour. But now that I've told the leisure centre I'm definitely not going back to work as a swimming teacher, I need to start earning. I never earned a fortune, but it helped and now Ed's feeling the pressure and that's not fair on him.'

They'd moved into a new house last year when they were expecting Arlo and I'd always known money was tight. Oh what the hell . . .

'Look, I need your creativity in the kitchen. I can't do it without you. We're a team. How about I pay you to come up with a new menu for the Lemon Tree Café?'

'Really?' Lia leapt out of her chair and hugged me till my ribs hurt. 'This is brilliant! Are you sure?'

'Absolutely. But not today. You should go. Call Ed to collect you and go home. It's the weekend; you should be with your family. I'll . . . I can work out how we're going to advertise our new menu.'

She looked at me and frowned. 'You should go too; bank holiday weekends apply to you as well.'

I wrinkled my nose. 'The café is all I've got, Lia. If I don't work, what else do I do?'

She looked appalled. 'Have fun?'

'Fun,' I repeated, rolling the word around in my head. I waved a hand over my iPad. 'Isn't devising business plans fun?'

'No. It's work.' She tutted. 'It's OK to love your job but it can't be all you do. What about chilling in front of a film, spending time with people you love?'

I felt my chest tighten. Yeah, right, because people were queuing up to fill that vacancy.

'You've always been better at that than me,' I said, clicking on my emails to avoid looking at her.

She eyed me suspiciously. 'So you're saying I'm lazy?'

'I'm saying you're lucky.' I smiled and this time she smiled back warmly. 'Ring Ed and leave me in peace.'

'Pizza,' she said suddenly. 'You wanted something that people will eat every day. It's cheap and quick to make and has the added bonus of being one of the most authentically Italian things in the world. We can make fresh, hand-stretched pizza. I guarantee the Cabin Café won't be able to do that.'

She folded her arms smugly and grinned, her eyes sparkling.

My heart gave a thump. I loved that idea: Barnaby's first pizza café. It was certainly different yet at the same time, in keeping with our Italian theme, and not too adventurous . . .

'And how will *we* do that? Doesn't it need a special oven?'

'We'll cook it in a traditional wood-fired pizza oven. You sort out how we're going to promote it and leave the oven to me.'

She pulled out her phone. 'Ed? Can you come and fetch me, please? And you know we're due at your parents' tonight? Do you think they'd lend me their pizza oven? Really? I love you too.' She blew kisses and ended the call.

'Sorted,' she said, tucking the phone and her new recipe book in her bag. 'See you back here tomorrow afternoon to try out some pizzas.'

'I thought it was a bank holiday?'

'It is.' She winked at me. 'But it will also be fun.'

'You are BRILLIANT,' I cried, grabbing her hands and bouncing on the spot. 'I knew you'd come up with something.'

'Culinary genius me,' she said, feigning nonchalance.

Ten minutes later Lia had gone home with Ed and I got stuck into some promotional ideas as Lia suggested. We only had a couple of days to make an impact, but after the success of the Spring Fair, I was confident that I could use Twitter and Facebook again to launch our new-look menu. We didn't have time for big changes to the decor, I thought, tapping a pen to my cheek as I surveyed the café. But it would be good to have something new to feature in our relaunch as well as the food. The tables already looked good, thanks to Gabe, and it looked like he'd finished the old dresser too. My eyes searched every corner of the café looking for inspiration, but to me the café was authentically Italian and already full of character, nothing needed changing. I closed my eyes trying to conjure up Bar Bufalo and suddenly remembered Nonna's reaction when she saw those old black-and-white photographs: the pictures of her family business in the cobbled streets of Sorrento.

Yes! Paolo could send me digital versions of those and we could frame them. Now that was real heritage. You don't get much more authentic than that. The Cabin Café could keep its plastic tables and chairs, the Lemon Tree Café had real history!

I fired off a quick email to Paolo and rubbed my eyes. It had been a long day and I was beginning to flag. I stacked our mugs in the dishwasher, turned off the coffee machine, cleaned down the milk pipe and switched off the lights before locking the door and heading for home.

It was already dark when I set off across the village green, but it wasn't cold or raining and I hummed happily to myself, pleased with what I'd managed to achieve today. It was only when I reached my cottage that I remembered I'd left the key behind the counter in the café.

Thank heavens for the spare! I put my hand into the bird feeder and found the key, remembering how Gabe had teased me that he'd be able to break in now he knew where it was.

As I opened the front door Lia's words came back to me, about weekends being a chance to spend time with people you love. And I suddenly felt very alone.

Chapter 29

Bank holiday Monday was not a holiday for the staff of the Lemon Tree Café. Although it was a lot of fun.

I'd begun work as soon as I'd woken up, posting on Facebook that tomorrow we would host a pizza party, with a free slice of home-made Italian pizza to every single customer. And the first person who'd seen the news was Doreen who immediately phoned Juliet. Both of them turned up to work even though the café was closed and I'd been so grateful I'd kissed them and had made a pact that whatever happened on Tuesday, they'd both be getting a bonus in their wages.

Ed and Lia had set up the pizza oven, on loan from his parents, in the tiny yard at the back of the café and Dad had gone to find Mr Beecher, who apparently had a stash of firewood going spare at the school. Mum and Nonna were having a quiet day catching up on everything Nonna had learned on her trip, including showing Mum the pictures of her father that had been stuffed in that Manila envelope I'd been searching for and a handwritten book of family ice-cream recipes which Alba had thought we might like to have for the café.

While Lia and Juliet had experimented with getting the oven temperature right and deciding on pizza toppings, Doreen had set to work on a huge batch of dough and I'd chopped wood into oven-sized pieces and concocted a Facebook campaign to spread the word about our pizza party.

Over a celebratory bottle of prosecco when all the work had been done, I'd given everyone a pep talk.

'Remember, folks, "loose lips sink ships". Garden Warehouse is the enemy from now on. I know that you've got a friend who's working there, Doreen, but our business has to stay that way: *our business*.'

Doreen nodded faithfully and mimed zipping her lips.

'The next couple of weeks are critical,' I continued. 'The Cabin Café will have an unlimited marketing budget and if their opening strategy of free cappuccinos and copying our bestselling cake is anything to go by, they won't take our free pizza strategy lying down. I fully expect them to retaliate and I don't want them to know what we're up to. We've got to beat them on everything – ambiance, service and, of course, food.'

'What about price?' Doreen had asked.

I shook my head. 'I draw the line at that. I'm not devaluing my staff or our café. Take our coffee, for example. You want to drink cheap dishwater coffee, fine,' I said with a defiant shrug, 'go to the Cabin Café. But if you want—'

Doreen and Juliet pressed their hands to their mouths.

'What?'

'That shrug,' said Doreen, her shoulders shaking with laughter.

'Fine,' Juliet mimicked, lifted her shoulders doing an impression of Nonna's trademark Latin gesture.

Lia giggled. 'You've got Nonna's shrug to a tee. Two days in Italy and you've gone native.'

I laughed, acknowledging that they were right. But who cares; I came from a family determined not to be brought down by their circumstances. If I'd inherited some of Nonna's feistiness and perhaps absorbed some of Paolo's commitment to succeed, so much the better.

'As I was saying, they've got the marketing budget to

fight back. We might have free pizza tomorrow, but after that all we've got is—'

'We've got you, you're our secret weapon,' said Doreen, her pink cheeks dimpling as she smiled. 'I'd never have thought of doing this.'

'True that.' Juliet nodded, pounding her clenched fist into the palm of her hand. 'We'll wipe the floor with the bas—'

'Actually, the pizza was Lia's idea.' I raised my glass to my sister and then to Doreen and Juliet. 'And none of it would have been possible without either of you.'

It was Tuesday already and Garden Warehouse opened its Cabin Café at nine o'clock, by which time we'd prepped enough pizza toppings to feed the Italian army and had huge signs on the road leading to the Garden Warehouse advertising our pizza party.

The celebrity appearance they'd advertised turned out to be a local TV weather girl, someone I'd never heard of. She arrived dressed to the nines in a tight low-cut red dress and heels and flashed her impossibly white teeth at a small crowd of onlookers. She posed between the store manager and my nemesis, Jamie Dawson the catering manager, before cutting the ribbon. She then tottered behind the counter to pour the café's very first cup of tea for the winner of the in-store prize draw for tea and cake for two.

Garden Warehouse had organized for a photographer to take publicity shots. But that was the sum total of any media coverage. According to Robin, our friendly junior reporter, in his email to me last night, his newspaper wouldn't cover it because the weather girl was 'from the competition'. I compared their poor turnout to the media splash we'd had for our Spring Fair and tried not to feel too smug about it.

I'd also received word about their food. As predicted, nothing spectacular to report. The sandwiches were so-so, the cake selection lacklustre and the coffee was not a patch on ours.

The news report came from Mum who had taken her friend Karen up there to spy on my behalf. The two ladies had shared a prawn sandwich that was heavy on mayo and light on prawns and a slice of walnut loaf which Mum suspected had been made before the bank holiday; she said it was so dry she didn't know whether to eat it or scrub the hard skin on her feet with it.

So, all in all, perhaps not quite the auspicious start the Cabin Café had been hoping for.

Oh what a shame.

The radio station wasn't covering the opening of the new café in their 'where to eat this week' slot either. And I knew *that* because they were on the phone to me. Live.

I'd planned on taking the call from the radio station in the café kitchen, but the constant arrival of customers holding their 'free pizza with this voucher' screenshot on their phones was making it difficult to concentrate.

I managed to nab the last free table in the conservatory, just as the producer warned me to stand by.

At the last moment, Tyson and Lucas, each carrying a mug of beef tea and a slice of pizza, appeared at the table. They pointed at the two empty chairs hopefully and I nodded for them to sit down. I looked for somewhere else to go but the producer was back in my ear whispering that the studio was coming to me in three, two, one . . .

'And on the line we have Rosie from the Lemon Tree Café who is going to tell us . . . WHERE TO EAT THIS WEEK!' Jeff, the radio presenter, boomed. 'Hey there, Rosie!'

'*Buongiorno*, Jeff!' I plugged my free ear with my finger to block out the noise of our pleasingly packed café.

'I understand you're throwing a pizza party as we speak in the little village of Barnaby?'

'That's right. You'll find us opposite the village green between Biddy's Pet Shop and Nina's Flowers and we're giving a free slice of pizza to every customer today.'

'Sounds fun! What gave you the idea for that?' he asked in a jaunty voice.

'My sister Lia is a talented cook and suggested that it was time our menu became more authentic, in line with our Italian heritage. My grandmother is from Sorrento where they serve the best pizza in the world.'

Somewhere behind me I heard Lia squeak. Lucas and Tyson looked from me to each other and pulled impressed faces.

'Is that right?' Jeff laughed. 'So—'

'Our pizzas are cooked traditionally in a wood-fired oven,' I gabbled on, determined to say my piece. 'The toppings are fresh and bursting with flavour, but the base is light, so it's the perfect thing for lunch.'

'Hear, hear,' said Tyson, folding the last mouthful of his Parma ham and mascarpone pizza into his mouth.

Lucas dabbed a spot of tomato sauce off Tyson's chin and tutted affectionately.

'And will you—' Jeff began to ask.

'We'll be introducing the changes gradually, but in order to get feedback from customers, we decided to celebrate our new menu by giving all our customers a chance to try it. Completely free of charge. One large slice per person.'

I paused for breath, aware that I had talked over the poor man, but I knew I only had one chance to get the message across. I turned towards the counter and caught Lia's eye.

You are ACE, she mouthed, giving me the double thumbs up.

'Well ...' Jeff began hesitantly, probably thinking I was going to interrupt him again. I was tempted, but managed to hold my tongue. I didn't want to appear too rude, after all. 'I don't know about our listeners, but my mouth is certainly watering. Make mine a pepperoni, I'll be right over.'

I laughed coquettishly.

'I'll hold you to that, Jeff. Our cakes are pretty good too, and our coffee, if I say so myself, is the best you'll taste in the region,' I said boldly. 'The Lemon Tree Café is *the* place to be in Barnaby right now if you want a *pizza the action.*'

The radio presenter guffawed at that and chimed in with his own cheesy joke, which included the leaning tower of pizza as its punchline. I reminded his listeners of our Facebook page and after bidding him a thickly accented '*Ciao*', I ended the call and I blew out a long calming breath, pleased to have that over with.

A round of applause broke out behind me and I turned to see Doreen, Juliet, Lia and even a few customers clapping and cheering enthusiastically.

'You are amazing!' Lia squealed, darting towards me, arms wide. 'A media star in the making!'

'I don't want to tempt fate,' I said, unable to get the huge grin off my face, 'but this is going even better than I imagined.'

'That'll put us on the map, hen, right enough,' said Juliet.

'We had every faith, didn't we, Ju?' Doreen nudged Juliet.

'We did, Dor, we did.'

I raised an eyebrow; when did these two get so pally? Not that I was complaining.

'Group hug!' Lia extended her arm to include Doreen and Juliet and to my surprise they both dived in to be hugged.

'Come on, girls,' said Doreen, nodding towards the counter where a cluster of people was queuing up and glancing our way. 'We've got customers. What's Italian for let's get a wiggle on?'

I left Doreen to serve the queue, Juliet to stretch dough

into rounds and Lia to load the oven with a fresh batch of Caprese pizzas, while I cleared some tables and handed out some hastily printed new menus to customers.

We'd been blessed with a lovely day today. The spring sun was out in full force, bringing people out of their homes in droves after such a chilly weekend. Everywhere looked fresh and new; from the bluebells nodding gently along the edge of the stream opposite the café right up to the tops of the distant hills, which now glimmered in a hundred shades of green.

Inside, the café looked dressed for spring too. I'd splashed out and ordered posies of freesias for every table from Nina, which smelled heavenly. Mum had washed all the cushion covers and plumped up every cushion on every chair. I'd bought a few new toys from Lucas's shop – heavy-duty wooden ones that even Alfie Sargent would struggle to break – and of course along the wall next to the old dresser was the row of photographs that Paolo had kindly emailed to me and I'd had blown up and framed.

But it was the sheer number of customers that was the biggest difference. There was someone at each table both inside and out on the pavement and while the pizzas were no doubt a big hit (Lia and Juliet, who'd been taking it in turns to shovel pizzas into the oven were both looking pink from the heat), we were selling everything else on the menu too. This level of business was unlikely to continue, but for now I felt incredibly grateful and more than a little proud.

At lunchtime, Ed came in with Arlo. The way my brother-in-law had the baby casually tucked under his arm made me smile; no pushchair, no changing bag, just him and his boy.

I sent him into the back yard to see Lia and he came back five minutes later munching a slice of garlic mushroom pizza, which Arlo was desperate to get his hands on. Ed pulled a piece of the crust off for him and placed a shy kiss on my cheek.

'I just wanted to say thanks for giving Lia some responsibility,' he said, scuffing his toe against the corner of the counter. 'It means the world to her, you asking her to come up with this pizza menu.'

'Some *paid* responsibility,' I reassured him. 'I do realize that I should have done that earlier, but we're not exactly awash with cash.'

'It's not about the money,' said Ed, meeting my eye finally. 'It's about self-esteem. She idolizes you, you know. She gauges her achievements by how she measures up to you and she constantly finds herself wanting.'

That made me feel very sad. My sister had always followed a different path to me, but it wasn't better or worse. In some respects, I thought, looking at Arlo giving the piece of crust a good sucking, hers was a lot richer.

But if working at the café would help give Lia the self-esteem she lacked, I could sort that out right now. It probably wasn't viable straight away. But what the hell? I was learning that taking risks and letting your heart rule your head was sometimes worth it and I felt that this might be one of those times.

'I haven't mentioned it yet,' I whispered, checking no one was in earshot, 'but I'm going to offer her a job. I know that'll help out at home too.'

'She'd like that.' Ed laughed softly under his breath. 'But I'll let you into a secret. If I had my way, I'd like her not to work at all. Coming home to her and Arlo is the best bit of my day. And the food she's been making . . .' He looked down at his stomach. 'I'm going to have to watch my figure. I know it's an old-fashioned view, and I wouldn't dream of holding her back, but there you have it.'

He hefted Arlo on to his shoulders. Arlo looked very precarious but he was beaming with gummy delight.

I looked at him quizzically. 'I thought things were tight?'

He shook his head. 'Cash flow was under pressure due to the office move, but the company is expanding. We don't need her to work. But that's not the point, she needs to feel valued.'

'Understood.' I tapped my nose. 'And believe me, she is completely valued. It has just taken me a while to realize how much.'

Customers and friends continued to pop in all afternoon and I was thrilled to see Gina at three o'clock, just before the after-school rush, with the two little boys she'd been looking after last week.

After settling the boys at a table with the new wooden toys and a slice of pizza cut up into finger-sized morsels and a glass of water each, she joined me at the counter.

'So,' she said, pushing her pink hair out of her eyes, 'tell me all about your Friday night.'

I finished slicing a fruit scone, set it on a plate with butter and jam and passed it to Doreen before answering and smiled at my old school friend.

'It was like coming home,' I said simply.

'Ah, I'm so pleased,' said Gina, her smile going all melty.

'It was my first time, and some things were hard to hear. But I can't wait to go again. Probably the best weekend of my life.'

'Wow.' Her eyes popped out on stalks. '*Weekend*?'

I nodded, happy to float off in a reverie of Italian memories for a moment. 'There's something about being so close to the ocean,' I sighed, 'the sky seems bigger and there's more room to breathe.'

'You are funny.' She giggled and shoved my arm. 'I think ocean is stretching it a bit, and I can't imagine there's much room on Gabe's boat, but anyway . . . What?'

I was staring at her. Clearly we'd been talking at cross purposes. My stomach plummeted.

'I wasn't with Gabe; I took Nonna to Italy for the weekend.'

'Whoopsie.' She pressed a hand to her mouth, appalled by her own blunder. 'I babysat Noah at my house on Friday.

Gabe didn't say who he was meeting, but he was all dressed up and smelled divine . . . Sorry.' She cleared her throat and shrugged sheepishly. 'I just assumed it was you. I wonder who it was, then.'

Hmm, I wondered that too, and I couldn't help feeling a bit miffed. I'd seen him on Friday morning before my Italy trip to let him know I'd be away. He had told me he planned to work on the dresser on Saturday but hadn't mentioned anything about 'a date'. And of course, while it was none of my business, I thought he knew me well enough to confide in me, that was all. Especially after he'd literally been my shoulder to cry on the other day.

'It's fine, really,' I said brightly, pasting on a smile. 'I told you, Gabe and I are just friends. That's all. He's his own man, entitled to his secrets.'

'Right.' Gina didn't look convinced.

I felt a sudden urge to extract myself from this conversation.

'Here.' I passed her a cup of tea. 'On the house. And er . . . I think the boys are trying to attract your attention.'

Gina looked down to see two faces smeared in tomato sauce. One was in tears and the other had a piece of pizza wedged up his nose.

'Oh joy,' she groaned. 'I'd better go and . . .' She pressed her lips together. 'Sorry about the Gabe thing.'

I smiled bravely and waved her apology away.

Good for Gabe, I told myself resolutely, *dipping his toe back into romantic waters.* This was an excellent thing. So why did I suddenly feel like crying?

Chapter 30

The café continued to be busy all day and I wasn't at all surprised when a larger than usual after-school crowd began to arrive.

'Good grief, it's an invasion!' Lia pointed out of the window at a sea of small people dressed in the grey and red uniform of Barnaby Primary School which was advancing across the green towards the café.

'Battle stations, everyone,' I said. 'I think we are about to be bombarded by some very hungry children.'

'Four Napoletana pizzas going in the oven now,' said Juliet, rubbing a floury arm across her face. There was flour in her red hair too and on her black apron, and the back of her jeans had two white handprints on it where she'd had her hands on her hips.

'We need more cheese.' Lia started to panic, grabbing the cheese grater and raiding the fridge for anything vaguely cheese-like. 'We're running out of mozzarella.'

'Spread it thinly,' Doreen suggested, reloading the cake stand with the last of the fairy cakes. 'Like the workers in this place.'

That comment may have been aimed at me because as the rest of the team scampered into action, I stood perfectly still, scanning the oncoming crowd of parents and children for a man with a thatch of sandy-coloured hair and a matching small boy . . .

And then moments later, I let out the breath I hadn't

realized I was holding as there he was in front of me, his grey eyes smiling as he pulled his hoody off to reveal a faded T-shirt that clung to his broad chest and showed off his biceps.

I felt something twang at my insides and my heart gave a little flutter and it was all I could do not to throw my arms round his neck and give him a hug, as I'd done a week ago in my cottage when I'd opened my heart to him. I'd missed him.

'Hi!' I beamed.

'How are you?' he said gently. 'How's Maria?'

'Good. Well. Happy,' I burbled. 'I'll have to tell you all about it sometime when we're not quite so snowed under.'

He took in the packed café and shook his head. 'You've done an amazing job. I called into Garden Warehouse earlier and it was like a morgue.'

I folded my arms triumphantly. 'Ha ha, my dastardly plan is working. It's cost us a fortune in giveaway pizza, but it's going down a storm and it's worth it just to ruin the Cabin Café's first day.'

'That's a bit harsh.' Gabe looked uncomfortable. 'It doesn't have to be that way, you know. They're appealing to a very different consumer to you – to all the Barnaby businesses, as a matter of fact.'

'Oh really? Well, they started it,' I retorted, sounding childish even to my own ears. I unfolded my arms. 'Anyway, how about you? Good weekend?'

'Um, yes.' He nodded. 'Interesting—'

He broke off as Noah skipped over, dripping melted cheese on to the floor from the slice of pizza he was waving about. He said a cursory hello to me and asked his dad if he could go to Robbie's for tea and then stay late to play in his garden because they'd got baby rabbits and could they keep one because they were free.

Gabe laughed and ruffled his son's hair, waving across at Robbie's mum and agreeing to the play date but not the rabbit. Noah stuck his bottom lip out until Gabe told him about the baby owls he'd spotted in a tree this morning which made him gasp.

'Owls sick up their own poo,' Noah informed me gleefully and ran off to tell Robbie the news.

'I do love that boy,' I said with a giggle.

I looked up at Gabe to find him staring at me as if I was a pot of gold at the end of the rainbow.

'What?' I laughed.

'Nothing, nothing.' Gabe cleared his throat. 'So, I was saying . . . Yes. It was an interesting weekend. I've got something to tell you, I've—'

Suddenly I didn't want to hear about it. I didn't want to know about his date on Friday night and how well it went and who she was and when he'd be seeing her again.

Because I wanted it to be me.

There. I'd admitted it to myself. Gabe was the loveliest man I'd met in aeons and if I hadn't been so wrapped up in my own issues I might have stood a chance with him and now it was too late.

'Gabe.'

I placed a hand firmly on his chest to shut him up. But instead of looking surprised as I'd expected, his eyes lit up and a wide smile spread across his face. Then he covered my hand with his, and squeezed it.

For a moment I was so taken aback I forgot what I was going to say. He stepped closer until the toes of his dusty boots touched the tips of my flat red pumps.

'This is important, Rosie.' He ran the tip of his tongue over his top lip.

The sounds of the café faded away until all I could hear was the whooshing of my blood in my ears. I didn't know what was coming, but it was clearly significant enough to make him nervous. A feeling of dread gripped at my insides.

'OK,' I whispered croakily. 'I'm listening.'

'I've got a new job. I start in three weeks once I've fulfilled all my French polishing projects.'

I blinked at him slowly, totally speechless. I hadn't seen that coming. New girlfriend, yes, but not that. I nodded for him to go on.

'I saw an advert for a job using my law background *and* it was local enough to fit in around Noah and I thought, Why not?'

I was nodding away to his story like one of those toy dogs you see in the back of cars, but still my mouth couldn't seem to remember how to speak.

'I got through the first round of interviews and then the managing director came down from York on Friday night and interviewed me over dinner. Gina looked after Noah and I could tell she was dying to ask where I was going but I didn't want to tempt fate in case I didn't get offered the job. Same reason I didn't tell you. But I did get it. And I feel . . . great! I feel like it's time. Time to get my life back on track. Time to . . .' he peered at me from under long golden lashes, 'maybe invite a beautiful woman out on a date? That's you, by the way. In case I'm not being clear.'

He grinned sheepishly and my heart started doing the fandango.

He hadn't been on a date with anyone else. It was an interview. And on top of all that he thought I was a beautiful woman.

He brushed his hand across my face as a tiny tear of joy slipped down my cheek.

'I'm sorry, I've made you cry.'

I launched myself at him, throwing my arms round his neck.

'You haven't, you've made me happy!'

I pulled back laughing and kissed him lightly on the mouth. 'Really happy. I am so proud of you. And RELIEVED.'

His brow crinkled at that. I laughed again, deciding not to elaborate.

'Thanks. After what you just said, I was a bit nervous—'

'We'll have to celebrate.' I grinned. 'Perhaps Gina could babysit again this Friday.'

He nodded and then slapped his hand on his forehead. 'It's a new moon again that night. I've already promised Noah we'll stargaze. I don't suppose you fancy a repeat performance? Singed sausages and cremated marshmallows?'

A new moon . . .

'You've been here nearly a month already,' I said, shaking my head in disbelief.

The new moon was coming round again and Clementine's old myth came flooding back to me: if you can peel a lemon in one single strip, you'll attract a new love before the next new moon. And even though everyone had agreed it was a load of mumbo-jumbo, I'd taken the last lemon home with me. I'd sat at my kitchen table and focused all my concentration on it. I'd peeled it painfully slowly, keeping an even pressure on the knife, making sure the strip of peel didn't get too narrow or too wide, and afterwards I'd sat there with one bald lemon and one long strip of yellow peel and laughed at myself for being so silly.

He smiled at me and I smiled back. Maybe I wasn't being silly after all. Maybe he could be my new love . . .

'I'd love to,' I murmured. 'Thank you.'

'Great, great.' He gave me another brief hug and I breathed in the delicious scent of him – Gina was right, he did smell divine. 'And I want to hear all about your trip.'

I nodded excitedly; I couldn't wait to tell him all about Sorrento and the story of Nonna's marriage and Paolo – he'd love Paolo, they had so much in common.

I heard a sharp cough.

'Oh there's someone behind you.' Gabe stepped away as I felt a tap on my back.

I turned to see a woman in her forties with brown hair so straight it looked like it had been ironed. Blue eyes blinked rapidly behind chunky glasses beneath a long, even fringe. Two dark-haired children with freckled cheeks clung to her sides.

'Excuse me,' she said in a staccato voice, 'can you tell me where the owner of this café is?'

'I'm the manager. Can I help?'

I smiled at her two children. There were tell-tale signs of recent pizza demolishment around their mouths. I passed them a napkin each from a pile on the counter and pointed out the toys to them and, after asking their mum's permission, they scooted off.

'The manager?' She looked from me to Gabe pointedly and we instantly shuffled apart. 'No. It's an old lady I'm after. Is Maria here?'

'My grandmother?' I shook my head. 'She's spending the day with a friend. In fact, she rarely comes in these days.'

Nonna had sent her apologies for not coming in to lend us a hand today but she was intent on getting back into Stanley's good books and wasn't going to rest until it was mission accomplished. Now that she was officially a widow, she wanted to make up with him and explain why she had lied in the first place. I'd told her that I was sure Stanley would come round once he knew the full story. She was probably there now camping out on his doorstep, singing Italian folk songs until he caved in and opened the door.

The woman huffed and a flicker of recognition lodged in my brain. Something about this woman looked familiar and yet I was sure she hadn't been in the café before.

'Right. Well, can you give her a message?'

'Sure.'

She reached into a very large handbag and rooted around in it and I caught Gabe's eye and we smiled at each other. Whoever she was, she wasn't very friendly.

Finally, she reappeared from the depths of her bag with a small notebook which had a thin pen clipped to the side of it.

Then it came to me; that framed photograph in Stanley's hall of his daughter and her family. That was where I'd seen her and the children before.

'Are you Stanley's daughter, by any chance?' I asked.

She blinked rapidly, surprised. 'Yes. Angela.'

'Oh pleased to meet you!' I beamed, sticking my hand out. She frowned at it and indicated that she couldn't take it because she had a small book in her hand. I dropped my hand and shoved it in my apron pocket. 'That's who Nonna has gone to visit.'

Angela folded her arms tightly. 'Well, she won't find him, not unless she looks in Chesterfield Hospital.'

'Stanley's ill? What's wrong?' I gasped out loud. Gabe moved closer to me.

She harrumphed. 'What *isn't* wrong? Silly old sod hasn't been looking after himself properly. I warned him ages ago about throwing old food out. He was bound to do himself a mischief sooner or later.'

I exchanged worried glances with Gabe. It sounded like a bad case of food-poisoning.

'How long has he been ill?' Gabe asked.

Angela flushed and started fiddling with her glasses. 'Five days or so.'

Poor Stanley. The thought of him lying in a hospital bed without any of us knowing about it broke my heart.

'But he only went into hospital last night. Anyway,' she coughed and tore a page out of her notebook, 'he's been asking after your grandmother. Here's my number, tell her to call me and I'll fill her in.'

I took the piece of paper from her and folded it in two. 'Thank you. I'm sure she'll want to visit as soon as she can.'

Angela sniffed. 'They're fussy about visitors in intensive care.'

'So it's serious?' I gulped, feeling the blood drain from my face.

I turned to Gabe, glad to have his presence beside me. 'Nonna is going to be heartbroken. I have to go and tell her.'

'Would you like me to drive you?' he offered. 'I'll just let

Robbie's mum know what I'm doing, swap numbers and stuff. We can pick Maria up and go straight to the hospital if you like?'

'I'd like that very much,' I murmured, already untying the strings of my apron.

He squeezed my arm and strode across the café.

We had to hurry, if anything were to happen to Stanley and Nonna hadn't known where he was . . . I shuddered, not wanting to contemplate the consequences. I needed to let Lia and the others know where I was going.

'Excuse me a moment,' I said.

'Now hold on just a minute,' Angela barked, barring my way with her arm. 'My father is the one who's heartbroken. What sort of woman strings a man along and then turns down his marriage proposal? Which I might add, I wasn't happy about at all.'

That didn't surprise me; I couldn't imagine her being happy about anything much.

'Your grandmother's probably the reason he's ill in the first place,' she finished with a scowl.

I felt my hackles rise. Nonna had upset Stanley, that was true, but hadn't Angela just mentioned something about him eating out-of-date food?

'Nonna made your father very happy and vice versa. Now are you going to tell me which ward he's in,' I said, hands on hips, 'or do I have to try to find it out myself?'

'Intensive Care, unit four.' She wagged a finger. 'But I won't have her causing him any more trouble. The doctor says he needs peace and quiet.'

'I would think,' I said sharply, wondering how such a kind and gentle person as Stanley had produced such a miserable old boot for a daughter, 'that a visit from someone who loves him will be just what the doctor ordered.'

Stanley looked tiny, barely making a mound under the crisp hospital sheets. How was it possible to lose so much weight in such a short time? Gone were his plump cheeks and bright smile. The face that peered up at me was grey and gaunt, his eyes dull and watery. He had an oxygen mask over his mouth and nose, and thin tubes protruding from his hand and chest. He was linked up to all sorts of monitors and two different drips and machines were beeping on either side of him. Nonna gently took his hand and pressed it to her lips and it might have been my imagination but one of the beeps seemed to speed up a little.

'*Signore mio*,' she murmured, 'what happen to you?'

He tugged his oxygen mask down to his chin, raised his head and opened his mouth but all that came out was a rasping sound. He coughed and dropped his head back weakly against his pillow.

I found a jug of water with a cup and straw on his nightstand and supported his head while Nonna carefully held the straw to his lips. He took a sip and smiled his thanks to me.

'Maria,' he whispered, 'you came. I thought I would die without seeing you again.'

'What you talking about dying for, dicky head?' She tutted. 'You not going anywhere, Stanley Pigeon.'

'It was awful. I was in the house on my own, and—' He broke off, exhausted with the effort of speaking.

'Shush, I am here now.' She moved her chair as close as it would go. 'And I never, never leave you alone ever again.'

His eyes filled with tears.

'Do you mean that?'

'Yes, Stanley, I do.'

He reached for her with his other hand until she was completely tangled in amongst his tubes and wires. And then he rested his head back on his pillow as silent tears of relief trickled down his face.

I left Nonna to talk to him in private, popped outside to check on Gabe who was waiting in the corridor and then went back on to the ward to find the nurse.

I'd thought we might be refused entry when we'd arrived at the ward but as soon as I'd mentioned Nonna's name, a nurse had led us straight to Stanley.

'Only two visitors at a time,' she'd said, asking Gabe to wait in the corridor.

'He's been asking for her since he arrived,' the nurse had told us, looking delighted to see Nonna. She had dark skin and even darker eyes and spoke in quiet soothing tones. 'But when we tried the next-of-kin number for him, it just rang out.'

I found her at the nurses' station explaining on the phone to someone that flowers weren't allowed on the ward, but get-well-soon cards always cheered patients up and balloons were fine, but no latex.

'It's the allergens,' she said cheerfully after putting the phone down. 'We've got enough to deal with as it is.'

We looked over at Stanley's bed. There were no cards and certainly no balloons and a noose of guilt tightened round my heart.

'Has he . . .' I swallowed. 'Has he had many visitors?'

The nurse, whose name according to her badge was Mamta, shook her head. 'Just his daughter this morning. But she only stayed a few minutes.'

'I'm not strictly family,' I said, 'but we do love him. Can you tell me what is wrong with him?'

She told me that Stanley had suffered with a terrible bout of gastroenteritis and had been too ill to get out of bed to answer the door when Nonna had gone round last week. It had got worse instead of better and had eventually triggered internal bleeding which, due to the anti-coagulant medication he took for his heart condition, hadn't stopped. By the time he realized how ill he was, he'd been almost unconscious and the ambulance had only just made it in time.

A wave of pure sadness crashed over me.

'Thank goodness it did,' I said, and the nurse nodded. 'And why is his breathing so ragged?'

'Pneumonia,' she said. 'But that's under control.'

Poor old chap, Angela hadn't been exaggerating when she'd said what *isn't* wrong with him.

Suddenly Nonna cried out.

'*Santo cielo!*'

The machines at Stanley's bedside stopped making the soft beeping noises and alarms started going off. 'Nurse!'

The nurse bolted over to his bed and began reading the dials and adjusting the drips and fitted the oxygen mask back over his mouth.

'Keep speaking,' said the nurse to Nonna encouragingly. 'He needs to hear your voice.'

'Stanley Pigeon,' Nonna said in a wavering voice, 'you not leave me now.'

Stanley's eyes were closed and his breathing was harsh. I tried to keep out of Mamta's way and squashed myself in between Nonna and the end of the bed. I rested my hand on her shoulder.

She covered it with her own and gazed at me through her tears.

'I left it too late, *cara*. I not even tell him I love him.'

A lump the size of a tennis ball formed in my throat.

'Tell him now,' I croaked. 'Just tell him.'

She leaned forward and pressed her cheek to his.

'I love you, Stanley. It take me fifty years to love again, but I do it now and I am sorry I not say it before. I hope it not too late. I love you, Stanley Pigeon.'

There was a commotion at the door to the ward and Nonna, the nurse and I turned to see who it was. It was Angela, unsurprisingly, raising her voice and Gabe doing his best to calm her down.

'Well, I need to see him,' she snapped, waving a sheaf of papers at the ward sister. 'I need to get this power of attorney signed. Tell that lot to leave.'

The ward sister, whose hair was scraped back into such a tight bun that it looked painful, was apparently not tolerant of this sort of behaviour and marshalled Angela straight out of the door and into the corridor. Gabe followed. My heart gave a little leap; he was such a star.

The nurse brushed past me to make a note on Stanley's chart when suddenly his eyes opened and he made a noise, muffled by the oxygen mask.

'May I?' I asked the nurse.

'Of course,' she said, her dark eyes full of compassion, 'he may be trying to tell you something.'

I gulped, understanding what she meant, and carefully lowered the mask.

'Say it again, Maria,' he croaked.

Nonna kissed his cheek. 'I love you, Stanley Pigeon.'

He closed his eyes and his face seemed to relax.

'Then . . . I die a happy man,' he whispered.

'No,' Nonna said, her voice cracking with emotion. 'Don't you dare.'

His hand fluttered up to find hers. I felt the nurse put her arms round my shoulders and realized I was shaking, tears coursing down my cheeks. This was so unfair, this couldn't end now, not just when they'd found each other.

Stanley's eyes flickered open again and a faint smile appeared on his lips. 'But not yet.'

Gabe and I stayed at the hospital for another hour after that. Stanley seemed to be out of immediate danger. He was going to need surgery as soon as possible to stop the internal bleeding but his system would have to be a bit stronger yet for that to happen. But now that he had Nonna by his side, I had the feeling that he would gain strength quickly; he already seemed to be a better colour.

I came off the ward to let Angela take my place at her father's bedside and chuckled to myself when I saw her trying to get Stanley to sign the paperwork she'd brought with her; Nonna was having none of it. I phoned Mum to let her know what had happened and she arranged to come down and bring Nonna home later. Nonna wasn't ready to leave yet and nobody had the heart to force her.

It was already a quarter to seven by the time Gabe dropped me off outside the café. He'd had a couple of messages from Robbie's mum and I could see he was getting anxious about being late to pick Noah up. It was a shame, I thought, stealing a sideways glance at him as I undid my seat belt and collected my bag, because a few minutes in the car, just the two of us, did have a certain appeal. But never mind, there'd be other times. Soon, I hoped.

'Thank you.' I smiled at him, shy suddenly, but conscious of his fingers drumming on the steering wheel. 'Having you there made all the difference, especially dealing with the delightful Angela.'

'You're welcome.' He grinned, but his eyes slid to the clock on the dashboard.

I leaned over and brushed my lips to his cheek before getting out.

'And congratulations again on the new job,' I said, leaning into the van, my hand on the door. 'You never said who it is?'

'Um, who who is?'

I giggled. 'Who the job is with?'

Gabe's eyes didn't leave mine as he drew in a long breath.

'I'm the new head of legal services for Garden Warehouse,' he said with a tight-lipped smile.

I stared at him in horror, not sure I believed what he'd just said.

'Seriously? You're going to work for them?' I gasped. 'You're going to work for the company that is threatening my livelihood?'

I swept my arm out, taking in all the other little shops. 'Threatening all our livelihoods? How could you?'

'Rosie, listen.' He pinched the bridge of his nose between his thumb and finger.

'No I won't listen. You know what this means to me, this café.'

'And me?' he said in low voice. 'Do you know what this job means to me? What it represents? How much I need to do this?'

'I know this,' I said, biting back the tears which I refused to shed in front of him, 'you are a snake. And if you take that job we can't be friends any more.'

'WHAT?' He stared at me incredulously. 'Rosie, wait. It's just a job, you can't . . . Listen, oh shit, I'm so late for Noah, I've got to—'

'GO! Just go!' I slammed the door and ran to the café but not before I heard him yell and thump the steering wheel.

Gabe's van sped away so fast that it left a cloud of dust in its wake and I knew I'd made him angry. But I was angry too. When would it end? I'd had a week, a whole week, of living on an emotional rollercoaster, and now, just when I thought the journey was finally smoothing out and coming to a happy end, whoosh, I was off again. I'd waited so long to let myself get close to someone, to trust another man after what happened with Callum, and now that I was finally beginning to let Gabe into my heart, I suddenly find myself sleeping with the enemy.

I looked up at the soft grey lettering across the front of the Lemon Tree Café, and dissolved into tears. I'd just sent away the man who'd touched my soul in a way no other man had ever done.

The café meant a lot to me and I wouldn't let Garden Warehouse take it away from me. And Gabe, I asked myself, did he mean a lot to me too? And if so, would we ever be able to come back from this row? I opened the door to the empty café, my heart heavy with pain.

Rosie Featherstone, will you ever learn . . . ?

PART FOUR

A Fresh Brew

Chapter 31

I was up and on my way to work far earlier than I needed to be. Just like yesterday and the day before that. Despite working twelve-hour days and driving Nonna backwards and forwards to the hospital to visit Stanley in my new little car (a bargain from one of our café regulars who'd sold his to treat himself to a new cabriolet for the summer) and sitting up late into the night researching pizza ovens, the oblivion of sleep eluded me.

And all because of that row with Gabe on Tuesday night when he'd confessed to accepting a new job with Garden Warehouse. I had been avoiding him ever since and as he hadn't been into the café, I could only assume he was doing the same to me.

The awful thing was that I'd been secretly hoping that he would put himself first for once, really think about what he wanted to get out of life. Any other company and I'd have been delighted that he'd decided to return to his legal career. But not Garden Warehouse; I couldn't get my head round that.

On my first trip to *The Neptune*, when Gabe moved to Barnaby, I'd been touched by how much he'd given up for Noah. He'd been so determined to give that little boy the start that he and Mimi had always wanted for their child that he had pared down his life so that he could manage it. Gone back to basics. And while I could see that 'working to live' to fit in around being a single parent had had its bene-fits, I could also see that Gabe might be ready for something more. And not just career-wise; he'd called me a beautiful woman and said he'd like to go out on a date with me . . .

But why oh why did he have to choose the company whose very existence posed a threat to my little café?

That question rolled round and round in my head during the lonely hours of the night to the point where I was relieved when five o'clock came around and the sky changed from grey to pink, accompanied by such a cheerful sym-phony of birdsong that it almost put a smile on my grumpy, sleep-deprived face. Almost.

And today, I remembered, as I stomped across the village green where a low mist hovered over the dewy grass, today was the first Friday in May. Today heralded a new moon. So much for Clementine's theory about my lemon-peeling skills attracting a new love before the next new moon; the only thing I'd fallen in love with this month was Lia's extra-thin-crust rocket and goat's cheese pizza. I honestly think I could eat that every day for the rest of my life and never get bored.

Yes. Much better. Think happy thoughts; I congratulated myself on changing the subject. Thinking about pizza and my plans to radically alter the Lemon Tree Café was a far better topic. All I needed was to get the go-ahead from Nonna. I slowed my pace as ahead of me, two baby rabbits, tails bobbing, scampered through a clump of bluebells and disappeared into a tuft of grass near the edge of the stream. Baby rabbits, spring flowers and a blue sky . . . I sighed a happy sigh: life wasn't so bad after all. Once this mist had cleared I reckoned it was going to be a lovely sunny day, clear skies perfect for . . . stargazing.

The thought brought me back down to earth with a jolt.

Tonight I had been invited to *The Neptune* to celebrate Gabe getting a new job. He'd suggested a night under the stars with him and Noah and supper al fresco.

Except that Gabe had taken the one job I couldn't celebrate. And seeing as we now weren't even speaking to each other, I could confidently say that our evening was well and truly cancelled.

I picked up my pace again as I approached the road, ready to cross to the café, and tried to regain my fleeting good mood . . .

Lia's ideas for the menu had been inspired; the pizza party had gone down a storm and our customers had all but abandoned our regular food in favour of them. And for the last three days, she had devoted herself to satisfying demand. Lia was über-talented in the kitchen. This week had given her a huge confidence boost; she had an amazing palate, she was a super-quick worker and completely unflappable under stress, and no one was more surprised to discover she had these skills than Lia herself. And now that I'd bitten the bullet and offered her a job, she was in the process of sorting out some proper, regular childcare. Although Mum was happy to do a few hours a day, Lia wanted more. And as soon as she'd organized that, she'd be bringing her talents to the kitchen of the café permanently. So that was good news.

The other good news was that Stanley, with plenty of love from Nonna, had stabilized and the doctor had told him that he should soon be fit for surgery to mend the ruptured ulcer, which had been detected.

So, on balance, I thought, taking out the big brass key to the door of the Lemon Tree Café, there were plenty of blessings to count.

'Eh, Rosanna!'

I turned round at the unmistakable sound of my grandmother's voice. She was hanging out of the window of Clementine's van and waving at me from the other side of the green. Clementine reversed wonkily around two sides of the green until the van was outside the café.

'Morning, you two,' I said, walking to Nonna's side.

'You up early?' Nonna's beady eyes scanned my face. 'What happen, you wet the bed?'

She nudged Clementine and they both hooted with laughter.

I did a double take at Clementine. Her hair still looked like she'd let Tyson loose on it with a pair of hedge clippers, she was still wearing scruffy men's clothes, but she had lost her haunted demeanour; she looked happier and more relaxed than I think I'd ever seen her.

'Couldn't sleep,' I said, leaning in through the window and kissing Nonna's wrinkled cheek. 'Clementine, you look well.'

'Thank you.' She circled her shoulders back and took a deep breath in as if she was about to start yoga. Then she smiled serenely. 'I'm going to the coast for the weekend after work tonight; staying with a cousin in a caravan. Got my regular radio slot this morning and then finishing digging a raised salad bed at the school this afternoon. Then I'm free. Free!'

Her thick eyebrows shot up at the last word as if she'd surprised herself.

'Sounds great; a weekend off. Remind me what that feels like.' I pretended to sigh and then smiled. 'Actually, Nonna, I'm glad I caught you. I want to invest in a proper pizza oven. We've only got that one on loan from Ed's parents and really it's not commercial standard. It's expensive but I've drawn up a plan . . .'

Clementine crunched on an apple while Nonna half listened to my idea to remove one of the ovens and replace the griddle with a smaller one to make room for a pizza oven. While I was talking she was rummaging through her purse counting out change.

'What are you doing?' I said eventually, a bit miffed that she wasn't concentrating when I'd been up half the night finding a supplier who actually had a small oven available for immediate delivery and a willing workman whose next job had fallen through. If I gave him the nod today he'd come next week.

'I need coins for hospital car park,' she muttered, counting out silver into her lap.

'Oh right,' I said, chastised. I opened my handbag and took out my purse. 'I didn't realize that's where you were going. Is everything all right?'

'Hope so.' Nonna sighed. 'They operating on my Stanley this morning. That nice Indian nurse phone me. Clementine say she take me in early so I can see him . . . you know, see him before he goes.'

I nodded, I did know. Mamta, the nurse, had explained that there was a risk with surgery; Stanley's spirit was willing, but his heart was very weak. And the longer his internal injury continued unchecked the weaker his body would be. Establishing the right time to operate on him was difficult; it was catch-twenty-two.

'That's good news; they must think he's well enough! Give him my love,' I said. 'Ooh, just quickly before you go, sorry to push you about the pizza oven. I spoke to Paolo last night about it, he said—'

'Paolo?' A big smile spread across Nonna's face. She looked at her friend. 'My great-nephew. In Italy. Lovely boy.'

'You might have mentioned him,' said Clementine drily. She polished off her apple, core and all, opened the glove box and took out a leather coin purse. 'What do we need?'

'One more pound,' said Nonna.

'I've got that.' I held up a gold coin but Clementine waved a hand.

'Got loads of change in here.' She closed the purse and started the engine again. 'Let's beat the traffic, Maria.'

'Wait,' I said, grabbing Nonna's arm through the window. 'I know you want to get off, but can I order the oven? There's only one in stock and the installer has got a window next week.'

'I dunno.' Nonna shrugged. 'You the manager.'

Clementine gave a short bark of laughter. 'Rosie's right, Maria. You're the owner and a big investment like this has got to have your approval. I don't envy you, my friend. Best pound I ever earned when I sold the garden centre. Now the biggest decision I have to make is which herbs to have in my tea.'

'I don't want decisions!' Nonna cried. 'I had enough of business. I old lady now, I just want to be with Stanley and enjoy time together.'

I cocked an eyebrow at her but said nothing. Wasn't this exactly what Mum had been saying to her for years?

'I understand,' I said, extracting myself from the van. 'You go; we can do this another time. Give him a kiss from me.'

I'd miss the order deadline and might lose the oven I'd set my heart on, but her mind was on Stanley, quite rightly. I was wrong to push her for an answer right now.

'Right. Give me the pound,' Nonna demanded, holding out her hand.

I held the money out to her, startled by her sudden change of mind.

Nonna prised it from my fingers. 'Okey cokey. Sold.'

I blinked at her. 'What is?'

She held up the pound between her finger and thumb. 'Fearnley's sell for a pound and now café too. Congratulations, *cara*, you just buy my café. You the new owner. You decide about oven.'

I stared at her. 'Me, the new owner?'

She flapped a hand. 'Yes. Can't be bothered any more; life not all about work, you know.'

Clementine snorted.

My heart began to quicken. I'd never planned to run a café let alone own one. But . . . why not?

'Really?' I said, completely calmly even though my heart was beating so loudly I could barely hear my own voice.

'Really, one hundred per cent,' Nonna confirmed.

I could do this; I knew I could. And it was a damn sight more meaningful than a career in social media, cheerleading other people's business, other people's dreams. Besides, now that I thought about it, turning the Lemon Tree Café into an Italian pizza café had become a bit of a dream and what better than to completely own that dream, to be responsible for its every hiccup, its every triumph? Paolo had taken on his family business and made it his own, transforming it into something special. And I could do the same. The Lemon Tree Café could evolve and grow and be the hub of the community and be there for the next generation of Nonna's family after me. I'd already got some ideas too; I had thought up so many during the last three sleepless nights that the notebook by my bed was covered in scribble.

'About bloody time.' Clementine was grinning from ear to ear. 'Congratulations, Rosie. I can't think of a better custodian to take on the mantle from your indomitable grandmother. Any tips on those lemon trees, come to me.'

I swallowed. 'Thank you.'

My head was spinning. There was so much I needed to learn. About tax and employment law and environmental health . . . And really, let's face it, I was a rubbish cook. But all that could wait.

I met Nonna's gaze. Her eyes had a film of tears. Despite the nonchalance of handing over her business for such a paltry sum, I knew the price she was really paying. The café had been her life, her *lifeline*, for years. A way to stay in control, a place where no one had power over her. And now she was handing that to me.

'I love you, Nonna.' I opened the van door so I could give her a proper hug. 'I promise I'll make you proud of what we do.'

A thought struck me as I said 'we', and I realized exactly what I had to do.

'Can we keep this between ourselves, just for now?'

Nonna shrugged. 'Sure. Whatever you say, you the boss. Now, Clementine, put your foot on it, I got a man to kiss.'

'Whoo hoo!' cried Clementine. 'Now we're both free!'

'*Ciao*, Rosie!'

The engine on the old van lurched off throatily into the early-morning sunshine and Nonna and Clementine waved hands out of the windows like an elderly Thelma and Louise.

I stood for a second, feeling dazed and wondering whether that just happened. And then I looked down at the brass key in my hand and started to laugh.

Rosie Featherstone, owner of the Lemon Tree Café . . .

I fitted the key into the lock, pushed open the door and breathed in the smell of all my tomorrows. The coffee machine was calling me, but before I could turn it on, there was something else I needed to do.

Dropping into an armchair, I took out my phone and called my soon-to-be business partner.

'Lia,' I said, unable to keep the smile from my voice, 'this might seem an odd question at seven o'clock in the morning, but have you got fifty pence?'

Chapter 32

And so it was that Lia and I, quite unexpectedly, became the proud new owners of the Lemon Tree Café.

Nonna devoted her time to Stanley's recovery, spending every hour she could at his bedside. She fended off his daughter's demands to sell his bungalow and move into a retirement home in Bristol and she oversaw his move from the Intensive Care Unit to a general ward (neither of them liked the word geriatric). They were both counting down the days until he could come home.

We'd told Juliet and Doreen straight away, of course, as soon as Lia had accepted my proposal to each take a fifty per cent share in the café. Juliet had burst into tears, which was so totally out of character for her that we were most concerned until she explained that she'd been worried that Nonna would sell up or close down and she really, really couldn't afford to lose this job; the money helped pay for her mother-in-law's care. Doreen had congratulated us and then promptly asked to reduce her hours. Nothing personal, she added, but she had another grandchild on the way and wanted to be around more to help.

After that the next ten days had flown by in the busiest whirl that the little café had ever seen. Work on the new kitchen began immediately; we ordered the oven, booked the installer to come and knock the living daylights out of the kitchen, redesigned the menus, revamped the website, issued a press release, interviewed a new accountant . . . The to-do list had been extensive and exhausting. Even when the café had had to be closed for three days last week while the kitchen was out of action, we hadn't stopped; we'd simply relocated to Lia's house. We'd worked up some delicious brunch recipes and, following feedback from the pizza party, had finalized a pizza menu.

The paperwork had been straightforward enough; I'd used the same solicitor as I'd used to buy my cottage last year. And if my mind wandered occasionally to the fact that I'd really like to chat things over with Gabe, to get him to cast his sharp eye over the new lease that the café's landlord had offered us, or the employment contracts we'd drawn up for Doreen and Juliet which included a yearly profit share, or mine and Lia's new partnership agreement, then I quickly reminded myself that he was, from today as it happened, part of Garden Warehouse, ergo, the enemy, and the last thing we needed was the competition knowing our business.

And today, Monday, in the middle of May, we were re-opening and the new pizza oven was about to be put to the test. Sitting outside, tilting my face to the morning sunshine, and waiting for Lia to arrive so we could open up together, I could scarcely believe my good fortune. The café was a world away from the media career I'd envisaged for myself, but it was a tangible thing and I loved how something as simple as a good cup of coffee could brighten up someone's day. At eight o'clock on the dot, Ed's car appeared and pulled up at the kerb. Lia jumped out and Ed followed.

'How was Arlo?' I asked, conscious that the upshot of all this excitement and upheaval was that my nephew was being shipped off to Gina's for three days a week.

Ed puffed out his chest. 'Took it in his stride. Hardly a peep out of him.'

'Good,' I said, nodding and wondering why I felt a bit tearful. 'That is good.'

I met Lia's gaze.

'Our first day,' she said with a shy smile.

We looked up at the café and then back at each other.

'Yep.' I nodded, my throat tightening with emotion.

Which was ridiculous because it was only a job, only a little café . . . But it wasn't, a little voice nagged at me as I submitted to Lia's silent hug. It was far more than that. The Lemon Tree Café had been a refuge for Nonna, a small piece of home in a strange land, a happy safe place, and now it was ours. Together.

'Smile, you two,' said Ed, holding up the camera on his phone. 'One for the family album.'

He took the picture, kissed Lia goodbye and, wishing us both luck, he set off for work.

Lia watched his car disappear and sighed fondly.

'Hashtag perfect man. Look what he gave me this morning as a surprise.' She thrust her hand in my face. Resting on top of her wedding and engagement rings was a new platinum band studded with tiny diamonds. 'He's bought me an eternity ring.'

'Gorgeous,' I said, bending over her hand to inspect it in a bid to disguise the flush of envy to my cheeks.

That was three rings now that my sister had got from a man. I couldn't even get a phone call. And whose fault is that, an annoying voice niggled in my head, when you yell 'we can't be friends' at the only decent man you've met this millennium?

She gazed at it. 'Apparently we're not strapped for cash any more. The family business is doing well and Ed's just had a bonus. And his dad is shifting more responsibility on to him so he can think about retiring.'

'And he's happy for you to do this?' I eyed her carefully.

Ed would really like her to be at home and not work at all and if they didn't really need the money which Lia would bring in, I hoped that he didn't harbour any resentment towards her new business.

She nodded. 'Being a parent is still my number-one job, but I need to think about myself too. I want to challenge myself, I know working at the family café isn't exactly *MasterChef*, but it's a new start for me. It's close to home, so it fits in around Arlo, and I'm secretly quite proud of being responsible for our new menu and for kick-starting a career. Ed understands that.'

'Good. And I'm proud of you too,' I said, handing her a set of keys.

'It's hard finding a job you love and still be there for your family. I'm so lucky to have this one,' she said.

I flushed, remembering how Gabe had said that his new job appealed partly because it would fit in around Noah's school.

'Well open the door, then,' I said gruffly.

'Sorry, boss!' she tutted.

I tugged her hair, just like I'd done when we were kids. 'Hey, partners, remember?'

'Partners,' she repeated and as the two of us stared at each other, I felt excitement bubbling inside me and I was sure she felt the same.

We pushed the door open together, flipped the 'Closed' sign over and we were in business.

By eleven o'clock the sun was high in the sky and Barnaby was getting its first taste of summer. The café's pretty new outside tables had arrived just in time.

Customers sat under the awning enjoying the sunshine while sipping their coffees and chatting with friends. Sun-cream had been smeared on to freckly noses and pale shoulders and the air was fresh with the smell of cut grass. Across the road, small children played on the village green in T-shirts and shorts and summer dresses, and a couple of teenagers lolled on top of each other on a rug by the stream, probably thinking no one could see them.

The view out of the café's windows was about as

quintessentially English as it could possibly be and we'd propped the front door of the café open to let in the gentle breeze.

A breeze which was very welcome indeed because the new pizza oven, we'd quickly established, generated an awful lot of heat and Rick, the photographer, was making us stand in front of it.

'Excellent. OK, Rosie in the middle this time. Arms round each other and big cheesy grins!'

No one could accuse him of not being thorough, I mused, switching places with Lia.

'Come and give us a cuddle, Juliet,' I said to our prickliest member of staff. 'You know you want to.'

'If I must, hen,' Juliet grumbled when I forced her to come closer. 'But I'll warn you; I'm sweating like a race-horse with this furnace behind me.'

I'd booked Rick to mark the pizza oven's first day with some professional pictures so I could tell the world about our new menu. Both Juliet and Doreen were working today, just to ensure everything ran smoothly on day one. Rick had been here for an hour doing interior and exterior shots of the café, close-ups of Doreen rolling out the dough, Juliet sprinkling mozzarella and Lia shovelling pizzas into the oven. My pose had been on the doorstep under the Lemon Tree Café sign with my arms folded. Although privately I thought he'd captured my combative stance on business very well, I got him to do another one of me at the coffee machine looking smilier. Now we were having some group shots done, much to the amusement of our customers who found it very entertaining.

Rick lowered the camera and ran a hand through his unkempt shoulder-length hair.

'Lovely. Lia, let's try holding the pizza up to the lens again, not at such a steep angle this time,' he said with a regretful look at his trainers. 'And the rest of you stand in a horseshoe around her.'

'I'll do my best,' said Lia with a giggle.

She carefully held out the metal paddle on which she'd got a freshly baked Diavola pizza studded with chillies and pepperoni. The first attempt at this had gone wrong and the pizza had slid straight off the paddle and on to Rick's feet.

'Nice one.' He grinned.

'Are we nearly done?' I asked, massaging my cheeks. 'I've been smiling for so long, I think I've given myself lockjaw.'

'And I'm having a hot flush,' said Doreen, blowing her fringe out of her eyes.

'And my arms are aching,' Lia added, putting the pizza paddle down on the work surface.

Doreen was surreptitiously checking her watch and Juliet was scowling at Stella Derry who was trying to open the till by herself to pay us for her tea.

'Yep. Just one last one, this time with serious faces, arms folded, like you mean business.'

Which we did, I thought, catching a glimpse of Lia tilting her chin proudly at Rick. We really did mean business.

The Cabin Café up the road might have big corporate backing, but small was beautiful, and with a bit of dedication, imagination and quite possibly the longest hours I'd ever work in my life, the Lemon Tree Café would not only survive but thrive. Besides, our food was a million times better . . .

'OK, at ease,' said Rick, lowering the camera.

'Wait, one last one.' Lia grabbed the pizza paddle. She looked at me wickedly. 'Do you dare me to toss it?'

I laughed and nodded. 'You nutter.'

'Ready, Rick?' she said. Her tongue poked out as she concentrated.

Funny how I was always labelled the brave one in the family, I thought, watching as she flipped the pizza up in the air like a pancake and caught it again, much to the delight of our customers. Actually, she was the one to step out of her comfort zone, to embrace new things and forge ahead without a backward glance. I could learn a lot from my sister, I reckoned, feeling a rush of love for her.

'And that's how to toss a pizza,' she beamed.

'Every day's a school day,' I replied.

'Mamma mia,' cried Nonna, fanning her face as she walked through the door half an hour later. 'It hot in here!'

I made a mental note to investigate air-conditioning and opened the back door a bit more as she said hello to our regulars and made her way over to the counter.

'Nonna!' I said, kissing her cheek. 'You've just missed the photos. We could have had one with you in it.'

'Good,' she said with a grunt. 'I not want my old wrinkle face in photo. Much better you two beautiful girls. I just pop in to wish you well before going to hospital.'

Lia and I enveloped her in a hug and thanked her for the millionth time for letting us have the café until Juliet yelled that the pizzas were ready to come out of the oven and Lia squealed and ran to pull them out.

Nonna led me to a recently vacated table, still with its used crockery on it.

'Sit,' she ordered.

I obeyed and began to stack the mugs and plates but Nonna stopped me.

'Listen, this is important.' She took my hands and looked at me over her glasses. 'I know you want to work hard but the café is just a business. Remember that. Don't hide behind it; don't forget to live as well, eh? And make room for love. I only just learned that.'

'I'll try,' I said truthfully. 'But I don't find it easy.'

I didn't want to be alone; I wanted what Lia and Ed had, and Mum and Dad and now Nonna and Stanley. I wanted it, I just wasn't sure how to get it.

'You know what I think?' Nonna smiled and pinched my

cheek, just like she'd done when I was little. 'You make life too tricky for yourself. Gabe is—'

'Nonna,' I warned, inhaling sharply, 'don't go there.'

She held her hands up. 'Okey cokey, but give him a chance and see what happen.'

I rolled my eyes. 'What happens is we argue.'

'That is good sign.' She wagged a finger at me. 'He light a fire in you. Don't let it go out.'

'Which reminds me,' I said, getting to my feet, glad to change the subject, 'I need to check on the wood situation for the oven. Can I get you anything, now you're a customer?'

'Oh.' Nonna blinked as if that had just dawned on her. She looked at the clock above the door and nodded. 'I just got time for espresso. Hurry up.'

I laughed and pressed a kiss to her cheek. 'There's fire in you too.'

'I know,' she chuckled. 'Where you think you get it from?'

I left her smiling to herself and made my way to the coffee machine, first poking my head into the kitchen to check on Lia.

Nothing could wipe the smile from Nonna's face these days, I thought fondly. Now that Stanley was making such a good recovery, the two of them had had the chance to really talk and share their histories, which in Nonna's case meant telling Stanley all about losing her first love Lorenzo and her catastrophic marriage to Marco. Now the pair of them were inseparable and she spent every moment of visiting time at his bedside.

I made Nonna's coffee and then whizzed round the café clearing plates and wiping tables. Suddenly, I felt my scalp prickle as if I was being watched and when I looked up everyone was here: Clementine and Tyson, both wearing kneepads and dirt smears; Lucas from The Heavenly Gift Shop carrying two neatly wrapped boxes; Nina from the flower shop, carrying two large bouquets; Ken and Mrs Ken (I could never remember her name); Adrian from the

336

pub with Frances, his cleaner; Mr Beecher from school; Biddy who'd brought Churchill in with her who was lapping at the floor where Lia had dropped the pizza earlier; Stella Derry, who never missed a thing, if this was in fact *a thing*, and finally Mum and Dad.

They were all hovering in the centre of the café, grinning.

Lia appeared by my side, pink-cheeked and wide-eyed. Most of her hair had come down from her ponytail and formed ringlets around her face. She looked beautiful and bubbling with happiness.

'Is something going on?' she murmured.

'Just a hunch,' I said, wrapping an arm round her waist. 'But I think so.'

Chapter 33

'Everyone's here,' she hissed, pressing herself close to me, 'except—'

'Gabe.'

'Gabe? I was going to say Ed.' Lia raised an eyebrow.

'I meant Ed,' I said, fooling no one.

'Gabe's in London for a meeting, isn't he?' She chewed her lip. 'Didn't you know?'

'Yeah, yeah, I remember now,' I muttered, doing my utmost to conceal my disappointment, although what exactly I was disappointed about was tricky to pin down. Also, the grinning crowd seemed to be inching closer. 'How do *you* know?'

'Gina told me when we dropped Arlo off. Gabe had been in a flap, apparently. It's his first day in a new job today and they sprung this meeting on him at the last minute. He asked Gina to take Noah in after school, but she's at capacity and couldn't help him.'

Oh God. Poor Gabe, poor Noah.

'So where is Noah going?' I said, feeling a bit sick and knowing that if things had been different, Gabe would have asked me. I so wish he'd asked me.

Lia shrugged and then yelped with joy. 'My men!'

'Sorry I'm late!' cried Ed, running in to join the crowd with Arlo bouncing along, clutched to his side. He grinned at his wife and squeezed in between Mum and Dad.

And then Juliet and Doreen pushed into the middle of

the café with trays of prosecco and people dived in until Nonna clapped her hands and everyone, even the bemused customers, fell silent.

'No big speeches,' said Nonna, passing Lia and me a glass each. 'But I wish you lots of luck and *love* in the Lemon Tree Café.'

I couldn't help noticing that she looked directly at me when she said 'love'.

Everyone clinked glasses, Nina leapt forward with flowers for both of us, Lucas presented us with a gift-wrapped box which he insisted was nothing special and Lia and I were nudging each other to respond with a toast of our own when Juliet cleared her throat ominously and turned a furious shade of red. We all stopped talking again.

'On behalf of Doreen and myself, I'd just like to say that in a café, of course, there are going to be bad days, when customers complain over nothing, or bugger off to that shite-hole café up the road to drink cat's pee—'

'Thank you,' I said, stepping forward to cut her off, 'for pointing that out.'

Doreen dropped her head into her hands.

Juliet continued obliviously: 'Or we run out of wood, or dough, or the loos get blocked but—'

'But mostly, there will be GOOD days,' Doreen interrupted loudly. 'And we wish you lots of those. Congratulations to Rosie and Lia!'

Everyone applauded, Doreen dragged Juliet back to the counter where they whipped out a huge celebratory cake and after a slice of that and downing their drinks, the other business owners said their goodbyes and went back to their shops. Ed kissed Lia and dashed off to take Arlo back to Gina's and himself back to work, leaving Stella Derry, Mum and Dad to lend a hand clearing up.

'We thought the occasion should be marked,' said Dad, collecting up the empty bottles to hide the evidence of illegal alcohol consumption in unlicensed premises.

'We are so proud of you both,' said Mum, looking pink after her prosecco.

'Thanks.' I gave her a hug. 'I'm really happy. It's not what I expected to be doing, but I'm proud of what Lia and I have done too.'

She leaned into my ear.

'Plus you succeeded where I failed, getting Nonna to finally hang up her apron,' she said in a stage whisper.

But Nonna hadn't had anything to hang her apron up for before Stanley, nothing to fill the gap, I thought, and simply hadn't been ready to do so. But now, having faced up to her past, she was set to make the most of her future. She was quite an inspiration, my grandmother.

'Mum has some news too, don't you, Luisa?' Dad prompted, putting an arm round her shoulders.

'Oh?' I smiled at her. 'Do tell.'

'I wasn't going to mention it, I don't want to steal your thunder on your opening day,' said Mum coyly, clearly bursting to tell us. 'It can wait.'

'Are you ready to take over at the WI again? That is good news,' said Stella unconvincingly.

Mum shook her head. 'I'm afraid I'm going to have to ask the committee to release me from those duties permanently, Stella.'

She paused dramatically and Stella's mouth formed an O.

'Because I've been offered a position at The Chestnuts Cancer Hospice as fund-raising officer,' Mum finished, smoothing her hair.

The cancer charity? I stared at Mum wondering when this had all happened.

Dad frowned. 'Oh. I thought you were just volunteering two days a week?'

Mum elbowed him sharply and coughed.

'Congratulations!' I said. 'You'll be brilliant, but—'

'I'll be planning my first event very soon, Stella,' said

Mum, interrupting me smoothly. 'I hope I can count on the Women's Institute's support?'

'Of course!' said Stella, darting to the counter with the last batch of dirty glasses. She hiked her handbag on to her shoulder. 'So that's definite, then, you're *definitely* not coming back as president?'

'Definitely,' Mum confirmed.

'I'll go and let the rest of the committee know right away. Bye, all.'

I stood aside as Stella nearly knocked me over in her haste to spread the word. Lia led Dad away to show him the pizza oven, leaving Mum and me alone.

'Where did this come from, Mum? I thought you were going to cut back on your voluntary work?'

'My *committees*, yes,' Mum corrected, looking shifty.

'What's the difference?' I said, already feeling sorry for Dad, who had cherished the extra free evenings that his wife's less cluttered diary had afforded them.

'Remember the second-hand book stall that The Chestnuts Cancer Hospice had at the Barnaby Spring Fair?'

I nodded.

'I bought a couple of books and got chatting to the volunteers and I realized that I've still got a lot to give. I'm only in my fifties, I want to make a proper contribution to something important, something that will make a real difference,' she said self-consciously. 'I was on the verge of offering to help in their charity shop when Helena, one of the managers, asked me who had organized the Spring Fair and . . . well, I may have embellished my role somewhat.'

'Mum!' I shook my head affectionately; she had attended all the meetings, and along with Lia had been responsible for the children's activities, but strictly speaking, it had been a team effort.

'I know,' she said, nibbling her lip. 'Before I knew it, Helena was begging me to bring my event-management skills to Chestnuts and I was so caught up in the whole notion of being useful that I agreed. Goodness knows how I'm going to live up to my own promises.'

'I'm sure you'll be fine,' I said confidently. 'You're very good at . . . delegating.'

'Giving orders, you mean.' She gave me a knowing smile. 'Don't worry, I admit it.'

'Well . . .' I grinned.

'All the committees I've been on . . . they filled the days after my redundancy and after you girls flew the nest. It's hard, you know, one minute being the hub of the family and superfluous the next. And my own mother didn't want me at the café, so I made myself indispensable in other ways, by doing what I was good at . . .' She blushed. 'Which turned out to be bossing people around.'

'At least you're honest,' I said with a grin.

Mum gave a sheepish laugh. 'But happily, that's precisely what the cancer charity is looking for. And yes, I did tell your father it was only two days a week, but it can be more if I'd like it to be, and although it's a voluntary position now, the manager said there is a chance of some budget for a salary later in the year and I'd like a bit of independence again.'

'But what about your plans to spend more time with the family?' If I knew Mum, two days would soon turn into five and before long she'd be too busy to take any time off to go on holiday with Dad.

'Arlo is going to the childminder's three days a week now and he won't need me so much, and my evenings will still be free to go gallivanting with your father. But during the day I can do something useful, something less self-indulgent. Do you remember when my friend Karen had cancer and a group of us did a charity walk in our bras?'

I nodded. 'You raised a fortune.'

The press had covered it and had printed a big picture of Mum and her friends in their bras decorated with feathers and sequins. Nonna had been horrified.

'Doing that gave me such a buzz. I'd like to get that back,

perhaps even do something in the village, like, I don't know, set up a little support group, somewhere to go when you need to talk. They say charity begins at home, don't they?'

She took a deep breath and smiled at me, her eyes were shining and I could almost see the ideas whirring round in her head.

'They do and I think that's a brilliant idea.'

I hugged her, thinking how proud I was of her and, come to that, of all the women in my family. Lia and Nonna were just the same: full of surprises, willing to take risks, daring to tackle new things and brave enough to admit their faults. They could teach me a lot, I reckoned. A sudden thought dawned on me.

'What time does school finish?' I asked.

'Three fifteen,' she replied.

'Thanks.'

Gabe might not feel he could ask me to look after Noah, but there was nothing to stop me offering . . .

Gabe didn't have anyone else in Barnaby, no backup, no support team to rely on when he was stuck at work or, like today, had a last-minute meeting foisted on him. My fingers itched to phone him, to let him know I'd help, that I'd always help out if he needed me. But I couldn't. I'd yelled at him that we couldn't be friends, I couldn't just ring him now, in the middle of his first day at work and say, 'Oh by the way, shall I look after Noah this afternoon?'

But I really wanted to. I missed him. I'd shoved all the nice bits about our friendship into the corner of my mind. For the last few weeks I'd focused on building a strong business, buttressing the café, protecting it from Garden Warehouse and that was partly because the Lemon Tree Café was very important to me, but partly so I didn't have to think about what I might have thrown away.

Poor Gina, I bet she felt awful when she had to say no to Gabe; but there were serious penalties for looking after more children than you were licensed for, Gabe would have understood that. I pictured Noah's cheerful little face, watching all his friends go home with their mums or grand-parents and having to wait behind with the teacher until his dad came for him, and my heart squeezed for him. There was no need, no need at all.

Charity, as Mum rightly pointed out, begins at home.

Gabe and I might have our differences of opinion, I thought as I marched towards Barnaby Primary School with a crowd of others, but I wasn't going to let that get in the way of doing the right thing where Noah was concerned. I'd take him back to the café until Gabe was able to pick him up and simply send him a quick text to let him know Noah was safe with me. That way I wouldn't have to speak to him. Lia and I had spent most of our after-school afternoons in the café when Mum had been working: making up dance rou-tines to Steps songs, chatting to customers and eating, a lot of eating. And there was no reason why Noah wouldn't enjoy it too, although maybe not the dance routines . . .

The bell rang and Mr Beecher appeared from behind the wheelie bins and unlocked the gates and adults slowly over-took the playground, chattering in their little clusters. I looked around for Gina but couldn't spot her so I stood awkwardly on my own where hopscotch had been painted on to the concrete, clutching the piece of cake I'd brought with me, and trying to work out where Noah might appear from. Then two school doors were flung wide and neat lines of children appeared behind their teachers. I scanned from one line to the other trying to spot Noah as each child was made to wait and dismissed individually when their expected adult was identified.

My confidence wavered for a moment; I hadn't realized there would be such tight security. Never mind, Noah would vouch for me, it would be fine; it wasn't as if I was an axe-murderer or anything. I stepped a bit closer to find him in the line-up.

'Noah?'

I whirled round to see who'd called his name and recognized Fiona, Robbie's mum, waving at the two boys as they stood next to their teacher at the top of the steps.

'Hi,' I said, joining her.

Fiona blinked at me in surprise. 'Hi?'

'Is that Noah's teacher?' I asked, pointing towards a young woman in a denim shift dress with big patch pockets and a whistle round her neck.

'Miss Cresswell, yes.' Fiona nodded and waved.

Robbie waved back and both boys were released by the teacher. Noah saw me and waved with both hands in the air.

'I'll go and explain to her that I can take Noah,' I said as we walked up to meet the boys.

'You can't.' Fiona looked at me. 'Gabe asked me.'

'Did he?' I said, feeling a tiny stab of jealousy. 'Right.'

It was my own fault. Of course Gabe would have asked Fiona. How idiotic of me to think he wouldn't have made some arrangements for his boy.

'Although I was a bit surprised,' Fiona added sniffily, 'after the last time.'

'Oh?' I looked at her, waiting for her to elaborate.

'Anyway.' She gave her head a little shake. 'I hope Gabe's not going to make a habit of it, it's really not convenient.'

That did it. Noah wasn't going where he wasn't wanted, not when there was someone who really cared about him.

'Excuse me, Miss Cresswell!' I skirted a group of mums in front of me and waved my hand in the air to attract her attention, just as Noah's firm little body barrelled into me.

'ROSIE!'

'Hey, dude.' I bent down, laughing, and gave him a one-armed hug, while trying not to squash the cake in the other hand. I risked pressing a swift kiss into his unruly sandy hair before he pulled away.

Fiona and Miss Cresswell both arrived together.

'Hello?' said the teacher, smiling helpfully.

'Hi, I'm Rosie,' I began, wondering the best way to word this without offending Fiona who struck me as the sort to get easily miffed.

'Is that cake?' said Noah, wide-eyed, looking at the contents of the napkin.

Robbie, who was taller than his friend with pale blue eyes and spiky red hair, licked his lips. I'd only got one piece, but it was big enough to share.

'It is.' I beamed. 'Would you like some too, Robbie?'

'Do you know this lady, Noah?' Miss Cresswell frowned as if I was some sort of child-catcher trying to lure him away with my buttercream icing.

'Of course he does.' I desperately tried not to frown; Miss Cresswell had been into the café, and although we hadn't spoken, technically she knew me too.

Fiona produced two peeled carrots from a Tupperware box and pursed her lips. 'I don't condone sugary snacks after school.'

Robbie sighed and crunched into a carrot. I stifled a tut. Who begrudges a hungry boy a slice of home-made cake?

'Yes, miss,' Noah nodded, slipping his hand into mine, 'Rosie is daddy's friend.'

Hooray! I smiled triumphantly.

'Rosie helped me cut up Mummy's wedding dress with scissors.'

Fiona and Miss Cresswell recoiled as if they were in the presence of a she-devil.

'It wasn't quite like that,' I stammered.

'And she told me to make a slide out of my bedroom window.' He nodded proudly.

Miss Cresswell stared at me. 'Doesn't he live on a boat?'

Fiona leaned into the teacher. 'That's why I won't let Robbie go round to play. Floating death trap.'

This was not going well. At all.

'I was joking,' I said weakly, 'because Noah wanted a bed with a slide.'

Miss Cresswell pressed her lips into a thin line and folded her arms; Fiona gave a humourless laugh.

Noah turned to Robbie. 'You know Katy Perry?'

Robbie shook his head glumly, still sad about the carrot.

'She's a girl singer,' Noah carried on blithely. 'Daddy says Rosie looks like her. He says he wants to hear her roar.'

Miss Cresswell and Fiona exchanged appalled looks as Robbie and Noah began to roar like lions and run round the playground. At which point I realized I'd got as much chance of leaving school with Noah as Cruella de Vil would have adopting a puppy from Battersea Dogs Home.

'You've clearly got this covered, Fiona,' I said stoutly, and risking a public stoning, kissed Noah and thrust the cake into his hands. 'I'll leave Noah with you.'

'I think that's best,' said Miss Cresswell, shooting a look of relief at Fiona. 'Under the circumstances.'

Chapter 34

The good weather had continued for the next couple of days. And when the other shop owners all converged on the café at the same time as each other quite by chance on Wednesday afternoon, Lucas suggested we sit outside for a coffee and a catch-up. We were all there except Adrian who'd gone on a lads' golfing week to the Algarve, and Clementine, who though not technically a village retailer any more I still thought of as part of our little business network. She was in a meeting with an editor about the possibility of a regular monthly magazine column and Tyson was spending the afternoon helping Lucas in the gift shop.

It was only two thirty; too early for the school crowd to start arriving, but that didn't stop me keeping one eye on the green as everyone sorted themselves out with drinks and cake at the tables I'd hastily pushed together.

I thought I might hear from Gabe after my playground humiliation, but I hadn't so far. I wasn't sure if this was a good or a bad thing. I'd thought he might appreciate my attempt to help him out. On the other hand, he might be furious with me for trying to abduct his child. Lia pointed out that I was overthinking it; starting a new job was exhausting and he was probably falling into bed as soon as Noah went to sleep. But that didn't help because then I couldn't stop thinking about him lying tangled in the sheets, those long lashes resting on his cheeks, broad chest rising and falling and possibly a muscular buttock, just visible under . . .

'Cheeky,' said Lucas, smacking Ken's hand away from the crumbs on his plate. 'Get your own French fancy.'

'Not allowed. The missis has put me on a diet,' said Ken, patting his belly. 'Told me I should get "lean in fifteen", whatever that means.'

'It's the Instagram hashtag for a hot sports guy in shorts,' said Lucas who blushed and popped the rest of his cake in his mouth. 'Allegedly.'

Nina and Lia giggled; Biddy and Ken looked none the wiser.

'Come and work with me, Ken,' said Lia. 'Making pizzas for a living is the best way to lose weight ever. I'm sick of the sight of them; I've gone right off my food.'

'Ahem,' I said, dragging my eyes away from the road and giving my sister a pointed look. 'Although our pizzas are delicious, is what she meant to say.'

Lia clapped a hand to her mouth. 'Whoops. Are you sure you want to be in business with me, Rosie? I'm hardly known for my business skills.'

'Nor me for my cooking skills,' I reminded her. 'Yet here we both are.'

'Teamwork,' said Biddy, slipping a piece of frankfurter under the table to Churchill, whose tail gave a happy thump against the table leg. She passed the rest to Ken who wolfed it down equally appreciatively. 'We all benefit from that.'

'And on that note, I'll leave you business bods to discuss world domination, while I prepare some pizza samples for the cardboard box man,' Lia said.

I smiled, watching her go back inside singing away to herself, stopping at the potted lemon trees either side of the door to pick off dead leaves just like Nonna used to do.

The 'cardboard box man' was actually a major supplier of pizza cartons. Lia had had the bright idea of offering a take-away service – just a couple of times a week to start with, she thought. If any of us was planning world domination it was her. She was far more savvy than she gave herself credit for. I'd been too busy mooning over my disastrous love life to do anything more than take people's orders accurately this week.

'It must be nice having a partner,' said Lucas wistfully, gazing over at his shop window where Tyson was inside, swishing cobwebs away with a feather duster. 'Someone to lean on after a tough day.'

Nina rearranged the vase of greenery in the centre of the table, putting the larger stems in the centre and fanning out the more feathery sprigs. Fresh flowers were my little indulgence. We should really invest in some plastic posies but there was something lovely and authentic about having real ones. And I knew from a bit of secret snooping that the Cabin Café had plastic carnations, which already looked dusty. Besides, it was worth it to see Nina's face light up when I went into the flower shop and placed my fortnightly order.

'How about another charity event?' said Nina. 'Like the Barnaby Spring Fair. That was brilliant teamwork.'

'That was a lovely day,' agreed Biddy, removing her chunky crocheted cardigan and hanging it on the back of her chair. 'We could call it the Barnaby *Summer* Fair.'

'Anybody got any charity links?' said Ken. There was a sheen of sweat on his forehead. He picked up a napkin, wiped his head, refolded it perfectly and set it on the stack with the others.

'Mum has,' I said, making a mental note to collect every napkin from the table when we left, even the ones that looked unused. 'The Chestnuts Cancer Hospice. Maybe any money raised could go to them. I'd like that, actually; it would give her some brownie points with her new boss.'

'Perhaps we should sell veggies and stuff again?' said Ken. 'Keep with the gardening theme?'

'Shame we can't grow chestnuts,' said Biddy. 'Ooh, what about chestnut mushrooms?'

Everyone agreed that was a good idea, Ken said he'd talk to Clementine about growing mushrooms and I opened up my iPad to look at the calendar. A debate followed about suitable dates, trying to fit in around a dog show in Derby, various weddings that Nina was doing the flowers for, Lucas and Tyson's weekend trip to Brighton and Ken's annual pilgrimage to Blackpool. I didn't have any events to plan around so I opened the café's Twitter account to send a couple of promo tweets while they chatted, and found we'd had a lot of new notifications since I'd last been on this morning.

A hundred to be precise. One hundred new notifications. That was a record. I scrolled back through the activity to see if I could spot what might have triggered it. New followers, apparently: we'd had over fifty new followers in the last twenty-four hours. How odd. I was so engrossed in the task that Lucas had to nudge me twice.

'First Saturday in July,' he said. 'OK with you?'

'I expect so,' I said distractedly as one particular new follower stood out from the rest. 'Wow. Lucinda Miller has just followed us on Twitter! I've worked with her, or her agent at least.'

'Who?' Biddy and Ken said together.

Nina sat up tall. 'The actress? Quick. Ask her if she wants to do a celebrity opening at our event.'

'She's followed us on Twitter, not asked to be friends in real life.' I laughed, secretly hoping that she might ask exactly that.

'I like her in *Raw Recruits*,' said Lucas. 'A proper woman with curves.'

I looked at him in surprise. He shrugged and rubbed his neck sheepishly.

'And totally kick-ass,' Nina added.

I clicked on Lucinda's profile to check it was *the* Lucinda Miller: Actress currently in *Raw Recruits*, love my French bulldog Purdie, polka dots and tea. Yep, definitely her. That couldn't be a coincidence, could it, that she'd followed us? It had to be because of our mutual connection? I followed her back. Seconds later a direct message popped up:

Is this Rosie from the social media agency?

I typed one straight back.

Yes! Thanks for the follow! How are things?

God knows what I expected her to say to that. Anyway, before she had a chance to reply Ken dropped a bombshell.

'We could ask Garden Warehouse if they want to sponsor our event,' said Ken, offering a packet of sugar-free mints round the table. 'Raise a few more quid.'

I glared at him. 'Ken!'

He shrugged. 'Why not? They'll attract lots of people.'

'Because, because,' I stammered crossly, 'they'll take over, that's why and they're a threat to our village identity. This is a *village* event. Village businesses only. Agreed?'

I looked at the others for support.

Biddy was stroking Churchill's head so vigorously that his fur was coming off in her hand. Nina was plucking fronds from a sprig of fern and Lucas was concentrating on collecting all the crumbs from his French fancy and putting them in its paper cake case.

'Agreed?' I said again.

Biddy raised her hand.

'I know you're very angry about them opening up, but I must be honest,' she said timidly. 'Since I converted a quarter of the shop into a grooming salon, business is doing better than before. I'm also doing a roaring trade in pamper products for dogs.'

'I'm not angry,' I said crossly. 'I'm just—'

'Pamper products?' Nina pulled a face. 'What like shampoo and conditioner?'

Biddy nodded. 'And much more besides. We've got paw

balm, detangle serum, breath spray, even doggie perfume. And,' she looped her hair behind her ears self-consciously, 'shoes and clothes.'

Nina giggled and said she thought Barnaby's dogs weren't looking so 'ruff ruff' these days and Lucas said he might like a dog, especially if he could dress it smartly.

'As I said . . .' I tapped the table with a spoon to get their attention.

They looked at me, startled, and I set the spoon down gently.

'Sorry. We were all agreed; that company has invaded our territory, our *small rural* territory. I thought we were going to stand against them. Put up a united front.'

Ken chuckled. 'Don't get your knickers in a twist, love. This is Derbyshire, not Dunkirk.'

Biddy clasped her hands together meekly. 'I'm sorry. But they've done me some good. Having them on my doorstep has forced me to rethink my range. I'm going upmarket and I rather like it.'

Having said her piece, Biddy went pink and buried her head in her mug.

'I'm really happy for you, honestly,' I said with a sigh. 'Would anyone else like to include Garden Warehouse in our event?'

Lucas shrugged. 'I'm easy. I have lost some sales of greetings cards, admittedly. They have a range of "five for a pound" cards; and that sort of product doesn't belong in The Heavenly Gift Shop. But on the flip side, I'm selling more big items. One lovely lady came in this morning with an envelope full of money from the café—'

I eyed him beadily and folded my arms.

'That awful *Cabin* Café,' he clarified, realizing his mistake. 'Someone is leaving and they had a whip-round. Spent fifty quid on a giant giraffe and a hip flask. That's a lot for my shop and I've been dying to get rid of that giraffe; its neck was going limp.'

So someone was leaving the café already and it had only just opened. Odd.

'What about you?' I said, turning my attention to Nina, who was stripping the leaves off a eucalyptus twig.

'Oh balls,' she said heavily. 'I don't know how to tell you this, but I'm doing better as well. And as usual, I have no idea why. Honestly, it's a miracle I'm even in business at all.'

'And I was never against it,' Ken reminded me gruffly, patting my shoulder. 'Remember? We all have to adapt, I said. And I have to say, girl,' he gestured towards the pizza menu tucked between the vase and the pot of sugar sachets, 'you've done that with knobs on.'

Adrian had had more customers in the pub too, especially for Sunday lunch. I seemed to be the only one still with an axe to grind.

'Right. First Saturday in July. That's agreed. Thanks very much, meeting adjourned.' I snapped my iPad closed and stood up.

'So *are* we going to approach Garden Warehouse for sponsorship?' Lucas asked, turning to take a photograph of his own shop where Tyson was building a leaning tower of gift boxes in the window.

'Not yet,' I said vaguely. 'Let's, well, let's just see, shall we?'

'Back to work, then,' said Nina, standing up and leaving some money on the table.

'Me too,' said Biddy, dropping half a frankfurter as she got to her feet.

Ken swooped down and picked it up before Churchill and popped it in his mouth with a gleeful, 'Ha!'

The dog gave a disgruntled woof and they all walked off to their respective shops leaving me with the uncomfortable feeling that instead of a village-wide crusade against Garden Warehouse, there may just be a one-woman campaign.

Later that evening I was walking home from work, as I was about to turn into the path beside the churchyard a car pulled up alongside me. It was Gabe in his new car. Noah was in the back on a booster seat with a football and his dinosaur on his lap.

A frisson of heat rippled up through me, settling annoyingly on my cheeks; this was the first time I'd seen him since we'd argued. Over two weeks ago. Not that I was counting. Oh God, I'd missed his lovely smile.

Gabe wound down his window. 'Hello.'

He leaned an arm out. He was wearing a white shirt and the sleeves were pushed up to the elbow. He looked very smart. This was the new corporate Gabe, the Garden Warehouse Gabe in his posh car.

'Hello,' I replied.

The word came out all croaky and awkward and I had a sudden flashback to being sixteen and a boy from sixth form, who I worshipped from afar, asking me out and me trying to sound cool but instead sounding like a Dalek. I cleared my throat and focused on Noah instead. He was wearing shorts and a T-shirt and had mud on his face.

'Hi, been playing football?' I said, smiling at him as he held up the ball for inspection.

'I scored a goal!' he said and then aimed a kick at the seat in front.

'Nice wheels.' I risked a brief look at Gabe before admiring the car, which I assumed came with the job.

'It was,' Gabe said, shooting his son a warning look, 'until they let us in it. Although a certain person prefers the old van.'

'I like sitting in the front best.' Noah scowled. 'Now I have to sit in the back like a baby.'

'Listen, Rosie, I've only just heard what happened at school on Monday,' said Gabe, running a hand through his hair. It was standing up in peaks. I could just reach a hand in through the window and smooth it down . . . 'Miss Cresswell told me when I picked Noah up from football club.'

'Ah,' I said, unsure whether I was in trouble or not.

He massaged his eyes briefly. His shirt was crumpled and he looked tired. I wondered how much of a strain it was on him, starting this new job and constantly having to worry about being there at the end of the school day for Noah.

'Did I do the right thing? Well, obviously not,' I laughed self-consciously, 'because I was virtually frogmarched off the premises.'

'Have you got any more cake?' Noah piped up from the back.

I shook my head.

'Come into the café,' I said automatically, before catching Gabe's eye.

'I thought I was *persona non grata*?' he murmured, tilting an eyebrow challengingly.

'True.' The pink flush to my cheeks ramped up to fuchsia. 'But Noah isn't.'

Gabe's lips twitched at that.

'Anyway, I didn't stop the car to have another argument with you; I just wanted to thank you. It meant a lot that you'd pick Noah up from school.' He fixed his soft grey eyes on me. 'Even without parental permission.'

'I didn't think.' I shrugged. 'When *I* went to that school they just opened the doors at the end of the afternoon and we all wandered off. I hadn't bargained on such tight security. But it's a good thing. Better to be safe than sorry.'

'Definitely, but I'm sorry if you were made to feel uncomfortable.'

'If I ever have children I'll just have to hope Miss Cresswell has left by then, I can't show my face again.'

Gabe laughed softly, shaking his head. 'I can imagine. She and Fiona together are a force to be reckoned with.'

I smiled and felt ridiculously happy all of a sudden. It was so good to be talking to him again. I said the first thing that came into my head.

'I've missed you.'

He held my gaze and nodded. 'Ditto.'

This time his voice was the one that cracked. He flushed and coughed, banging his chest extravagantly.

'Dad, what's for tea?'

Gabe rolled his eyes at me and grinned at his son in the rear-view mirror.

'Will fish-finger sandwiches do you?'

'YAY!'

'Verity's favourite,' I said and smiled.

It was on the tip of my tongue to say 'mine too' in a subtle so-why-don't-you-invite-me way. But we were making friends again, building trust; I didn't want to push things. Besides, I was totally aware that I owed him an apology. And I'd do that any second . . .

Gabe looked wistful. 'She and Mimi used to make them for me when we were students. My cooking skills haven't evolved much since those days.'

I held a hand to my mouth and whispered behind it: 'Don't tell anyone, but you and me both.'

'Congratulations to you and Lia on the café, by the way; everyone's been telling me about your new pizza oven. Sounds great.'

He left the comment hanging in the air, but I knew what he was thinking; he hadn't been in because I'd told him we couldn't be friends . . .

I was an idiot. Everyone else, even Clementine who was most affected by the new store opening up right next to her house, seemed to have accepted them. It was only us at the café who were still so anti Garden Warehouse. And now, facing this man, who I had to admit made my heart skip like no one else had ever done, I couldn't remember exactly what it was I had against them.

'How's the new job?' I said, trying to keep my face neutral.

Gabe blinked at me in surprise and then rubbed a hand over his forehead. 'Knackering. Totally knackering. We're pulling a proposal together to take over another company, a family-owned retailer in homewares with about fifteen branches. They've got some great locations, but aren't making money. I'm seeing my boss about it tomorrow to put a rescue package to the bank.'

I bristled and folded my arms tightly across my chest. There it was. That was what I had against them: their total disregard for the people behind the numbers. It was all about turning a profit, about how many pounds per square metre generated.

'Not another family business? For goodness' sake, Gabe, Garden Warehouse are a bunch of vultures, what are you going to offer them this time, ten pence per shop? How do you sleep at night?'

I glared at him, feeling my heart thudding angrily as the friendly atmosphere between us leached away into the cracks in the pavement at my feet.

'Dad, I'm hungry. Can we go?'

Gabe glanced over his shoulder at Noah. 'One second.'

Noah took another swipe at the seat with his foot.

'It's not like that, Rosie,' he said evenly. 'What sort of person do you think I am?'

'Honestly? I thought you were the very best kind.'

He held my gaze with such an intensity that I felt my insides quiver. '*Were?*'

'I don't know any more,' I murmured, not wanting to argue in front of the little boy. I managed a smile. 'Bye, Noah.'

Gabe muttered something not fit for small ears and I turned on my heel and began to walk away from the car, towards the footpath at the side of the church where he couldn't follow me. The car door slammed and I heard footsteps running towards me.

'Rosie, I'm not letting you run away from me.'

He grabbed hold of my arm and spun me round to face him. A flame of anger crackled through me.

'You're not *letting* me? How dare you?' I shouted in his face.

What was it with him and me? Five minutes in his company and I exploded with fury? And he . . . he'd used his size against me. Just like Callum. I couldn't – wouldn't – be bullied into doing something just because he had more physical strength than me.

He released me instantly and held his hands up in defence. 'I'm sorry, God, I'm sorry. Rosie, I didn't think—'

'You of all people,' I said breathlessly. My legs had turned to jelly and tears of anger weren't far away, 'should know that forcing me to do anything is unforgivable.'

He bowed his head. 'I apologize unreservedly, but—'

'Dad?'

'Stay in the car, Noah,' he ordered.

'I've dropped the football out of the window.'

'OK,' he shouted. 'I'll get it.'

The sound of an engine approaching made us both turn to the road. And then time slowed down, each second stretching into a full-length horror movie as Noah flung open his car door just as a white van overtook Gabe's car. There was no time for the driver to react. A sickening crunch of metal on metal splintered the evening air as the rear door was smashed back towards the car.

Screams seemed to bounce off every surface as Gabe and I tore back down the path to the road, both of us yelling Noah's name. The van screeched to a halt and the driver, a man in his forties wearing work-stained clothes and sunglasses perched on his head, held his arms out to the side.

'What the . . . ?'

Gabe grabbed at the other rear door, wrenched it open and dived inside. I was right behind him, gulping at air to stop myself from being sick, filled with dread at what we might find.

'Daddy,' sobbed Noah, 'I'm sorry.'

Oh, thank God.

Noah's little face was white with terror, but he was still in one piece, clutching his dinosaur.

'Are you OK?' Gabe gasped, dragging the little boy from the car.

The van driver wiped a hand over his face and swore viciously. 'I'm so sorry, mate; I didn't see the door. Is he hurt?'

The door was a mass of twisted metal and shattered glass. Noah, miraculously, seemed completely unscathed.

'No, I don't think so,' said Gabe, glancing at the driver. 'And it wasn't your fault.'

Gabe sank down on to the pavement, cradling his son in his arms.

I didn't think twice. I threw my arms round both of them and hugged them like I never, ever wanted to let them go.

Our stupid row evaporated into the evening sunshine. Nothing else mattered. Only these two.

Later that night when Gabe had taken Noah home, I poured myself a glass of wine, pulled on a thick jumper and sat in my garden in the dark and went over and over what had happened this evening with Gabe on the pavement and then afterwards with the crash.

Two things I knew: first, I wasn't over Callum after all. Far from it. What had happened with him had made me lock away my heart where no one could hurt it. And second, Gabe and Noah may just hold the key.

Chapter 35

The next morning at the café, I did my best to put that grabbing incident with Gabe behind me. He'd be busy working on his 'rescue package' today, so there was no chance that I'd see him. That and explaining to his new boss how his car door had come to be crumpled. I tied on my apron, plastered on a smile, and if anyone noticed that my eyes were a bit watery now and again, thankfully they didn't mention it.

We had the nicest customers, I decided, later that afternoon. I counted up the tips and divided them into three envelopes, marked 'Juliet', 'Doreen' and 'staff night out'. The show of support we'd had since Lia and I had taken over at the café had blown me away and not only in the size of their tips. It wasn't just the pizzas either; people had been keen to try out our new brunch menu too. Even Doreen, who'd sworn blind that no sane person would ever eat avocado on toast, had had to eat her words.

Bookings for larger groups had also picked up again: Stella Derry had been in earlier to book the conservatory on Monday afternoon for an emergency meeting of the WI committee. She'd ordered afternoon tea for eight and had told me confidentially that the number-one issue on the agenda was Mum's resignation and the election of a new president. The vicar had asked if we could do an extra-large pizza for the parish council meeting and we'd had two enquiries from mums wanting to know if we'd host children's birthday parties, which Lia had been thrilled to say yes to. And everyone, without exception, had expressed how happy they were to see the café move with the times and most importantly remain in the village at the heart of the community.

Monetary matters sorted for the moment, I picked up my cleaning cloth and made a start on the serving area. It was almost the end of the afternoon, Lia had already gone to collect Arlo and Juliet was cleaning the outside tables. I might get my trainers out later, I thought, bending down to retrieve a dropped slice of salami, and go for a run down to the river, but not as far as *The Neptune*. I wasn't ready to see Gabe again quite yet. Although in a village this size we wouldn't be able to avoid each other for ever. Noah's accident had called a halt to our argument and we'd ended up with our arms around each other but there was still a lot unsaid between us and I fully expected our next conversation to be heated.

'A-hem.'

I straightened up to find myself face to face with Jamie Dawson, Garden Warehouse's catering manager. He had a suitcase on wheels behind him and a stuffed giraffe under one arm.

So he was the one leaving. With a giraffe. No sign of the hip flask.

I fought the urge to laugh out loud and gave him the cool stare I saved especially for difficult customers.

'What do you want?'

'Gee, thanks for the welcome.' He gave me a lopsided smile.

'I don't know how you've got the nerve to show your face in here,' I said, spraying a mist of cleaning liquid on the counter and rubbing it vigorously.

'It'll be the very last time, I promise,' he said meekly. 'I'm leaving Barnaby tonight.'

'If you want to know what this week's bestseller is,' said

Juliet, barging into him on her way past with a full tray of dirty crockery, 'it's courgette and lime cake; I'll let you have the recipe.'

I smirked.

We'd served it a couple of weeks ago when I'd over-ordered on courgettes for Lia's courgette and parmesan soup. Juliet had used up the excess in a cake but it was green and sour and customers had voted with their feet. We'd happily share that one with the Cabin Café.

He scratched his beard and looked from Juliet to me. 'Just a guess, but you don't like me very much, do you?'

I fluttered my eyelashes innocently.

Jamie held up a hand. 'I come in peace. And also for pizza.'

'No can do,' I said, pointing to the oven, which wasn't lit. There wasn't enough demand to offer pizzas after three o'clock; we had to think of our running costs. 'You can have a dry scone and be grateful I'm serving you at all.'

'Ever thought of entering the national warmest waitress of the year competition?'

There was a snort of derision and a clatter of plates from the kitchen. *She can talk*, I thought, shooting a dark look over my shoulder.

'Take it or leave it,' I said, slapping the scone on a plate; it was actually light and fluffy and not in the least bit dry.

'Mmm, delicious. Better have a coffee with it too then.'

'Anything for your friend?' I nodded at the giraffe.

'Very funny.'

He sauntered over to the nearest table, tucked his suitcase out of the way, set the giraffe down on a chair and returned for his order.

He held out a five-pound note and when I went to tweak it out of his hands he held on to it.

'Don't suppose you fancy joining me?'

I looked at the floor which needed a proper wash and the coffee machine covered in dried-on milk foam and coffee grounds and the pizza toppings which needed covering and putting away until tomorrow and sighed. 'If I must.'

Pouring myself a glass of water, I took a seat opposite him and next to the giraffe.

'Gladys, meet Rosie,' said Jamie, stroking the giraffe's neck. He turned to me. 'Gladys isn't a real Rothschild's giraffe.'

'Just as well, I don't think we're licensed for wild animals.'

'Wild?' He clapped his hands over Gladys's ears. 'Don't listen. My team have sponsored a real giraffe at Chester Zoo, Gladys is just to remind me.'

'So you're leaving?' I said, straightening up the coaster in front of me and setting my glass down in the corner of it.

He sliced into his scone and pressed a finger on the springy inside. He looked up at me and grinned. 'I'd say this is fresh out of the oven.'

I shrugged, cursing the smile that threatened to give me away.

'Yes. Going home to Kent for a long weekend. Then straight on to a new project in Bath on Monday.'

'So the rumour is true.' I quirked an eyebrow at him. 'The Cabin Café isn't doing very well and you've got the sack?'

He threw back his head and laughed. 'Thanks for the vote of confidence. No. Sorry to disappoint. My job is to get our cafés up and running smoothly. As soon as that happens, I get moved on to the next store opening.'

'And is the plastic paradise running smoothly?'

His lips twitched. 'Is that what people call it?'

'Amongst other things.' Actually, I'd just made that up but everything was plastic: the tables, chairs, the cutlery, the flowers and some unkind people might say the food . . .

He frowned and dug his knife into the pat of butter and spread it roughly. 'Early days. Why, who told you it isn't doing very well?'

I puffed out my cheeks and counted on my fingers.

'Andy the postman, Doreen's friend who shall remain nameless, Biddy's sister who's got mobility issues and got stuck in the doorframe in her motorized scooter and some idiot sent her flying down the ramp when he tried to free her.'

Jamie winced. 'I think I remember that.'

'Three members of the parish council,' I continued, 'the cleaner from the Cross Keys pub, a man who comes in here with two whippets. And my mum.'

He bit into his scone and munched for a few seconds. I folded my arms.

'Can we talk off the record?' he said softly.

'No.' I sipped my water. 'I don't trust you further than I can see you.'

Jamie shook his head and laughed softly. 'How's the new pizza oven doing?'

'Keep your beak out.'

'Rosie.' He stretched his legs out in front of him, crossed his ankles and smiled lazily. 'Off the record, Bath is my last job for Garden Warehouse; my wife is having a baby and I'm fed up with all the travelling. We plan on opening up our own café, or a bistro, not sure exactly.' He shrugged. 'But something special, somewhere without disposable spoons. Like this place. There. I've told you a secret. You could get me in trouble with that piece of info. I haven't told the boss yet.'

I stared at him for a long moment. 'What do you want, Jamie?'

He leaned forward, resting his elbows on his knees. 'To part as friends. We're both in the business. And I love what you've done with this place. I admire you.'

'I had no choice,' I retorted, secretly pleased nonetheless. 'We would have been ruined if I hadn't done something. Remember the five hundred free cappuccinos? And you nicked our blueberry crumble cake!'

He held his hands up. 'I know and I do regret that. If it's any consolation, it didn't sell for us.'

'Frozen blueberries,' I said. 'You should have used fresh.'

He inclined his head, conceding defeat.

'True that,' Juliet piped up from the kitchen.

Jamie looked startled and I grinned at him.

'But the free coffee thing, we always do that as an opening offer, it wasn't to sabotage you. Scout's honour.'

'Well, thank you for your admiration,' I said magnanimously. 'And off the record, we probably wouldn't have gone down the pizza route if Garden Warehouse hadn't forced us to examine our offering. At least not as quickly, anyway. So we have you to thank for that.'

'You're offering something a bit different. And it has certainly taken us by surprise.'

I raised my eyebrows, pleased with myself.

'Oh yeah, that day you had the pizza party wiped the smile off everyone's faces at head office. The publicity you had on the radio, it blew our celebrity weather girl out of the water.'

'That's reassuring,' I said, not bothering to wipe the smile off my own. 'How's your scone?'

'Good,' he said in a muffled voice through a mouthful.

'Buttermilk,' yelled Juliet. Her head appeared round the kitchen door, she bit her lip. 'Shite. Didna mean to tell him that.'

Jamie laughed.

'Anyway, they've learned their lesson. Garden Warehouse is an urban business through and through. They stuck their neck out with this Barnaby site, in a rural location. The price was irresistible and the boss had read an article about rural communities in crisis, not having access to shops, and had this romantic notion of being a knight in shining armour and saving the day.'

'With a branch of Garden Warehouse?' I sniggered.

'Fair point.' He grinned. 'We will never be a destination store, not like the shops you've got in this village.'

'What do you mean?' I leaned forward, interested in his opinion, trying to remember why I'd disliked him so much and sort of wishing he wasn't leaving any more.

366

'"Let's take a trip out to the Lemon Tree Café, make a day of it" is destination as opposed to: "let's pop into Garden Warehouse while we're in the area". Basically, people won't make a special trip to visit us.'

'Unless they're people who are really into plastic tat,' I suggested.

'They're learning that not everyone wants that,' Jamie said tactfully. 'And we've got the menu wrong for this area too.'

'Even though you copied from the best?' I gave him a pointed look.

He winced. 'I have apologized. And if it's any consolation even our scones aren't a patch on yours.'

'Well, that's something, I suppose.'

'In fact,' he gave a half-laugh, 'someone at the management meeting yesterday suggested we started doing pizzas.'

I sat bolt upright in my chair. 'You are kidding me?'

'Nope. That new guy in legal services.' He swigged the last of his coffee and set the cup back down. He smiled wryly. 'Though what the café menu has got to do with him is debatable.'

Gabe. My head began to spin. I could hardly believe it. Gabe would do that? I expected he'd want to create a good impression in his first week by coming up with good ideas but that was a low blow. A very low blow indeed.

I swallowed. My face was all crumpled and cross.

'And what happened? What was the outcome?'

'I'd put that glass down if I were you.' Jamie frowned at my hand.

I was gripping my glass of water so tightly that my finger ends had gone white. I set it on the table and looked at him. 'Well?'

He shrugged. 'I told him we didn't have the facilities. Mark the boss seemed keen, though. Anyway, it's up to them; my work here is done.' He pulled a face. 'Only one more "plastic paradise" to install and I'll be on the phone

367

picking your brains about opening my own café. In Kent,' he added. 'No competition to you.'

'Yeah, sure, I'd be happy to,' I said distractedly.

I knew we'd had our differences, Gabe and I, but this took the biscuit.

Jamie beamed. 'Great, I could do with a mentor.'

'Hardly,' I scoffed. 'We're just a small rural café and I don't know what I'm doing half the time.'

Jamie opened his mouth as if to argue, but the café phone rang. I shot him a look of apology and stood up to get it but Juliet beat me to it.

'Who, hen? Will she know what it's regarding? Oh, OK.' She covered the mouthpiece with her hand. 'Rosie, it's Lucinda Miller, for you; says she's an actress.'

Jamie's jaw dropped. '*The* Lucinda Miller?'

I nodded. 'We worked together, so yeah, probably.'

He got to his feet, laughing. He picked up his giraffe, collected his case and held out his hand.

'Only a small rural café?' He shook his head in amazement. 'I think the Lemon Tree Café is far more than that. And you, Rosie, are one hell of a special girl. I hope we meet again.'

'Bye,' I said, shaking his hand. 'And good luck with the new baby.'

I was still grinning when I took the receiver from Juliet. 'Rosie Featherstone, can I help?'

Chapter 36

'Rosie? Is it really you? *The* Rosie Featherstone who did that online charity campaign thing for domestic violence?' Lucinda sounded out of breath.

'Yes,' I said, thinking how surreal this was and that it should be me who was star-struck having an actress on the phone. 'That's me. Are you OK? You sound out of breath.'

Juliet and I exchanged glances.

'I can't believe I found you!' she panted. 'And I'm on an exercise bike. Pedalling my butt off.'

I smiled and gave Juliet the thumbs up.

'Well, it's lovely to hear from you,' I said tentatively, 'but I don't work for them any more.'

'I know! I heard about what you did, how you got the sack for not airbrushing my photograph to make me look slimmer. And I wanted to get in touch to say thank you, I don't often get someone sticking up for me, but my agent said no one knew where you'd gone. And then, there I was on Twitter, and someone had retweeted a picture of you looking all kick-ass outside a café with your arms folded and I thought that has GOT to be her. And it is!'

Lucinda's voice was a bit like gunfire and after Jamie's languid tones, it took me a moment to catch up.

'Well, that's not quite what happened at Digital Horizons,' I said. 'Far from it.'

She gasped and said, 'Oh. My. God' a lot as I explained

that I'd known she was happy with the pictures from the photo shoot to be used to front the campaign and that when the charity and my company had wanted me to airbrush them to reduce her waist and thighs, I'd refused and walked out.

'Good on you,' she said fervently. 'I mean, I'm not that fat, am I?'

'You are not fat *at all*, Lucinda,' I said hotly. 'And anyway, the point of having your picture there was to empower women who found themselves in a difficult situation, not to highlight the circumference of your thighs.'

'They should have used you to front the campaign instead of me. Walking out like that over something you believe in . . . you are totally my hero,' she said in a small voice. 'I wish I was more like you. You're just so sure in your own skin, you know your own mind. You've got an opinion and you stick to it.'

'Thank you,' I said, touched. I lowered my voice. 'But actually, that isn't always a good thing. I'm beginning to worry that I'm getting as bossy as my mother.'

'I never really knew my mother.' Lucinda sighed. 'She died of cancer when I was three. Dad couldn't cope and my sister and I went into care.'

'I'm sorry, I remember that from reading your profile from your agent,' I said softly. 'Which makes everything you've achieved so impressive.'

'I miss her. I miss having a mum. I'd just like someone to talk to sometimes, who's unconditionally on my side, you know.'

'I do,' I replied, thinking how blessed I was to be surrounded by family, who if I ever needed them would be there for me in a heartbeat. 'I'm no substitute, I know, but if you ever need a sounding board, you know where I am.'

Down the other end of the phone was a noise that sounded like a sob.

'Thank you. I can't tell you how hard it is in this industry to stand up to all that image stuff. It's like you have no control over your own body. I had an audition for a part two weeks ago and they told me to come back when I'd lost a stone.'

'That's outrageous,' I said, appalled. 'I hope you told them to get stuffed?'

There was a pause on the other end of the line and all I could hear was the whirr of the exercise bike and Lucinda's panting. 'I've lost four pounds so far, but I'm so hungry. I could inhale one of your pizzas now, just scoff it down, crust and all.'

My heart tweaked for her. How stressful to have to monitor your every mouthful. And how awful that someone else thinks they can dictate how another person should look.

'Come and work for me,' I said, looking at the containers of olives, sliced Italian sausage and fresh mozzarella beneath the counter. 'I bet I can cure you. You won't want to touch another pizza after being surrounded by them all day. My sister has gone right off them.'

'Five hundred calories! Smashed it. I'm done.'

The exercise bike stopped and there was a glugging noise as presumably she had a drink.

'I'd love to,' she said breathlessly, 'but I got another part. Which I'm probably, well, possibly going to take.'

'Oh good!' I said heartily. 'One you don't need to lose weight for, I hope?'

'They haven't asked me to but . . .' Her voice faded and I heard a heartfelt sigh.

'Lucinda? What is it?'

She sighed. 'It's my first film role. Only a small role. But it's a great cast. Tom Hiddleston's in it.'

'Take it!' I cried. 'And I'll be your PA.'

She laughed. 'I want to take it but there's some nudity in it.'

'Ah,' I said. 'And I take it you have to provide the nudity?'

Her voice went all muffled as she explained that it was

bum and boobs only, which wasn't too bad. But she wasn't sure whether to do it and as I'd been so passionate about not airbrushing her curves, she thought she'd ask me for my advice.

Suddenly her voice was clear again. 'Sorry about that, just stripped off for a shower. So what do you think? Should I do it? I really want to but . . .'

'I think it's about staying in control. Being comfortable with the situation at all times and making it clear what you will and won't show. This is about you, Lucinda. You and your body.'

'But what if I say yes to bum and boobs and when I get there they say "oh just turn round" or "just drop the sheet"? I'll be pressured to do as they say.'

Pressured . . .

I thought back to my last night in London when Callum forced himself on me. Making me do things I didn't want to do. It was completely different to Lucinda's situation, of course, but I had lost control; the power he had over me had taken away my right to choose. And what was worse was that I had let him get away with it. I should have done the right thing, the brave thing, and reported it. It was rape; he should have been punished. Instead, I had slunk back to Barnaby and tried to forget the whole incident. That one night had had repercussions for my love life for ten whole years. Telling Gabe about it had done me the world of good; he'd made me see that it hadn't been my fault, that what Callum had done was wrong in every sense. But it still niggled me: because I hadn't done anything about it – hadn't made Callum face up to the fact that he had committed a crime – what was to stop him doing it again?

What if I could have prevented that by reporting it to the police? What if someone else had suffered the same thing? So in a way I was guilty . . .

'You're disgusted, aren't you?' said Lucinda, after my continuing silence. 'I'd better go.'

'NO!' I blurted out and then calmed down. 'I'm in awe. Totally. And I think your mum would be too.'

'Seriously?' she said in a small voice.

'Yes. But don't let anyone force you to do anything you don't want to do. I know it's not quite the same, but *no* means *no* and you have to make sure your director understands that. And if anything happens that you're not comfortable with, speak out, don't accept it. Tell someone – promise me you'll tell someone.'

Like I should have done at the time . . .

'OK.' Lucinda sighed. 'I'm not ashamed of my body. I'm looking at it now in the mirror. I'm just not sure I want anyone else to see my foofoo. But this could be my big break. If I say no, I might never get asked to do a film again.'

I chewed my lip, wondering what I'd do.

'Put yourself in your shoes a few years ahead from now. Imagine you're an older successful actress looking back at your career, what would you tell your younger self?'

'Er . . . oh gosh, I'd probably say, take every opportunity that comes your way, but always be true to yourself, be proud of your body, it'll never look any better than it does right now.'

I grinned. 'Spoken like a legend of the silver screen.'

'You are seriously good,' said Lucinda with a giggle. 'I'd never have thought of that.'

There was a beep from her end and she gave a little squeak. 'What was that?'

'Just made a sale on *Depop*, you know that sales app?'

'Yes I do know,' I said with a grin. 'I was in social media, remember?'

'So much better than eBay with all its grouchy old people moaning about feedback and postage.'

'What did you sell?'

'A Stella McCartney suit. I'm going through my wardrobe while I've got a couple of weeks free before the filming starts.'

I laughed. 'So you're definitely taking the part.'

She giggled. 'Yeah, why not? I'll just channel you when the cameraman tells me to drop the towel. Can I call you again? From my trailer in Hollywood?'

I shook my head affectionately, thinking that Lucinda was going to be fine. 'Of course, now bugger off, I've got some baking trays to scrub.'

She gave a squeak. 'Bloody hell, there's a car coming for me in half an hour! At this rate I'll be appearing nude sooner than planned. But listen, if I can ever help you out, you know, with anything, please ask. Although possibly not washing up. And thanks for the new mantra, I needed to hear that: *no means no.*'

We exchanged mobile numbers and she rang off to go and prepare for a film premiere in Covent Garden and I picked up some cake-encrusted baking trays and thought there was somebody else who still needed to hear it too . . .

I was tired when I brushed my teeth before bed later that night, my back ached from stacking the outside tables and chairs, but my brain was still buzzing; I couldn't get Callum out of my head. My conversation with Lucinda had triggered all sorts of worrying thoughts. What if he had done it again – attacked another girl? What if what had happened to me was part of a pattern that I could have prevented by pressing charges? What if he needed to hear *no means no* too?

I was ten years older now, I wasn't afraid of him – I hadn't been at the time, actually. He'd been a moody sort of boy, not my usual type. He'd always seemed a bit tortured, as if everyday life was a challenge for him. Looking back, I have no idea why we got together; we were so unsuited. Up until Callum, I'd always gone for the loudmouths, the life-and-soul-of-the-party boys. I should have known then – they always say it's the quiet ones you have to watch.

We'd both had too much to drink that night. Perhaps if I hadn't been in such a deep tequila-induced slumber I'd have had the strength to fight him off and it would never have happened.

I pulled back the duvet and was about to get into bed when I stopped. It might be too little too late, but all of a sudden I knew I had to do it. I had to find Callum and see what sort of life he had led since we split up.

I ran downstairs for my iPad, settled myself back into bed and asked Google to find Callum O'Connor from Leeds, last seen in Putney in 2006. My first search produced nothing. He wasn't on LinkedIn or Facebook. Which was odd; he'd just started out in a career in media when we met; assuming he was still in that line of work, I'd have expected him to have a profile on every social media platform on the planet. I stared out of my bedroom window, racking my brains for ideas. I'd left my curtains open and even though it was late, it wasn't completely dark. The sky shimmered silver from the light of an enormous moon.

I thought of Gabe; he'd no doubt be in bed now too, possibly gazing up at the moon like me. I picked up my phone from the nightstand and flirted briefly with the idea of sending him a text: Guess what? I'd say, I've decided to try to find Callum, what do you think? And if he was awake he'd probably text straight back; he'd want to help. My heart fluttered. He would, I knew it; he was kind-hearted like that.

And then I remembered what Jamie had said about Gabe's idea of introducing pizzas on to the Cabin Café menu and I tossed my phone back down. I took a deep breath and went back to my search; Callum O'Connor couldn't have simply disappeared . . .

Half an hour later my heart was racing; I was pretty sure I'd found him, or at least his family.

I'd found an O'Connor family living in Leeds and as I'd dug around, more and more details of Callum's life had come back to me: his dad had run a small building firm; he had three brothers, one of whom, Patrick, had played rugby for Ireland; and his mum was called Nuala. I knew that because one of the other brothers had just had a baby when I'd met Callum and his mum had asked to be called Nanny Nuala.

Nuala O'Connor's Facebook page was full of proud pictures of her family. Her husband had evidently passed away, but last Christmas she'd posted a picture of 'me and all my babies' and had tagged all four of the people in the picture. She was standing in the middle of the group, surrounded by three burly men and a woman wearing party hats and Christmas jumpers. Nuala was holding a selfie stick and she'd shaved the tops off two of the tallest men in the picture and a couple of comments made reference to her dubious selfie skills. But that wasn't what stood out for me. The person I couldn't take my eyes off was the woman. She was wearing a lot of black eyeliner, had an angular jaw and her Adam's apple jutted out over the neck of her jumper. I was sure Callum didn't have a sister but this girl smiling shyly at the camera had the same blue eyes as the rest of her family. I stared at her picture and a shiver ran down my spine. There was no mention on Nuala's page of Callum. But plenty of Candy O'Connor . . .

My mouth went dry. Could Candy be Callum? My finger hovered over the link to Candy's profile page. I clicked on it and held my breath.

All of Candy's posts were private, but I scrolled through her profile pictures and what I saw made my heart beat like fury; there, over the last few years, was the gradual transformation from male to female. And even though Facebook would only let me scroll back so far, I could tell it was him.

Callum had gone through gender realignment and now lived as a woman. I'm not sure quite what I expected to gain by Facebook-stalking my ex, but it certainly wasn't this. This wasn't closure; this was opening a whole new can of worms . . .

I checked the time again. It was nearly midnight, too late

to be doing this but I knew I wouldn't sleep now. I had to contact him, *her*.

I clicked on the Facebook messenger icon and tried to think what to say. It took me half an hour to compose a three-word message:

Can we talk?

I pressed send and waited, optimistically, for an instant reply. But none came.

I lay back against my pillows for another hour, my heart still thumping. The moon disappeared behind the clouds and the room grew dark, the only light the blue haze from the screen. My eyes became heavier and heavier until eventually, half-asleep, I slid my iPad on to my nightstand and drifted into an uneasy sleep.

At six o'clock I jolted awake, my heart pounding as if I'd been having a nightmare. I automatically reached for my iPad to check for messages. My inbox was showing one new message.

Candy O'Connor had replied.

Chapter 37

Candy's message simply contained a phone number.

I didn't give myself the chance to think it through, or talk myself out of it, or worry what the hell I was going to say. With my heart still racing, I called the number and on the first ring, Candy picked up.

'Hello?'

I swallowed, my mouth dry. I wished I'd made some tea first, but it was too late now.

'This is Rosie. Sorry to ring so early.'

I rolled my eyes at myself. Why on earth was I starting off with an apology?

'I'm glad; I've been staring at the phone since I sent you my number.'

Candy's voice was soft and low, a trace of a northern accent. I could hear her nerves too: rapid breathing, a slight tremble in her words. I didn't recognize it as Callum's. That might be because ten years had gone by, or maybe it was hormone tablets; I didn't know much about these things. Suddenly I felt unsure of myself; do I blurt out 'are you Callum?' or was that un-pc? Or did the final moments of our relationship allow me to say what the hell I liked?

'Look,' said Candy in a rush, 'I have to ask, are you going to the police? Is that why you're ringing, because of that last night at the flat?'

'So it is you,' I murmured. 'Bloody hell, Cal—Candy.'

She blew out a long shaky breath.

'Yeah, it's me. A lot has changed since I last saw you.'

I'll say.

I didn't really know why I was ringing, other than to finally close the door on a chapter in my history as Nonna had done in Sorrento. I suppose I'd expected to contact someone who'd be apologetic, who'd reassure me that he was a changed man. Instead, I found a changed woman. But I wasn't going to involve the police. What purpose would it serve? Callum didn't even exist any more; he was a she, not even the same person.

'No. That's not why I wanted to find you. I guess I'd hoped you would tell me that nothing like that had ever happened before or since. I guess I was just curious to find out what sort of man you'd become.'

'Thank you, thank you.' There was a pause. 'I bet you didn't expect to find I'd become a woman?'

'Well, no.' I smiled. 'Bit of a conversation stopper.'

'I'm glad you called,' she continued. 'I've lived under the shadow of what I did to you for the last ten years.'

'You and me both.'

'Oh shit,' she groaned. 'The stupid, *stupid* thing was that you were the best thing that had happened to me. If I hadn't been such a coward, we could have been friends all these years, instead of me living in fear of this phone call.'

I swung my legs out of bed, pulled on a dressing gown and padded downstairs.

'So tell me over a cup of tea,' I said, switching on the kettle. 'Tell me how Callum became Candy O'Connor.'

'OK.' I heard her making similar noises: the gush of water, the tinkling of spoons, the clunk of a mug.

'Do you still have huge cups of tea with the tiniest splash of milk?' she asked.

'Yes,' I said with a hint of a smile. '*I* haven't really changed at all. Now come on, spill the beans.'

'I'd struggled with my gender for years,' Candy began.

'But I didn't want to face up to it, I was afraid to. In my family, men are men and do manly things all day long . . .'

I made my tea and took it out into the garden. I wiped my sleeve over the damp seat of a chair and sat down, and in the still of the morning with the mist hovering over the distant peaks, Candy told me her story.

Mr O'Connor Senior was a builder and two of his sons, Jacko and Patrick (once he'd retired from rugby), both worked for him and took over the firm when their father died eight years ago. Kevin, the other brother, worked on the oil rigs. All of them were so undisputedly masculine that there was simply no space for the conversation Callum needed to have as a teenager, so he didn't have it. He left home for university and tried to push aside the feelings of shame and guilt, just wishing he could be like his brothers, be the man his father thought he was. Nobody at home seemed to notice that he'd never brought a girl home until Jacko got married and had a baby. Then the pressure was on and the jokes from his brothers started up: are you gay or something?

'*Or something,* I wanted to tell them,' said Candy with a sigh. 'But of course I didn't. I did the most stupid thing I could have done: I decided to prove them wrong.'

'So you hadn't had a girlfriend until you met me?'

'Nope. A virgin at twenty-two.'

I tried to cast my mind back to whether I'd suspected that, but nothing obvious sprang to mind.

I squeezed my eyes shut. This conversation was nothing like I'd imagined having. Instead of anger and accusations, I felt only sorrow and regret. I could see my younger self in my mind's eye: full of fun, excited at life's opportunities, totally self-absorbed, oblivious to the needs of others. My life revolved around me: my wants, my needs, my dreams. Callum had needed something, someone entirely different; I must have been blind not to have picked up on it.

'Cal— Sorry Candy, I'm sorry, really sorry that I didn't

know any of this. And if it's any consolation, you, well, you know, did OK.'

'Oh God. I watched a LOT of videos,' she said and suddenly we both laughed.

'And please don't apologize,' she said. 'We're working up to the hard part here, remember?'

It was cool outside, the air was damp and even though I'd slipped my feet into my trainers and was in a thick dressing gown, I was shivering.

'We don't have to go over it, Candy,' I said quietly. 'Both of us know what happened.'

'Let me say it; the very least I owe you is an apology and an explanation.'

'OK, I'm listening,' I murmured, wishing I'd listened more at the time.

'I tried, I just thought if I could . . . I feel stupid even saying it out loud now, but I thought if I could just pretend, get a girlfriend and live like a man, I'd be OK. I couldn't believe it when you agreed to go out with me; I had the social skills of a mollusc.'

'You weren't that bad,' I insisted. 'Besides, I like a challenge.'

'I loved you, Rosie, but it was a desperate kind of love. When you started showing an interest in me, I thought, this is it, I can do this, this beautiful creature thinks I'm a man, so I am. And for a few weeks, it seemed to be working out.'

'And then I ended it,' I said heavily.

'Yes. At the time it felt that my only chance at "normal life" had gone. I tried to cling to what we had. I'm so ashamed of what I did. I've looked back on that night a million times, shouting at myself to do the right thing, but of course that's not possible. Callum raped you and there's not a day goes by when I don't think of that.'

A thread of cobweb caught my eye. It ran from the back of the other chair to the stone wall, glistening with dew. I watched as a tiny spider skimmed across it like an acrobat on a tightrope and disappeared from view. Callum had been living like that, on a tightrope, clinging on to me for balance. Until I cut him loose. And now Candy had cut him loose and had distanced herself from the events of that night.

I gripped the phone to my ear and listened to her breathing.

'Was that the catalyst that made you face up to your gender issues?'

'Oh yeah, without a doubt. I left London straight away, didn't even take up that job offer I'd had. Left the UK, actually – spent a couple of years travelling. Only came back when my dad died. Felt really bad about that. Losing my dad hit my family really hard. But about a year after the funeral Mum sat me down and asked me if I was gay. That she'd always wondered, even when I was little, I seemed so much more delicate than her other boys. And it all came out. She's been brilliant, actually, helped me get counselling, supporting me through my treatment and the surgery. My brothers were a different story . . . anyway. Water under the bridge. They're coming round to it now.'

We chatted some more about family and careers; she was still in media, working for an independent film-maker in Leeds; she lived with her mum. We'd been on the phone for nearly an hour; it was time to get ready for work.

I picked up my empty mug and made my way back into the warmth of the cottage. I put the mug in the sink and went upstairs.

'What made you get in touch now?' Candy asked.

I thought of Lucinda and the advice I'd given her: about staying in control, about making others aware of what you will and won't do.

'I was angry – still – and I wanted you to know that I'd survived, I've made a success of life, I'm not a victim and I'll never let anyone overpower me again.'

There was a heavy silence for a moment.

'Right.' Candy sounded thoughtful. 'Do you mind me asking, are you single?'

I tucked the phone under my ear while I made my bed. It was a double, pillows each side, I slept on the left. The right side was neat and unremittingly unruffled. I wondered which side Gabe slept on.

I sighed. 'Yes. That night left me with an overwhelming resistance to people, well to men. Actually, to be accurate, one man in particular.'

'Go on.'

I closed my eyes and indulged myself with images of Gabe Green.

'He's called Gabe. I'd like to get to know him better, but I've developed such a tough suit of armour that it gets in the way and I repel him like oncoming fire.'

I told her about our near misses, our almost dates and mostly our arguments. And I told her how scared I had been to fall in love in case history repeated itself.

Candy groaned, repeating my name over and over, and saying how sorry she was.

'The chances of you meeting a man who's actually a woman living in a man's body who then goes nuts and attacks you twice in your life are pretty slim. Listen, I've been in therapy for years. Take some advice from me, take the armour off, lower the drawbridge ever so slowly and tell him how you feel; let the guy in, love him and I bet he'll love you right back.'

I conjured up Gabe's face and wondered. Could I love him, would he love me right back?

I let out a long sigh. 'I wish, I wish . . .'

'What?'

I let myself flop down on the bed. 'Oh that I could give you a hug, that'd I'd called five years ago, or before . . . I wish I'd been braver.'

There was a sniffle on the other end of the phone.

'Me too, Rosie love, I wish all those things for me too.'

'Funny really. Well, not funny exactly, but in those first few weeks after I left London, I thought you deserved to have your willy chopped off. So you couldn't do it again.'

'But I beat you to it,' she said.

'UGH, Candy! Too much information.'

I felt oddly peaceful after talking to Candy. In fact, there was a small serene smile on my face which refused to budge for several hours. Talking to her couldn't change the past, but it did put it into perspective. Rightly or wrongly, I'd forgiven her and as a consequence I felt good. As Nonna had said, a door had closed on an unhappy part of my life. And the rest of my life was an open door.

I stayed like this until it dawned on me around mid-morning that the last time I'd felt so light and happy was after I'd confided in Gabe. I remembered how we'd both got soaked to the skin in the rain and he'd taken me back to the cottage, lit a fire and made me hot chocolate and listened, properly listened, and then made me feel safe and secure. When he'd been a true friend.

Oh God.

He had been such a good friend that day, but since then, he'd started working for Garden Warehouse and, if Jamie were to be believed, he'd suggested to his boss that pizzas might be the way forward in the Cabin Café. Not to mention grabbing me so roughly the other evening. I was so confused . . .

Friday mornings were always our busiest at the café. And today I was particularly glad of the distraction. By noon Juliet, Lia and I had served countless pots of tea and rounds of avocado on toast, umpteen cappuccinos and slices of cake and the vicar had been in to collect his extra-large pizza order. Juliet was having a clear-up outside and Lia was bracing herself for the lunchtime pizza orders when Mum popped her head round the door.

'Any chance of a coffee and a chat, darling? My nerves are in tatters,' she said, sinking down into an armchair and closing her eyes for an instant.

'Sure,' I said, taking a mug from the shelf. 'But I . . .'

Mum's eyes popped open. I'd been about to say that I couldn't join her for a chat as I had lots of jobs to do, but Lucinda's words were still ringing in my head about how much she missed having her mum to talk to.

I decided to turn a blind eye to the spilt milk on the floor and picked up a second mug. ' . . . but I think I'll have tea.'

I added a plate of biscuits to the tray and brought it across to the table. 'How have your first couple of days at The Chestnuts Cancer Hospice been?'

Mum groaned, leaned forward and pressed her palms into her eyes. 'Full on.'

'That bad?'

'I may have bitten off more than I can chew. My boss showed me into a giant cupboard yesterday, stuffed to the gunnels with second-hand designer clothes – too good to sell on the rails through the shop. Everything from Valentino to Versace. Wedding dresses, ball gowns . . . right down to designer jeans. She wants me to come up with a way to make money with them. An event.'

'Sounds exciting, what are you thinking of?'

She pulled a face. 'I haven't got a clue. I've been racking my brain ever since, I barely slept last night. I think Nonna's revelations about my father and our escape from Italy in the sixties have taken more out of me than I realized. I just don't seem to have the energy or the focus, Rosie.'

It was so unlike Mum to admit any sort of weakness that I nearly spat out my tea. I peered at her; she did look a bit under the weather. And it struck me just how much she had gone through since finding out about her real father. Maybe she should put herself first for once and relax a bit. Not that she was likely to listen to me.

'Perhaps you should postpone this volunteering job?' I said tentatively. 'Give yourself some time off?'

Predictably, she looked appalled.

'I'm fine physically.' She waved a hand dismissively. 'And compared to the other volunteers, my life is a piece of cake.

I met a lady called Sharon who is still having chemo. She goes on her own these days because she's had so many appointments that her friends and her husband can't take any more time off to go with her. Besides, I need to be busy.'

I raised an eyebrow. I wasn't sure that was true, but seeing as I rarely took a day's holiday, I couldn't really argue.

'So I have to pull myself together and organize an event,' said Mum staunchly, taking a biscuit from the plate. 'This charity is so important because there are hundreds of people just like Sharon.'

'How can I help? What can I do?'

She lifted a shoulder. 'Want to buy any second-hand dresses?'

'I could,' I said thoughtfully, an idea beginning to unfurl like a new spring leaf. 'But I think I might know a really good way to sell them.'

I persuaded Mum to leave her fund-raising conundrum with me over the weekend and told her that we'd already thought that The Chestnuts Cancer Hospice could be the beneficiary of our next village event and maybe we could incorporate a clothing angle to it.

She was only too happy to take my advice and dashed off to the hospital where Nonna and Stanley were waiting to come home. The patient was finally being discharged but would need someone with him for the next couple of weeks. Angela had been most insistent that he come back to Bristol with her. But Stanley, seemingly quite enjoying being fought over, had convinced her that she already had far too much to do looking after her own family and he'd be better off at home. So Nonna had packed a case and was moving in with him for a while.

Later that afternoon, I was carrying a Margherita pizza to one of the outside tables when a big silver car glided swan-like around the green, came to a halt and reversed effortlessly into a parking space directly in front of the café. A short man in his fifties, with curly greying hair, an expensive suit and a squashed nose, bounced out of it. He glanced at the sign above the door and then at the potted lemon trees and waited for his passenger to emerge. And out climbed Gabe.

My heart jumped at the sight of him. Then I noticed his navy suit with a jacket that emphasized his broad shoulders and slim-fitting trousers showing off a rather shapely bottom and it jumped a bit more. Gabe was a man made to wear suits, I thought idly.

'Enjoy,' I said, setting the pizza down in front of the elderly couple who were sharing it.

'That must be the big boss from you-know-where,' Juliet hissed loudly, appearing beside me with a tray to collect empties.

'Hmm,' I said and began helping her load discarded plates on to her tray. 'Fresh from ripping off some poor unsuspecting small business owners like Clementine, no doubt.'

'Looks like they're coming for a working lunch,' said Juliet. 'Cor, Gabe fills that suit very nicely, I must say.'

The boss-man and Gabe were reaching into the back seat for briefcases and things. I remembered Gabe holding a dust sheet over my head on that very spot and covering me with sawdust. It was almost impossible to reconcile that memory with the city slicker who stood before me, directing the other man to an empty table at the far end of the café's stretch of pavement.

'Hello, Gabe!' Juliet called. 'Nice to see you back again, isn't it, Rosie?'

'You too, Juliet.' Gabe raised a hand, slipped his jacket off and took a seat quickly, studiously avoiding my eye.

'Isn't it?' she repeated, nudging me.

'Rumour has it that Gabe has suggested adding pizzas to the Cabin Café menu,' I whispered to her. 'So don't be too nice.'

'Says who?' She scowled. 'I don't believe that of him. Not for a minute.'

I flushed. 'Jamie Dawson, their catering manager.'

Juliet still didn't like him, even if I'd warmed to him.

'It was probably a joke, like: ha ha, perhaps we should start serving pizzas like the Lemon Tree Café. Rather than a plan to ruin us,' she suggested.

'They've certainly been scrutinizing the menu long enough,' I said, nodding to Gabe's table.

'Because no one has taken their order, have they?' she said severely and hefted the heavy tray back inside.

'Right,' I muttered under my breath, 'let's get this over with.'

I took out my order pad and stood at Gabe's table, looking from him to his guest and hoping he couldn't sense my nerves.

'So, gentlemen, to what do we owe the pleasure of your company here at the Lemon Tree Café?' I said brightly, as if Gabe and I had never exchanged a cross word.

'Mark, this is Rosie Featherstone, joint owner of the café.' Gabe's eyes met mine briefly and then dropped back to the menu. 'Rosie, meet Mark Cooper, managing director of the GW group.'

'Pleased to meet you.' Mark shook my hand firmly and gave me a friendly smile. 'We've been stuck in an office all day working on a very boring deal. Gabe suggested we had a change of scenery for lunch, get some inspiration from your wonderful café.'

'Inspiration?' I flicked my eyes to Gabe who shifted uncomfortably in his seat.

'He was right as usual,' Mark continued. He took a pair of sunglasses from the breast pocket of his jacket and popped them on. 'What could be nicer than being outside, with a view of the village green?'

'Inspiration for what?' I repeated, staring at Gabe. Jamie was right; they were seriously looking at our pizza menu.

'For real life,' said Mark. 'I'm guilty of not seeing past the figures, whereas Gabe's rather more philanthropic; he reminds me that we have to consider the people behind the shopfronts. He suggested we leave the spreadsheets for a while and get some sunshine. We make a good team.'

He clapped Gabe on the shoulder.

I folded my arms. 'Is this the takeover you were telling me about? The proposal to—'

Gabe coughed suddenly and began banging his chest.

'Sorry,' he gasped. 'Swallowed a fly.'

Mark leaned forward in his chair. He looked from me to Gabe. 'Are you two an item? Because this is confidential.'

'No,' Gabe and I both said together.

'Just friends,' Gabe added.

I glared at him. 'That's debatable. And don't worry, Mark, he didn't tell me any details, and frankly I'm not interested in hearing how Garden Warehouse plans to ruin another chunk of England's retail landscape.'

Gabe inhaled sharply.

'Wow,' I heard Mark mutter as I strutted away. 'She's a feisty one.'

I glanced down at my order pad, which was completely blank. Damn it. I turned round and marched back.

'Can I take your order please?'

They both ordered pizza, naturally. Before I left the table Mark stood up and pointed inside.

'I'll just go and find the little boys' room.'

Leaving me facing Gabe. I felt my heart beat faster.

'I'll go and put your order into the kitchen.'

'Rosie.'

Gabe gently put his hand on mine. His touch shot through me like a bolt of electricity.

'I really am sorry about the way I behaved the other day, before Noah had that accident. I hope you know that I'm not someone who would push a woman around. I grabbed you and I, of all people, should have known how that would make you react.'

I nodded, not knowing what to say.

I really wanted to tell him about Callum – about

Candy – about how I'd talked it through with her and made my peace with what had happened. How I regretted not being more sensitive to someone who was crying out for help. But this wasn't the place. Not now, and certainly not here.

He looked at me with those soft grey eyes and I felt my insides melt.

'The stupid thing is that I stopped the car to try to mend our broken friendship, to thank you for trying to help out at school, but all I did was push you further away. I am truly, truly sorry.'

I nodded, feeling close to tears all of a sudden. This was an olive branch, a peace offering, a chance to put our argument behind us. Anyone else would have taken it gladly. Unfortunately, I seemed to have been born for battle.

'Then why bring him here?' I said sadly, nodding towards Mark's chair.

Gabe blinked. 'You don't want our custom?'

'Not if it comes at a price.' I looked through the café windows. 'Look – Mark's in there now talking to Lia.'

'I thought he might.' He smiled. 'I knew he'd be interested in the pizza oven.'

'So it's true.' My throat tightened. 'You want pizzas for the Cabin Café?'

He half laughed. 'Blimey, news travels fast.'

I stared at him, not believing what I was hearing; how could he be so blasé about it?

'It's just an idea but I thought as it is working so well here, why not expand the reach? The Cabin Café could—'

I balled my fists. 'I'd like you to leave.'

'What?' Gabe's face drained of colour and he raked a hand through his hair.

'You've done enough damage and I want you to leave,' I said, far more calmly than I felt.

'What have I done now? And what about Mark? My

boss is going to wonder what's going on. You've already nearly dropped me in it by mentioning the Home Stores takeover.'

'I wasn't to know.' I shrugged, although privately I did feel a bit bad about that.

'Rosie,' he said calmly, 'believe it or not I need this job. I'm already skating on thin ice after trashing my car door on day three.'

My heart tweaked for him, despite myself.

'All right, you can stay for lunch. But then that's it; you've had your final chance with me.'

Gabe's jaw dropped.

'Bloody unbelievable,' he muttered. 'You are the most difficult person to help in the entire universe.'

He thumped the table and the couple next door to him stopped chewing on their pizzas and flinched.

'Help? *Help?*' I hissed, trying to keep my voice down. 'In case it's escaped your notice, Boy Wonder, I don't need help. And if I did it would be because of the newly opened café trying to steal our business. And who do we have to thank for that?' I tapped my cheek with my pencil, pretending to think. 'Oh yes. That would be you.'

Gabe's eyes burned angrily. I could feel my chest rising and falling as I tried to get my breathing under control.

'OK, OK.' He threw his hands up. 'Got the message.'

'Good.' I span round on my heels, eager to get away before the tears came.

'Rosie, wait.' Gabe's voice was barely audible.

I froze, not wanting to turn back, not wanting him to see my expression.

Why do we do this? I wondered. *Why do I do this? He makes me so mad and yet . . . and yet I'm crazy about him too.*

'I've spoken to the school. You're approved to pick Noah up from now on. Because . . . because I need help some-times, even if you don't.'

His words hit my heart like tiny arrows.

'OK,' I said hoarsely, nodding. 'Fine.'

I marched inside, brushing past Mark on his way back to the table. I handed Lia their order and then I carried on going through the café and out into the courtyard where I let the tears of frustration roll down my cheeks and felt like an utterly, utterly terrible person.

Chapter 38

It was Saturday. Stanley had been home for twenty-four hours and Nonna was moving in properly today. I arrived at his bungalow after work with a chunk of Stanley's favourite chocolate cake and some biscotti for Nonna as Dad was unloading some of her things from the boot of his car.

'Honestly,' he said, shaking his head as he pulled out a box marked 'empty jars', 'women.'

'On behalf of women everywhere,' I said, kissing his grumpy face, 'I apologize.'

I left him grunting to himself and went inside.

The bungalow already seemed a brighter place: there was a vase of tulips and hyacinths in the hall, replacing the faded fake flowers I'd seen on my last visit. The air smelled fresh and there was something delicious wafting from the kitchen.

I found Stanley in the living room on a recliner chair, two brown slippers peeping out from under a blanket. His face looked a little pale and he'd lost quite a bit of weight, but his blue eyes still held a sparkle.

'Welcome to Antarctica,' he said, holding up his cheek to be kissed.

The window was open and a fresh breeze ruffled his white hair which hung round the back of his head from ear to ear like bunting.

'Shall I close that?' I asked, shivering as I sat on the sofa next to him.

He shook his head and pulled the blanket under his chin. 'I need fresh air, apparently. Amongst other unpleasant things. Normally I like air. In moderation.'

'And cake?' I said, lifting the lid of my cake tin.

'Cake,' he said, eyeing the contents greedily, 'is contraband. Quick, let me hide it.'

He held his hands out for the tin just as Nonna opened the door by pushing her bottom through it. He shoved the tin back at me.

'Your grandmother's derrière always arrives first.' He winked. 'Not that I'm complaining.'

'Eh, cheeky. Green tea,' she said officiously, planting the tray on the coffee table. 'Full of anti-somethings. Good for heart. And some biscuits. But not for you, mister.' She wagged a finger at him. 'You can have tablets.'

I attempted to hide the tin behind my back but she held her hands out.

'He can't eat this. It is poison.' She lifted the lid and sniffed. 'Mmm, but you can leave with me.'

Stanley and I exchanged resigned smiles.

She straightened up, pressed a hand to his forehead and frowned.

'You look tired, Stanley. Rosie, just five minutes. He need plenty of rest.'

Nonna was wearing an apron with a bib and she'd got a watch tied on to the front straps. She looked scary and nurse-like and she was obviously really enjoying herself.

'OK, I only popped in to check everyone was getting on all right,' I said.

Dad shouted something from the hallway and Nonna went out to answer him, the cake tin gripped firmly in her hands.

'Couldn't be happier, my dear.' Stanley sniffed his green tea and took a brave sip. 'I shan't want to get better at this rate in case she moves out. It was so nice last night to say goodnight to someone. She's agreed to live here for two weeks and after that . . . Well, I shall miss her.'

I stifled a smile; judging by the enormous pile of boxes in Dad's car, it looked like she was planning on moving in permanently.

'Maybe she doesn't have to?' I raised an eyebrow. 'Maybe you could pop the question again?'

Stanley shook his head. 'It's too late for us. I couldn't go down on one knee again. For a start, I probably wouldn't get up.'

He was making light of it, but his shoulders sagged and he gazed into his mug.

'But it would be different this time,' I said, taking his hand. His nails had grown in hospital and his skin was soft but cold, icy cold. 'She's footloose and fancy-free.'

'Exactly. Look at me. I'm on so many drugs, I've had to make a list to remember what they're all for. I don't want to saddle her with an old crock like me. I couldn't marry her now, it wouldn't be fair, she deserves a husband not an invalid.'

I opened my mouth to argue but Stanley held up a finger.

'I know you mean well, but she'll be glad to get back to her own home. Back to her greenhouse and a summer spent in the garden, I'd put money on it.'

'Maria?' Dad barked. 'For goodness' sake. Where on earth do you want me to put this Christmas tree?'

I caught Stanley's eye. 'You sure about that?'

From the hall came a crash, followed by a stream of expletives from Dad. I left Stanley looking thoughtful and went to investigate.

One of Nonna's suitcases, which by the look of it she'd brought with her from Italy in the sixties, had burst open. A mountain of pale pink nylon spilled over the hall floor, Nonna was on her knees scooping it up and Dad stooped to help.

'Don't look, Alec, these are my smalls!' she yelped.

'Not that bloody small,' muttered Dad, holding up an

enormous pair of knickers. He caught my eye and a reluctant smile crept over his face.

I smothered a giggle as Nonna grabbed them back off him and thrust them in the case.

'Right, that's the car emptied,' he said, brushing the dust from his hands. 'Now I'll go and fetch the rest of your clutter.'

'Eh, not clutter! But don't you want a cup of tea first?' She tried to do the zip up on the case and gave up.

But Dad was already out of the door.

'No,' he shouted over his shoulder. 'Let's get this over with.'

I picked up the broken case, laid it on the single bed in Nonna's room and went back into the kitchen.

'What's up with him?' said Nonna, handing me a tea towel and pointing to the drainer full of clean mugs.

'Derby County lost in the semi-final something-or-others,' I said with a sigh. 'Mum says he's had a face like thunder all week.'

I picked up a mug and stared at it. It was one of hers.

'How long are you staying, Nonna?'

She took a piece of biscotti from the tin and snapped it in two.

'I don't know. Couple of weeks. Until he doesn't need me. How long a piece of wool?'

I pressed a kiss to her cheek. 'He'll always need you, I reckon.'

She grunted and lifted a shoulder. 'I not so sure.'

'Well, I am,' I said firmly. 'You've brought this place to life, and he adores you.'

She looked down at her hands, plump and wrinkled and completely ringless.

'He want me here as his nurse because it is better than going to stay with Angela, but I think I miss my chance with him. He not say anything about marriage ever again. I missed the bus; story of your nonna's life.'

My heart squeezed for her. I wondered whether to repeat what Stanley had just said, but decided against it. This was something they'd have to figure out for themselves.

I opened all the cupboard doors until I found where to put Nonna's mugs and began squeezing them in alongside Stanley's.

'He's only just come out of hospital, remember. Isn't marriage supposed to be one of the most stressful things a person can go through?'

Nonna harrumphed. 'Certainly was for me. But then I married a dicky head.'

I smiled at that. 'Perhaps Stanley feels he's had enough stress for the moment. I'd give him time. Besides, didn't you always say you wanted to live with him first anyway?' I nudged her playfully. 'This way you get your wish.'

'No I don't.' She rolled her eyes. 'We're in separate bedrooms.'

'Well,' I cleared my throat, 'I'm sure there'll be plenty of time for that.'

I didn't like to dwell on what *that* might be.

Nonna looked wistful and put the last piece of biscotti in her mouth.

'Plenty of time?' She tutted. 'I seventy-five. Mind you, we had our first lovers' tiff last night. That good sign. If you row with a man it show you hot for each other.'

'Really?' I perked up.

In that case maybe there was hope for me and Gabe yet; we did nothing *but* row . . .

The sound of Dad's car returning dragged us both back from our reverie.

'I'll go and help him,' I said, hanging the damp tea towel over the kitchen door handle to dry. 'See if I can get a smile out of him.'

Outside Dad was lifting a rusty old exercise bike out of the back of his car.

'God knows what she wants to bring this for,' he grumbled, setting it down.

I perched on the edge of the open boot and waited until I had his attention.

'Dad, what on earth is wrong with you?'

He shoved his hands in his pockets and kicked out at a few loose stones on Stanley's drive.

'I know I shouldn't say this, but when your mother gave up all those committee nights, I felt happier than I'd done for years. It was just her and me. We booked a holiday, we planned some work in the garden and we looked after Arlo together when I wasn't at work in the Easter holidays. I felt I'd got my wife back. I thought she'd enjoyed it too. But now she's as bad as ever. And I know she wants to help this charity, but I honestly think she's exhausted.'

I nodded thoughtfully. 'I agree. Can't you persuade her to take a break, even for a long weekend somewhere?'

He shook his head.

'I've decided. I'm going to insist she gives up this hospice job,' he said defiantly. 'It'll be the death of her.'

I sucked in air. 'She won't thank you for interfering, Dad.'

His brow furrowed and he dived into the car to pull out a box marked 'winter boots'.

'I'm not interfering. I'm looking after her. I'm loving her. Doesn't that count for anything?'

'Of course it does.' I rubbed his arm. 'But sometimes people just have to make their own mistakes. All we can do is be there when they fall. That's how they know we love them.'

Dad appeared to accept that and after I'd kissed Nonna and Stanley goodbye I went for a long walk down to the river where I sat outside the Riverside Hotel at the table furthest from the water's edge, huddled low behind a tall glass. As the sun sank lower in the sky and the moon, full and round, began to cast its silvery shadows on the water, I watched Gabe and Noah playing and laughing together on the deck of *The Neptune*. And I wished with all my heart that I was playing too.

No sooner had I opened up on Monday morning than Doreen called in a flap. Her daughter was in labour six weeks early and she was very sorry but she wouldn't be coming into work. I knew Lia wouldn't be in either: she was taking Arlo to the doctor for his jabs first thing. I called Juliet to see if she could help out but her phone had gone to voicemail.

I was flying solo for breakfast duty.

I didn't mind; I was in a good mood and felt like I could conquer anything. Sunday had been very productive: I'd got a brilliant plan sorted to help Mum out with her designer clothing and I'd had a second chat with both Lucinda Miller and Candy O'Connor.

The rain we'd had the night before had cleared, making everywhere sparkle, and the grass on the village green was steaming in the warmth. This time next week, the school children would be on their May half-term holiday and we'd have a run on milkshakes and cookies. I made a mental note to refill the sweetie jar on the counter. I wondered what Noah would be doing; Gabe wouldn't be able to have time off already. He could perhaps come here for a day or two; we could entertain him between us, like Nonna had done when Lia and I were small. Assuming Gabe and I could be civil to each other for long enough to sort out arrangements, that was.

I was setting up the outside chairs and tables, when Nina flew round the corner and began fumbling with the keys for her flower shop.

'Morning, Nina!' I called. 'You're early.'

'Busy, busy, busy. Big, massive, HUGE bouquet order from Fone-A-Flower. That big boss from Garden Warehouse. Oh balls, I can't get the key in the door, I'm all flustered.'

'Mark Cooper?' I strode over, took the keys from her and opened the door smoothly.

'That's him.' Nina could barely stand still with excitement. 'He's gone for the Couture Collection. Fone-A-Flower wanted Garden Warehouse to do it, but apparently he insisted on us. Eighty pounds! *Eighty!*'

'That was good of him,' I said, meaning it. Presumably he'd have got a staff discount if he'd bought from Garden Warehouse.

She chewed her lip. 'I just hope I've got enough eryngium.'

'Me too,' I said with a smile. 'Whatever that is.'

I walked back into the café, flipped the closed sign to open and turned the hot water on for the coffee machine.

The café landline and my mobile both rang at the same time. I dashed for the landline but I was too slow, the answerphone picked it up. I was just answering my mobile when Stella came into the café carrying some leaflets.

'Juliet, thank goodness,' I said into the phone, giving Stella a wave.

WI jumble sale, Stella mouthed, leaving a pile next to the bookcase.

I gave her a thumbs up and she carried on her way, calling over her shoulder, 'See you later for afternoon tea.'

'Hello, hen, sorry I missed your call,' said Juliet in a whisper. 'What's up?'

'I'm short staffed, any chance you can help?'

Juliet groaned. 'No can do, I'm at a funeral. In Glasgow.'

'Oh my condolences, I didn't know.'

'My mum's old next-door neighbour. Only found out about it yesterday. Thank heavens for cheap flights.'

Just then Mark Cooper's car swooped into a space outside and both he and Gabe got out. Mark jogged into the florist and Gabe headed directly for the café.

'Hope it goes well. Got to go,' I hissed down the phone. 'Customer.'

I smoothed down my hair and took a few deep breaths.

Do not argue with him, repeat, do not argue . . .

'My first customer of the day,' I said as he approached the counter. 'What can I get you?'

'Rosie,' said Gabe in a serious voice, 'have you got a minute?'

'Yes.' I spread my arms, indicating the empty café. 'I'm all yours. Is anything the matter?'

No sooner had I said that than two separate groups of people trooped in: a party of cheerful women, wearing walking boots, sunhats and matching 'LISA IS 50 TODAY!' T-shirts and an assorted group of all ages each with a dog, or in some cases two. For the next ten minutes I ran backwards and forwards with pots of tea, frothy lattes and dog bowls. I mashed avocado, grilled bacon and toasted bread, refusing all offers of help from Gabe who sat fidgeting at the counter, watching me get warmer and warmer.

Eventually all I had left to do was grill a portobello mushroom and gruyère panini. I laid the filling on the bread, sandwiched it together and put it in the sandwich press.

'Right,' I turned back to Gabe. 'You wanted me?'

'Rosie,' Gabe spread his hands on the counter, 'all I wanted to say was that—'

'I don't suppose you've got any wholegrain mustard?' said a man with bushy eyebrows and a droopy moustache. He had a grey Miniature Schnauzer under his arm and they looked uncannily like brothers.

'We do.' I retrieved it from the cupboard and passed it to him.

'Sorry, Gabe, you were saying?'

He swept a hand through his hair.

'This is probably not the time or place,' he murmured.

'When is it ever?' I said wryly.

I hope I sounded cool; my body was about as cool as a basking hyena on the Serengeti plains. My pulse rate was in competition with the coffee machine for high-pressure whooshing and I had a sneaking suspicion that my face was glowing like a radioactive tomato.

'I don't know why I keep saying and doing the wrong thing,' he began. 'I don't know why I keep messing it up. It should be so easy, to tell you that . . .' He cleared his throat portentously. 'What I'm trying to say is that no matter how hard I try to impress you and get your attention, it always seems to backfire. But the truth is that you are the best thing that has happened to me – to me and Noah – in a long, long time.'

'Am I?' I said innocently. 'Have I *happened* to you?'

He nodded. 'I think you have. We're both suffering from Rosie withdrawal symptoms.'

'Oh.'

I quite liked that idea. We both grinned.

'And there's more,' he began.

The landline rang again and I realized that the previous caller hadn't left a message.

'I hate to interrupt you,' I said, still beaming, 'but I should get this.'

I dragged my eyes away from him to pick up the phone just as Mark came in, staggering under the weight of Nina's bouquet.

He slapped Gabe on the back in a manly fashion. 'Have you told her yet?'

'Not yet,' said Gabe hurriedly. 'Hold on, Mark . . . wait, I was just . . . working up to it.'

My eyes narrowed. 'Told me what?'

'You should get the phone,' said Gabe.

Mark set the flowers down gently on a table. 'About the pizza oven.'

'No, he hasn't,' I said coolly, staring at Gabe. He looked away, his jaw clenched.

I darted for the phone before I missed another call. 'The Lemon Tree Café; can I help you?'

'Hello, this is Helena from The Chestnuts Cancer Hospice, who am I speaking to?'

My heart began to pound.

'Rosie, Rosie Featherstone, Luisa's daughter.'

'Oh good. Well, *not* good, I'm afraid your Mum's collapsed; nothing to worry about. Well, not much.'

'WHAT?' I gasped.

Chapter 39

I blew out a sharp breath, willing myself not to panic as Helena told me how Mum had looked pale as soon as she'd arrived but denied feeling poorly only to pass out minutes later, catching her head on the corner of a desk as she fell.

'She's come round again now, but she's very woozy,' said Helena. 'I don't think she needs to go to hospital, but she does need to go home. I tried your father's number but it went to voicemail. Can you fetch her?'

'On my way.'

I put the phone down and glanced down at my shaking hands.

'Rosie?' Gabe took hold of my arms, very gently, I noticed. 'Rosie, what is it?'

'I need to get to The Chestnuts Cancer Hospice,' I said, frowning, 'right away. It's my mum. Dad said she was doing too much; I should have listened.'

I looked around me frantically. For my keys and my phone and oh . . . the panini.

I ran to the sandwich press, burned my finger and swore as I slid the panini on to a plate. I hadn't got a clue who'd ordered it; my mind had gone blank.

'One panini?' I yelled indiscriminately.

One of the fiftieth-birthday lot came to fetch it.

'My car,' I said, my heart sinking. 'It isn't here.'

I'd have to run all the way home and collect it. I regretted not driving here now, but there was such limited parking and I liked to leave space for customers.

'We'll drive you to collect her,' said Mark, picking up his flowers.

'But I can't just leave the café with customers in it.' I swallowed. 'I'm on my own this morning.'

'You're the only member of staff?' Mark's eyes widened as they roamed the café.

I could almost hear his thoughts: *This would never happen at Garden Warehouse.*

'Look, Lia's at the doctor's with the baby,' I said irritably. 'Juliet is at a funeral and Doreen's in the labour suite.'

'Doreen?' Gabe's eyes popped open wide.

'We're just people,' I said, feeling myself getting tearful. 'It's a family business about people, not just about profit and footfall and square metres, and sometimes life comes before work.'

'Bloody unlucky people, by the sound of it.' Mark put his flowers back down and rolled his sleeves up. 'Luckily for you I used to be a barista. Gabe can drive you, I'll stay here.'

'You'll stay at the café?' I eyed him beadily. He was still the competition after all. 'Alone?'

He cast an eye over the serving area. 'Nothing here I can't handle.'

'Are you sure you won't redirect all our customers to the Cabin Café?' I tilted my chin.

Mark laughed and looked at Gabe for support. 'You were right; she is a tough one.'

'Rosie, he won't do that,' Gabe said, holding my gaze.

I looked away and frowned at Mark. 'Haven't you got an empire to build or something?'

Gabe raised an eyebrow and I flushed.

The door opened and two women with expensive pushchairs headed over to the toy corner.

'The words "gift horse" and "mouth" come to mind,' Gabe said sternly.

'Actually, it's my wedding anniversary,' said Mark with a twinkle in his eye. 'I'm supposed to be having the day off; Gabe here is having the afternoon off. Because sometimes life comes before work.'

'Oh. Happy anniversary,' I said meekly.

'Mark and I just had one quick job to do; well, two if you count visiting you, and then he was going home,' Gabe explained and then winced. 'Are you sure you trust me with your car?'

Mark reached into his pocket for the keys. 'Yes, but no opening doors into oncoming traffic. OK?'

'Very funny,' said Gabe sheepishly.

I allowed myself to study Gabe while Mark explained which key did what.

He was in a suit again, not that he wasn't equally gorgeous in his scruffy shorts and ripped T-shirt, but there was something about him looking so smart that gave me a frisson of excitement. And also made me want to undress him immediately.

I looked away quickly before anyone noticed my face heating up.

Mark stepped closer to him and the two of them began a mumbled conversation sneaking completely indiscreet glances in my direction.

Gabe turned and caught my eye, mouthing that he'd just be a minute. I smiled back and walked slowly to the door, waving to the mums, one of whom was still unpacking bags of baby paraphernalia, the other had hoiked up her T-shirt and had a baby attached to her boob.

From my position in the doorway, I watched Gabe pass an envelope to Mark who clapped him on the back and laughed.

Gabe had always seemed happy in his own skin, content with his life choices, but now he exuded something else, an aura of contentment so complete that it was impossible not to feel joy for him. I eyed him again casually and counted the reasons for putting all this nonsense behind us and stopping fighting.

Firstly, God knows he'd been through a crappy enough time over the past few years, he deserved every scrap of happiness.

Secondly, what would I have thought of him if he had said, 'Oh OK then, I won't take this job if you don't want me to'? Not a lot, probably. I much preferred people who stood up for themselves.

Also, thirdly . . . I swallowed a big knot of guilt. If I could forgive Candy-formerly-known-as-Callum for what she had done, surely I could get over Gabe's working for Garden Warehouse, pizza oven or no pizza oven? And wouldn't it be worth it, to call a truce? It was all right Nonna saying that arguing with a man was a sign of passion, but presumably arguing all the time wasn't?

But right now, Mum was my main concern and time was ticking on.

'Gabe, can we please leave?'

Mark and Gabe exchanged looks.

'Yes, boss,' said Gabe, pretending to tug his forelock.

Five minutes later we were cocooned in Mark's big posh car and I was sliding about on the leather seats while texting Dad and Lia to let them know about Mum and asking Lia to come in to work as soon as possible to get the pizza oven on.

'Mum doesn't listen,' I said to Gabe, torn between being cross and worried. 'She thinks she's invincible, won't accept help from anyone. She has to take charge, be in control, and she can't see that life would be so much smoother if she let others in.'

'Hmm,' said Gabe non-committally. 'I know someone like that.'

'I'm talking about the right sort of help.' I sniffed, folding my arms tighter. Then I remembered my promise not to fall out with him today. 'I'm accepting help now, aren't I?'

It dawned on me that this was the third time since he'd arrived in Barnaby that Gabe had had to drive me somewhere for some drama or other: first when he drove me home sobbing and soaking after I found out about Nonna's secret past, then when Stanley was in hospital and now to fetch Mum. He always seemed to be around when I needed him and I really ought to show a bit more gratitude.

'And I'm very grateful,' I added quickly.

'Reluctantly grateful,' he said with a smirk. 'But it's a start. About what Mark said, about the pizza oven—'

Gabe's phone began to ring and I answered it for him.

It was Mark telling us to turn the radio on, which we did.

'. . . And now over to the London news room for our national headlines.

'Troubled retailer Home Stores has been thrown a lifeline this weekend by the outdoor discount chain Garden Warehouse. An offer has been made not only to keep all the existing branches open, but also to retain the majority of staff, thus protecting over three hundred jobs in the Midlands.

'A spokesperson for the buyers, Gabriel Green, Head of Legal Services, says he's looking forward to implementing changes that will see the retailer nudge out of the red and into profit within the next twelve months. Our reporter spoke to Mr Green earlier from our Midlands studio:

'"We recognize that the strength of any business is in its people. Behind every member of staff is a story: a family, maybe children and mortgages and responsibilities. We respect that and will do whatever we can to ensure both Home Stores employees and customers benefit from the company being incorporated into the Garden Warehouse family. Of course we'll be looking at the bottom line, at ways we can improve the business, but not at the expense of our people."'

The more I heard, the hotter my face became. Gabe had basically just repeated what I'd said in the café a few minutes ago. I couldn't believe that our two businesses had the same philosophy, it was heart-warming, not to mention mortifying.

Gabe snapped the radio off with a groan. 'I sounded like an idiot.'

'You are KIDDING!' I stared at him disbelievingly. 'You were amazing, Gabe! Seriously. I'm so proud of you. And what you said about families was lovely, really lovely.'

And embarrassingly similar to what I'd just said to Mark in a far more accusatory tone.

'Thank you.' He stared ahead as the car's satnav informed him to turn left at the next junction.

'Perhaps I was a bit quick to judge Garden Warehouse,' I admitted. 'Everyone else seems in favour of it. You're enjoying this job, aren't you?'

He wrinkled his nose. 'I am. It's just hard, you know, with Noah. I thought it would be easier now he's a bit older, but,' he shrugged, 'he's only been in school five minutes and already they've got a week off next week. Luckily Verity has offered to have him, but it's not going to be easy.'

'I'll help whenever I can,' I said. 'Now I'm officially approved.'

'Thanks.' His face broke into a smile and then dropped again. 'The thing is Mark really wants me to go to head office.'

'When?' I reached for my phone. 'Because I can look after Noah, I'll put it in my calendar now.'

'Well, it might be more of a . . .' He coughed and looked uncomfortable. 'Regular thing.'

'I don't mind,' I said cheerfully. 'Did I tell you Lia and I used to spend every afternoon in the café as kids? Noah could do the same. Oh hold on.'

A text came through on my phone. I opened it quickly, hoping it would be from Lia. But it was Gina:

Feeding ducks with the kids and came across this!!! Where's he going?

I stared at the message, wondering what on earth she meant, when a second text came through from her. This one was just a photograph of a woman in overalls next to a houseboat by the river. I zoomed in on it to see that the woman was nailing a FOR SALE sign to Gabe's boat.

My heart plummeted.

Was that what he wanted to tell me? That he was selling up and leaving Barnaby?

I looked across at his handsome profile, the tip of his tongue protruding as he checked both ways at a junction. I didn't want him to leave. But what did he have to stay for? I'd done nothing but argue with him and shout at him since he arrived. And he'd just said how much he loved his job.

I wish I could strip everything away – our jobs, our differences, our pasts – and just *be*. Just be together. The three of us. But life wasn't like that, was it? It was messy and complicated and we were all to a greater or lesser extent a product of everything that has gone before.

Yes, Callum had made me reluctant to let anyone close to me, but I'd faced that now and whilst I'd never forget what happened, I could forgive, move on. I could go through the open door, just like Nonna, and love again.

We turned into a leafy lane and I stared at him, watching the dappled shade flicker across his face.

'So you're enjoying it, this new job, you've found your place in the world?' I said softly.

He nodded. 'Mark's a good boss. He listens to my ideas – that means a lot to me, especially after being out of the

410

corporate loop for so long. It's reassuring to know that someone appreciates me.'

We pulled up at traffic lights. Gabe's hand was on the gear stick. I took a deep breath and gently laid my hand over his.

'I appreciate you too.' I looked at him from under my lashes. 'And I know we have our ups and downs, but we're friends, aren't we?'

He looked at me briefly just as the lights changed to green. He thrust the gear stick forward to change gear and my hand fell away. 'I thought that wasn't allowed any more?'

'That was a mistake,' I said, looking out of the window to hide my embarrassment. 'Heat of the moment. You know what I'm like.'

'Do I?'

'Well, I . . .' The words died on my tongue.

My heart throbbed as adrenalin flooded through me. I stared at his lovely face, not caring if he was aware, imprinting his smile, the curve of his cheek, the way his hair stuck up at the crown just like his son's.

But there was so much more to Gabe than a handsome face. He was worldly-wise and hard-working and ambitious with strong family values. He'd loved and lost, but was still prepared to love again. He was quite simply, I realized, a good man. That was what made him attractive to me. Instinctively I felt that my heart would be safe in his hands. Or would have been. Because stupidly, I'd done exactly what Nonna had warned me not to do: I'd left it too late.

We drove past The Chestnuts Cancer Hospice charity shop, the last in a row of similarly despondent-looking façades, and then a sign for the hospice appeared on our left.

Gabe touched his top lip with the tip of his tongue and flicked the indicator on.

'Rosie, when I said Mark wants me to go to head office, I meant permanently. To take a seat on the board.'

411

Hence selling the boat.

'Oh right. Congratulations.'

I couldn't think what else to say. I certainly wasn't about to stand in his way, but the thought of him and Noah leaving Barnaby made my toes curl in my shoes.

We pulled into the car park of the hospice; Gabe scouted round for a space, not looking at me.

A woman in her fifties with shoulder-length blonde hair and big glasses appeared on the steps and waved at us with both arms.

'I think that must be Helena.'

The Chestnuts Cancer Hospice was a large square building made of chunky red stone; it must have been a lovely smart residence at one time. It was still rather lovely now. It stood set back a little from a busy road and had a decent-sized car park at the front. I spotted Mum's car in the end space, squeezed between a minibus and a row of prickly bushes.

'Rosie?' The woman marched towards us, hand outstretched. 'She's a good bleeder your mum. Only a tiny nick to the back of the head, but she's made quite a mess of the carpet.'

'Sorry about that,' I said, shaking her hand. 'This is Gabe.'

He nodded at her. She cast an eye over him approvingly.

'Do you run marathons? Triathlons?'

He shook his head. ''Fraid not.'

'Pity,' she said, marching back towards the building, her tweed skirt swishing against her thighs. 'We're always looking for fit volunteers to raise money. Come on through.'

Helena skimmed us through a wood-panelled reception so rapidly that I barely had time to smile at a girl in a headscarf with carefully drawn-on eyebrows behind a desk and take in the smell of beeswax and old wood and the delicate scent of a bunch of freesias on a table in the corner.

She turned abruptly through a doorway and Gabe nearly ran into the back of me as I changed direction to follow her.

Mum was slumped on a chair at one of two desks in the

412

dim office with a bloody cloth pressed to the side of her head, a glass of water on the desk beside her and a bucket at her feet.

'Darling!' She sat up straight too quickly and then grimaced, blinking her eyes. 'There was no need for you to come, I'll be fine after a sit-down, I'm just overtired, that's all,' she said. And promptly threw up in the bucket.

Helena's nostrils flared. She stomped to the window and opened it wide. I handed Mum the glass of water and stroked her hair and Gabe stepped forward with a handkerchief.

'Mum, this has got to stop,' I said. 'You need to listen to your body even if you won't listen to anyone else.'

She nodded weakly and grasped my hand. 'I know. And I've decided to put this job on hold for a little while, just until I get my strength back. I'm sorry.'

'Oh,' said Helena, pouting, pointing to a small storeroom leading off the office. 'But I thought you were going to organize an event for me?'

'Well,' said Mum with a sigh, 'I suppose I could just do that one job.'

'No,' said a voice firmly. 'You'll do no such thing. Luisa, I'm here now, to pick you up.'

We all turned to see Dad standing in the doorway. He swept across the room, giving me the tiniest wink and then with an extravagant manoeuvre, he took Mum in his arms, tipped her back and kissed her passionately.

If that isn't a sign of true love, I thought, pushing the sick bucket out of the way of Dad's feet, then nothing is.

'Oh,' Mum squeaked.

'I'm taking you away from all this, right now,' he declared. 'I love you, Luisa, you're selfless and kind and always the first to help others. But enough is enough. Now it's time for me to take care of you.'

We stood back as he picked Mum up and staggered towards the door.

'Oh, Alec,' Mum said breathily. 'That was so masterful.'

'Actually, darling,' he said with a wince, 'my back . . . Do you mind if I put you down?'

Gabe and I grinned at each other and I turned to Helena who'd walked to the far side of the office and was staring into the storeroom in dismay.

'Oh bugger,' she said. 'Luisa promised to help me with the designer stuff.'

The perimeter of the room was bulging with rails of clothes.

'If you don't mind hanging on for a couple of weeks,' I said, tapping her on her shoulder, 'I think I can help you out with this lot.'

Gabe reached in, tugged at the sleeve of a charcoal suit jacket and whistled. 'Paul Smith!'

Helena regarded me over the top of her big glasses. 'Are you volunteering?' She swished across to her desk and picked up a clipboard. 'Rosie, isn't it?'

I had the feeling I needed to be firm with Helena.

'Yes, but I'm only volunteering to help once,' I said, holding my nerve, 'on social media, but I need to confirm a model first.'

'Well,' she sighed, 'beggars can't be choosers. All help gratefully received, thank you.'

Helena's eyes flicked over to Gabe who was shrugging his arms into the rather smart jacket. 'You can try on the trousers if you like. I'll shut the door.'

He looked at me. 'Do you mind? It'll only take a minute.'

I shook my head. 'I'll just call the café to check up on Mark.'

The phone at the café rang and rang and eventually switched to voicemail, which I tried to see as a good sign that we were busy and not a bad sign that Mark had got fed up with waiting for us and had disappeared with the takings, which was hardly likely seeing as in my haste I'd forgotten to charge this morning's customers and there was a grand total of £4.49 in the till.

'What do you think?' Gabe asked, self-consciously turning full circle.

'Made to measure,' Helena purred.

'Lovely,' I said with a dry mouth, thinking that I'd quite like to see him without the suit on too.

'Fifty pounds to you,' said Helena.

Gabe pulled a face. 'Will you take an IOU? I don't have cash on me.'

'I'm afraid not,' she said with a sniff. 'I don't have time to chase creditors.'

'I'll buy it for you, I'd like to,' I said, swallowing the lump in my throat. 'As a leaving present.'

Gabe's eyes met mine and he nodded and somehow I managed to smile back.

'Thank you,' he said simply and stepped backwards into the cupboard, reappearing thirty seconds later with the suit over his arm.

I handed over the cash to Helena and promised to be in touch soon.

'Let's get you back to your café, then,' said Gabe. 'And then Mark and I can finish our meeting and leave you in peace.'

'Great,' I said, trying to summon up enthusiasm.

Chapter 40

'Oh my giddy AUNT!' came an unmistakable squeal from inside the café.

'Lia's back,' I said to Gabe as we approached the door.

'And it looks like Mark hasn't sent all your customers to the Cabin Café,' he replied, arching an eyebrow at the busy scene before us.

The café was humming with customers, some of whom were braving a brisk breeze under the awning and the sound of laughter and clattering crockery spilled out through the open door.

'He may have tried,' I said sweetly. 'But our customers know what's good for them.'

Gabe laughed and very gently rested his fingers against my back as we walked in together. The sensation was tantalizing and I slowed down, just so he would bump into me and for one second our bodies would be touching. I turned quickly, catching the scent of him before he murmured an apology and I walked on.

'Quick,' Mark said to Lia when he spotted us, 'look miserable, your sister's here.'

He wasn't looking quite as dapper as when he'd arrived. His forehead was shiny with perspiration, his curly grey hair had an awful lot of flour in it and he had a big blob of tomato sauce on the seat of his trousers. The serving area looked like there'd been a food fight and both he and Lia were giggling and dancing about to the radio, which was on much louder than normal (no wonder they didn't hear the phone) and they both seemed to be enjoying themselves.

'Ooh yes.' She swept the hair from her pink face with her forearm and pulled the corners of her mouth down. 'Mark and I have had a terrible time. How's Mum?'

'She'll be fine.' I reached for my apron from a peg behind the kitchen door, slightly annoyed at being cast in the role of killjoy. 'She was whisked away by a tall dark handsome hero and they rode off into the sunset together. And Arlo's jabs?'

'Screamed the place down,' said Lia, peering into the oven to check on a pizza. 'And that was just me.'

'Poor thing,' I said with a smile.

She stood up and rubbed her tired eyes. 'He was OK. It's his teeth that are bothering him, his cheeks – both sets – are as red as . . . Mark's . . . and he's got terrible nappy rash. But hey, sleep's for wimps anyway.'

'Try crushed ice, Lia,' said Gabe, 'wrapped in a clean cloth, to suck on, not to put on his cheeks. Noah liked that.'

I felt a rush of affection and had to stop myself flinging my arms round him; there was nothing this man couldn't handle.

'I will, thanks,' said Lia, raising her eyebrows thoughtfully.

'That's what I could do with.' Mark pressed the cold can of squirty cream to his face and sighed. 'And for the record, only one set of my cheeks are red.'

'Wrong.' Lia snorted and elbowed him in the ribs. 'Have you seen your trousers?'

Mark, much to her amusement, tried to see behind his own back and groaned.

Gabe cleared his throat. 'Mark, have you mentioned . . . ?'

'No.' Mark's face grew serious and he looked at Lia and then me. 'When that next pizza is done, can we all have a chat? All four of us?'

I opened my mouth to say that we couldn't all leave the counter (in true killjoy manner) but as luck would have it Doreen arrived, a little tearful, and after telling us that baby Bethany and her mum were doing well she bustled straight into action and shooed us all out of her way.

Five minutes later Lia and I were sipping cappuccinos in the conservatory and listening intently while Gabe and Mark outlined their pizza plan. To say I had got the wrong end of the stick was an understatement. Their proposal was for the Lemon Tree Café to completely take over the running of the Cabin Café.

'So we'd have *two* cafés?' Lia's jaw dropped and she stared at me with a big goofy grin.

'Correct,' said Gabe. 'We've suggested a one-year lease to begin with, with us putting up some of the initial investment for the kitchen.'

'Is this the pizza oven I keep hearing about?' I asked.

He nodded. 'I only received the figures last night; I wanted to have the full details before we discussed it. With both of you. What do you think?'

I hadn't expected this in a million years; Lia and I were still getting to grips with running one café let alone two, but it was a fantastic opportunity.

'I'm . . . well . . . speechless,' I stuttered.

'God, that's a first,' Lia said with a smirk.

Gabe scratched his chin and I got the distinct impression he was trying not to laugh.

'All our other branches are urban,' Mark explained, stirring his coffee. 'Our menu, our set-up, our ethos is geared towards that. We got it wrong here, and I hold my hands up, it was probably my fault. My wife said can't we have a Garden Warehouse somewhere nice for once and with Fearnley's coming on the market, I just snapped it up without enough research. Don't get me wrong, the rest of the business is doing well. It's just the café. We're no competition for this place.'

'Well, the Lemon Tree Café is a destination café,' I said, parroting Jamie. 'People make a special trip for our food.'

'We agree,' said Gabe, 'which is why we thought that putting a second pizza oven in at Garden Warehouse would be such a winning idea. It would double your capacity, plus you could employ staff who want to work longer hours on the evenings that our store is open until nine at night.'

'It would give you more flexibility too,' Mark offered. 'For when life gets in the way of work and you find yourself short staffed.'

'That might be useful,' I conceded.

'Takeaways!' said Lia. 'We could offer takeaways from the Cabin Café – there's much better parking there. Did I show you the boxes I'd found, Mark?'

The two of them began discussing printed over plain cartons and I found myself gazing at Gabe.

'So this was always your plan?' I murmured. 'It was never to try to muscle in on our business.'

Gabe smiled ruefully and shook his head. 'I thought you knew me better than that.'

'I'm sorry,' I whispered, feeling wretched.

Lia reached for my hand under the table and squeezed it. 'I'm so excited.'

'It's all in here,' said Mark, laying a thick white envelope on the table. 'Our proposal, well, Gabe's proposal. All his idea. We'll leave you to mull it over. Now if you don't mind I'd better get back to celebrating my anniversary while I still have a marriage to celebrate.'

We all stood up and shook hands and I thanked Mark again for coming to our rescue in the café this morning and for the proposal. He collected his flowers from Nonna's watering can out in the courtyard and said that if Gabe wouldn't mind giving him a lift to the train station, he could keep the car for the weekend.

I grabbed Gabe's sleeve as he made to leave.

'Can we talk? Later before you pick up Noah?'

He nodded just as his phone rang. I caught a glimpse of the screen before he answered it: the call was from Haywood Boat Sales.

'Excuse me, Mark, I need to take this.' He strode outside, walking up and down the pavement, talking and listening.

Mark followed my gaze. 'That lad is the best appointment I've ever made. In the space of one week, he's improved my life immeasurably. I just hope he makes the right decision about joining the board.'

Gabe came back holding his phone and looking surprised.

'Good news?' I said, the effort of keeping my voice light almost killing me.

He blinked up at me and smiled in amazement. 'I think so, yes.'

Mark clapped him on his shoulder. 'Great stuff, looks like everything's falling into place.'

The two of them walked out to Mark's car and as Gabe turned and raised a hand in a goodbye wave, I had the terrible, terrible feeling that for me everything might actually be falling apart.

By lunchtime, Doreen and Lia were fed up with me. I couldn't concentrate on anything, I either completely forgot orders or muddled them up, I'd lost my ability to give anyone the correct change and I floated about in a trance, seemingly oblivious to anyone else. Finally, Doreen pointed me in the direction of the village green and told me to get some fresh air.

As I wandered aimlessly across the grass, Gabe's words kept coming back to me: *I thought you knew me better than that.*

I thought I knew him too but I'd made so many assumptions and jumped to so many conclusions that I just wasn't sure any more. I needed advice and there was one person who knew Gabe better than anyone else.

I sat down on a wooden bench and dialled her number.

'Verity, I need your help,' I said with some urgency when she picked up the phone.

I heard her laugh and the squeak of a chair before she answered.

'OK, I'm sitting comfortably, is it about the coffee machine again because you know it's probably time you invested in—'

I took a deep breath and butted in. 'I've fallen in love.'

'Oh,' Verity whispered with a sigh. 'I'm so pleased for you.'

'With Gabe.'

Neither of us spoke. The seconds ticked by until I couldn't bear it any longer.

'Verity, is this really terrible news for you?'

At first I couldn't make out what she was saying, there seemed to be an awful lot of high-pitched noises and not a lot of words. But eventually I picked out 'no' and 'happy' and after she'd blown her nose and cleared her throat, she managed a whole sentence.

'I know I shouldn't cry, but this is a big thing, you know, after Mimi, and Rosie, this is brilliant news, the best, I couldn't have planned it better myself. Of course, I did hope this might happen once he'd moved down to Barnaby. And . . . oh.' She sighed again. 'I can't think of a better person to be in Gabe and Noah's lives.'

I exhaled with relief. 'I wasn't sure how you'd take it. I know I've got a bit of a reputation for loving and leaving boyfriends, although perhaps *liking* would be more accurate, but with Gabe it's different.'

'Well, of course it is,' she said with a shaky laugh. 'You, my lovely friend, have been waiting for the right man, that's all.'

'You really think so?'

'YES! Oh, I can't BELIEVE it!' she finished with a shriek.

'Unfortunately, I don't think he feels the same way.'

'Rosie, he talks about you all the time,' she assured me.

'He's besotted. I was going to say something before but it sounded as though he had it all under control and so I decided to stay out of it, let him do his thing. Especially as I'm friends with both of you.'

'He talks about me?' I said, perking up briefly and instantly curious to know what he'd said. Then I remembered the phone call from the boatyard and groaned. 'The problem is we don't always . . . ahem . . . see eye to eye.'

'As in you argue a lot?' I could hear the smile in her voice.

'An awful lot.'

She laughed. 'Knowing both of you as I do, I can only think that's a good sign. Rosie, he's a man with baggage, he needs a strong woman in his life who can pick that up and run with it, and vice versa. You'd get bored of a man who didn't know his own mind.'

'That is very true,' I said ruefully. 'I wish we'd had this conversation ages ago, because now I think I might have left it too late.'

'Why?'

'I found out today that his boss wants him to relocate to head office, which is up north somewhere miles away, and on top of that I think Gabe has sold *The Neptune*. He's planning on moving away, Verity. So he can't feel the same way as I do. Noah will have to move schools again and—'

'Rosie, you can't let this happen,' said Verity all in a rush. 'Noah has only just got settled in Barnaby. You have to take matters into your own hands.'

'But if I do, how will I know what he really wants?'

'This is a man who's been on his own for three years. Before that he'd been with Mimi since he was sixteen. His dating technique is non-existent. In fact, I think the way he got Mimi's attention was to throw frogspawn in her hair.'

'Urgh.'

'Precisely.'

'I'm beginning to see why we're having problems

communicating. The last boyfriend who I allowed to fall in love with me was Callum and that didn't end well . . .'

'Hmm. I always thought there was something you weren't telling me about him.'

My heart thumped. 'And yet you never pried.'

'Everyone has secrets, Rosie,' she said darkly.

'Oh?'

'Callum,' she said swiftly, 'tell me about him.'

So I gave her a condensed version. And when I got to the bit about that last night in London she called him an absolute git. But as the rest of the tale unfurled, her gasps grew longer and longer until I worried she was going to run out of oxygen.

'So now he's a she?'

'Yes.'

'Bloody hell. I feel like a terrible friend for not knowing this thing about you.'

'I hid it underneath a lot of meaningless flings,' I said briskly. 'Now tell me what to do about Gabe.'

She blew out a long breath. 'Well, either you wait for him to find some frogspawn to fling at you or you give him a clue about how you feel.'

I bit my lip. 'Aren't . . . well, if we're going to do this properly, shouldn't I wait for him to come for me?'

I thought about Dad's heroic rescue of Mum and how nice it would be to be swept off my feet like that.

Verity snorted. 'You could. But put it this way: if I'd waited for Tom to do that to me, I'd still be single.'

'OK, OK, so what *do* I do?'

'Just show him what he'd be missing if he leaves.'

'What, like take him on a tour of the village?'

'Idiot.' She tutted. 'Let him see what's in your heart.'

'Right.' I nodded, pushing down a tremor of fear. It was now or never. 'I'll do that.'

I stood up with the intention of going back inside the café just as Gabe, driving Mark's car, pulled to a halt outside Ken's Mini Mart.

'Let me know how you get on.'

'You won't have long to wait,' I said in a wobbly voice. 'He's just arrived. Wish me luck.'

I ended the call and dropped the phone in my apron pocket.

Don't overthink it; just tell the truth, I told myself as I strode purposefully across the green towards him.

If this had been a film, Gabe would have seen me and run towards me, arms outstretched, and I'd have run to meet him and he'd have swung me round without secretly thinking I was heavier than I looked. Unfortunately, it wasn't a film and Gabe went into Ken's shop instead. I immediately changed direction, feeling a bit silly, and headed towards a patch of bluebells, stooping to pick a few as if that had been my plan all along. They were past their best and smelled slightly of wee. I'd picked half a dozen of the least dead ones when Gabe reappeared with a bottle of what looked like champagne. He opened the door of Mark's car and stowed the bottle inside.

My stomach quivered nervously; I'd heard of smashing a bottle against the hull of a boat to launch it, perhaps you did the same when you said goodbye too? I stood up, possibly too quickly, and felt dizzy and unsure. I didn't want to think about goodbyes. Not until I'd done my best to persuade him to stay.

He took off his jacket, opened a door at the back and hung it up. Now it looked like he might be driving away. This wasn't going well at all.

I began to scurry towards him, hoping he'd spot me, but despite waving both my arms in the air and yelling his name he didn't seem to notice me.

Instead, he bent down until his back was flat and, bracing himself on his thighs, he began to creep slowly around the car until he reached the other side and disappeared from sight almost as if . . . Could he be hiding from me? How embarrassing.

I slowed down, pondering my next move, when out of the corner of my eye two small people came shuffling round the corner from the direction of the school.

Why was everyone suddenly skulking about? I wondered. But as they got a bit closer, I realized it was Nonna and Stanley, arm in arm, going for a walk at a pace that would have put a tortoise to shame. Stanley was wrapped up in a winter coat, hat and scarf, despite the warm day, and leaning on a walking stick. They seemed to be heading to the far side of the green.

I waved at them but Nonna was too busy chattering to notice and Stanley was concentrating on the path in front of him.

'Churchill, come back here!' I heard Biddy's voice just as Churchill launched his nose into my groin.

'Hey, you,' I said, stepping back. 'Off.'

'Sorry,' Biddy said, flustered, clipping on his lead and trying to pull his sturdy body away from me. 'There must be a bitch on heat somewhere, he's been howling all afternoon. I've brought him out for a piddle and a sniff.'

How simple to be a dog. I bent down and scratched between his ears. 'Good luck, Churchill, I hope you get your girl.'

'I don't,' she said mournfully. 'It's virtually impossible to get him to listen once he's got his eye on the target. Even frankfurters don't work.'

Outside Ken's Mini Mart, Gabe stood up from his hiding place. I wondered if I'd have the same trouble getting him to listen to me. My heart lurched; even if he did listen I'd kept my heart in check for so long now I wasn't sure if I'd find the right words.

'Mind you, there's no one around,' Biddy was saying, 'so I might risk it and let him have a run. Come on, boy.'

They ambled off together with Churchill snuffling at the pockets in Biddy's crocheted tunic for treats.

I felt Gabe's presence beside me before I heard him.

'You look like Queen Boudicca standing there, hands on hips, hair blowing off your face in the breeze,' he said. 'Ready to do battle.'

I turned to face him, all my emotions bubbling just below the surface; there was so much I wanted to say and yet . . . I felt all panicky suddenly and worried that I was going to mess this up, that I'd lose him, or, worse still, start another argument.

'I feel like I've been battling for ages,' I said softly, my breath coming in short bursts, 'against one thing or another. Against men, against any perceived injustice, against Garden Warehouse, and . . .' I swallowed hard. 'Against you.'

He regarded me inquisitively, a soft smile playing at his lips. 'I had noticed.'

I stepped closer. 'Don't go.'

He shook his head. 'I'm not, I've got the afternoon off.'

'I mean ever.'

He looked at me confused. 'Rosie, are you OK?'

'Have you sold the boat?' I blurted out.

He looked startled. 'How did you know that?'

'So it's true.' My heart sank. My eyes felt hot and I blinked the tears back. 'I thought you loved it here.'

He nodded. 'I do, but it's time to leave *The Neptune*. I bought it because I wanted to strip my life right back to the basics and live in the moment, bring up my baby boy, not thinking about the future, the mortgage, the bills, just get through each day. It's been a home for us for three years, but time has moved on. *I've* moved on.'

Something whipped at my legs and when I looked down, a pretty cocker spaniel, tail swishing madly, had run past, and a lady in a smart Barbour jacket, a paisley scarf tied at her neck, was in hot pursuit, trying to hook the end of the dog's lead with her golf umbrella.

'Ginger! Ginger! Come back to Mummy!'

'Gabe, think about Noah, he's just got settled here, he's made friends, started school.'

'I am thinking about Noah and I have needs too.'

'Oh Churchill!' cried Biddy in despair.

Unsurprisingly Churchill had made a beeline for Ginger's rear end; Biddy was lobbing treats at him in an attempt to stop him trying to mount her. Ginger's owner was going for a more hands-on approach, prodding him with a golf umbrella and tugging at her own dog's lead. Churchill wasn't paying the humans a blind bit of notice and Ginger seemed to be enjoying all the attention.

'Come along, come along.' The dulcet tones of Stella Derry rang out as she herded the Women's Institute committee from the church hall towards the café where afternoon tea for eight was being set up in the conservatory.

'Watch the car with your handbags,' murmured Gabe anxiously as the committee ladies squeezed between Ken's shop and Mark's car, still in their tight pack.

'What were you doing earlier?' I asked, nodding towards the car. 'What was that crouching lap of honour all about?'

He laughed softly, still keeping an eye on the progress of the women.

'Checking it for existing damage. I wanted to know if it already had any scratches on the paintwork before I let Noah near it.'

'And has it?'

'Sadly not. Totally pristine. I'm worried to death. I've already told Noah that I'll be docking his pocket money to help pay for the car door he trashed, to give him a sense of the value of money. He can't afford any more accidents.'

'Very sensible.'

Gabe huffed.

'It would have been, but then he reminded me that he doesn't get any pocket money and that all his friends do. So now I'm having to pay him fifty pence a week.' He rolled his eyes. 'Shot myself in the foot there. Outwitted by a four-year-old.'

He grinned goofily and a big wave of affection swept over

me for this man and we both burst out laughing and then the words that came out of my mouth next slipped out so naturally that later I wondered why I had taken so long to say them.

'Oh I do love you,' I said with a catch in my voice.

Gabe's eyes widened.

'You,' he murmured, 'love me?'

I nodded.

Gabe looked so shell-shocked that I felt a bit hot and silly all of a sudden.

'That's . . .' He swallowed hard and blinked. 'That's the best news I've had all . . . well, for years, actually.'

'With all my heart,' I said, emboldened by the light in his eyes. 'And Noah.'

I stepped a tiny bit closer and took hold of his hands.

'But I understand now, your career is important to you and I'm glad and I'm proud of you. Mark clearly thinks the world of you and you should be on the board, because you're brilliant. And why stay here?' I said, forcing a laugh. 'Let's face it, I've been nothing but a pain in the bum ever since you arrived.'

'Oh Ginger,' came a desperate wail.

Churchill had finally got his girl. Even from this distance I could see the victorious grin on his doggy face. Biddy and the other woman began swapping phone numbers.

'Actually, I *am* staying here. I'm going to buy a house.' Gabe's smile threatened to take over his whole face. 'Because I fell in love with a gorgeous girl who's turned my world upside down and keeps me thoroughly on my toes. She's brave and ambitious and never afraid to take risks. And because she's right: Noah doesn't need any more upheaval just yet.'

'Is that me?' I whispered.

'It's you. It's been you since the moment I steered my boat up to the Riverside Hotel.'

My heart fluttered as he stepped closer. I could feel the

heat of his body pressing against mine. He curled his hand around the back of my neck and I tilted my face to his.

'I have been a *bit* afraid to take risks,' I said, my body melting into his. 'With men.'

Gabe nodded, his eyes scanning my face tenderly. 'And now?'

'And now,' I whispered huskily, 'I want to . . .'

I couldn't even wait to finish the sentence, I just closed my eyes and showed him exactly what was in my heart.

Gabe kissed me back hungrily and our bodies pressed as close as they could be, his arms round my waist, my hands in his hair. It was so intense, so exquisite, that I felt a sob building in my throat and a pounding in the pit of my stomach and I knew instinctively that I would give my heart, my soul and my everything to this man willingly for the rest of my life.

Breathless and giggling slightly hysterically we broke away from each other. I opened my eyes and tried not to notice that quite a crowd had gathered on the green. But I didn't care who saw us. There was only one person I was interested in right now and he was here, his soft grey eyes dancing with happiness and his sandy hair standing up in tufts quite possibly because I couldn't stop running my hands through it.

'But what about *The Neptune*?' I said suddenly. 'You've sold it?'

'You mean you don't know who's bought it?' He smiled secretively.

I shook my head.

Gabe mimed zipping his lips. 'He needs to tell his wife first. So the offer is still subject to marital approval. But I'm confident she'll say yes. Anyway, we need more room. Noah's bed is really tiny.'

'And he wants a slide,' I reminded him, pressing a soft kiss to his lips.

'And that too.' He slid his arms lower until his hands

rested casually on my bottom. The way my pulse was racing was anything but casual. My hormones were zipping about like crazy inside me.

'Although *my* bed is big enough.' His eyes flashed wickedly. 'For two.'

'GO STANLEY!' yelled Ken, cupping both hands to his mouth.

Across the green Stanley had lowered himself on to one knee and removed a small blue box from his coat pocket.

'YES!' Nonna yelled. '*Grazie a Dio!* I will marry you, Stanley Pigeon.'

Everyone began to clap and whistle: Stella Derry and the ladies from the WI; Lia and Doreen came out of the café and waved tea towels in Nonna's honour; Lucas and Tyson appeared from the gift shop, arm in arm, Tyson passing Lucas a tissue for his misty eyes; even Biddy and the lady with the cocker spaniel stopped arguing about vet's bills to join in. Nina ran across the green and thrust a posy of peonies into Nonna's hand and then a huge cheer went up as Stanley wobbled to his feet and pressed a loving kiss on to the lips of his blushing fiancée.

'Oh,' I said, realizing who was missing. 'Mum and Dad would have loved to have been here.'

'I think your dad will be busy persuading your mum she needs a narrowboat.'

I gasped. 'Dad? Good for him!'

Gabe pressed his cheek to mine and murmured in my ear.

'There's a bottle of chilled champagne in the car, and one hour until I have to fetch Noah from school. I think we should celebrate.'

No one noticed as Gabe and I slipped away, back to *The Neptune* and into Gabe's bed, which as promised was indeed big enough. And in the tiny cabin with the blinds drawn against the sunny day as the boat bobbed gently against the riverbank we did celebrate. More than once.

Epilogue

Lucinda Miller's gold Versace dress was so tight that she had to hop sideways up the steps from below deck of *The Neptune*.

I attempted a wolf-whistle and she giggled. Her sense of fun had helped us all through what had had the potential to be a very difficult day. And to think that if I had airbrushed her photo, like my boss had wanted me to do back in March, none of us would be standing here now.

How things had changed in a few short months; now I was happier than I'd ever thought possible.

The fabric of Lucinda's dress was so dazzling in the sunshine that I was glad I'd got sunglasses on. Gabe helped her up the last step and then climbed off the boat to join me on the jetty.

'Does my bum look big in this?' said Lucinda, trying to look over her shoulder. 'There's no long mirror in Gabe's bedroom.'

'Huge,' said Candy, winking at me, 'I might actually need to change to a wide-angled lens.'

Lucinda stuck out her tongue. 'Oh shut up and get on with it.'

'I won't forget today in a hurry,' Gabe murmured in my ear, wrapping his arms round my waist, 'a famous actress in designer gear being photographed by your ex in a dress on my boat.'

'Dad's boat,' I corrected. 'And I hope that's not the only reason you'll remember today?'

I turned within the circle of his arms and pressed a lingering kiss to his lips. A kiss that promised there'd be more where that came from.

'No, of course not,' he said with a grin, 'it's also the Barnaby Summer Fair today.'

I smacked him playfully.

Candy held up her iPhone and took the picture. 'Damn, girl, you look hot.'

Gabe raised an eyebrow at me. He was doing his best to warm to Candy, but I knew he was struggling to forgive her for what had happened in the past. I loved that Gabe was so protective of me and every day I felt blessed that I'd finally allowed him into my heart.

Lucinda grabbed the phone off Candy to approve it. 'It's all right, I suppose. Right, let's upload. How much do you reckon we'll get for this on Depop?'

'One hundred?' I said with a shrug. 'Two?'

Lucinda had a huge following on social media and it had almost doubled when the press announced she'd be starring in a new film with Tom Hiddleston next year. When I'd asked her if she'd come and model the clothes from Helena's cupboard, she'd offered to sell them through her own page too.

'What's Depop?' Gabe whispered.

'It's an app; imagine if Snapchat and eBay had a baby,' I replied.

'Oh right,' said Gabe, looking none the wiser.

I peeled myself away from him and clambered back on to *The Neptune.*

'We're off,' I said, kissing them both on the cheek. 'Thank you for doing this. I can't tell you how grateful I am.'

'You're kidding me!' said Lucinda, turning round so Candy could unzip her. 'We'll raise loads of money for the hospice. My mum would be so proud of me. And then after I've officially opened the village summer fair thing I've got an interview lined up with a top reporter from the *Derbyshire*

Bugle later on, so it'll be great publicity for the charity and for me.'

'The reporter – his name isn't Robin, is it?' I asked.

Lucinda nodded. 'Yup. He said to ring him when we got to the swimwear shoot.'

'Did he really?' I said, suppressing a smile. That cheeky chap would go far, I reckoned.

She picked up her skirt and climbed clumsily back down the stairs to change into another outfit, leaving me with Candy.

'And I think I owed you one hell of a favour,' said Candy, taking my hands. 'Thank you. For your forgiveness and for your understanding. You too, Gabe. It means a lot. I never expected . . . I don't deserve . . .' Her voice cracked and she shook her head.

'You make a happier woman than you did a man,' I said, pulling her into a hug. 'Anyway, those eyelashes were wasted on a man.'

I hopped back on to the jetty, Gabe holding his hand out to steady me.

'Right,' I smiled at him, 'I'm all yours.'

He stroked my cheek with his finger. 'Is that a promise?'

'Cross my heart,' I said, grabbing his finger and making an 'X' on my T-shirt with it.

Paolo rang as we climbed into Gabe's van (the plan had been to sell it, but it was useful for ferrying supplies between the Lemon Tree Café and the Lemon Tree Pizza Cabin, and also it was more Noah-proof than Gabe's posh work car, so he'd kept it).

'*Ciao*, Paolo, is everything OK, have they arrived?'

'Hey, baby! I just pick up your parents from the airport, we are driving to Sorrento now. Wow, Luisa is one hot mamma. Wait, I put them on hands-free.'

'Oh Paolo, you charmer,' I heard Mum say with a titter.

'Keep your eyes on the road, there's a good chap, these bends are a death trap.' Dad sounded petrified.

'You'll be safe with Paolo,' I giggled. 'How was the flight, Mum?'

'Smooth as silk, but more importantly, how are you, how's the day going so far?'

'Nonna's now completely moved in to Stanley's. Angela is helping them set up their new king-size bed. Gabe and I are just leaving *The Neptune* and all of his stuff is out. And once Candy and Lucinda have finished taking the photos for the hospice, the boat will be ready for you to take it on its first outing.'

As expected, even though Stanley had been well enough to live on his own for weeks, Nonna never did come home again. She'd put her house on the market and yesterday the sale had been finalized and she'd handed over the keys. Mum and Dad had jumped on the first plane to Naples for a second honeymoon (the third would be on *The Neptune*, according to Dad) and Paolo had insisted that they stay at Bar Bufalo.

'And what about you, darling?' Mum said with a catch in her voice. 'How are you?'

'We,' I reached across for Gabe's hand, 'are almost home.'

As soon as Gabe stopped the van outside Nonna's cottage, Noah burst through the door, swiftly followed by a girl with brown wavy hair and dancing green eyes . . . It couldn't be . . . It was . . . !

I leapt from the van and dived on my friend.

'VERITY BLOOM!' I gasped, looking from her to Gabe. 'When you said babysitter, I didn't realize . . .'

'It was my brilliant idea,' Verity beamed. 'I thought you and Gabe might like some time, you know, on your own.' She jerked her head towards the cottage.

'There's a trapdoor in my bedroom!' cried Noah, punching his arms in the air.

'Noah's bed arrived while you were out so I asked the men to assemble it directly *over* the trapdoor,' said Verity pointedly.

'And how's the slide, dude?' Gabe pretended to pick Noah up by his ears and kissed him on his forehead.

'The slide is the best thing in the world,' said Noah, eyes shining. He put a hand to his mouth. 'Auntie Verity's bottom got stuck down it, but she said not to say anything.'

Verity rolled her eyes. 'And on that note . . . Come on, we've got a summer fair to go to. We'll see you two later.' She winked. 'As late as you like.'

Noah slipped his hand into Verity's and the two of them set off towards the village green where Stella Derry was directing proceedings with her usual aplomb ready for a noon kick-off. Suddenly Noah broke free from Verity's grasp, darted back towards the cottage and threw himself at me.

'Hello again,' I laughed, kissing his adorable little face.

'I've changed my mind,' he whispered loudly in my ear. 'The slide on my bed isn't the best thing in the world. You are.'

Gabe and I exchanged gooey smiles.

'Oh Noah Green,' I said, biting back tears, 'carry on saying things like that and I'll end up spoiling you rotten.'

His eyes popped open wide. 'Can I have one of Churchill's puppies?'

I looked at Gabe questioningly, he lifted a shoulder as if to say, *Why not?*

I nodded at Noah. 'Go and tell Biddy, she'll be thrilled.'

He ran back to join Verity and I turned to Gabe.

'So this is it.' I looked up at the man who had reawakened my soul. 'Our first home together.'

I gasped as Gabe scooped me up into his arms and kissed me with a passion that sent my heart soaring.

'Are you carrying me over the threshold?' I said when we came up for air.

'I am and yes, I know we're not married,' he murmured, gazing at me with such intensity that there was no mistaking his love for me. 'Yet.'

And then without taking his eyes from mine he took the first step to our new life. The door was open and we went through it. Together.

The Thank Yous

As ever I couldn't write at all without a tremendous team cheering me on and keeping me motivated along the way. So a big thank you to the Transworld posse: Aimée Longos, Becky Hunter, Janine Giovanni and Nicola Wright. And especially to the fabulous Francesca Best, my editor, who is tasked with coaxing me to the finish line – no mean feat! Thank you to the wonderful Hannah Ferguson, my agent, and her colleague Joanna Swainson, who together have looked after me so well during a trying year.

Thank you to the Literary Hooters, I love you all and really couldn't manage without you. Thank you for listening and bolstering and mostly, all the hooting.

The Lemon Tree Café features an Italian lady of mature years and as I'm not an Italian speaker, I'd like to thank those who helped me with Nonna's Italian sayings: Isabel Tartaruga, Gennaro from the Iberostar Torviscas Playa hotel in Tenerife (although his suggestions turned out to be too explicit!) and Francesca Best.

Thank you to Tony for all your help with the astronomical details. Thank you to Kath, my stepmum, who shared her story with me. Thanks to my brother for once sewing his curtains to his duvet cover and thank you to my friend and former colleague, Nina Whitby, who kept me entertained during many a boring meeting. Thank you to Carey Shelton for your help with my technical café questions and, of course, the recipe for Ginger Whoops! A special thank you to Ella Thompson; whatever floats your goat, Ella!

I made two research trips for this book, both of which helped enormously: The Wee House On The Hill, a tiny cottage in Wirksworth, became not only my haven at the start of writing this book, but also the inspiration for Rosie's cottage in Barnaby, so thank you to Sarah and Mal, its owners. Thanks also to the wonderful staff of Il Roseto, bed and breakfast in Sorrento, who looked after me when I went to research the Italian thread of Rosie's story.

Of course, writing wouldn't be any fun without my amazing readers. Thank you for buying my books, thank you for the reviews, the tweets and Facebook messages and thank you for the lovely emails too. Please keep them coming!

Finally, to Marian Keyes, my favourite author. I was struggling with the first draft of this book and Marian came to the Nottingham Playhouse theatre to do a Q&A session. 'Sometimes,' said Marian wisely, 'you have to go back to go forwards.' Those words became my mantra. It was exactly the right advice at the right time and more than that, her message became the theme of *The Lemon Tree Café*. Thank you, Marian, meeting you was the highlight of my year.

You've reached the end of
The Lemon Tree Café

But now you can escape to the seaside and meet a fantastic
new cast of characters in Cathy Bramley's next novel:

A Match Made
in Devon

Available for pre-order now! It will be serialised in four
ebook parts, and then come out as a full paperback and
complete ebook edition in early 2018.

Part One – The First Guests

Part Two – The Hen Party

Part Three – The Frenemies

Part Four – The Leading Lady

Or the irresistibly uplifting

Flirtatious, straight-talking **Jo Gold** says she's got no time for love; she's determined to save her family's business.

New mother **Sarah Hudson** has cut short her maternity leave to return to work. She says she'll do whatever it takes to succeed.

Self-conscious housewife **Carrie Radley** says she just wants to shift the pounds – she'd love to finally wear a bikini in public.

The unlikely trio meet by chance one winter's day, and in a moment of 'Carpe Diem' madness, embark on a mission to make their wishes come true by September.

Easy. At least it would be, if they hadn't been just the teensiest bit stingy with the truth . . .

With hidden issues, hidden talents, and hidden demons to overcome, new friends Jo, Carrie and Sarah must admit to what they really, really want, if they are ever to get their happy endings.

Available now

Holly Swift has just landed the job of her dreams: events co-ordinator at Wickham Hall, the beautiful manor home that sits proudly at the heart of the village where she grew up. Not only does she get to organize for a living and work in stunning surroundings, but it will also put a bit of distance between Holly and her problems at home.

As Holly falls in love with the busy world of Wickham Hall – from family weddings to summer festivals, firework displays and Christmas grottos – she also finds a place in her heart for her friendly (if unusual) colleagues.

But life isn't as easily organized as an event at Wickham Hall (and even those have their complications . . .). Can Holly learn to let go and live in the moment?

After all, that's when the magic happens . . .

Or the irresistibly charming

Appleby Farm

Freya Moorcroft has wild red hair, mischievous green eyes, a warm smile and a heart of gold. She's been happy working at the café round the corner from Ivy Lane allotments and her romance with her new boyfriend is going well, she thinks, but a part of her still misses the beautiful rolling hills of her Cumbrian childhood home: Appleby Farm.

Then a phone call out of the blue and a desperate plea for help change everything . . .

The farm is in financial trouble, and it's taking its toll on the aunt and uncle who raised Freya. Heading home to lend a hand, Freya quickly learns that things are worse than she first thought. As she summons up all her creativity and determination to turn things around, Freya is surprised as her own dreams for the future begin to take shape.

Love makes the world go round, according to Freya. Not money. But will saving Appleby Farm and following her heart come at a price?

Available now

Irresistible recipes inspired by
The Lemon Tree Café

St Clement's Cake

'Oranges and lemons, say the bells of St Clement's . . .'

This works brilliantly as a cake or as a pudding and looks so impressive that you get loads of 'oohs' and 'aahs'. And to top it off, it's really easy to make. If you want to make it gluten free, check the details of your baking powder before adding.

You will need . . .

380g of fruit made up of 1 lemon and roughly 3 or 4 clementine oranges

7 medium eggs

225g golden caster sugar

250g ground almonds

1 tsp baking powder

Remove any remnants of stalk from the fruit, place in a saucepan, cover with cold water and boil for two hours. Drain and discard the water. Cut fruit into quarters and remove the pips. Then put the lot into a food processor and blitz until really smooth (I often do this the day before making the rest of it).

Grease a 9-inch springform cake tin really well and pre-heat the oven to 190°C (fan 170°C), gas mark 5.

Beat the eggs in a mixing bowl, add the sugar, almonds and baking powder and mix until everything is incorporated. Then add in the orangey puree and stir thoroughly. Tip the mixture into the tin and bake in the oven until a skewer inserted into the middle comes out clean. It will take roughly an hour, depending on your oven.

Enjoy warm or cold with a dollop of crème fraiche and a small glass of dessert wine.

Almond Croissants

My husband really loves these. The ones covered in flaked almonds and filled with frangipane. But delivering them fresh and warm to the breakfast table is a step too far living where we live. However, I devised a cunning plan and these work wonderfully well for a special breakfast (like over a bank holiday weekend or birthday).

You will need . . .

A can of Jus Rol Bake-it-Fresh croissants

120g softened unsalted butter

150g caster sugar

200g ground almonds

2 eggs

1 beaten egg for making egg wash

A handful of flaked almonds

Icing sugar for sprinkling

Cream the butter and sugar together with a hand mixer until pale and fluffy. Add the ground almonds and eggs and blend well. (There should be enough mixture to fill the croissants and spread some on the top after they have baked.)

Preheat the oven to 200°C (fan 180°C), gas mark 6. Open the can of dough and unroll and separate the triangles as per the instructions. Spread some of the frangipane mixture over the entire triangle. Roll up from the wide end to the pointed end of the triangle, tucking the pointed end underneath, and place on a baking sheet. Repeat with all six, brush lightly with egg wash and bake in the oven for 10–12 minutes until golden but not too brown, and remove from the oven. Take the remaining frangipane, spread a small amount over each one and top with a sprinkle of flaked almonds. Pop them back in the oven for 2 minutes. Remove and dust with icing sugar. Enjoy with coffee in your favourite mug!

Honey Cake

My family are big fans of honey – on toast, on breakfast cereal and even on ice cream. So this recipe is especially popular in this house. Perfect with a cup of coffee or add a drizzle of cream to jazz it up for pudding.

You will need . . .
100g margarine or butter (softened)
2 tbsp golden caster sugar
4 tbsp clear honey
2 eggs, beaten
175g self-raising flour
½ tsp baking powder
1 tsp ground cinnamon
1 tbsp water

Preheat the oven to 190°C (fan 170°C), gas mark 5 and grease a 20cm (8-inch) cake tin – I use a square silicone one for this recipe. Then simply add all the ingredients to a large mixing bowl and beat until thoroughly mixed. Transfer the batter to the cake tin and bake in the centre of the oven for 30–40 minutes until golden brown and the top springs back up when you press it. Cut into squares to serve. Pop any leftovers in an airtight container and it will taste even better tomorrow!

Ginger Whoops

My friend, Carey, is the best cake maker I know. A couple of years ago, she realized a dream to open her own café called Fintons in Derbyshire. As you can imagine, the menu is to die for and she has kindly shared this recipe which is one of their best sellers. It was invented by accident one day – hence the 'Whoops' part!

You will need a 23cm square loose-bottomed tin or silicone baking mould. Line if necessary. Preheat the oven to 180°C (160°C fan), gas mark 4.

For layer 1 you will need . . .
150g plain flour
100g oats
150g light brown sugar
125g margarine

Place all the ingredients into a food mixer until combined into a dough. Press the dough into the bottom of the tin.

For layer 2 you will need . . .
Approximately 250g ginger jam

Spread the jam over the layer of dough.

For layer 3 you will need . . .
3 medium eggs
175g light brown sugar

175g soft margarine

175g self-raising flour

2 tbsp of ground ginger

Place all the ingredients in a food mixer until combined into a cake batter. If you are doing this by hand then use the creaming method – combine margarine and sugar until light, add eggs and combine. Then add flour and ginger.

Cook in the centre of the oven for about 30 minutes, ensuring the middle is cooked. Leave to cool.

For layer 4 you will need . . .

350g sieved icing sugar

200ml lemon juice

Chopped candied ginger (optional)

Slowly add the lemon juice to the icing sugar until you have a thick paste. You might not need all the lemon juice. If it goes too runny just add more icing sugar. Spread this on to the top of the sponge layer. Sprinkle some chopped candied ginger on top of the icing if desired.

Blueberry crumble cake

This is heavenly with a dollop of clotted cream. Yum.

You will need . . .

125g plain flour

1½ tsp baking powder

Pinch of salt

50g softened butter

100g caster sugar

A few drops of vanilla essence

1 egg
75ml milk
300g fresh blueberries

Crumble topping
100g caster sugar
125g plain flour
½ tsp ground cinnamon
130g softened butter

Preheat oven to 180°C (160°C fan), gas mark 4 and grease and flour a 23cm square cake tin.

Place the flour, baking powder and salt together in a mixing bowl. In a separate bowl, cream the butter and sugar together until pale and fluffy. Add the egg and vanilla essence and beat together, adding a spoonful of flour if it starts to separate.

Tip in a third of the flour mixture and combine, then add some of the milk, then more flour, alternating until all of it has been incorporated. Transfer the mixture into the prepared tin and cover with the blueberries.

Make the crumble topping by combining all the ingredients in a bowl with a fork. Sprinkle over the blueberries.

Bake for approximately 35–40 minutes until a skewer inserted into the cake comes out clean. Allow to cool in the tin before serving warm.

Almond biscuits

These look really elegant. But they are very easy to make and gluten free!

You will need . . .

3 egg whites

1 tbsp amaretto*

150g ground almonds

150g caster sugar

25 whole almonds

*if you haven't got amaretto, milk will do

Preheat the oven to 200°C (180°C fan), gas mark 6. Line a baking tray with greaseproof paper.

Whisk the egg whites until frothy. Very gently, fold in one third of each of the ground almonds and sugar. Pour in the amaretto or milk. Add the remaining almonds and sugar.

Take a teaspoonful of mixture and drop it on to the baking tray, using a second teaspoon to push it, leaving at least 3 centimetres between each biscuit. Top each one with an almond.

Bake for 10–12 minutes. They should be light golden brown but still have some 'give' and they will crisp up as they cool. Leave on the tray to cool and store in an airtight tin.

Rachael Lucas's Cranberry Biscotti

If you follow me on Twitter or Facebook, you'll probably know that Rachael and I are good friends. She helped me a lot through this book, actually, she helps me through life on an almost daily basis! This is her recipe, in her words. (That's why it's longer than my usual ones!)

You will need . . .

200g plain flour

150g soft brown sugar

50g butter

3 eggs

1 tsp vanilla essence

2 tsp ground ginger

2 tsp ground cinnamon

1 tsp baking powder

75g dried cranberries

75g flaked almonds

Preheat your oven to 190°C (170°C fan), gas mark 5. You'll need one large or two smaller greased baking trays.

Throw the flour, sugar, eggs and butter into your mixer (there are no words to describe how much I love my Kitchen-Aid – even more so when it's a bit grubby through hard work), add the vanilla and the spices (I know, that seems like LOADS, but somehow the flavours are really muted if you use a normal amount) and baking powder and mix briefly before adding the cranberries and almonds.

What you have now is a rather splodgy dough. Divide in two, and plop on to the baking trays. Shape into sort of rect-angular shapes. Whether this is a case of gently prodding or giving up as it lies in an uncooperative manner depends on some kind of strange baking alchemy. Doesn't make much difference, anyway. (I blame the eggs.)

Pop it in the oven for 15–20 minutes. You want it cracked on top and feeling quite firm to the touch.

Take the giant biscuits out of the oven. Do NOT eat. Not even a tiny taste. Let them cool for five minutes, then slice them into biscotti-sized pieces and place them on another non-stick baking tray, cut side up.

Pop them back in the oven for ten minutes, until they look toasted on the outside.

Then you have to let them cool without eating any. Not

even one. I'm really good at this, honestly. Whilst you're waiting for them to cool, you can deal with the resultant mess.

The end result is the best biscotti ever. The children said so, so it must be true.

Happy baking!

Lemon Shortbread Biscuits

Call your friends, tell them you're baking these and watch them appear at the door!

You will need . . .
250g salted butter, softened
100g caster sugar plus a tablespoon for sprinkling
250g plain flour
125g cornflour or rice flour
Grated zest of a washed, unwaxed lemon
More flour for dusting

Preheat the oven to 170°C (150°C fan), gas mark 3½. Cream the butter and sugar until pale and then stir in the lemon zest. Sift in the flour and cornflour a couple of tablespoons at a time, mixing as you go until it has all bound together. Dust your hands lightly with flour and knead gently to make a smooth dough. Wrap the mixture in cling film and chill for 30 minutes.

Remove the dough from the cling film and turn out on to a floured board. Using a rolling pin, roll out to a depth of 5mm and then use a biscuit cutter to cut into your desired shapes. Line a baking sheet with baking parchment and place the biscuits evenly on the sheet. Bake for 15–20 minutes. Remove from the oven and before removing them from the baking sheet, while they are still warm, sprinkle with the extra tablespoon of sugar. After ten minutes, transfer to a cooling rack.

Tiramisù

This recipe comes from my editor, Francesca, who had her very own Italian nonna, Bruna. This is a real family favourite of hers! '*Tiramisù*' means 'pick-me-up' and is recommended for those times when you need the little boost that only coffee and chocolate (and alcohol!) can bring.

NB. You'll need to chill this in the fridge overnight, or for at least four hours, before serving.

You will need . . .
5 large eggs, separated
5 tbsp caster sugar
500g mascarpone cheese
500ml brewed black coffee, left to cool
50ml Marsala wine, or cognac/brandy (optional)
A packet (generally about 30) savoiardi/ladyfinger sponge biscuits
Cocoa powder
Some dark chocolate for topping

Add the sugar to the egg yolks and beat until pale, thick and creamy. Add the mascarpone and beat well again. With a clean whisk, beat the egg whites until you have stiff peaks. Fold the egg whites into the mascarpone mixture. Pour the Marsala wine (if you're using it) and the cooled black coffee into a shallow dish. Working quickly, dunk each sponge biscuit into the liquid one at a time (you want the biscuits to have soaked up the coffee but not to become soggy or break, a couple of seconds will do it) and line the bottom of a glass dish, approximately 20cm square. Top with half the mascarpone mixture, making sure you go right into the corners of the dish with an even layer. Dust with a little cocoa powder. Repeat with another layer of soaked biscuits, then the rest of the mascarpone, and another dusting of cocoa powder. Add some grated dark chocolate to finish off. Chill in the fridge for at least 4 hours before serving.

Limoncello Meringue Ice Cream

Isn't this the perfect recipe for *The Lemon Tree Café*?! My friend Lucy, who owns a restaurant called Lucy's On a Plate in the Lake District, gave me this recipe. Delicious for a summer dinner party!

You will need . . .
4 egg whites
225g caster sugar
300ml double cream
Grated rind of 2 lemons
Zest of 1 lemon
2 tbsp limoncello liqueur (plus one for the chef ☺)
2 tbsp lemon curd

Preheat the oven to 110°C (90°C fan), gas mark ¼. Whisk the egg whites until stiff. Add the caster sugar a spoonful at a time until the meringue is really stiff.

Spoon into even-sized dollops and place on baking parchment and bake in the oven for 3 hours.

Whip the cream until firm. Add the limoncello and fold in the lemon curd. Stir in the zest and rind of the lemons.

Crush the cooled meringues into bite-sized pieces and stir into the cream mixture (don't worry as you fold, it binds together well). Put the mixture into a plastic tub and freeze for at least six hours.

Triple Chocolate Cookies

These cookies are absolutely delicious and are best eaten while still warm. The trick is to take them out of the oven before they set even though they don't look quite ready!

You will need . . .
200g butter or margarine
300g caster sugar
1 large egg
275g self-raising flour
75g cocoa powder
A little splash of milk
100g milk chocolate
100g white chocolate
100g dark chocolate

Preheat the oven to 200°C (fan 180°C), gas mark 6. Line two trays with baking paper or a silicone sheet. Cream together the butter and sugar in a mixing bowl until soft and pale. Crack in the egg and add the flour and cocoa powder. If the mixture is looking dry add a small amount of milk to bring it together. Break up all of the chocolate (I use a rolling pin while it's still in the packaging) and add to the bowl and mix thoroughly. Now, with clean hands, divide the mixture into ten portions and pop them on the trays leaving plenty of room between them – they will spread in the oven!

Bake the cookies in the oven for 10–12 minutes. Remove from the oven while they are still squidgy and leave on the trays to cool. As soon as you can pick one up without it disintegrating (about 25 minutes!), they are ready to eat.

'Healthy' Flapjacks

This recipe hits the spot when we fancy something sweet but want to feel a bit more virtuous. It is great to take as part of a packed lunch because it really fills you up. Please feel free to make substitutions depending on your tastes or what you have in your cupboards; for example, sunflower seeds for pumpkin, dried cherries for cranberries, or figs for apricots . . . the combinations are endless!

You will need . . .

6 tbsp coconut oil, plus extra for greasing

115g honey

½ tsp vanilla extract

3 tbsp soft brown sugar

180g rolled oats

100g chopped nuts (almonds, pecan or cashew)

50g pumpkin seeds

50g chia seeds

40g unsweetened desiccated coconut

85g dried cranberries

85g chopped dried apricots

Preheat the oven to 180°C (160°C fan), gas mark 4. Grease a 30cm x 20cm cake tin and line with baking paper. In a large saucepan, gently heat the coconut oil, honey, vanilla extract and sugar until the sugar has dissolved. Add all the dry ingredients and stir well. Tip into the cake tin and press down firmly with the back of a spoon. Place in the oven for 25 minutes until golden brown. Take the tin out of the oven and leave it on a rack to completely cool before cutting the flapjack into squares. This will keep in an airtight tin for about two weeks.

Cathy Bramley is the author of the best-selling romantic comedies *Ivy Lane*, *Appleby Farm*, *Wickham Hall* and *The Plumberry School of Comfort Food* (all four-part serialized novels) as well as *Conditional Love* and *White Lies & Wishes*. She lives in a Nottinghamshire village with her family and a dog.

Her recent career as a full-time writer of light-hearted romantic fiction has come as somewhat of a lovely surprise after spending the last eighteen years running her own marketing agency.

Cathy loves to hear from her readers. You can get in touch via her website: www.CathyBramley.co.uk,

Facebook page: Facebook.com/CathyBramleyAuthor or on

Twitter: twitter.com/CathyBramley